MY NAME IS MATILDA

MY NAME IS MATILDA

David White

Book Guild Publishing

Sussex, England

First published in Great Britain in 2009 by
The Book Guild Ltd
Pavilion View
19 New Road
Brighton, BN1 1UF

Typeset in Baskerville by
Ellipsis Books Limited, Glasgow

Printed in Great Britain by
CPI Antony Rowe

A catalogue record for this book is available from
The British Library.

ISBN 978 1 84624 324 0

Dedicated, of course, to Matilda.

And to Ollie Drew,
her youngest great-great-great-great-grandchild
(at the time of writing).

Contents

Acknowledgements

This book would not have come about if my aunt, Ella White, had not told me of a 'skeleton in the cupboard' and her sighting of a lost document that was written some time in the 1850s. Its rediscovery led to the idea of this book.

Nor would the book have had so many people included if I had not been helped by so many wonderful elderly ladies in the parishes of Dalwood and Shute. It was the freedom they gave me to clamber into attics and under stairs, and go through dusty boxes of letters and records, that let the stories of Madeline, Dick and many others be told. Thank you all, ladies, you made a difference.

Thanks to the staff who showed me where to look, and how to use their resources at: National Archives, Kew. Devon Record Office, Exeter; Dorset History Centre, Dorchester; the Lyme Regis Museum; Taunton Library; Anna Sander at Balliol College, Oxford University; Matti Watton at Lambeth Palace; HM Courts Services, York; the ladies of St Mary's Church, Timsbury, who showed us around; Sara Welch at Scott Rowe, Solicitors, Axminster, for locating the original debenture; Elsa Chapman, who allowed me to delve into her brother's work on the history of Dalwood—she knew where to find things! And Pete, for allowing us to ramble around Dalwood Hill and view Matilda's plaque again.

I used the tremendously helpful website Findmypast.com extensively, and its link pages to obtain copies of births, deaths and marriages.

Thank you to all the kind folk of Dalwood who welcomed us into your homes—you all added something. Thanks to Roger Pym for showing me how he makes cider the traditional way. The tasting was memorable, the photos much clearer than my head! Thank you to all my cousins in England, who encouraged me along the way.

Most importantly, thanks to my ever-patient wife, Pamela, who saw five weeks of our last holiday in England vanish, while I visited all the above.

Chapter 1

1827: A Young Entrepreneur

This Axminster market day was in all appeareances no different to any other. It was certainly a crisp dawn and moving on to a pleasantly warm morning; the stock was moving steadily through the yards under the auctioneer's hammer, their calls providing a constant background to the babble of the stallholders' cries. The day had progressed enough for the regular merchants to have parted with a goodly amount of their produce to their favourite buyers, and their modulated calls reflected their acceptance of a favourable day to come. Those of lesser quality could be heard with a more urgent cry, with stalls still too full for their liking.

Pushed into a corner furthest from the cattle yards and away from the main passage of the village buyers was a new stallholder, and she had not been made welcome by many. At thirteen she was old enough to be working there, but her family had never been stallholders and changes to the traditional family inheritance of space were not accepted by many of her neighbours. Last market day had been a tragedy for her, but as usual, her pride hid her tears until she got home. She had set up with a small trestle by the Old Bell Hotel, hoping to catch the trade as folk took refreshment. Old Edith had offered her her spot as she herself needed to attend her sick sister, and felt the young girl had worked hard enough to be able to sell her own produce that Edith had previously sold on her behalf.

The day started well enough: her strawberries were of excellent quality and her small pots of clotted cream were the envy of many older women. She was canny with keeping her prices close to others so as not to appear to undercut them and antagonise other merchants. She was keenly aware that they were supplementing family income to support a hungry family, whereas she was a newcomer whose father and brother were already known to be doing well with the stock they sold.

The first sign of trouble started when the elder of the neighbour's boys knocked her stall with callous intent as he passed by with increasing regularity to sup cider in the Old Bell.

'Bit of a gurl like you should be upalong with her mother getting meal done for menfolk, not 'ere doing grownups' business.' His tread became more unsteady with each pass till finally he spilled her remaining strawberries on the ground.

'You great lump, Tom Burrows—look what you done now! You should be helping your father, not drinking his profits!' Angry at the truth of her accusation, he swiped the last of her stock to the ground and stamped on some strawberries.

'Dornee talk to me like that, young brat, or you'll learn lessons older gurls learn.' He leaned over her, his sour breath covering her face. 'Fancy you can learn 'em anyways.'

Not one of the stallholders had moved to intervene, the incident worth watching further. Only a solitary voice was heard saying, 'Careful Thomas, there's plenty hearing what you say, you dornee want to cross 'ee bruther.' Matilda stood, unable to make herself move, and did not see what caused Tom to rise back from her and his fetid breath leave.

'Watch 'em doing to 'er Tom?' The bulk of Dick's large body appeared behind Tom as he dragged his older brother away. 'You'm not making trouble for Miss M, are you? Dad be wanting you, you better not be drinking already, you be getting kick in arse!' With the ease of lifting a kitten, he swung Tom around, his braces strung taut under his weight, and shoved him away through the crowd. 'Sorry Miss M, he be no good with cider in 'im.'

Dick's world was simple: there was right and there was wrong, and he knew the difference. His great size and strength was not matched with intellect; school education was never considered as a possibility for him, and so the farm animals became his classroom.

Matilda was shaking but refused to let those around see her discomfort. She knelt and tidied the mess from her stall, put the remnants in her hamper and, with chin held high and her curly hair flouncing, walked away to her father's cart.

Once home, it took only a glance from her mother for her to realise that all had not been well with the day. Mary was too well used to her husband's ways to say anything until they were alone.

'What happened, child? Tis all very well for Father to go on so about your first day and clearing threepence for your efforts. Full of pride he be, but not an eye in his head to see the cost to you! Now tell me if I'm wrong.' Matilda long ago learnt that she couldn't hide from her mother what she could hide from all others, but she knew in telling, that she would probably stop her from going to market again.

'Twas something and nothing, Mother. That Tom Burrows got too much cider in him and messed up my stall. He knocked the last of strawberries over, but Dick got him away quick like. No real harm done, just that Tom is getting worse toward me.'

'There be your problem, my girl—you're fast leaving being a girl behind and boys be looking at you differently soon abouts. There's pity all I can do about the likes of that pisspot Tom and his mates. But what to do? Now that you have done one market well enough, I can't see you not wanting to do another, nor will Father want you to stop, seeing as how you made us something for the purse. But you need looking after there and I can't see William leaving his father's side to check you be getting along all right, Charles be too young to make no difference. Not right for Dick to be always about, and animals are his world, not people. Treats you like a little sister, he always has and probably always will, but poor lad can't think much beyond the now, and he be a Burrows, so that Tom will just make his life more miserable than he does already. I got the two little ones to tend and would be wrong anyways for me to attend. If you want to be at next market you will be doing it alone; tis not the best choice, but life is never going to give you the best choice. You decide, I doubts that I can hold you back, but think on what if Dick hadn't come along when he did.'

Matilda's joy at not being stopped from going to the next market glowed in her face, her seemingly ever-present smile twitching at the corners of her mouth.

'I'll be fine, Mother. I have to learn to handle the likes of Tom, and sooner the better. There are always lots of folk around and no one will let anything get out of hand. Don't worry, I can look after myself.'

And so it was to be—a mother having to let her child leave her protective nest, cursing their lowly existence that stopped them sending her to school. If only, she would say of Matilda more than once in the future, if only she could have gone to school and learnt proper. She is the brightest of the family by far, as quick as her dad at sums, with no need to write them down to get the answer faster than the boys, and sometimes Father as well. Reading and writing is for the boys if they can grasp it, Mary

3

would tell herself, and plenty do fine without, tis not necessary for girls such as us who stay on farms, let them up the Manor teach their girls, for their girls be no use on a farmyard. No, Matilda will be just fine, she's as sharp as a tack and no one will put one across her.

Matilda soon put Tom from her mind. Edith had let them know she would not be back for the next market day, and as Matilda had done better than she expected, she could have her stall again. *This time I will do better*, she said to herself. *If I treat Henrietta to extra feed she may give more cream, which will give me more for making clotted cream. I need something to cover the strawberry plants so I lose less to those birds and have more good ones to sell.*

She went in with William the next market day. He left her there while he went on to help repair a field wall. It was a splendid morning, every bird trying to out-sing the other. Her anticipation rose at being left alone to tend her stall like an adult, as did her feeling of importance in being able to bring something in for the family purse through her own efforts. Full of excitement, she said, 'Oh William, is this not a day God made in Heaven?'

William, whose only thoughts were of a long hot day ahead at a stone wall, replied, 'If you wish, sister, if you wish.'

'William White, sometimes you are so blind to all the lovely things around you!'

'Aye,' he muttered, thinking more of having to miss his turn of cider at the end of the day on his mother's repeatedly stressed instructions to collect Matilda not a minute late. He should have known better than to tell his mother to keep her at home and save him the bother of having to look for her.

'Aye,' he muttered again, 'p'raps you're right.'

Nor was William going to be let off so easily when they got to the market.

'Now Will, you have time to help me carry this lot to the stall, then make sure you give Dobbin a drink before going on to your wall repairs at Denslows, or are you only doing it so as to be near that Ann Denslow? You be sure to tether Dobbin in the shade while working and don't dally about in collecting me after, now will 'ee!'

When William finally got away and out of her hearing, he could be heard muttering, 'I don' rightly know who's worse, she or 'er mother!'

'Well you've come back then,' Matilda's neighbouring stallholder said in greeting. 'After you went off last time I reckon'd we seen the end of you. At least you got the pluck not to give in, but I doubts you seen the last of 'im. You bring any clotted cream again? Old Ma Rowe reckons it's the cleanest she's seen in many a day. Takes a steady hand to get it that good, she said. Best ways I take some home m'self, if you don't mind, young lass.'

Matilda was delighted with the compliment and gladly handed over a pot.

'Here young lass, you take home a couple of my buns and see if your mother donne reckon she could do no better.'

Matilda could not have been happier. She had been accepted in the market place, she was starting a life off the farm and standing on her own feet. She knew the importance of being able to contribute to the family purse, and the bubbly excitement inside her showed in her shiny eyes and unsuppressed smile. The morning flowed by. She was pleased to recognise some who came to buy from her again, including the girl in another pretty dress that she had admired last time.

''ere lass, you just sold to the gentleman squire up hilltop way. That be his daughter that bought them strawberries, he be watching her from over yonder at edge of grass. You got a good customer if 'e comes back.'

'You know a gentleman squire then? How be that so?' Matilda was amazed that anyone could possibly know someone of such importance.

'I donne know 'im personal like, just seen 'em about, knows who he be. He lives up Charmouth Road in the big house, I lives downalong in cottage where I bakes from. He got all his own staff now and don't buy much in town no more. Tell you what though, his gardener can't be much if he be buying your strawberries!'

'You've had a grand morning, young'un,' she told her later. 'Just six punnets left and all clotted cream gone—your folk will be fair proud of you, I reckons. Be my guess on you becoming a regular fixture now.'

'Well thank you, but I am only here till Edith comes back from nursing her sister. I didn't expect to be here today—she must be more poorly than we thought. I don't suppose that she will be away much longer, I shall miss it when Edith returns.'

'I donne think you will miss it much longer—lookee yonder, here comes that trouble boy and two of his hanger-ons! You give us the nod if you want a hand, you be one of us now and old badger-hat there will be 'appy to do some sorting if need be.'

With a sinking heart, Matilda looked over and saw Tom and two of his friends heading towards her. The smirk on his face forecast the fun he was intending to have at Matilda's cost, and the sneer on the faces

5

of his two companions showed they were expecting some sport with her.

'Well, if it isn't little Matilda White back on the stall. Look lads, she has but six punnets left and not very good ones at that. Shouldn't we help her with the rest and look after her till her brother comes back?'

Matilda summoned her courage, determined not to show any fear in front of them, but she also tried to see where the badger-hat man was out of the corner of her eye.

'I am perfectly all right, thank you. I can sell the last of my strawberries without your help. I think it would be best if you moved away.'

'Ooooh! Listen to it, lads. Is that not fighting talk from a little bantam hen? A feather needs plucking, I believe!' Their leery grins broadened.

'You boys should go,' said the old girl next door, 'you have no place here.' One of Thomas's friends went over to her, leaning roughly on her stall, pushing into her.

'Mind your own business, you old crab. We got time to deal with your stall as well. Keep your snotty nose out of it, it's between Thomas and the girl, see!'

Thomas moved closer to Matilda, speaking quieter so as not to be overheard. 'I've just come to help you, Matilda. Now you're such a big girl with a stall of your own, I'm going to show you how to do some real business—man style.' He began moving the last punnets to her hamper. Matilda glanced desperately to her left to see if the badger-hatted man was coming, but couldn't see with Thomas beside her, one of his companions in front of her and the other blocking the old lady next to her.

'Now let's see here, all nice and tidy and we can go out back.'

Matilda wanted to scream when she looked back at his eager face and saw he was dribbling down the corner of his mouth. Suddenly afraid, she could barely shout at him, 'You get out now, Thomas Burrows! You think you can bully us around?'

He leant toward her to steer her away, then she heard a dull thud and he suddenly disappeared into the doorway of the Old Bell. His companions realised too late that their plans had gone astray, and their option of walking away diminished as the badger-hat man hauled one of them off the old girl's stall and the other spun around to flee, straight into Dick's barrel chest.

'Morning Miss M. I been watching them, but they slipped aways when Pa and I was busy. Reckoned he be coming here, 'e just gave Pa lip 'bout misbehaving last time. Reckon 'e learnt his lesson this time though. These two need a cooling down, I be back for Thomas soon enough,' Dick said, looking down at his brother who was lying, curled on the floor with eyes wide open and trying to gasp air. 'You look stupid holding yourself like that, Tom,' were his unconcerned parting words as he and badger man took the other two away.

'Cor, deary me!' exclaimed the old girl, not sure she had really seen what had happened. 'Did you ever see such a booting? Just one fair up his britches, and he's through the door like a rabid dog. I reckon he got his manhood shifted fair up to his belly! That be real justice, that be.'

Matilda was not sure what to do. Dazed, she looked at Thomas who was clearly in great pain and needed help to move. Some woman was standing by saying something she couldn't quite hear.

'Come on, Matilda, dear,' said the old girl next to her, 'this lady is asking for strawberries, you got a few in your hamper, don't you?'

'Yes, sorry ma'am. We got a bit distracted just now, here we are.' Matilda fought for calmness to serve her customer and the old girl cackled in victory.

'I think your problem has been sorted good and proper now. He be a proper fool to try anything now, that gurt sized boy left no misunderstanding what 'e faces for his actions. That's if he can get 'is bits back out of his belly again! Cor!' she mused. 'I'd pay good money to see that again.'

Dick was soon back to collect his brother, who had moved little since.

'Where be the other two?' the old girl asked. Ignoring her, he quietly spoke to Matilda.

'They be in the water trough with that fellow in the badger-skin 'at stood on top of 'em, they be needing cooling off, you see. He be doing a proper job of it, so I come and shift Thomas out of the road of good folk.'

With more fear than agility, Tom got to his feet. Still hunched, with elbows tight to his sides and hands belatedly protecting his privates, he minced his way from the stalls.

'I'm sorry Miss M, he shouldn't treat 'ee so. I'll make sure 'e knows to leave 'ee alone—I'll give 'im a wee reminder during the week.' He took a few steps and turned. 'We be castrating pigs come Wednesday, I make sure 'e watches closely and I'll sharpen the blade slow, like. He'll still be hurtin' bad then.' The huge boy turned away and followed his brother, trying to hide a smile.

'Tis true, Matilda, you been given us more entertainment than a side show since you come. I donne wish ill on Edith's sister, but I do hope she don't get well too soon!' The old girl grinned devilishly. 'You best ways call me Margery. I hopes we see more of you.'

Matilda couldn't help a smile.

'It's a sad truth, Margery, but I rather wish the same.'

Chapter 2

1827: Playing Father Right

Matilda's wish did not come true. Edith's sister did regain her strength, and Edith was back on her stall the next market day. The fact that Matilda's venture into marketing produce from their vegetable plot had ended before she could claim it her own, left her frustrated. She felt that she had lost something unique to her, a skill that no other member of the family had an interest in emulating. It saddened her that she had lost her tiny foothold of independence, then she immediately felt ashamed for not feeling grateful to Edith for showing her what she was capable of. She knew now that she could do more than work on the farm— though her contribution there was substantial. The vegetable garden was her domain more than any of the others; she knew she was contributing well by getting the best from it, and the family fed well through her efforts. There was little interest from the other children in helping collect the cow manure and spread it watered down on the garden, or covering the ground around the plants with old straw from the barn, even though they understood that they had better vegetables to eat when the crop was ready. And eat them they did, often before they got to the table.

It had also become Matilda's role to milk most of the cows by herself. This she took real delight in, knowing that she had the softest hands in the family. Her touch on the cows' udders had more gentleness and even pull than the practised hands of her elder brother and sister, always filling the pail more than either of them or her father, and the cows were content and calm enough to let her milk them out in the pasture.

The best time was in spring, when so many flowers were out, adding colour to the hedgerows and fragrance to the air. Birds all sung their

9

best tunes, but she always listened out for her favourite, a skylark that would trill a flow of music from somewhere suspended high above her. Her day would be complete if she caught sight of a buzzard gliding lazily high above all else, as if not caring when its next meal would present itself, and then almost nonchalantly, gracefully sweeping down to earth to satisfy itself with a ready meal. Her gaze would take in the rolling green hills that formed the Devon valley that was her world, and she was content in it.

Henrietta always wanted to be milked second, so that she got all the benefits of ready warmed hands, before Matilda began to slow down with the later cows. Matilda knew this and on more than one occasion, when the teasing took her, would stand up when finished with the first cow, give it a pat and say, 'Good girl,' letting the cow know she could move away, but then move away herself. In umbrage, Henrietta would trot around with udder swinging, stopping squarely in front of Matilda, cutting her off from going any further to any other cow.

'Why hello, Henrietta, I was wondering where you were,' she would say in mock innocence. But Henrietta was not to be fooled. Her look of superiority over the other cows left no doubt that order had been restored and milking could commence.

There were usually about five cows to be milked by one of the others and inevitably needing to be roped and taken to the parlour to be tied and milked there. On a successful day, a wet, cow-dung-covered tail would be flicked onto the milker's head and back. Such a covering Matilda was always pleased to see, and never hesitated in telling the smelling sibling what a good mess they were in.

'One day,' they told her, 'one day it will be your turn. And what a day that will be!'

But the day never arrived. All the animals had their role, and all were necessary to the success of the farm, but none rose to the stature of Henrietta and the herd, in her eyes.

The routine of the farm gave her a settled and comforting life—she was born to it, after all—but occasionally her thoughts turned to the market-place stall and she felt a tug of longing to go in again. After all, it was just a morning and the farm could go on without her, and she had brought home something extra for the family purse. Perhaps it was the fact that the next market day was less than a week away that brought it to her mind.

She had seen Thomas Burrows after attending a church service, and he was walking quite naturally again, but he hardly gave her a glance before moving off. 'Stupid boy,' she muttered. There were plenty of stories about as to why he had been left at the farm, and why only Dick went in with his father to market now.

When they got home her father came out to greet them.

'Well enough, was it then?' he asked. Interested in proceedings, but not interested enough to attend himself.

'Yes Father, well enough.'

'We've had a visitor—just as well I was here to see them for you, lass.' This didn't indicate who the visitor had called to see, as he called all the women 'lass'. Mother was only called 'Mother' when one of them needed to be corrected, as he was hopeless in correcting the children's behaviour himself.

'The table's ready,' he said, turning to go indoors, without any enlightenment on who had come. It took nearly half the meal before Mary could wait no longer.

'So who was the visitor who wanted to see one of us?'

'Didn't I say?' he said with surprise, but fooling absolutely no one. He tore another piece of bread, mopped up some gravy and went to put it in his mouth.

'Oh no you don't, John White!' admonished his wife, putting a hand on his arm to stop the flow of food. He knew he was in trouble when she called him John White, particularly when she put so much severity into it.

'Ah,' he said, knowing the game was at an end. ''Twas Edith. There's been talk at last market. Seems as how our Matilda here made her mark with folk in there.'

'Why should that surprise you? And don't put that in your mouth, there's more to be told!'

'Ah yes,' he said again, 'seems as how the old dolt on the next stall has been talking to Edith about our Matilda.'

'She is no old dolt, Father! Her name is Margery, and she is kind!' Matilda firmly stated to her father, and then more carefully, 'Old, but kind.'

'Well,' Father said, drawing in a breath, 'seems as how she made a mark on you too, then—what was that about?'

'John, what did Edith have to say?' Mary interrupted before Matilda needed to speak, being sure that what she had been told of Thomas's inability to walk well for a week was very near the truth, and that was something that her husband need not know about.

'Ah, yes,' he murmured, trying to work out what he had missed out on. 'Edith, it seems, has had a lot of comments about how well Matilda handled herself on her own in there. Seems some customers have been back looking for her strawberries and clotted cream, it seems some reckon they haven't tasted better, even some gent came back, the old dol . . . Margery said. 'Course Edith couldn't help them and you know how much that would hurt her, losing a sale, even if it wasn't her own. Seems as how those two old cronies reckon they would be better off if our Matilda was to be there regular like. Seems as how Edith wants to share a bit of her stall with you, lass. What do you make of that then?' he finally finished in a rush, not sure yet if he himself saw it as good or bad news. She was still too young yet for him to be thinking of placing her somewhere, but if folk were asking for her services already, well by joves, she will be taking her pick of what suits her best. And when did that last happen, 'eh? Lost in his thoughts of Matilda's future successes, he could hear himself telling folk, 'Aye, and our Matilda's doing well for herself.' With thoughts too far hence, he didn't notice Matilda's face light up. Then the smile slowly faded and a frown began to wrinkle her brow.

'It's too late now, the strawberries are past their best. How can I go in with those tail-enders? Folks will be wanting the good'uns and there be none left, just colour but all soft and watery and no taste. That isn't any help to Edith, she said folk wanted what I had, not this lot. What to do, Mother?'

'Hush child, don't fret so. Edith did say you could share a part of her stall, not take it over! You couldn't take in all you did before, t'would not be fair to Edith. You bestways just to make your clotted cream, I don't know of any who can make it better and Edith will be happy with that.'

'Of course.' Matilda sighed with relief, her standards maintained.

'I suppose that means Henrietta will be getting extra feed again,' John grumbled under his breath. 'I not so daft yet that I didn't see ye feeding her up last time 'round.'

'Aye Father,' Matilda acknowledged, 'but it helped the purse by doing so.'

'I'm not that blind, girl,' her father retorted, 'before I lets 'ee go in, you reckons on how we all have to do more to cover your chores around 'ere. Dornee go wasting our efforts here by not selling all your stock at a good price. T'was easy afore. Lucky you was. Edith gave you a privilege in her absence and that be gone! You work with her on her stall and you got standards to keep, and only hard work will keep you there. She can't afford no slap-dash efforts from you. William and I go in but one in four, how are you reckoning on getting in other times? Us have no time to cart you about, I won't be having any of us running after you for no gain on the farm. You want to work off the farm like your older brother and sister, then you got to start thinking like them, grown-up! No place now for bit of a girl, day dreaming. You've a long way to go before we see any good of you traipsing in there!'

And with that, he returned to finish his meal in silence. No one else spoke a word, except for a quiet reply from Matilda.

'Yes, Father, I understand.'

Only careful glances passed among them around the table. Never before had their father said so much at one time and never with such severity. Something about it worried him very deeply. When he had finished, he rose and went solemnly out, and for the first time in their lives together, failed to thank his wife Mary for the meal. The others followed, only their eldest child, also called Mary, staying to help her mother clean up, not daring to ask why there were tears in her mother's eyes.

'Now Mother, whatever do you make of that?' her daughter eventually asked. 'Father never went on like that to me when I been doing work away, and be doing it on and off at every chance from younger than Matilda is. What's got his shirt tail in such a knot?'

'Truly I don't know. Time enough will tell though, just give him room to come out with it. Here, take these scraps to the hens and talk to Matilda a while. She will be there or in the garden trying to make sense with a confused mind. It will come better from an older sister than me— she will just expect me to have answers to it all.'

Matilda had sought refuge in the vegetable garden, a place where she could rely on being left alone. She hated feeling this upset. Whatever had got into Father, she couldn't imagine. As hard as she tried, she could never remember any more than a few soft words of kindness, or gentle instruction on farm work. It was as if he had put a wall up and she felt quite alone.

She looked up, seeking a buzzard circling high as though it was watching out for her, but none were there. Not even a skylark sang in the clear blue sky; there was nothing for her to talk to there. With random tugs she began to clear some weeds and try to clear her head. She had to find a way of enlisting Mary and William's help as she felt it was clear that her father would not be a part of it. A scraping sound from the lane side of the garden wall made her rise and see what was there. As she walked over, Dick's head appeared over the top.

13

'Hello, Miss M—you'm be not troubled are ye?' he quietly asked. 'You'm don't seem yourself, you know.' Matilda couldn't help smiling: all that was visible of his face was from his top lip up and two sets of fingers clinging on each side.

'Just deep in thought, Dick. But if you wanting to talk, you be better off coming around before you slip back off the wall.'

'No, I'm just passing by on my way to fish ponds. Fancied saying hello. Mary is coming in so I will head downalong.' Matilda turned to the garden gate expecting to see Mary, but she wasn't in sight. She turned back to Dick, but he had already slipped down the wall and there was only a faint crunching of his steps to be heard.

'What a strange day,' she sighed. 'Dad upset, then everyone disappears, no buzzards, no skylarks, no Mary, and now no Dick!'

'Talking to yourself now, are you, Matilda?' called Mary as she came through the garden gate. 'I do hope you're getting good answers.'

'Oh Mary, it's all confusing and I can't make sense of it. First Father goes on so, like I've never heard before, and I really don't know whether he wants me to work with Edith or not. Mother says nothing at all, and when did that last happen when we been talking at the table? Dick peers over the lane wall and wants to know what's worrying me, then says you are coming and you are nowhere in sight; I turn back to Dick and he's gone, then you do come in behind me from nowhere. Of course I'm confused!' Her usually happy face was wrinkled in utter confusion.

'Poor Matilda, come and sit on the bench and we'll sort it out together,' Mary suggested, linking her arm in Matilda's and keeping it there as they sat under the flowering clematis.

'Now I don't know all the answers, but this is how I see it. Dick, I cannot answer for you, for it's likely you know him better than any. He's not the idiot the village take him for, but he has never said more than "Hello Mary" to me. It's the same with everyone—he knows all our names and never gets it wrong, but says no more. With you I've only heard him call you Miss M, but he knows your name very well, so why doesn't he use it? On top of that he actually talks to you, sometimes in whole sentences. Even with lots of folk about he will only talk with you. What I cannot understand at all is how he appears when you are in trouble or upset—he's done so since you could first walk. It would seem that Father is the only person this side of Lyme Regis who doesn't know why his brother had trouble walking backalong.

'But Father is troubled and I don't know why. He has never gone on so about leaving the farm short-handed when William and I work away;

he's never said a word to me about putting my earnings in the family purse. You are going to be away for only the morning on market day, where William has been away a week without fuss. Whatever father is raddled about, I think we have just got to work around.

'So, we have to find a way to get you to market when Father and William don't go as well. I've not spoken to William yet—he be with Father, so best left alone. You do know he's sweet on Ann Denslow and he only goes in to repair that hedgerow so to see her? Well, if we play him right, I reckon we can get him to do wall repairing every market day. I don't think he will say no to the chance, do you?'

'No, I don't think he will. But that makes you two short here.'

'That doesn't matter. You remember your first stall day, when Mother and I did the milking? Father didn't fuss that day, so he's lost argument before he starts. It will be all the better if we can get Mr Denslow to pay William a bit. I will get Ann to work on her father—she says the only time any real progress is made on the wall is when William is there. So getting him there regularly is good for us all. Milking will be fine; it only takes two of us, and Mother will gladly step in for you. Father is right though, it is your responsibility to do a proper job of making the cream every time. You will be better off not going in if a batch is not to your high standard—folk talking will quickly work against you.' Mary paused. 'I think with all that, we will have got you to market to Father's satisfaction,' she finished with a satisfied sigh.

'Oh Mary, you are such a help. Will you and William talk to Father with me?'

'There's no need to worry over that. We will talk it over during dinner tomorrow, then we will all be present. Now get along, you need to attend to Henrietta and do the milking.'

The rest of the day passed quietly enough for all of them. Mother kept her peace, calmly working through to bedtime, as though her husband's tirade had never occurred. Once snuggled up to him and the candle blown out, she quietly said to him, 'So, my dear, what is it that really troubles you with Matilda?'

His reply was a long time in coming, but to ask again would only irritate him. Eventually, with a shuddering sigh, he told her.

'She is growing up too fast, she's no longer my little girl—she's too young yet, surely. She has always been the sharpest, so quick to learn, so sure of herself. Aren't we rushing her out of the house?'

'Oh you soft old fool. She'll be fine,' Mary consoled him.

'Aye, maybe. I can't help feeling it's not right. There be so much

15

innocence about her. Yet from somewhere, I got to see her now as a young woman—when did that happen? I don't want to lose her for good.'

A tear rolled down his cheek.

'Oh you soft old fool' Mary whispered to him again. 'Your boys don't grow up fast enough for you, and your girls grow up too quickly for your liking. You just got to be prepared for their growing. When them were babes, they were heavy on your arms and as they be grown up, they be heavy on your heart. You be their dad and you'm got to be ready to care for 'em at any age.'

'Aye,' he murmured, 'perhaps you're right, but it don't go to say I like it any.'

Chapter 3

1827–1828: The Matchmakers

Matilda could not believe how smoothly she was able to begin her mornings in the market. William got up early the next morning to help her milk, with an enthusiasm that he rarely showed.

'By all that's mighty, tis a beautiful morning!' he beamed as he greeted her.

'I'm sure it will be,' she said, looking through pre-dawn darkness towards the hills where the sun would shortly rise, 'but not like you to be so cheerful so early! Not like you to be here at all! What has happened for you to be here instead of Mary?'

'Well, little sister, Mary had a word in my ear about you last night. She be as cunning as any vixen after her prey, that one. Pity help the lad that marries her, he won't stand a chance will 'e? She'll pick out the one she wants, have 'im up the aisle and bedded, afore 'e knows what hit 'im. Cor, poor fellow will be tugging 'is forelock and begging permission at every turn! Glad I'm her brother, for she be setting me up lovely, like.' He paused to collect a stool and pail as Matilda had, and went to leave the parlour. Matilda just stood and looked at him and waited. 'Aye, per'aps you're right,' he said with a sheepish grin, returning them in place and collecting a rope instead. 'Well she be a corker sister to us both, what a plan, eh? Cause I'll take you in, and I get to see my sweet Ann, and she'll see to it that I be paid for my efforts as well. Can you just see 'er dad asking Father if I can go help 'im as though twas all 'is idea, and father being right pleased that he got approached for another of us for doing outwork. Then we got to keep straight in the face when we get told by him that I got an offer! Cor, we be in a dandy position!'

Milking was never done in better humour. They went in for breakfast still in a fine mood and more hungry than usual because of it, passing their father on his way out. Surprise showed in his eyes at seeing William.

'You'm been milking then?' he queried of William's unusually early start. 'Be sure you be ready soon abouts, you not forgotten we are helping on the Big Farm with hay today?'

''Course I'll be ready,' William replied, trying to look confident, though he had forgotten all about it. 'Be right along. Get breakfast down and get a jar of cider from cellar, I'll be waiting for 'ee.'

But his father had moved on.

'He's not that much happier this morning, then,' William said to his mother while helping himself to some hot tea, and she filled his plate.

'You may well be best working away from him today. You lads work at scything and let your father rake over with one of 'is cronies. He just needs a little time to work his worries out in his mind and having you jack-bobbing about in earshot won't help. Get 'im to take Dobbin with 'ee and hook on rake—talking to 'is horse all day will do more good than hearing silly notions 'is daft friends will fill his head with,' their mother advised. 'And you, young lady, had best ways get on with clotting cream. Did you keep Henrietta's milk separate?'

'Yes Mother. I have kept hers and Daisy's as well. I should take in plenty—I don't want to run out too early—and what's left I will bring back, and use what's here now to make into butter. We will be out come Friday.'

Mary wondered at her daughter's overnight return of self-assurance and quiet contentment, at William sitting there as though he was trying to hide a smile, and at their older sister Mary, gone already to help the other women prepare food for the haymakers, and having already had breakfast started when she came down. *They be up to something that Father and I can't see. They went up along to bed all quiet and solemn, like a row of monks, keeping out of Father's way. Now they act like it never happened; they all be up to something and poor Father will never see it coming. He worries that Matilda is too young—I don't wonder if she be already too old.*

'You are looking full of thought,' Matilda said to her mother as she reached to get the scalding pan down. 'You worrying about Father and what he said yesterday, is that it?'

'Aye, that I am. I am surprised you are not.'

'Mother dear, Father was saying what he thought needed saying. He will be fine soon enough.'

I wish I had their confidence, she mused, *but I wish more that I knew what you three are up to.* But there was nothing to be gained by pursuing it further—rather, be grateful that the children seemed to be getting on without staying moody over it all. She watched Matilda pour the fresh milk into the scalding pan and another large dish, then carefully place them in the parlour to settle.

By this time, Mary was in the neighbour's kitchen, with several others there to help. As she had expected, Ann had arrived with her father and brother.

'I'm pleased to see you so early, Ann,' Mary greeted her, nudging her along to a quiet part of the kitchen. 'I need your help to get us out of a bit of bother at home.' She went on to explain her plan to Ann, who was absolutely delighted to play her part, and not doing very well at hiding her emotions at the possibility of having William visiting so regularly. *If I play my hand right,* she thought, *by time farm hedgerow is all repaired I'll be set to have William courting me proper.*

And so it was to be, all done by the time the sun set.

By the time morning victuals were prepared, Mary and Ann had set together a faultless plan.

By end of morning break, Ann had set her father to thinking that to get William to come regularly to do wall repairs was his idea. He sat with his daughter, munching on a chunk of fresh bread with a slab of fine cheddar in it, watching William as he and two others strolled over from where they were scything. With some satisfaction, he noted that William was a clear ten yards further along than the rest, and his big hands seemed to grip the scythe in a way that allowed him one mighty sweep to the others' two. *A lad worth watching—be sensible to pay the boy to keep him coming back. Might be a bit of a catch for my girl here if he measures up,* he mused, wondering how to broach his idea with the boy's father. 'Durned if old John hasn't been on quiet side away with 'is 'orse all morning.'

By the end of the midday break, William had a job repairing the hedgerow. Ann's father timed his place in the queue to come in behind William's father, nodding toward a shaded place where they could eat undisturbed together.

'Making reasonable progress, so far,' he began, not sure how to start on what he wanted to say.

'Aye, good enough,' John responded quietly.

'Your boy been right helpful getting hedgerow mended when 'e gets over,' he continued, hoping a bit of flattery would help his cause. 'Seems more gets done when he passes by.'

'Aye, be a good lad,' muttered John between mouthfuls.

'Could do with more of 'im, get job done and finished.'

'Oh, aye.' Silence followed with thoughtful chewing.

'Reckon be worth my while to pay the lad for regular days to get job done, if 'e can be spared, mind.'

'Oh, aye.' John started to think on the prospect—be good to have a bit extra come in, now and then like. No harm in 'im being away the odd day, no harm at all. He be going soon enough to work in full employ, do 'im good to get used to having other man's rules. 'Do you want me to talk with the lad then?'

'Aye, if he can be spared. It will help me out, right enough.' A satisfied silence fell over the pair, both thinking what a grand lunch break it was.

By afternoon break, William was desperately trying to look thoughtful and not break out with a tremendous grin as his father explained the proposition.

'Be all right I suppose, Father,' he said, stuffing a mouthful of apple in, with the juice dribbling down his chin. 'Providing you can spare me.' John looked at his boy, puzzled that he should eat an apple with his face pulled like that—must have got a sour one, perhaps.

'Just be sure to do a proper job of it. You be getting paid, then you got standards to meet. You'm be looking to be working away from home soon enough now and you'm got a chance now to show what you be made of. No more room for your larrikan nonsense with them lads down yonder cutting, no race about it now, you be cutting more than 'em, but dornee get so far ahead, you just piss 'em off. Cut yourself a wider lane and stay together. Menfolk will see what 'ee be about and get a measure of 'ee without this smart-arse show-off nonsense you be doing,' his father concluded, not at all sure that the boy understood the importance of the situation. He returned to work not sure if he understood any of his children any more.

Mary was watching her father talking seriously to her brother and his stupid great grin appearing on his face and spilling apple juice down his chin. 'Be careful William, you'll be giving the game away with silly looks like that. Father will realise we be up to something and all will be ruined.' With relief, she saw her father rise and her brother looked over and gave her a well-satisfied nod of his head and returned to work. When she got back to the kitchen with the dirty plates and empty baskets she was met at the door by an anxious Ann wanting to know what had happened.

'I didn't speak with William, but he and Father did eat together, and

William didn't half have a stupid great grin on his face when Father went back to work. Not a lot unlike the stupid great grin on your face, Ann.'

By the time day's end came, they all were wearily making their way home with a good day's work done in many ways.

'You may be pleased to know that my idea worked, Ann,' a tired Sidney Denslow said to his daughter. 'Young William White will be coming a day a week to work on hedgerow. I reckon I won on that deal as 'e be the best cutter out there today, 'e be a worker worth 'is pay, I reckon. If 'e measures up, I'll put 'im onto other chores, I be needing a man's help with. Aye, a pretty good day's effort I reckon on.'

Fortunately the gathering dusk helped hide Ann's delighted smile at the prospect of William's permanent visits. 'Aye, Father, you can be well pleased with such a satisfactory result to your idea.'

Likewise, Mary and William walked along with their father as he contentedly rubbed Dobbin's neck and told his son, 'Well lad, that be a grand day's work in the end. You cut more'n your share o'hay like a man and I got 'ee regular day's work with wages from old Sidney Denslow. T'is well we go back aways, Sid and I, for you to get an offer like that. Mother will be pleased.'

None more pleased than us, thought Mary, giving her brother a clip on the ear, to stop him laughing out loud.

Matilda and her mother were both secretly delighted to hear the three of them chatting among themselves as they came into the yard, Mother thinking that her instruction to leave Father alone with his horse had had the desired result, and Matilda guessing that Mary's plan had worked. Father was first through the door.

'Well Mary,' he pronounced, giving his wife a mighty hug and kiss on top of her head, 't'is been a fair old day, lad worked like a man and old Denslow and I came to an agreement for 'im to have regular day's employment over 'is farm. He to be paid in cash, too, not cider as 'e usually do, that be a first for 'im!'

Mary's glance past her husband's shoulder at her three eldest children's knowing faces told her that they knew more than they were going to let on. Getting William to get his father to work alone with Dobbin had had nothing to do with it—this was all their doing, along with that young Ann Denslow. They had set their fathers up and they hadn't a clue that their children had led them along.

'Well you must all be very pleased with your day's efforts,' she said, looking at her children, letting them know that fooling their father was

21

one thing, but fooling their mother was another. 'That's all right then,' she concluded, as if giving her approval as to how they had returned their father's humour.

Supper was a chatty, light-hearted meal. Tired as they were, they were still all privately jubilant at what the future now held for each of them. All retired to bed in a much more contented mood than the previous evening, to sleep and dream of attainable ambitions. Father took Mother in his arms with delight that what had worried him so much last night seemed of no concern tonight.

Much later, Mary wondered where her husband got his energy from, and whether there might be another child on the way.

The next morning, once the haymakers were on their way, Matilda collected her pans of settled milk and carefully placed them on the still-warm stove top. She tested the heat to be sure it was not too strong, as the best clotted cream came from a slow scalding of the milk below the now-floating layer of cream. Too much heat would stir up the milk and remix the cream and milk together. Slow and gentle, her gran had taught her, slow and gentle, and keep an eye on it. Leave it to do other things at your peril, she always said, as it is always best to lift it from the heat once a crust forms on the top. Knowing how much crust to allow to form was what dictated the quality of the clotted cream below. Too little and it all would not clot, losing some cream back into the milk; too much crust and the cream below would taste almost burnt, a bit of whey flavour tingeing the cream. Lifting at just the right moment produced a smooth, spreadable clotted cream with the cleanest taste, that brought out the best flavour of any jam that was added with it on scones or bread. To produce clotted cream like that was an art, and Matilda was considered one of the best. She carefully carried the pans back to the parlour to cool, making sure she did not disturb the milk and cream layers.

She went out to help her mother hang out the last of the washing, to be met with a despairing sigh.

'Can you do something with Charles, Matilda? He's made such a mess of cleaning the milking stall, it looks worse than it did before he started, and look how much he got on 'imself! Little wonder they don't want 'im over haymaking, all hindrance and no help.'

'Come on Charles,' said Matilda to her younger brother. 'We'll pick up the apples in the orchard, go and fetch an armful of sacks.' She turned to her mother, smiling. 'That will slow him down, pulling a sack of apples along.'

They headed off to the orchard, Matilda determined to direct Charles' constant chatter and energy into collecting the windfall apples ready for cider making. There were very few left of the popular early Morgan Sweet apples that could be used on their own to make the first cider of the year, and they were soon among the mixed planted trees of Kingston Black, Pound Apple, Billy Down Pippins, Plum Vinney and Crimson Kings. Her father had shown her that the orchard was planted out to suit the trees' ability to produce the fruit. The Morgan Sweet trees were together at the orchard's entrance, while the rest were planted in mixed rows flowering and producing much later. They were drinking this season's Morgan Sweet cider over at the haymaking, its apples falling from September. Cider from the rest of the trees was always mixed, as none of the apples individually made a nice cider, but mixed they produced a very palatable drink. Often enough, she had noticed, too palatable, as the drinkers had walking difficulties along with rather awful singing and laughing.

They worked their way along the rows pulling a sack behind them until it got too heavy for them to drag, and then she would lean the half-empty sack against a tree, continue to fill it by filling her apron and dropping them into the sack, while Charles would continue to partially fill a sack and take it over to one that he would fill to the brim.

Now if he could only work like this all the time, life would be so much more peaceful for me and Mother. It was a wish she knew would never be granted, as there was a sudden 'Tallyhoo!' and he went hurtling through the trees, throwing apples ahead of him.

'Gotchya, ya bliddy varmit!' he shouted in triumph, still running. 'Fall over, ya bliddy fowl-eating, plague-ridden, bliddy useless animal ever created, poxed pest!'

Matilda looked up to see a fox running off down to the bottom field, easily out-distancing Charles for all his efforts. Trying not to laugh at his outclassed performance and trying to sound stern, she called out, 'You stop that cussing this minute, Charles! You be swearing like your father at 'em and you be feeling your father's hand around yer ear! You knows what 'e thinks of that sort of language from young mouths and don't come at me that if 'e says it, so can you!' She turned quickly and went giggling back to her mother for lunch.

By the time the haymakers returned home that evening, Matilda had finished the afternoon milking and was carefully skimming off the clotted cream from the milk with a wooden spatula and filling punnets ready for sale. She held each punnet at a sharp angle, pushing the clotted cream

23

up into it so as to force any drops of milk out, watching with satisfaction the consistency of each ladleful. 'Tis a good brew, Gran,' she said to herself, acknowledging her departed gran's tuition. She put her punnets in the cool of the parlour and the remaining milk into a large jug to be used in cooking.

William walked in and leant against the doorway. 'All done, Sis? You ready to give me a hand to bring the apples in? You hold the cart steady and I'll load 'em and we can pull cart in together.'

'Only if we make two trips of it. I can't go pulling that lot in one load, even with you doing twice me.'

'Come on yer little sprat, I'll be kind to 'ee.'

'I be no sprat! I can do my share but that cart be bigger 'n me!'

'Cor dear oh dear! Pity help any silly bugger that takes you on. Wonder yer didn't march the bliddy apples in on their own!' he retorted, artfully dodging a flying spatula and heading out to get the cart.

Later they both surveyed the stacked apples they had brought in with some satisfaction.

'We'll do these Sunday, be more than enough for a cheese then. Reckon you can bring in the straw for me to save time? We be going on to next farm than ours while weather holds,' William said, looking down at his blistered forefinger from when the handle slipped.

So the pace of summer was set. The round of haymaking came to an end with not a drop of rain falling.

Matilda was always ready for market days and her trade was steady, her presence on Edith's stall benefiting all concerned, Matilda more so than she realised. Edith had long ago appreciated Matilda's sharp mind, and was determined to help her make the most of it. Each market day she would quietly correct the girl's speech, suggest a new word to describe something, and show her how to form proper sentences. She had a willing pupil, with Matilda showing her advancing skill on each subsequent visit. Edith took joy in it, never having thought when she first took on the stall to maintain her widowed lifestyle that it would become a classroom.

William earned the extra wages and more work was found for him. As one task finished, Sidney found another he had been leaving because he couldn't do on his own, but didn't want to admit it.

William and Matilda's extra time away from the farm had little impact on the rhythm of farm life, while adding to the purse.

It came to be held as one of the better years for production in the valley, with every farmer telling stories of their best yield, be it from crop or cow, each story developing depending on the volume of cider consumed, and the ability of the teller to remember what he had told previously, often forgetting what vegetable was involved, or which cow.

But more often, forgetting when to go home.

Chapter 4

1830–1837: A Wedding, Three Years On . . .

A dry summer had been followed by a harsh winter. Many farms had used all their meagre store of food, already diminished by a poor hay crop caused by the lack of summer rain. The ground had been hard and cracked for months, giving little real growth when haymaking needed to begin and producing awkward low stacks that were difficult to build.

The autumn barely existed as the temperature dropped and winter came marching in. Stock had been brought in early and the sudden snows that covered the valley in a complete blanket prevented them from being let out during the day a lot sooner than many could remember. It would be the winter that they would measure future winters by.

'Bin 'aving it too good for too long,' older farmers were heard to say before the cold dampness of winter had really set in to stay, 'be due for a shake-up'—spoken with stoic optimism before they realised what it would cost them. Much later, when they were living with the harsh reality, little was ever said beyond, 'Let nature take 'er course.' Only a few had guessed it would be so bad and had sold stock off in the early autumn market days, facing criticism for doing so.

'Leaving 'e a bit short for spring, ain't ee?' some said as they bought their neighbours' stock and looked forward to a bonus start in the spring for themselves. John was one that sold, but he would never reveal how he knew to do so. To be fair, he was not all that sure that he was doing the right thing, and William had certainly let him know he thought he was wrong.

'Why be 'ee selling so many, Father? You'm be leaving us short for new season. You gone three cows too many, and them heifers be coming in summer time would've upped our milking. We gonna 'ave sod all milk to sell at this rate and none left for Matilda to make 'er clotted cream from. I don't want to be near when 'ee tells 'er that and 'er market days are over!'

His father very softly said, half to himself, 'I think she already knows.' He thought back to the last days of summer when it was their farm's turn to be the last one for haymaking. His disappointment at the low yield he was to get was tempered by how low all the others had been; even the big farm's 10-acre field made a miserable stack.

The last of the helpers were finishing off the cider from the stone jars, Matilda strolling among the men filling their cups while Dick followed her carrying the last jar. She approached her father, and Dick moved forward.

'I give'm from this 'un, it be cooler, Miss M,' he said as he filled John's cup.

'Thank you, Dick, and thanks for your help today. Stacks a bit low, but no worse than others, we been got through a winter with less, I reckon,' he said, ever hopeful he could get a conversation out of him.

'Hello John,' was Dick's customary reply. He half turned to Matilda and added in a soft voice as if John wasn't there, 'Tell 'ee father he be way too short, he dornne a chance with present stock, we be in for snow 'ee neber seen the likes of,' and he started to walk away.

Matilda turned with him, saying, 'Thank you, Dick, I'll let him know.' She was so used to Dick's ways that it never occurred to her that it was an odd conversation, seeing as how her father would have clearly heard everything they said, he being not two paces away. John too was puzzled. *Snow!* he thought, looking at the parched ground and clear blue sky. *We will be lucky to get rain at this rate.*

That evening, as Matilda passed by her father, she said, as though there had been no break from the afternoon's encounter, 'What are you going to do about it?' and left the question hanging in the air, not expecting a reply at all. John watched his daughter move on and help her mother with the dishes.

Something, he couldn't help think to himself, *and damned if some don't take me for a fool for doing so, but I will be seen as a bigger fool if they knew why!*

They did get through, but barely so. All the hay was used and anything else he could find was used as well. Turnips, carrots and potatoes were used from the store to help supplement the hay, the family having to go short because of it. Mary had rationed the food as much as possible from early on, helped by a late crop of potatoes that Matilda had put in.

The later part of the winter was the worst. Barely a soul was seen about, all locked in their own desperate cells bound by a deepening depression. All available spare hay and other fodder had long since been snapped up, there was no longer a market for those with too much stock to feed, with the last three market days showing dismal prices for the few that were sold, and most farmers taking their own stock back home with them. Condition on the beasts fell away quickly, making it inevitable for many to be slaughtered in an attempt to be able to make the feed last for the rest.

There were three lonely deaths. Eric never looked after himself at best of times, with too bigger proportion of his diet being cider, a fair bit of it being consumed at the inn of an evening. When he had had his fill, or run out of ability to pay for more, he would tell all present that he was 'flup to ears . . . I stop before it runs out'er 'em,' and with unsure steps make his way out the door and home. But this night he didn't quite get home. Stumbling by the gate, he fell and, lacking strength and balance, couldn't push himself up out of a snow drift. In his drunken stupor he felt comfortable enough and fell asleep where he lay. They found him there, frozen in place, only a boot showing out of the snow in the morning.

It was the squire himself who went into Wilkinsons' cottage to see how they were. One of his lads had reported seeing no smoke from their chimney and no sign of them about when he was coming down from other lane. Squire was concerned from the start as the Wilkinsons were both in their late seventies and had worked on the estate since his father's time, near on sixty years.

Wind-blown snow was pressed and frozen against the cottage door and he had to kick it free from its icy lock. The air was freezing inside, the fire had died, but there was a pile of dry wood beside it ready for it to be stoked up fresh when they came down in the morning. He called but got no answer. Almost nervously and with trepidation, he climbed the stairs to their bedroom, still calling their names as he went. He saw them at last as he pushed open their bedroom door, a cold draught blowing through a break in the window that had allowed a dusting of snow to be sprinkled across the floor and bed covers. They lay together to share each other's warmth, wrapped in each other's arms for the last time, still showing in death a love for each other that began sixty years before. He left them in their final embrace, returned to the manor and organised their funeral. He sent messengers out to their three remaining children, one as far away as Dorchester, with the sad news, and arranged for them all to be present.

It was in depressed times like these that the recruiting officers from the army regiments would appear, often from regions as far away as Derbyshire and Nottinghamshire. They would be full of cheer and stories of opportunity for young men in their regiment, buying drinks in the local inns and getting the word spread that they were looking to take on new lads. Many farmers saw this as a relief too good to be true, as the future for their sons was anything but sure. Many of the young men saw it as an opportunity for a whole new exciting life, a life without the restrictions and hardships that they had to endure in winters like these, and enrolled happily enough.

In many cases there was a direct immediate bonus for the lad's family as occasionally a bounty was paid, and this could be as much as a pound. In the grip of a disastrous winter, a pound could make the difference in seeing the bad time off. Little consideration was given to the extra workload created by one of the boys leaving; there was normally only room for one lad to stay on and the rest would be moving away at some point as a matter of course.

As spring warmed the land, folk took stock of winter's toll. Quiet condolences among the farmers who had had to reduce stock levels solely to survive, and were now trying to foresee how they would fare the summer months with a much depleted stock level. Buying replacement stock was out of the question as any money gained by selling the stock was used in feeding the family through a long winter, and a long period of waiting for the gardens to produce.

Some would face three good seasons to regain their previous years' standards. Women would compare ways of feeding a hungry family with so little, hoping someone would come forth with a recipe that would add much-needed variety to a dull and much-repeated diet.

But probably the saddest and longest loss to bear, and never spoken of, was borne by the maidens of the valley, who, once released from the snow's prison, found that the lad they had fancied had vanished with the snow into the folds of the army. Not only gone from the valley, but in all likelihood, gone for good, to be trained and sent to India and unlikely to return.

So the first reading of the banns of marriage announcing a young couple's hopes for their future brought a wave of relief and light-heartedness to the valley folk.

'I publish the banns of marriage for William White of this parish and Ann Denslow of the parish of Broadhembury. This is for the first time of reading. Should any of you know just cause or due impediment why

29

these two should not be joined together in Holy Matrimony, ye are to declare it.'

The vicar was sure he felt a wave of warmth flow up from the congregation; such familiar words, said often enough and not heard, but the names meant so much to those sitting in his church. He couldn't help smiling himself.

This time even John had attended, just to hear the banns mind, not for the rest of it. Barely had they got in the door than the first of their neighbours came knocking, bringing well wishes and a jar of cider. By the end of the hour, the womenfolk were arriving with smiles and hot scones and cakes. Laughter was heard coming from the kitchen and parlour, spreading like a contagious smile over the valley. Mary was particularly pleased to see Madeline come by with her two children, who quickly disappeared off to the barn and the noise of other children playing. Madeline had been a widow for three years now. Her husband, a miserable sod by all accounts, had died from being thrown from his horse one evening coming home. Miserable and penny-pinching though he was, he did leave her well-off and she lived a solitary life alone, looking after her children, with little involvement in the village life.

'Madeline, how very kind of you to come by and wish the youngsters well for the future,' Mary said, welcoming her in.

'I do hope you don't mind,' she began awkwardly. 'I was so pleased to hear the good news. To begin with love is so important and so often forgotten for convenience's sake. Oh dear, what I meant was . . .'

'Hush now Madeline, I do understand what you mean. Now come and have tea—there is so much here to eat with all that has been brought along. Matilda, go and fetch William back in here, he sneaked out back to the barn getting into the cider.'

Matilda returned a little while later with a dishevelled William and two dirty and dusty children.

'William!' his mother exclaimed.

'Hello Madeline, I be right sorry about the children,' said a contrite William. 'We be playing hide and seek and a rack of sacks came down on us, tis my fault. Matilda was going to get 'em scrubbed up before you saw 'em.' A breathless silence fell over them all as Madeline surveyed her grey and dusty brood half hiding behind William.

At first slowly, and then with a flash, a smile spread across her face. With hands to her cheeks she laughed and said, 'I wouldn't bother, be off and play you two. You can be cleaned up just the once when we go!'

And she added her congratulations to William. It was the first time any of them had seen Madeline smile for years.

Mary and Matilda slipped out to do the milking, sharing the unexpected success resulting from Mary's plan of years before to get Matilda to the market.

'Did you think Ann would play her part in your plan so well?'

'I thought she might, but I didn't reckon on William being so keen.'

'He was always late getting back to pick me up, always said it took longer than he thought. Seems as how it wasn't the work that was holding him up—funny how he never mentioned Ann at all.'

'Doubt if he will ever stop now it's announced. Old man Denslow will have to find someone else to work for him, cause Ann won't leave William alone if 'e goes over there now. Fathers will be watching 'em like a hawk from now on.'

'Mary, whatever do you mean? They've been ever so proper when they been in company.'

'Dornee be so innocent, Matilda. The only time I see William run is toward her and she can turn on a fair lick of speed when he shows up. They will need prising apart with an iron bar at the drop of a hat from now on.'

'Mary!' Matilda exclaimed, shocked, but she giggled uncontrollably at the prospect of it.

Once all the excitement had died down, Ann's mother began to worry about how they were ever going to be able to provide a suitable wedding for their daughter, one to be proud of. She knew only too well how pitifully low their cash was and they had very little left to trade with, and they wanted to marry so soon.

'Dornee worry, my love,' Sidney told his wife repeatedly, 'us'll be right on the day.' Her frustration grew as he could never tell her *how* it would come right on the day.

Mary couldn't see her son being any more ready to be married then than he was now. There was not enough for either farm to support him full time, and William had been working on both farms in equal share.

'What on earth does he think he is going to do with a wife to care for?'

'Hush lass,' John would tell his wife, 'dornee worry so. There be time yet to sort lad out before he get marched up 'e aisle.' But when pressed, he couldn't say how.

Ann herself would have been happy standing at the altar in work clothes, just as long as she could get married to William. The sooner the better. For three years they had courted with increasingly deepening love, first shyly and quietly, with no outward indication of their mutual feelings for others to see. But since last summer they had struggled with controlling unbidden surges of passion, leaving her breathless in anticipation with what might yet occur before her wedding night. Now the banns were read and everyone knew of their love, it was so much easier to show their feelings for each other in front of folk.

Recently, when they had been alone, she was puzzled as to how or who had released her bodice, blaming her pounding heart that needed the extra room to beat.

William was, to all appearances, his usual unruffled self, shy in the congratulations of his impending marriage, and unconcerned at his soon-to-be increased responsibilities. He carried on working wherever he was required, sure that it would all sort itself out in time. His only mild concern was actually getting to the church on time, as he was sure that the stitching in his trousers was not going to withstand too much more pressure.

His two oldest sisters were no help to him at all. Matilda, with increasing understanding, would tease him without mercy. Mary would tease Ann even more, often taking her away from William to have a 'big sister chat' and returning giggling and blushing from a conversation on which he was never enlightened.

The fathers, however, noticed none of this. There was farming work to do, and no time for any nonsense. But between them and their neighbours, they did get William and his future wife their own farm employment.

There was huge relief for the mothers that the couple were both to be employed. William was to work for the Burton's on their farm at Colyton, and Ann was returning to her work as a milliner with her old tutor in Colyton, making hats for a retailer in Exeter. Providing that a family was not too soon in arriving, then they should be just fine. While both fathers secretly enjoyed vivid memories of their early wedded enthusiastic activities, conception, they hoped, would bide its time.

With time to spare, there was enough material found to make Ann a most desirable gown, and a suit of almost correct size was lent to William.

The joyful wedding day finally arrived, with folk from miles around Umbourne crowding the church at Shute to witness the first and without doubt the most popular wedding since the storms.

Sidney's chest fair burst with pride as he walked up the aisle, while Ann concentrated on walking as slowly as possible beside him, trying to hide her eagerness to get there. Mary walked behind them as bridesmaid, doing her best to make her smile seem one of happiness and hide the temptation to laugh aloud at Ann's impatient steps to get beside William. William, his composure gone, stood by the vicar and grinned like a showground clown. John watched his son and hoped no one else could read his daft face as well as he. 'Bliddy fool needs concentrating on wedding first,' he muttered. He glanced down at his wife and was grateful that Mary already had tears filling her eyes and wouldn't see their son's expression.

Matilda was in awe of it all. Would it be like this for her? Was there someone she could feel that way about as Ann and William so clearly did for each other?

Chapter 5

1837–1838: An Unlikely Relationship

It was Father who finally pushed Matilda into returning to the market, even though she could only muster up a few punnets of strawberries of good enough quality.

'Let 'em be knowing you be coming in again, lass. Sooner folk knows you be in, sooner word gets by they needs to be there to get 'em. Sets 'ee up for when we 'ave enough milk spare for your clotted cream. That be not but a few weeks yonder, mind, so's them needs be telling it be coming along.'

Edith smiled like a child getting a lollipop at the fair when Matilda came toward her with her small offering.

'Goodness lass, you are a welcome sight.' She gave a shrug as Matilda showed her how little she had for her first day. 'Don't worry about how much, now we will get the punters back who have been asking for your strawberries and cream. The market has been like a funeral procession, full of long faces and empty pockets. They have been trying to get life back here since the snows shut it down. There has been nothing of quality to sell either, truth be known, and folks all know it. Nothing to sell and no cash to buy it with. Margery has not been back yet, lost her will to keep on like a lot of them that suffered badly. She will soon return now you are here, along with others. It will give them something to say for the report on the market in the paper, as a sign of better times arriving.' She took a breath and looked Matilda up and down. 'The winter has done you no harm– you have grown two years older in the five months gone!'

'Dornee be daft, bit of weight is all.'

'Bit of weight, true enough, and the lads will tell you where it's gone on. I hope that drunken lout be not paying you attention and causing trouble?'

'No, he be no bother any more, nor 'is cronies likely to. Dick went to castrate him along with the pigs and the stupid fool took Dick as serious and they daren't even look at me now!'

'Bit mazed as a sheep, is he? Does he talk to anyone but you?'

''Course he does, just not a lot,' Matilda replied. 'Just not got a lot to say.'

The next market day Edith was all a-jitter, waiting for Matilda to arrive.

'Look at this, Matilda, I told you so! It's as I said! You are in the paper as a new item with your fresh strawberries in the market report. Look here and read it yourself.' Matilda took the offered paper and gazed at the massed type, confused.

'I'll tell Father, he'll be so proud,' she said putting the paper aside. Edith looked at her in surprise that she hadn't bothered to read it straight away. Then with sickening regret, it came to her.

'I'm sorry, lass, but don't tell me you can't read?'

'Don't be sorry, Edith. None of us have been to school, nor can Mother and Father read. We have been on the farm, and farm work is what we do best, we have no need for reading and writing.'

'But lass, you talk so well with all about, you do sums in your head quick as you like, you know your money and give correct change. Goodness, you even stop smart alecs from cheating Margery without seeming to pay them any attention. How can you do that without being able to read and write?'

'I don't know Edith, just farm work I suppose. You can't farm if you don't know what it's all worth and how to bargain for it, can you?'

'I don't suppose you can, but wouldn't you have had to write it all down to know for next year? You have learnt new words quickly—more than I thought an unread person would be able.'

'I just listen a lot, I suppose, and remember.'

Edith was amazed by the revelation, more determined than ever to teach Matilda better English. Like Matilda's mother, she wondered what Matilda could have achieved if she had been literate. She was roused from her thoughts by a sudden bustling of skirts and chatter.

'Oh I'm so pleased to see you back. I was sure it was you they were talking about in the paper. Please say you still have some for sale and I am not too late to get some. Father was such a bore about coming in to get some with nonsense about paper work to do, as if eating was unnecessary, and next time will do, and just wasn't going to budge from his desk, even though he loved them last year and cursed having to come into Axminster to get them when our gardener should have been providing them from our garden, which is way big enough, and it's what he pays him for after all, and all he produces are small, sour hard things that father refuses to eat, so why he can't get organised to come and get them I really do not know. So I left him there and got Martins to bring me in without telling Father, who will be furious if I have done all that and go home without any, so please let me have some!'

This flood of words came from a pretty young lady standing breathless before Matilda, who waited, smiling, with a punnet of strawberries held out in her hand.

'Will these ones be all right, do you think?' Matilda finally got to say.

'Oh, how wonderful! They are perfect. Can I take two, as Father will eat one on his own when he sees them? I'm so lucky you still had them, I was getting worried what Father would say when we got home. Now he will have less to say, and I can handle that.'

At this point a dapperly dressed gentleman arrived.

'There you are, Miss Hannah, you mustn't go running off like that. You know your father will be most upset if he finds you had been off on your own in a place like this!'

'Do not worry yourself about it, Martins, he will only find out if you tell him, because I'm not going to. Now look at these and tell me if it hasn't all been worth it?'

'Yes, Miss Hannah, your father will be pleased to have them. But I doubt if he will be at all pleased on how they were attained. I do not think he will let the matter rest on the production of such fine strawberries.'

'Martins, you are such a worrier. I will go in first and see him, he will be fine. Now, miss, would it be possible for you to hold three punnets each market so we can avoid this unseemly rush and any bother Martins seems sure we are in when we get home? I will, of course, pay you in advance so that you suffer no loss should I fail to get in. Should I be detained I will send in Martins or one of the other servants, who will ask for our order. My name is Hannah Hill, from Fairfield Lodge. May I have your name, so they can identify themselves correctly?'

'My name is Matilda,' Matilda replied smiling, wondering if she ever stopped talking or even slowed down enough for her father to be able to reprimand her, 'Matilda White.'

'Well there we are then, Matilda,' Hannah said, offering her hand in agreement. 'That's just splendid, and a fine arrangement we have come to, even if I do say so myself. Quite a splendid day's work, as Father is often heard to say. Now come along, Martins, and do stop fidgeting like that. Nobody's going to kidnap me, but we must return before he notices you are missing.' With that, she whirled poor Martins about and marched him from the stalls. At the corner she turned back to Matilda, and waved.

'Well, that's a turn up for the books,' Edith said. 'That's Squire Hill's daughter from Lyme Regis. I'm sure she will get away with coming over, but I reckon that that Martins fellow will get a dressing down from the Master, no matter what the result, and he knows it!'

Matilda was too entranced to care. *She used my name as though I were a friend, not a stall worker.*

'Matilda, you're dreaming, customers waiting!' called Edith, smiling at Matilda's faraway look.

It wasn't long after that Matilda had sold the last of her stock, but she carried on helping Edith. There were several people coming by to buy strawberries who went away empty-handed, disappointed at missing out, but determined to be earlier next time. All of them were quietly pleased that the girl with the strawberries was back at the market; the horrible winter was at last fading away.

She was helping Edith pack away the last of her stall when she heard her name called quietly behind her,

'Hello Matilda, I wondered if you would still be here. Could you spare me a minute?' Matilda turned and met the inquisitive gaze from Madeline, who was standing with her two children beside her.

'Why don't you go off with the lady and talk on yonder bench, Matilda— I will finish off here,' Edith offered. She was sure she knew the woman from somewhere, but couldn't place her.

'Thank you, Edith. Come on, it will be quiet enough over there.'

'Thank you, Matilda, that is kind of you.' Madeline led her children to the bench and sat them at the end. She began hesitantly. 'I have been speaking with Mary, asking if she knew anyone who could help me in the garden occasionally. Perhaps I should explain a little—since we came over to share William's good news, your sister and I have met and chattered more often than ever before, and she has encouraged me to try and perhaps have women folk home on occasion, for tea. She felt that I was being too within myself since my husband died. She thought it would help the children, if others came to our house, and their mothers came by as well. Because no one does, you see, and nor have I really wanted them to. Mary thinks it wrong for the children not to have others in our house, and since they had such a delightful time at your place, then perhaps she is right. My problem is that I have rather let it all go and there is really nowhere for the children to run around outside—the garden is a wilderness of brambles and nettles and it needs clearing, which is really quite beyond me. It really is a man's work, but I no longer have the confidence to enquire into these matters directly. Because of my marriage, I feel quite afraid of men. I'm afraid that I thought that Mary had taken me to be rather a silly person and was wasting her time, and I almost walked away from her, as she took so long to say anything. But then she put her hand on my arm, smiled warmly, and said she had thought of just the person. She had a lad in mind who would certainly do the work well, and would always be courteous to me, but I should talk to you to organise it all, as apparently you will be able to get him to do as asked without any bother. I was so relieved at someone being able to help that I quite forgot to ask her who she had in mind. Has she spoken to you about it yet?'

'Well no, not really to such a point. But I can certainly get him organised.' Matilda was taken aback. Mary could only be thinking of Dick—but why? There were plenty of men needing work that could do the job just as well, that would be no bother for Madeline, so why Dick? What was Mary playing at now?

'Now you have gone quiet on me like Mary—why is that?' Madeline interrupted her thoughts nervously.

'Oh I'm so sorry, Madeline. I didn't mean to be rude. The truth is he may be a surprising choice to you. Mary is thinking of Dick, and too many people treat him as though he is the village idiot.'

Madeline tried to hide her surprise. Her initial thought was that they were making a joke of her, and she began to feel upset, as though betrayed by them when she had asked for help. But Matilda had carried on talking and she missed what was first said. 'I'm sorry Matilda, your choice surprised me and I was not listening. Mary didn't tell me on purpose, as she knew I would never have come to ask you if I knew who it was.'

'That's all right, but please don't judge Dick on the only way you have seen him, and the only way everyone speaks about him. He just doesn't know how to put words to things. I be not knowing why he will always do as I ask when he takes no orders from others. But he will do a proper job of it. He will be doing it his own way, but it works out as you would want. I doubts if he will talk to you, that is one thing I can't get him to do. I do know he will be always quiet, won't do anything to worry you,

38

or to be upset about. He will worry about what others will say about him being there. If he up and leaves in the middle of work, it's likely 'cause of some stupid remark made in his hearing about you asking him to do the job. Most times he comes looking for me when that happens and I go and sort him out. But it's up to you, Madeline—if you are ready to take him on then I will talk with him and I will bring him over for the first time to get him started and stay a while—he settles better that way.'

'Thank you Matilda, how can I refuse? He sounds just the person I need. When will you talk to him?'

'When do you want him to start?'

'As soon as he likes—I have no preference for any day for him to work.'

'I will get him organised then. There is just one thing you need to be ready for and it could be a worry to you. I have tried to stop his one bad thing he does—when he needs to relieve himself he will just go off by a tree or wall and pee. It just don't worry him any, be folk about or not. I have told him so many times and all I get is, "Yes Miss M, but the bull don't care either." His is a world of animals more than folk. I can only tell 'ee to walk away as though you have seen nothing, and come back later. He has lived all his life being put down and made a fool of at every turn, but 'e knows that what he has there is better than any other man, and none will challenge him on it. That be as far as his misbehaviour will go. He will come to me if he has upset you, and he will find me in his uncanny way, wherever I am, and tell me what has happened. So now knowing that, do you still want him in your garden?'

'Is it likely to happen? What has happened when he has worked for other women?'

'He makes no habit of it, it's just his way of dealing with the nature's call, and it means no more than that. He has left working for women a couple of times because they stood there and stared at him, he has always told me why he left them as he is a bit afraid of what they may do to him.'

'Then I am happy for him to come and do my garden. It is unlikely that anything will happen in front of me because I will be inside doing my needlework and writing. Thank you for being so honest—my uncertainty with men is because of the way my husband treated me and I have kept a distance from them ever since. If Dick does his work in the garden as you say, then I accept that, and I'm sure he will do a good job.'

39

Dick felt very proud when Matilda told him of the job; he had heard how many were looking for more work, and trying to get by on less, and here he had got a job ahead of others. Because of Matilda.

'Now you listen very carefully, Dick—Madeline is scared of men.'

'Yes Miss M. I seen 'er turn away from 'em when out.'

'You must be very gentle near her when she comes outside.'

'Yes Miss M, I keep back abit.'

'I don't want you going pee when she's outside.'

'No Miss M, but it no difference . . .'

'And dornee go on about a bull. You will just scare her, understand?'

'Yes Miss M, I'll watch out for her.'

'Her husband died when he fell from his horse, she told me he mistreated her. She is nervous of having a man on her property, just be very careful of her Dick, like you are for me, all right?'

'Yes Miss M, 'e busted 'is neck. He was a nasty man. She be better off without 'im.'

'She probably is better off without him, but who ever really knew what he was like to her? I didn't know his neck was broken, we were just told he had fallen from his horse.'

'I just knows, I suppose, but I be real careful with her for you Miss M,' he added quickly, worried that he had revealed too much of his knowledge on her husband's death.

Everything fell into place so very easily. Matilda took Dick along to Madeline and she explained what she wanted done; Dick followed behind them nodding his head, and saying yes to everything she wanted doing, and where all the rubbish was to be burnt. Mondays will be best as there would be no washing on the line, and when all was explained to Madeline's satisfaction, he said to Matilda, 'I'll be making somewhere for the children to play, then.' And he wandered off back down the garden to find where he would start.

'We will just be inside for a cup of tea, Dick,' Madeline called after him. He lifted a hand in acknowledgement of hearing without turning around. 'What do you think, Matilda? Do you think he will be all right here? Will he answer me at all?'

'I am very sure he will be just fine. I don't know if he will ever really talk to you, but he will with expression and gesture. That wave is more than Mother has had after years of him coming by. Yes, I really think you might be able to learn to relax when he is about.'

Madeline smiled a little more confidently.

So Dick became a regular Monday morning visitor in Madeline's garden. He came and went at his own odd hours and worked in an odd pattern, clearing and tidying. Madeline was happy to see her shambles being cleared, and the children came home from school each Monday keen to see what had been cleared next.

Chapter 6

1838–1840: Relationships Blossom

It was almost a relief to John and Mary when William left to set up house with Ann in Colyton. The rest of the family were growing up fast and they needed the room. John was never short of labour and even after William had gone the house seemed full of adults. None of them seemed in a hurry to leave, either for new work or for marriage.

'Ain't 'bout time they got 'emselves married?' said John to his wife. 'You be spoiling them too much, they still be 'anging on 'ere. Mary lass will be left on shelf if she don't 'urry up and take a lad, she be far too quick at seeing 'em off with a flea in their ear. She be thirty and old maid before 'er time. Matilda better be careful too, she be past marrying age for such a good catch as she, she be near on twenty-four. But doubts anyone game enough to get close since Dick tried castrating his brother for getting interested.'

Mary rolled over in their bed and leant up on one elbow. John realised too late he had said too much about her girls, and copped a clip on his ear and a tirade from his protective wife.

'John White. You need being grateful you got such good children! There be nothing wrong with Mary waiting for the right man, a lot more marriages would be successful if young'ns had waited to get the right partner. You look around at the miserable marriages about you because they rushed into it. Doan you tell me that you would want a daughter of ours to be bound in misery?' Mary paused for breath, and John tried valiantly to save the situation.

'Of course not, my dear. I only mentioned it . . .'

'You should think before you mention anything! What kind of mess

42

do you think Matilda would have been in if Dick hadn't turned up? You be grateful you still got such a smart girl in one piece! And there have been plenty looking but none good enough. And who got all mizzy-mazzy about her growing up, and not wanting 'er to leave home, eh?'

John held his peace—there was nothing to gain by pointing out how many years had passed since then.

'And you don't want Charles leaving yet, he needs learning responsibility now William's gone, you left 'im out of too much in preference of William. He needs sorting and working hard here and kept away from them land girls up big farm, though I doubts they would know who the father of their baby be, they be trying out the valley and we don't want 'im trapped in that sort of marriage. Young Ann be fine but not sharp. Matilda takes her in hand out of doors, but she don't seem to catch on like others. You get yourself busy with showing Charles what's right and what's wrong and leave 'em well alone on getting 'em gone! You sleep on that, John White, and see if I'm not wrong.' And with that off her chest, she gave him a kiss goodnight, rolled over and went promptly to sleep. John tossed and turned, trying to rid his mind of all the grumblings he heard from unhappy men about their wives, and knew full well how he would react if one spoke of his daughter like that.

As it was, their concerns for Mary were shortly about to come to an end. Oddly enough, it was Dick who had started it just a few weeks before. He had been passing by the church when they all came out, and Mary and Matilda both went over to him to see how the work for Madeline was going. He stopped by Matilda and quietly said, 'Hello Miss M, tis be a fair job o' gardening I be doing, she be mending I feel, she come out now at times to see what I be doing, neber saw her once to begin with, but I keeps me distance like you told me to. Morning Mary,' he added as an afterthought.

'That's very good to hear, Dick. Does Madeline follow what you are doing?' Matilda asked, pleased that the situation there was going smoothly.

'Aye, she talks and I shows her, she doan be so scared of me, I reckon.'

'Perhaps she might mend easier if you said an answer sometimes, just a word now and then, like name the plants you would like to put in, that she could then get for you to plant next time you go. You might help her mend that way.'

'I try for you Miss M, but words dorne want to come out.' He sighed mightily, then added, 'Mary might like to know there be a new man up at big house, be working inside for Master, he be called Richard Hoyle. Tell Mary he got somethin', be no mump'ead, 'e talked nice to me.'

And off he wandered, worried that he was almost certainly going to let Matilda down, and not find even one word he could say to Madeline. Mary laughed and took Matilda's arm in hers.

'Well now, how do you think he will find words for Madeline, who he hardly knows, when he still won't talk to me when I'm beside you? And since when has he been thinking I need marrying off, like Father does?'

'You know I don't know how he thinks, but I have to try to get him talking, anything is worth trying,' replied Matilda. 'It scares me that he sees into people and knows they need "mending". But if this Richard Hoyle has got something, then maybe you should find out what it is.'

'Matilda! Don't you start as well!' Mary exploded, then laughed. 'He must be a servant if he is working for the Master; how are we going to meet him out of the house to find out? How did Dick meet him, because Dick would never go inside the big house? Why didn't you ask Dick how he met him?'

'Lory be, Mary, one minute you go hissy-fit at me for wanting to set you up, and the next you blame me for not doing so! What am I supposed to do?'

They laughed together and hurried to catch up with the others.

There was little time to think more on it as they were met by John leading William's horse.

'Be quick Mary, William been home in a tizzy and be gone again. Ann be in labour and she be wanting you to help her. He came with two 'orses to make trip in quicker.'

Without a word she grabbed the reins and pulled her skirts about her. John helped her into the saddle and she promptly left at a fast trot for Colyton.

'Careful there Mary,' John called after the fading sound of clipping hooves. Even at a good steady trot through the narrow part of the lanes and as fast a gallop as she could handle on the flat, she was too late. She burst into Ann's room to find her sitting up holding a very pink and wet baby boy.

'He just popped out all of a rush, Mary,' Ann said, crying. 'I didn't reckon on it being so fast—William just got in the door and it all happened.'

With that, William rushed in with hot water and towels, the nurse following closely.

'Well bless my soul, we all arrived after the little thing I see,' the nurse jovially said and busied herself with tiding baby and mother up.

'Our first grandchild and it's a boy,' Mary murmured with tears running down her cheeks. 'John will be so pleased.'

By now Matilda had started making clotted cream for the market, with Henrietta and her girls yielding much more milk than previously. More often than not, Hannah would arrive at her stall by mid-morning to collect her strawberries; very rarely did a servant arrive instead. As with this morning, Hannah would wait until Matilda was free, so they could chat for a bit.

'Good morning, Matilda, I trust I find you well?'

'Good morning, Hannah, yes, very well indeed. Even better, in fact, I am now an aunt! My brother William has a baby son and it's so exciting!'

'Yes Matilda, it should be exciting, and I'm pleased for you,' Hannah replied with a smile, thinking of her family's formal reaction to her two nephews born into the family so far. *Why are we so dull about family matters,* she wondered, *when Matilda gets so much joy from it?* She smiled even more at the thought of how the household would have handled the situation if she had reacted as excitedly as Matilda. She held Matilda's hand and said, 'Yes, I truly am very happy for you.' She envied her luxury of openly showing her joyful emotions, and then she laughed aloud at the thought of Matilda in her house and her energy in those sedate surroundings.

'I'm afraid the strawberries are going to be past their best very soon, Hannah—the early start isn't going to make for a long season. A few weeks more and they will start to get watery and not be very tasty, be only good for jam. I do not think you should be paying in advance when I am not sure of the quality, but you could try taking some of my clotted cream.'

'We must have them for next market day as my brother will be home from Oxford for a visit before he goes on a European tour. I've told him how tasty your strawberries are, and he eats them more than Father. Let me take four punnets next time, and some cream as well. Mother is planning a dinner for him when he arrives.'

'Thank you, Hannah—I will keep a special lot aside for you.'

'Has the baby a name yet?'

'He is to be named John, after his grandfather.'

'That's my father's name as well, isn't that funny?' And so they chatted like two lifelong friends, Matilda serving customers all the while until Hannah's servant came to collect her.

'You have made a friend with her, Matilda—you're probably the only person who can handle that constant chattering!' Edith chided her.

'You must be getting too old to remember what it's like to be young,' Matilda shot back, with both of them smiling at their banter.

But it was not a nephew that got Matilda most excited, it was what her sister greeted her with when she got home. She could see that Mary was bursting to tell her something, and helped her out by suggesting that they get on with milking if she wanted. Mary could barely wait till they were out of the house before she burst out, 'I've met him!'

'Who have you met, Mary?' Matilda asked, not even vaguely sure who she meant.

'Richard Hoyle, you daft thing! Who do you think?'

'Oh, the mysterious Richard! How did you manage that, and why the excitement?'

'Dick was absolutely right, he is different and I met him because he takes Master's mail down for posting at village agents. Matilda, he is the most likely man for me I've ever met, and I intend to get to check his credentials, as you might say, before any other maid gets a look in!'

'Mary, forgive me the obvious, but how can you be in the village at the same time as Richard? You can't know when Master will want the mail taken in, and you can't know when you can be free to go in. It could be months before you meet again.'

'Dear Matilda, I do have a plan—don't be so naive to think that I haven't got that all worked out. And Richard has agreed!'

'What!' Matilda exploded. 'You already have him agreeing to meet you?'

'Once you meet him, you will know I cannot waste a day. It's quite simple, really. His master always has letters and papers he works on that he wants to go out that day. To save in trying to meet the early post, he keeps it all, and then sends it out by the last post. To be sure he doesn't miss it, he is sending Richard down every day at the same time in the afternoon. All I have to do is be there to meet him. From there events, will take care of themselves.'

'But Mary, how can you be sure Father will let you go? You may be in the middle of something for him.'

'I'm thirty and unmarried, Matilda—do you think he will even try to stop me?'

'No, perhaps not.'

'Anyway, it will do Charles good to work harder. It's my turn to disappear if it suits me.'

'Do let me know how he shapes up. Where has he come from for us not to know of him, and when will I meet him?'

'You can meet him when I decide that he is going to be my husband. Before that, there is no point.'

So Mary began taking walks later in the afternoon that gradually became longer. Richard always left the big house at the same time with the afternoon mail, but gradually returned a little later. Charles quickly learnt that it was not a good thing to complain to Father that Mary was doing less work in the afternoons, and he had to do more to cover for her. A short, sharp lash from Father's tongue made it clear that what Mary did was none of Charles' business, and Charles had better shape up with more attention to farm work if he was to do anything with his life.

Matilda watched and waited. It was clear from the glow on Mary's face and the lightness in her step, that so far, Richard was measuring up very well. The occasional sly wink from her sister over the dinner table told her that progress was being made.

Mary did say that she had met Madeline in the village and she appeared to be more assured. She said that she was more comfortable with Dick in the garden working, and the project was nearing completion. She went out at the same time with a cool drink for him, and chattered away about the garden to him and accepted his silence as part of his manner, although he often pointed and moved his hands as to what he intended to do next and where plants should go. They both agreed that big steps forward were being made by the two of them.

Madeline, in fact, was very pleased with the progress, both within herself and in the garden. She had not thought it possible that she would ever be able to talk in a relaxed manner with any male again, but then she had to admit that Dick was hardly a typical male. He never spoke a word, either in question or answer. He never stood near her, giving her plenty of space. He always moved so gently for such a big man, and showed no aggression or impatience. Even when clearing the most reluctant brambles, he would mutter at them, calling them 'bliddy taildor's niddles' as he tugged them free. He would nod and give a faintest smile in thanks when he handed back his empty mug and turned to resume his work. It was a strange emotion to her that after such a period of constantly being in fear of men because of the brutality of her husband, that she could now be near Dick and stay calm.

'Yes, that is what it is,' she said to herself. 'I feel calm, for the first time in this house, I feel calm. He's been gone nearly four years, and at last I am calm.' She put down her needlework, walked to the kitchen and leant against the door, looking down the garden where Dick was working, and where the children were already able to play. 'Yes, it will now be a proper home for my children, a safe home.' She smiled.

As she was up and in the kitchen, she decided she might as well make Dick his cool drink—it was nearly time any way. She got it ready and made one for herself too for a change, and wandered down to give it to him, further down the back than she last saw him.

She realised her mistake as soon as she saw him. As he would not have expected her this soon, he had taken the opportunity to answer nature's call before her due arrival. He looked as startled as a frightened deer when he realised she was there, fumbling with himself to hide what he was doing. She felt stupid and more embarrassed for him than herself, and desperately tried to stay undisturbed. She turned from him and called out. 'I'm sorry I interrupted you, Dick,' she said, thinking hard what to say, 'but it be no different for a bull in the meadow, and he don't care any, at all.'

She stood still in a silence that felt it would last for ever. Then softly, hesitantly, 'Be all right then, Madeline.'

She turned to him in shock. He had spoken to her. She looked at his face, searching for any sign of whether he had really spoken to her, or if it was her desperate imagination making it up to heal the damage she had done by seeing him thus. She saw his quiet gentle smile appear as he realised that he hadn't scared her back to a shell, as Matilda said she could be. He smiled because Matilda would not be upset by what he had done, and she had been clear he mustn't do it in front of Madeline. He smiled because Madeline had understood him to be doing a natural thing in his world, and she had kindly turned her back so he could finish. He smiled because he had finally got some words to come out and he knew Matilda would be very pleased with him for doing so. He tied his baggy britches together and went to get his drink. Madeline passed him his drink with a trembling hand, relieved that all was not lost and that the trigger had finally been found that had got him to talk.

'I brought one for me as well,' she heard herself saying rather unnecessarily. 'Do you think foxgloves would do well along the wall just there?' she asked him, doing her best to sound normal.

'Aye, Missus Madeline, needs clematis to cover the wall.'

'Of course, Dick.' She took a gulp of her drink to stop herself laughing out loud. He is talking to me, and then had trouble trying to hide a blush as in hindsight at that terrible interruption, she remembered seeing him holding himself. *Gracious Matilda, you were right, it is enormous compared to what my husband's was*, and she hurriedly took another sip to get her mind back to the garden. 'I will get some plants ready for you for next week.'

'Thank you,' he said, handing her his empty mug. 'I finish this bit and think of plants you need.' He turned with a satisfied smile—he had got more words to come out. She watched him while she finished her drink and then went back indoors.

She picked up her needlework, but kept making mistakes as her mind kept wandering back down to the garden. Unnoticed, she had stopped stitching, and sat thinking of the change Dick had made by speaking to her. Her reverie was broken when he coughed at the kitchen door.

'Missus Madeline, I knows the plants you need now.'

'You had better come in and I will write them down,' she called to him and placed a writing pad ready. He quietly stepped in with his feet bare, having left boots and cap at the back door, and stood beside her. She looked up from her paper sheet and found herself looking straight at the front of his britches that covered his large manhood. Its image leapt to her mind in wonder. *You can't think like that*, she reprimanded herself, and lifted her hand to her head with her elbow on the table and leant against it ready to write, cutting all else from view.

'What have you got for me?' she asked rather badly, then hurriedly, 'What flowers do you have in mind?' and he slowly began to recite a list. He looked down at her bowed head and noticed she had only written three words and her pen was still. He gently took her hand from her head and held it carefully in his own great hand.

'You'm been mending well, Madeline—has today been too much for 'ee? Does 'ee be too scared to keep mending now? Do 'ee want me to go?'

'I do not know anymore, I do not know how you knew I needed help in mending, as you put it. I just don't know why you don't scare me anymore, but all other men still do. I don't know how not to be scared, and I don't know how I should feel to be normal. I don't know anything at all anymore.' Her confusion saddened him.

'I doan know how I knew you needed mending, I just needed to try and help. I only knows what be natural to me, but I doan know why. I trys to help, but stops if it don't,' he said, now taking her hand with both his. She watched him in total surprise as he placed her open hand over his trouser front. She felt his size, and she felt him begin to harden. 'Do I scare 'ee by doing that?' he quietly asked.

'No,' was all she could reply. He took one hand away and loosened the tied string. As the top of his britches fell away he held them in place with his free hand; part of him was visible at the fold.

'Do that scare 'ee?'

'Not yet,' she replied, finding herself looking at what was showing. He took her hand and softly put it where she was looking.

'Do that scare 'ee?'

'Not yet,' she said, surprised that it didn't, as it was only when they were first married that she had touched her husband there. Dick loosened his trousers even more so that nearly all was showing. He moved her hand and placed it on the shaft and let her hand go. She felt its warmth as it hardened more, fascinated that she could watch it grow.

'Not yet,' she said without being asked. He let his britches go and they dropped to the floor. He placed his hands on her shoulders and turned her from the table to face him, her free hand making its own way to join the other. She felt strange sensations starting to shiver inside her. She couldn't stop staring at him. He must be twice as big as her husband had been, she thought in wonder, her finger and thumb not nearly meeting. Dick felt her fingers tighten and was glad she was still mending.

'Do 'ee feel scared yet?' he asked. 'Do 'ee want to stop?'

'Not yet,' she whispered.

'Then let me carry 'ee upstairs.' He bent and effortlessly picked her up and climbed the stairs. *She be coming along good,* he thought to himself, *she be still be holding on with one hand.* Her dress fell smoothly to the floor where his shirt already lay. She looked down at his full size, and said to him that it would never fit in, it was too big for her. He told her that it didn't need to, she only needed to feel the end touching her there to know if she was ready for more mending.

'I'm not scared yet Dick, and I got feelings there I forgot existed.' He slowly rubbed against her to find her wet and slippery. The end found the entry and the head of it moved partly in, just enough for him to be able to slide back and forth a little.

'Try putting in a bit more,' she requested, 'but slowly.' He eased the head in and eased out. 'Not so far out, in a bit more.' He moved back to her, introducing more this time, getting to where he was thickest, and he waited. She felt his size and marvelled at her own feelings. She found her legs were wide apart and couldn't remember spreading them there. She lifted her hips to try and take in his width.

'I'm not scared yet,' she almost moaned to him, and moved her hips again to aid his entry.

What would people think if they could see me now, being bedded by their village idiot? They would banish me for good. A shiver at the audacity of it shook through her, getting even more of him in. *Oh Dick, this is amazing,* she cried to herself, *is this really me here?* And she thrust up at him again just to prove to herself she really was. The motion kept at her, her legs raising her hips up to him. Dick had kept still above her, letting her take what she felt she could handle. After every few lifts, a tentative thrust pushed more in, and each time he was lowered down onto her a little more. She found she was trying to follow the surges of desire and need that pumped deep inside and her thrusts became more demanding, her moans more intense. Dick started to ride with her, meeting her calls for release and satisfaction.

'Help me Dick, the surges are coming faster!' And Dick helped, but he was having trouble holding back. Her legs came up around him, locking them both into one action, pumping desperately. She took all of him, gloriously, demanding satisfaction, unaware that he had no more left to put into her, but cried with joy at being filled so completely. Suddenly her whole body was shuddering, as all the surges met as one, shaking her to the core of her soul in one last shout of victory. She fell back exhausted.

'Oh Dick, surely I be mended now?' She laughed as never before, feeling the size of him in her still, and finally realising she had taken all of him.

'Now I feel as a woman should.' And with a knowing smile, she drifted off to sleep.

Chapter 7

1840: Another Wedding in the Family

Dick quietly left her lying there. He laid her dress over her in modesty, not sure if she was fully asleep as he looked down at her, her smile still in place. *You be mended as much as I can make 'ee*, he thought as he left her.

He went to find Matilda with an urgency in his step. He needed to tell her he had been able to talk with Madeline as she had asked him to, and he knew how happy that would make her. He found her in the garden tending to the strawberry plants. She was turning toward him as he came in.

'What is it Dick? What are you rushing for, what's happened?' She looked at him worried—he was not his usual calm self, hot and sweaty from walking so quickly.

'Doan 'ee be getting all upset now Miss M, I did what you asked and I dorne know how. I talk to 'er, Miss M, like only I can with you. I talk to Missus Madeline!' And he stopped suddenly, scared that she might still be annoyed with him because Madeline had seen him peeing in her garden, and that was what she had said he must not do. Matilda watched all the emotions sweep across his face, puzzled that he should look worried at such a tremendous achievement.

'Dick, that is wonderful! How did you get to do it?'

'Doan know, she came down the garden and said something and I knew she be suddenly understanding me, the way you always has from being a little girl, and words were able to come out. We talk more later and I feel she be mending good.' He stopped, hoping he had explained enough.

'I think you have done wonderfully well. I am sure Madeline will tell us how pleased she is with you as well.' Matilda was jubilant, but could see he was reluctant to say more. 'Wait till I tell Mary.'

'No! Miss M, you mustn't let on! What will others think if they knows I talk to her as well now, must be between us only. People will stare at 'er and think wrong of 'er if they knows I spoke words with 'er. 'Er mendings will all be undone if peoples start staring and talking about 'er. Peoples knows I bin talking to you from as a baby and that be my ways, but 'ers be harmed if they hears of 'ers and me talking.'

'Dick, Dick calm yourself, you are right and only us three will ever know. I am sure Madeline will not say a word to anyone and neither will I. You have done a wonderful thing for her, and I'm sure no one else need know. Now tell me how the garden is going.'

'It be cleared to see where it all used to be and paths be fixed for walking on. Garden wall can do with clematis and flowers need replanting maybe. Reckon lots of bulbs will grow now they not covered over no more. Vegetable garden be empty 'n not got to knowing what to do with it, being she not a gardener and vegetables needs working, maybe's make play place for the boys with swing, p'raps sows it over for more grass for 'em to play on. Rubbish be all burnt and bin fixing tools in shed I uncovered. Even grass cutter thing might work again if I can figure it. I be finished what I can soon.'

'I think you have done well. I am sure Madeline must be very pleased with the changes you have made for her—I think we deserve a drink on a job well done.' With that, she promptly led him off to the kitchen for some cider.

When she saw Mary later she said that Dick had been around and had told how well he had done with Madeline's garden, and that he thought he didn't have too much more to do before he had finished there.

'Already?' Mary said, gazing out the window at nothing in particular, and after a pause added, 'I might drop by and visit her on the way home, haven't seen her for a bit.' She stayed gazing a little longer, then with just a murmur of 'Hmmmm' left the room without a word.

Mary decided to leave the farm even earlier and went to see Madeline on the way to meeting Richard—she felt calling like that would seem more casual, and less enquiring that way. Madeline was surprised and delighted to see Mary coming in the gate and came out to meet her. *He hasn't fixed the squeaky gate yet,* Mary thought as she met her.

'Hello Madeline, I thought I might pop by on my way into the village. It looks as though Dick is making good progress on the garden.'

'Isn't he just! I am so pleased you thought of him, he has been tireless and we are ready to plant. Look at the difference now.' Mary did indeed look at the difference, and it was to Madeline that she was looking, not the garden. There was a confident woman before her now, a glow in her cheeks, a glisten of life and knowledge in her eyes that had never been there before. The unruliness of her hair may well have been the result of working in the garden, but Mary did not believe so. Mary watched her as she went down the path, such a graceful and fluid walk, there was no longer the rigid and tenseness about her. Madeline stopped and turned to her.

'Come on, you can't see much from there,' Madeline said.

'Actually Madeline, I see quite a lot. Having Dick come here working has done you a lot of good, and not just the garden.' Madeline began to blush and put her hands to her face.

'Oh dear, what do you mean, what makes you say that?'

'Madeline, my dear friend. Only someone like me who has got to know you well can see the difference in you,' she said kindly to her. 'I have finally found a man who knows and loves me as a person and with respect, he is tender with me and we have an understanding of each other's needs as only married couples are supposed to. Madeline, my dear, you look as I feel, having been with my Richard.'

'Oh God help me, does it show so much! What will become of us, I have surely put him in jeopardy!'

'Hush now Madeline,' Mary said taking her arm, 'no one else could tell, no one else but me would ever think to look, no one will ever make any kind of connection. Only Matilda may work it out, as only Matilda has ever known him to be anything other than the idiot people think he is. He will only speak to her and no one else, and he will never even tell her unless she asks him. She will never do that because she has spent her life with him, respects him and would never ask him anything personal. You have nothing to fear.'

'I do hope you are right, but nothing will happen again. He felt he was helping me get mended and I said as much to him when he left me this morning. I felt so fulfilled I said, surely I be mended now. He nodded and smiled as he went.' Then she added softly, 'He spoke to me.'

'What!' stunned Mary repeated, 'What?'

'He spoke. It started in the garden, I said something that Matilda told me that he used as an excuse for one of his actions for something she didn't like him doing, he responded to it, so I kept on talking and most times he replied. Later, inside, he talked to me, and I was doing the

54

replying. He said he knew I needed mending from a long time back, even before my husband died, and now the mending is done. He will see no reason to carry on. I know I am very comfortable in his company, but I still am afraid of other men.'

'To hell with other men! Believe me, with Richard and me, it gets better with each time. If you want more, then be a woman around him, and he will provide. And speaking of providing, I must go and meet mine. Thank you for telling me, Madeline—I have made up my mind to tell Richard we will be married within the month. You have our first invitation.'

Laughing, Madeline said, 'Shouldn't you ask Richard to marry you first?'

'Of course, then I will tell him the answer!' They parted, laughing at each other, both looking to the future.

When Mary got home, a little dishevelled and a little late for dinner, she told the family around the table, 'Richard and I are getting married in three weeks' time. He is coming here for dinner tomorrow evening to meet you all. Now Mother, I know this only allows for two banns of marriage to be read, but the third one can be read before our marriage service begins. Is that all right with everyone?' She gave a glimmer of a wink to Matilda, who tried to suppress a smile. There was a silence as the others took in her words. Charles started to say something and got a sharp clip on his ear from John, who stayed silent, leaving it to his wife to pass comment.

'That is very nice for you dear—perhaps a little more warning might have been helpful. What can you tell us of him?' she said, knowing full well that nothing any of them said would make any difference to her daughter's plans.

Mary finished her mouthful, put down her knife and fork and informed them, 'His name is Richard Hoyle and he is working for the Master at the big house as a servant and groom. He leaves his employ at the end of the month and we will be working on the farm at the Soap House at Dalwood. His family are from Honition and he is five years younger than me, not that it matters. What matters is that he is the only man that I have met who is good enough for me and we love each other. Any questions?' The silence continued. 'Good,' she said, and continued with her dinner.

When her mother had finished her meal, she said, 'What would you like for your wedding, Mary? Anything special?'

'There is a family service at 11 o'clock that Sunday—we will get

55

married at the end of it. Matilda will be my bridesmaid, Richard's brother will be his groomsman. Richard is not well known around here, and we want no fuss, so we thought a simple lunch here for those who might like to join us after the service would be enough. There will only be Curate Ashe and a few of the congregation wanting to be here anyway. That is all we want.'

'Very well, my dear,' her mother acknowledged, 'that all sounds perfectly reasonable. I do believe it will be a perfectly wonderful day, don't you, John?'

'Oh aye,' he quickly agreed, 'proper job it will be.' He was careful to say no more in case he said the wrong thing, not at all understanding how his wife could be so calm and accepting of such sudden news.

He finally got his chance to ask her if she had known beforehand and why he was the only one kept in the dark.

'Poor John,' she said taking his hand, 'you just cannot read your children, can you? Of course I had not been told anything, probably only Matilda had been confided in. Had you not noticed the change in her of an evening? Did you not question why she was leaving the farm at the same time every afternoon, washed and fresh looking? My only surprise was how quickly she decided.'

'Dornee think I be daft enough to be asking 'er what she be about! She be telling me she be leaving farm on afternoons, like she be me mother, in a tone that stops I even thinking I be getting told any more. I just says yes and get on working Charles as I been told. I dorne know who be head of this house, I really don't.'

'You poor dear man, you be of course. Just let the women here run it.' She gave him a hug and a kiss and went about her work.

Aye, he thought to himself, *has it ever been any other way?*

The family service and wedding was a cheerful event. Many village folk had heard of the wedding and attended, overflowing the church, with the less regular attendees sitting in the sun, chatting among themselves until the wedding service itself. They then silently filed in, filling the back of the church and aisle in solemn procession to witness what many thought would never happen. At the exchanging of the final vows an unexpected applause broke from them as their acknowledgement at the success of the union.

It followed that the lunch was no quiet affair, with the womenfolk all arriving with plates of food, the men with jars of cider. Curate Ashe, new to the area, was delighted to be included so warmly and with the success of the unorthodox manner of the wedding.

Madeline found Mary and gave her a hug.

'You look radiant, Mary,' she said, 'and he is so much in love with you, he looked at only you all through the service.'

'I know, it's blissful! How are you doing?'

'Very well, I think. He is very proper as he always was. Seeing he has mended me, as he puts it, that area has ended. But it is very comforting having him around and talking—he talks quite a lot now, but never in public. I am happy with that.' Mary looked at her and took her hand.

'No you're not,' she whispered in her ear, 'and it is up to you to do something about it. I know, I did with Richard, just judge your moment and take it. I must go—Mother's waving frantically.'

Matilda walked in, with Dick following close by. They were talking quietly together.

'Hello Mary,' he said quietly, and even more softly, 'hello Madeline.'

They smiled at each other and replied in unison, 'Hello Dick.' He bent and said something to Matilda.

'We have been looking for Richard—have you lost him already, Mary?'

'Haven't seen him for a bit,' she said, realising for the first time that she hadn't.

'We be trying the barn, Miss M. He be out there trying cider with the men, I feels. He be no good for Mary if he be out there too long.' He turned with Matilda close behind, leaving them laughing.

'Come along Mary, you haven't spoken to some of the ladies in here yet,' her mother fussed over to her. 'Do try and keep her to greet everyone, Madeline, I have asked her twice now, and what have you done with Richard?'

'He is with Matilda and Dick meeting the other men,' she replied, hoping they had found him in time. It was a slightly befuddled Richard seen walking around the yard before they brought him back inside. The men laughed.

'Another half glass would've had 'im, 'e would be praper gone then.'

'Maybe's bestways they got 'im now, would you be up to facing thicky Mary if he be fair sozzled?' And a solemn silence fell among them, none game enough to say they would.

It was one of the most enjoyable wedding days many could remember, a fine hot day with ample food and a great deal of cider taken, far later into the afternoon than Mary thought her simple lunch would go.

Many a cow was milked late that evening, and not very well.

When Matilda had milked Henrietta, she asked her if she was ever going to find a man as Mary had done. Henrietta only sighed in reply.

Chapter 8

1841: One Year On – The Introduction

It was the last day that Matilda was to take strawberries into the market for the season. They were still of good appearance and size, but were losing flavour and becoming too watery for her liking. When Hannah came in she would have to tell her they would be the last.

'Oh dear, Matilda, that's a bother. Father insists we use cook's clotted cream, even though he says yours is finer—he doesn't want to upset her as he has with the gardener over the strawberries. But do not worry too much, I will make sure that I have a reason to need to come in. Father will not want to put up with the fuss I will make to want to stop me for long. He came in today, said he had business to attend to himself. I told him to come and find me here when he is ready to leave.'

'There is a gentleman standing over the other side by the church—is that him?' Hannah turned and looked in the direction Matilda indicated.

Edith whispered to Matilda, 'That's him all right. He's been there a while looking over every now and then as though checking on his girl.' They exchanged puzzled glances as Hannah waved over to her father and turned back to Matilda.

'I am going to introduce him to you Matilda. It is only right I do so as I said so much about you to him, and it will do him good to realise I do have a good friend that is not involved with the family somehow,' and off she bustled to fetch him.

'Father, this is Matilda White, the one that I have told you about. Matilda, please meet my father.'

'How do you do, Mr Hill. It is nice to meet you,' she said, holding out her hand. 'Hannah and I always seem to chat away a bit, I hope we haven't kept you waiting.'

'No, not at all, Matilda. I am pleased to have met you at last. Hannah speaks so much of you after being in here that I feel I know you quite well already.' He took her hand and shook it very formally. 'It is refreshing to hear her chat about you as though you have been friends for many years. I must compliment you on your very fine strawberries—they are by far the best anywhere, and certainly well beyond anything that my gardener can produce, much to his discomfort.' He continued looking at her in a slightly surprised manner.

'That is very kind of you to say so, Mr Hill. I have been doing the garden since I could walk, and having the best manure to put on them helps, but I'm afraid that this is the last of them for the season—I don't like bringing them in once they start going watery. Sure you don't want my clotted cream so that I can still have Hannah call by?'

'My dear, I would like your clotted cream, but what I do not need is having cook bending my ear as the gardener has been bending the other because I don't eat his strawberries; there is only so much I am prepared to take from the staff. Now we must be getting along, Hannah. It has been very interesting meeting you, Matilda—thank you.' And with that he took Hannah by the arm and they walked away, with Hannah waving behind her as they disappeared from view.

'Well isn't that an odd thing?' Edith said. 'He gave you a proper looking over as though he was unsure of what to expect from you— polite enough, then off he goes as though he was late for something, having spent ages yonder hanging about.'

'I can't say I noticed, Edith, but he did leave in a bit of a rush.'

Hannah thought they had left a little too abruptly for good manners, and said so to her father when they were under way in the carriage.

'I remembered some unfinished business with your mother and I need to discuss it with her before she goes out this afternoon. I apologise if I seemed rude and I did not intend to be so in front of Matilda—please say so to her when you see her next, but it is rather important I see your mother quickly.' With that, he remained silent all the way home, clearly deep in thought.

He strode through the front door calling to his wife. 'Sarah! You haven't left yet, have you?' Then, turning to his butler who appeared, 'Ah Martins, be so kind and find Mrs Hill—she hasn't left yet, has she? I shall be in my study.'

'John, what is all the fuss about? I've never known you to storm into the house calling out like that before, nor have I known you to dismount the carriage and walk away leaving any lady, even if it was your own daughter, to get out on her own. What will the staff think? I couldn't leave, you had taken my gig! Now what can possibly be so important that keeps me from my meeting that you wanted me to have in the first place?' She gave him a hard look, puzzled at his behaviour when he had spent so much time getting to the stage of this afternoon's meeting that should solve his worries for his daughter, and now there was something more important?

'Sit down, my dear, sit down,' he said, pacing up and down the room. 'The answer has been under our noses all the time and neither of us took the hint, and a better answer we couldn't hope dream of!' He suddenly stopped and stood beaming at her.

'Is there a chance that you will tell me?' she asked.

'Of course, of course. It's Matilda!'

'Matilda? The strawberry farm girl?'

'Matilda is no ordinary farm girl, my dear. I met her today and I was taken aback—she would be perfect; who else does Hannah talk about so incessantly? Now I know why—she dressed far better than a farm girl on a stall would, she is clean and fresh looking, carries herself well, good posture, her hair was tidy and she speaks very well. Certainly well above her social status. I would guess her to be a couple of years older as well. She is used to responsibility and has a confident air about her. Good Lord, I believe she could even carry a conversation with Richard! She is all we could hope for and much better than those wishy-washy pasty females I've seen about so far. I suggest a trial so you can judge for yourself.'

'Really John, do you expect us to take in a farm girl? Whatever next!'

'Sarah, she is no ordinary farm girl! If you were to meet her in our drawing room for the first time, you would never think of her as a farm girl. Let us have an afternoon tea and ask some of your ladies along with Matilda present. I'll wager they will treat her as Hannah's equal!'

Sarah could not help feeling his excitement—but what a risk!

'John, we will look awful fools if she doesn't carry it off. We will be set further back than now—can we afford that?'

'I don't believe that we can afford not to—it will be one of the lesser risks I've ever taken. Do you think you can organise it so that Matilda arrives without any obligation? Perhaps a weekend here as a companion for Hannah while you invite perhaps some of your more elderly acquaintances?'

'That would be the best way. Martins can go and fetch her and take her home, but you had better raise it with Hannah as a distraction for her from the rest of the group. That will give me time to get a measure of her and see if she will do. Now I suppose that I had better go through the charade this afternoon.'

It was at the table that evening that John casually said to Hannah that Mother was having a ladies' tea and would she like a friend to stay as a companion for the weekend?

'Yes Father, that would be nice—but who would come, as they all know what Mother's teas are like?'

'Would Matilda come?'

'Matilda! She would be perfect, but Mother hasn't met her yet, and it would be unfair as she probably hasn't much of a wardrobe and I would never want to embarrass her. I'm not sure she would accept, if only because she has not enough changes of clothes. I could let her use mine as we are of a size, so maybe she could be persuaded. It would be quite wonderful if she could though, but do we have time, as she will not be in for two weeks yet?'

'I am sure we will have time. You just need to ask her—she may say no.'

It was an impatient Hannah who finally got to ask Matilda to stay. Matilda was at first delighted and surprised, and then slowly realised that it would be impossible.

'I'm sorry, Hannah. But I don't think I can. It would be a privilege for me but I do not have the wardrobe for it.'

'You can use some of my clothes—there is lots I've only worn once. Please think about it and say yes!'

Matilda was torn between the excitement of going and the certainty that she would make a fool of herself staying with such an important family.

'Yes,' she said, 'I would very much like to come for the weekend. But I will need to borrow some of your clothes. Are you sure that will be all right?'

Hannah's relief was immediate.

'Oh bless you, Matilda, you do not know what a relief it will be, having you there. Mother is forever trying to match me up with some pathetic creature as a companion when I don't need one at all, or worse expecting to match me up with some insipid son of one of the old ducks in the village. God help us all! That is the last thing I need, you have no idea what a change this will be! We will get Martins to collect you. How will he find your farm?'

61

'The lanes are a bit confusing when you are a stranger—it will probably be best if I waited up by the gates to the big house, which he can't miss.'

It was all arranged very easily. John and Mary kept their doubts to themselves, fearful for their daughter if it did all go wrong and what it would do to her confidence, and the nasty gossip that would follow among the villagers who thought her getting above her station.

Matilda's only moment of anxiety came as they pulled into the entrance of Fairfield Lodge, and she saw for the first time the mansion where Hannah lived, and thought it looked as big as Shute Barton.

A doorman opened the door of the gig and helped her down.

'Welcome, Miss Matilda, maid will show you to your room. Miss Hannah will be along presently.'

'You got here so soon!' said Hannah, rushing in. 'I'll quickly show you your room—I'm two doors down, the guest wing is too far away from mine and it would be just silly to put you there. Father did fuss over that, but what is the point of having you here if I have to walk all that way to find you? This arragment is much better. Get her bags up to her room, Martins—we will be in mine.'

'There is only one bag, Miss Hannah,' he said pointedly. Hannah spun around to him, glaring at him in fury at his insolence.

'Then you will be able to manage it in one trip, will you not?' she retorted, staring at him, waiting for an answer.

'Yes Miss Hannah,' he quietly replied, very aware he had said too much and hoped desperately his master would not hear of it.

'Stupid man,' Hannah whispered in Matilda's ear as she took her arm and led her inside.

Matilda worried how much more she would have to take from the staff who would all very shortly know that Miss Hannah's guest was no more than a farm girl, and quite below even their status. She became more uncertain of her decision as they went up a huge staircase and hallway that led to their rooms. The rooms were enormous, and the bed so large that she felt three would sleep in it if it were in Umborne. The mirror opposite was bigger than she was, and the doors on the wardrobe looked like they could hold the clothes of her entire family.

Hannah opened a door to one side, saying, 'My bathroom is through here, I'm afraid yours is smaller, but it is still quite nice.' She led her through into it.

'Lorre be! I could teach my little sister to swim in a bath that big!' Matilda exclaimed. 'It is all so big and different to home, Hannah—how am I going to cope here without making myself look a fool?'

'Probably a lot easier than you think at present. First let us unpack your bag and see what you have, then we will come back here and we will see what I have that will fit you and then we will go downstairs and meet Mother and Father in his study. He was rather keen on your coming this weekend and I rather suspect he will make sure you feel comfortable in our presence. He knows it will be a bit overwhelming at first for you and for that reason he has made it clear to my sister that there will be no others but family at the table tonight. Now let's see if Martins or his boy haven't strained themselves bringing your bag up.'

Her bag did look a trifling thing in her room—its contents would barely fill one drawer.

'Right,' said Hannah, 'let's get to work.' She whisked the clothes out and spread them onto the bed. 'There is no time to waste on petty fussing about. This, this and this are perfectly fine, this dress is too heavy for this weekend unless we go walking across the back fields and that is not likely to happen, as Father has stopped me wandering about them years ago. I am, apparently, not to be seen near the workers there unattended. This blouse top is beautiful, the stitching is so even, we need to show it off. Now back to my room to see what we can match up with yours.'

They bustled off, Matilda feeling some relief that Hannah had not disregarded everything she had, and was proud of her admiration of her blouse. Somehow not feeling quite so awkward, she was soon engrossed in going through Hannah's wardrobe, holding clothes up in front of herself and looking at the mirror. Hannah would take them away from her with an abrupt 'No good,' and would shove the offending article back on its hanger. After a hectic flurry of clothes, Hannah finally announced that she felt there were enough to select from. It was time to try some fittings. With equal zest, clothes were put on and taken off till only six were left, all of near fitting and suitability.

'I will get Jane to come up with her sewing kit. She is Mother's maid, and will have these looking like they were made for you in no time.'

When it came time for them to go down and meet Hannah's parents, Matilda had regained her confidence and a smile was back on her face.

'You look a picture, Matilda—your blouse top looks like it was made for that dress. Come on, we have kept Father waiting long enough.' She rapped sharply on his door and was entering almost before he had called them in.

He rose from his desk with a smile, carefully appraising Matilda's appearance.

'Good afternoon, Matilda. I trust Hannah has made you welcome?'

'Yes, very welcome indeed, Mr Hill. She has made sure that I will be most comfortable over the weekend.'

'That comes as no surprise,' he said with a wry smile. 'Perhaps you could ask your mother to come in, Hannah. Please sit down, Matilda. I will tell you of the weekend's events.' Sarah, Hannah's mother, must have been waiting close at hand, for they were both back in very short order. Matilda rose from her chair as they came in.

'Mother, this is Matilda, my friend that I have spoken of. Matilda, please let me introduce my mother,' said Hannah very formally.

Matilda gave the faintest bob of a curtsy and greeted Sarah.

'Good afternoon, Mrs Hill, it is very kind of you to ask me here to stay with Hannah.'

Sarah stood and looked at Matilda for a fraction too long for Matilda's comfort, then she said in a refined voice, 'You are welcome here, my dear. I must say that is a very nice blouse you have. I do appreciate good needlework, and that is decidedly tidy.'

'Thank you,' Matilda said, grateful for their tact with her as surely she must have recognised that it was Hannah's dress she was wearing.

'I was about to explain the weekend's events, but perhaps over some tea?' John Hill rose and pulled the bell rope. 'Do sit down, all of you.'

It was proving to be easier than Matilda thought possible; she found talking with them flowed in a natural conversation with no awkward silences. Tea was served and John spoke of the following afternoon's ladies' tea party that he expected both Hannah and Matilda to attend. It was not until Sarah suggested that Hannah show Matilda around the parts of the house that she would be involved with that Matilda realised that Hannah had not spoken.

'Certainly, come on Matilda, we will start with the dining room.'

'Does she always have to think of eating?' Matilda heard Sarah saying to John as they left the room.

'I will show you the dining room first as it will be laid and I should show you the cutlery you will be using without the servants watching.' She led her into the vacant room and proceeded to explain what each utensil was used for. Matilda was dumbfounded.

'How can I remember all that?' she asked in a quivering voice.

'We need a code,' Hannah suggested. 'This is how we will be seated: Father there, Mother there. I will be seated over there and you will be opposite me here. If my sister is back she will be beside Mother there. What you need to do is to keep your hands on your lap until Mother moves to pick up her cutlery. Watch my fingers, as I will lay one on each you are to use with each course. Just pick up the same ones I am touching—it is how Father taught me when I was first allowed to eat at the table with visitors present. I knew by then, but he didn't want me making a mistake. Just make your movement up with your hands slow and easy, and watch what I am doing across from you.'

'Yes,' Matilda agreed, not at all sure that it was going to be as easy as Hannah made it sound.

'Now let's go round the rest of the house.' The tour took some time as Matilda looked in awe of so many rooms, filled with so many possessions. None of it caused her concern until they went into the library, where books lined the walls and lay on the tables. It was to her the symbol of all that she was not, everything that she could not understand, the physical presence of what was completely beyond her world. The books stood in ranks, uniform in their bindings, side by side, row above row, as though in military precision they were there to remind her of the void between Hannah's life and hers. It was the only room she wanted to escape from and never return to.

'Come along, Matilda,' Hannah called and she realised that she had been standing there alone. 'It's nearly tea time and we need to change into more formal dresses for it.' Matilda followed with her mind still in that alien room, wondering how on earth she could ever consider herself Hannah's equal.

Dining that night went smoothly, with Hannah's finger signals guiding her effortlessly through the meal. But disaster struck when a particularly large dish was put on the table in front of Hannah and her hands were hidden behind it. Panic was fast rising and Matilda's inadequacy was about to be revealed. As if in readiness of apologising to John, she turned to him and was surprised to see him watching her thoughtfully. *He knows I don't know*, she thought to herself as she looked up to his face, not knowing what to say. He gave her the slightest of nods and his eyes lowered to his plate. There he had a finger of each hand resting on a knife and fork, waiting for her to follow. Only the briefest of smiles from him acknowledged the help he gave her.

Thank you, she mentally said, her blush of embarrassment fading as quickly as it arrived.

After that, she felt, nothing would rattle her. Try as they might, the ladies at the afternoon tea failed to get even the merest of reactions from her. They left doubting the quality of the gossip handed out through the servants' ranks, usually an impeccable source where guests of questionable status were concerned.

Chapter 9

1841: Higher Circles

That Monday, in early 1841, was to mark the beginning of changes for for many in the valley that would affect the rest of their lives.

Mary, with her certainty of planning, excelled herself and gave birth to twins. Francis and John Hoyle arrived with no excess of difficulty, with justifiable pride on Mary's behalf, but with complete confusion and consternation on Richard's. Mary had to laugh at him not knowing what to do next. Should he rush off and tell the family? Should he help the nurse, and get in the road again and be told so? Which baby should he hold? Which was which? Should he help Mary be comfortable, and be told again to stop fussing? Should a meal be prepared? Where did the other one come from, she was never that big? Couldn't she have warned him there were two?

For two hours he achieved nothing but wear out the carpet going from room to room. Finally Mary could take it no more.

'For heaven's sake Richard, saddle a horse and go and tell Mother.' He left with such speed, relieved at being given something to do, that he forgot to kiss his wife goodbye, but just stared in wonder at the two little bundles side by side in the bed with her. Peace at last descended on the house. Mary and the nurse looked at each other and smiled.

'He will get used to it, Mary, but did you have no idea you were carrying twins? You were never that big and they be healthy little blighters. Best ways I make you a cuppa while it's quiet and they be sleeping. Place be a mad house when he be getting back.'

Not two months later, William and Ann produced their second child, a boy they named Thomas. They were delighted that it was a son, as

John was now two and becoming a handful, forever disappearing out of the house to play in the garden in the dirtiest places. This was to Ann's annoyance and inconvenience, as she would have to stop working on the hat she was making to clean him up when he came in. In a good week the extra that she could make with her millinery could sometimes be close to William's earnings, and they were able to put more aside in their savings. Another boy would grow to be a playmate for John and maybe keep him occupied and out of the dirt, or perhaps she would end up with two dirty boys!

Madeline had decided that today she would have to stop thinking about any further mending with Dick. It was against all the principles of her upbringing to even consider taking any more pleasure with him. All that Dick had done was to give her the freedom from those tormented years and remind her what it was like to feel like a loved woman. He had behaved impeccably in her presence since then, with never a hint at what had happened. He never spoke to her away from her home, and never in the presence of others if callers came by to see Madeline, and some women had begun to call. She could carry on now, with confidence building and no recriminations; it had accomplished all that was needed. If only she could stop daydreaming back to that morning with such vivid memories of satisfaction.

She looked out her kitchen window to where he was working on building a swing for her children. How they loved playing out there now with what he had done.

She made him a drink and took it out to him.

'What do you think then, Missus Madeline?' he said, giving the seat of the swing a push.

'I think I need more mending,' she heard herself say, not realising she had had the courage to say so. He looked up at her in surprise.

'Ye said it then.' He studied her face. ''Tis been on yer mind, been seeing it in your eyes on occasion. Sure it's me you be wanting?'

'I still want no other man near me, I am still fearful of how horrid they can be to me because of him. You are not like them, you showed me only gentleness and kindness and I responded as I never thought I could. I would like to try again if you think you could help.'

Madeline turned and walked back to the house without another word, not wanting to hear what Dick might say in rebuttal. He watched her walk away in silence for a moment, then put down his empty glass, and followed her in.

Their affair, over the years it lasted on those Monday mornings, was never discovered. Their secret was held in trust by the only two who knew of it from the beginning, and Mary and Matilda never spoke of it, even between themselves.

Matilda spent much of the morning telling her mother of the weekend, of the largeness of Fairfield Lodge, of the clothes she wore, of Mr Hill's kindness, of the inquisitive ladies at Mrs Hill's afternoon tea, of the fun she had with Hannah at teasing them by not telling of her background, of her status, and them being unable to guess that she was a farm labourer's daughter, of Mrs Hill watching them intently to make sure they behaved with her guests, of Martins letting her know he thought her below the other servants and letting them know it, of her making him bring her all the way home just to teach him a lesson and acting like a lady all the way to their cottage door, of the real friendship Hannah shared with her and how she enjoyed Matilda's company, and of the size of the bath. But not a word of the library and all those printed words she could not read, all those reminders that she could not be an equal to Hannah.

Matilda was the centre of intense discussion in that very room.

John and Sarah had been in there for an hour, the door firmly shut against interruption, both wanting to agree to such an obvious decision, but both very aware it could also be such a wrong one. They had been sitting in silence for a few minutes, deep in thought, not wanting to repeat again what had been said already.

'What are our choices, Sarah? When did she show any disrespect to anyone? When did she not show how to behave as Hannah's friend and guest? Did she behave in any way that caused you concern with your ladies present? Did she ever speak in a common manner to anyone, even the servants? And I believe Martins was no help to her. Was there anything that happened that made her presence among us uncomfortable? Sarah Ann treated her well, I think, glad her sister had someone to keep her out of her way. What are your reservations?'

Sarah sat a little while longer in silence.

'There really are none, almost too good to be true. I believe we must approach her, as clearly Hannah will have no objection. We only need to advise Hannah that we would like Matilda to be her Lady's Companion, and you can be very sure that she will find a suitable way of arranging it all to everyone's satisfaction, and very quickly.'

And that is exactly what happened. Matilda could not believe that she was being offered such good paying work, to live permanently as she had over the weekend. All she had to do was to be a companion to

Hannah and go out with her as a chaperone, when her parents were unavailable, so that Hannah could be seen as a mature young lady of independent means.

John and Mary were delighted that their daughter had gained such an important form of employment. They had no doubts that they were not going to suffer from a labour shortage, as Charles had settled into his role on the farm and Ann was coming along well enough, considering her dislike for the outdoor work. There was only Henrietta who would permanently miss her—not even Ann's soft hands were as good. Matilda's only concern at leaving was in how she would tell Dick and how he would cope. She decided on telling Madeline of her new job so that she would be prepared when Dick arrived next Monday and be ready for his reaction.

It was the only time in her life that she underestimated him.

Dick surprised Madeline when he walked up to her kitchen door. She was concerned for him as he approached with a sad and puzzled expression on his face.

'Miss M be leaving,' he said quietly to her before she could speak.

'Where to Dick? Why is she going?'

'Dornee be knowing that, but she be going outalong.'

'Didn't she tell you where or why?' Madeline could not believe that Matilda would be so cruel to him by only telling him she was going away without spending time with him to make sure he understood the reasons.

'Not spoken to 'er yet, I jus' knows. She be 'ere soon enough, I do some garden work till she be getting 'ere, not long now,' and he wandered down to the garden, leaving her confused as to how he could be so certain. She decided on some baking as this would give her something to do and she could still watch the gate for when Matilda arrived. She felt more than slightly unsettled by Dick's statement on what was about to happen. The baking mix had not reached the oven when Matilda came through the garden gate. Her intense expression forewarned Madeline that it was not a social call, and that Dick must be completely right.

'Are you leaving?' Madeline couldn't help asking forthrightly without any greeting, almost scared of the answer. Matilda stopped, amazed that she could have heard so quickly.

'Yes, and soon, but how did you know?' Madeline didn't answer, but turned slowly toward the kitchen window. Matilda followed her gaze and saw Dick slowly walking up the path towards them.

'Oh God! What have I done to him?' Matilda gulped and ran out to meet him. She ran to him as she had done so often as a little girl and threw her arms around his barrel chest and sobbed.

Madeline came down behind them and heard him saying to her, 'There be, Miss M, there be, tis nought to be crying about. Yer've a need to be going and ye need to be there, more'n 'ee knows yet. Tis no crying matter, 'er got a job to be doing and when done, 'ee be back in time. You didn't get me talking with Missus Madeline for no reason, you know, there be a need for it now so you be free to go. I be fine with Missus Madeline now she be understanding me proper.'

Matilda relaxed her grip and looked up at his face. 'You great oaf, Dick, it's not the going that upsets me, it's that I stopped believing that you would already know, and that you knew where to find me.'

'Tis just as well that one of us remembers, then. You tell Missus Madeline all about it, for 'er doan know any of it. I best be going upalong to Pa now, but I will knows when 'ee comes back.' He wandered off, feeling a sadness in himself.

Matilda told Madeline all about the Hills and her role within the family, and that she would be gone by the week's end.

'I do not know about the coming back that Dick seems to think I will be doing—I will be gone many years before I come back, if at all. It is strange that he said that, unless he thought he was comforting me somehow.'

Madeline was lost for an explanation. The understanding between the two of them was beyond her comprehension, but she had come to realise that if Dick said something would happen, then surely it would.

Dick had moved away quickly, afraid that what appeared in his mind would be seen by Matilda. He did not want her to see that she would be back sooner than she thought and the circumstances were unpleasant and more tears were yet to flow.

Matilda and Madeline were still chatting about the wonderful opportunity that had come Matilda's way and the future that it held. When they said their goodbyes Madeline said, 'You have no idea how much you and Mary have helped me, and given me the confidence to go on.'

Matilda looked into her laughing eyes and replied, 'Only Mary and I?' she teased, and went home to pack.

Her acceptance into the Hill household was much easier than any of them could have hoped. Hannah introduced her to all the staff and it was quickly accepted among them that Martins had got it wrong. Miss Hannah's companion may very well have been a farmer's daughter of no standing, but the Miss Matilda that was now part of the family was a lady who appreciated the world that they lived in, and showed gratitude for what they did for her. More likely to offer help than rebuke tardiness, more likely to smile encouragement than criticise their efforts. It did not take long for Gordon the gardener to overcome his desire to be rid of her, to desire to have her visit him in his garden. Her bubbly approach and complete lack of snobbery soon had them discussing plants and cultivation.

'Good heavens, Gordon, we are gardeners, and how are we to improve the gardens if gardeners were to stop talking with each other? Now what on earth have you been doing to your strawberries?'

Hannah would watch in amusement at the two of them working together, wondering if Martins would ever accept her as totally as Gordon had, and he having been her greatest foe before she came.

John and Sarah were surprised at the transformation in Hannah. For the first time she had someone she would listen to, someone who she did not immediately start to argue with when she could not do as she pleased. Someone with whom she would share her thoughts without fear of criticism and denouncement, someone who would let her prattle on with patience and show interest in what she wanted and where she wanted to go. Someone who was quite prepared to go along with her, so long as they remained within John and Sarah's guidelines, and someone who was totally capable of pulling Hannah back into line without any apparent effort, an almost willingness from Hannah to comply with what her companion thought was acceptable to her parents as correct lady's behaviour.

Hannah saw it differently. She finally had a friend living in the house, not a stodgy and controlling paid servant glued to her side. She could not believe the freedom suddenly granted her so long as Matilda was with her. She had never before been allowed even down the hill to the Lyme Regis village stores with one of the servants to send her own mail, or visit one of the family friends for tea. Now there seemed to be no bounds; they went where she wanted unless Matilda said it was not in their best interest to be seen in that area, or walk that street. She accepted Matilda's instinct as to when it was safe to venture down, what sailors from which ship would leave them alone, and those that would not. She had no desire at all for trouble, or even the slightest difficulty, and so long as her parents allowed her such freedom, she would do nothing to cause her father to reinstate her former restrictions. Just why they put so much trust in Matilda to keep them both safe and above criticism, she could not understand, but they both appeared to have complete faith in Matilda's ability to decide where they would go, and the town events to attend that would only reflect well on the family as a whole. It came to a point where it was a sign of acceptability if Hannah and Matilda were seen attending such occasions, and within months, Sarah was delighted to see invitations arriving addressed to Miss Hannah Hill and including Miss Matilda White.

She mentioned this to John and reminded him of their doubts of taking her on and how the arrangement had succeeded.

'Mmmm,' said John, 'I only hope we have enough to keep her occupied. I dread to think of her getting bored with having to keep Hannah in line, and her going back to what must have been a very busy and demanding life. I fear Sarah Ann will go her own way with marrying that Hussey fellow, whatever we think of him. Richard at least will maintain the family standards that the rest seem hell bent on destroying. We need Matilda to stay and instil in Hannah that which seems to be natural to her. Without Matilda, I fear that she may lose her way again. I have severe doubts that Hannah will ever marry—her independence is too embedded, and she has always rebelled against sensible instruction until Matilda. It is a shame that Matilda cannot do the accounts on our books as well, and then she could teach Hannah some sense there too.'

'Dear John, you do expect a lot. Within six months the poor girl has taken Hannah further than anyone has managed in the previous six years. At this rate she will perform miracles. Let her talk money with Hannah—you must remember how well she coped in the market and how well she stopped the swindling of that old lady. It's how not to lose money that Hannah needs to understand, though I think Matilda might just be a help there too. And have the others really done so badly?'

'To the latter, not well enough, not nearly well enough, except perhaps Sophie. As to the money matter, perhaps you are right. It's the looking after it that counts, and Matilda can certainly look after it. If some of Matilda's savvy with money can rub off onto her, then maybe what we will be giving her will not be lost. How do we go about it so that she just doesn't go and buy more clothes that never get worn?'

'Let me think on it. At least now all those clothes are being worn, even if it is Matilda who is doing the wearing.'

The matter was left forgotten for a while as a letter arrived from Richard that had the whole family in turmoil of excitement. He confirmed much of what had been initiated earlier in the year.

Proudly, but rather stoically, he advised his parents that he had been granted the living at Timsbury, and he was to take up his duties as rector on the first of July. He had gained his MA and would be leaving Balliol College shortly. The Bishop's Chaplain, he said during the interview for the position, had been most impressed with his achievements during his seven years at Oxford, and felt that the St Mary's parish of Timsbury would benefit greatly from his presence there.

'Sadly it is the closest living available,' he wrote, 'but at least there is a direct coach service between Bath and Lyme Regis, which will aid communication and visits tremendously. I may need to avail Father's help initially, as I gather both church and parish have not been receiving true attention and care.'

At this John grunted, observing that it sounded like the boy was already paving the way for some funds. Not that he would begrudge him a penny—he would gladly pay, as Richard was still going to be setting the standards he wished the rest would follow.

He was undeniably proud of this son. He just wished he had a more relaxed approach to everything; even his letters home made stuffy reading. *He needs lessons on his approach to people,* thought John, *as he is going to bore them to sleep in the first five minutes of his sermon, at the present rate of his ponderous letters home. He will need to learn fast or there will be no congregation left for him to preach to.*

'He may be able to repair the church, but I fear for his ability to restore a congregation,' Sarah said, almost simultaneously with her husband's thoughts. 'He is such a bore at times, so pompous in fact. I can just see him standing up there, all clear six feet of him, chest out, and delivering a sermon in stentorian tones using his Oxford words that no one else has heard before. John, he will empty a church faster than the plague, they will all be gone before the offering. You will need to have serious words with him. Who do you know who can give him tuition?'

'The matter had crossed my mind,' admitted John. 'We can't use the local bloke, too close to home, rather embarrassing. Must be done though, must be done.'

Richard's arrival home was much anticipated and a large celebratory dinner was planned. A week to go, and Hannah was getting quite tense about his arrival; it would be the first time that Richard and Matilda would meet, and she particularly wanted them to get along. She was quite sure that they would, and that would cause her to have divided loyalties, Richard being the only one of her siblings whose company she enjoyed. She always considered him to be a funny old stick, always so much more serious about things, even than their father, but he never refused her his company, was never too busy on his brief visits home not to accompany her wherever she wanted to go. Now she had Matilda, and she didn't want him feeling usurped of her company, just for all three of them to get along together without any friction. He knew all about Matilda as his sister wrote regularly to him and he was well aware of how Matilda's presence had made a big difference in her life. In his letters to her he had said he was very pleased for her and was gratified that someone had been found to accompany her at all times. She just wished he would remain very pleased with the situation when they met and show Matilda the same courtesy.

It was an odd greeting Richard received when he arrived in the coach. Hannah ran up to him as always, excited to see him again, but with obvious nervousness this time. His parents stood on the top steps, as was customary, with a formal handshake and pat on the shoulder from his father and a brief hug and kiss on his cheek from his mother, just a little more cursory than normal.

They think I'm stuffy, thought Richard, somewhat wryly. *What has got into them?*

'Let us go into my office, my boy, just for a minute.' John turned before he could reply, and Richard joined his mother to walk through.

'Father thinks it best if you are to be introduced to Matilda on arrival, away from the servants' eyes, so after that, you will be on an informal standing with her,' she told him. 'John has become quite her champion, as she has made such a difference to Hannah's behaviour. He doesn't want anything to change that, and nor do I. You will be quite surprised how much has changed with her since Matilda arrived. Hannah has gone to bring her down from her room,' she finished as they approached John's office.

His father closed the door once they were inside, and he remained standing.

'Richard, I do hope you forgive this unusual greeting, I merely want to get any formalities in your meeting Matilda out of the way quickly and without servant commentaries. She has been more than I dared hope for in getting a companion for Hannah, and certainly never with the background I would have considered appropriate. But that is how it has turned out and I am extremely grateful. Please do not be hasty in your judgement of her, and any criticism you have you can keep to yourself. Your mother and I have finally got a peaceful household, and I don't want your arrival and meeting with Matilda to disturb that.' John looked at his son.

'Good heavens, am I really such a monster? Of course I will accept her without criticism! Hannah has been writing to me for months about her friend and companion. I can scarcely believe where they have been and what they have done; it amazes me you have let Hannah do so much compared with previous chaperones. Her letters have become so much more confident and informative—I quite enjoy getting them. Rest assured that I would never dream of saying anything to either of them that would upset that balance. Am I really so tactless?' he asked, surprised.

'Yes Richard, sometimes you are. You are going to have to learn to control your comments in your new role as rector. Temper your comments, young man, or you will have no congregation.'

John would have said more but there was a polite knock on the door. Hannah came in and headed for her brother, giving him a big hug.

Matilda came behind her, and quietly closed the door before following her to the centre of the room.

'Richard, this is my friend Matilda,' Hannah said, disentangling herself from him. 'Matilda, may I introduce my brother Richard.'

Matilda stepped forward to him, saying, 'I am pleased to meet you at last. Hannah has spoken of you so much that I feel that I know you already. May I congratulate you on your new position? Hannah is so very proud of you and your appointment.'

Richard was taken aback. So this was Matilda! No wonder Hannah had come alive with this woman as her companion. Quite beautiful really, clearly so confident and self-assured; her twinkling blue eyes looked straight at him.

'My pleasure, Matilda. But I could say the same, Hannah has written so much of you that I feel I know you already! I am pleased at last to make your acquaintance.' He bowed his head in acknowledgement.

John could barely suppress his surprise at his son's polite behaviour. *There is hope for the boy yet,* he thought, *if he can be this charming with a stranger. Don't tell me Matilda is going to drag Richard out of his cloistered, academic, dull and judgemental life, and make a personable man of him.* He wondered whether she could work her personality on him and turn him into the approachable vicar that Timsbury needed. Was it too much to hope that she could do for Richard as she had done for Hannah?

Chapter 10

1841: Wise Words of Advice

The dinner that night to celebrate Richard's elevation to rector of Timsbury was a joyous and happy occasion.

John beamed at him, and rose from the table.

'A toast is in order, I believe,' he proudly stated. 'This is to you, Richard. An unrivalled record to date, examinations and degrees gained, commendations from the Dean, and a rectorship within Balliol's living granted. Well done, my boy. Now here is to the challenge of making your name as the respected clergyman of Timsbury.' He raised his glass toward his son. 'To you, Richard!'

There was a clinking of glasses as the assembled gathering toasted him. When the enthusiastic congratulations and general chattering comments died down, Richard rose to his feet and spoke more humbly than usual.

'Dear family and friends, thank you. Perhaps it is right that I admit that I am nervous about my new role and the challenges ahead. So far life has been rather straightforward and easy, almost sheltered, in fact. I have been in some form of a class room all my life, nearly always as a student and occasionally, over the last two years, as a tutor. Quite suddenly, within a month, I leave those classrooms to go into an unknown arena where I must give guidance and help others to learn. Now I am this close to assuming the mantle at Timsbury, I am feeling in awe of my responsibilities up there. I have become aware of being only twenty-five years old, and short of life's outside experiences. I am very aware that I will be asked for guidance from people much older than me, who are very much wiser into the ways of the world. I only hope that common sense and the power of my prayers are up to the job. Do not be surprised if you all become my sounding board on how I am doing. I will be looking to Father often enough to get me started, and it is as well that he is coming with me for a few days to see what needs doing up there and where to start. Thank you for your best wishes, and in advance for the help you are going to give me.' He raised his glass, sipped, and sat down.

There was laughter and more clinking of glasses, and the chattering continued between courses. Sarah looked at her son and smiled her love at him. *Praise the lord*, she thought, *John has one son he can be proud of and, in all likelihood, the only one who will carry the family name forward with honour.*

John nodded his approval toward him and thought, *Thank God I have managed to sire one son who is capable of carrying on the family name to a standard that we can hold our heads up to.*

Hannah raised her glass to him and smiled. *My big brother looks so important*, she thought, *and at last doesn't sound as pompous as his letters usually do. At least he admits he is lacking in worldly experiences. I do hope he doesn't put his great foot in when he should have kept quiet.* She looked across to Matilda and caught her looking at her brother with an almost puzzled expression on her face. *Matilda would bring you down to earth about what it is really like to scrape by on nothing. I wonder if you will ever know what that is like.*

Matilda felt Hannah watching her and looked over to her friend.

'Doesn't he look so important!' Matilda whispered across the table between them, and Hannah laughed that they should both think the same of him, which made Matilda giggle as well.

John glanced down the table to see what the mirth was about and caught Hannah and Matilda smiling at each other. *What are those two up to, I wonder*, he thought. *I wouldn't be surprised if Hannah hasn't roped Matilda into some prank she is planning to pull on Richard. Probably do him good, as there will be no harm in it.*

The evening was a splendid success. All their guests felt privileged at being invited, and many thought that they had seen a new Richard. In the past he had barely a word to say to any of them at the best of times, but this evening he had made a point of talking to each one, making them all feel that they were important and a part of his future.

It was very late when Richard and John were alone in his study, quietly taking some fine port and reminiscing on the evening.

'Wish to discuss those dinner thoughts now, Richard?'

'Hear me out before you make any comment, please, Father. It is an idea that passed my mind at dinner and it seemed plausible, though you may well see it as completely unsatisfactory for any number of reasons.' John nodded, leant back in his chair and sipped his port. 'I said at the table that I had lived a sheltered life compared with that of my congregation. I quite literally have very little knowledge of how they live, how they support themselves, or what is important to them in daily life. To gain just a small insight before I am their vicar would help stop me from making some foolish spectacle of myself that would set me back at the beginning of my tenure, or worse still, lose their trust before I had a chance to gain it. Do you understand?'

'So far. Carry on.'

'My thought was that I might gain some insight if I spent some time in the company of Matilda, with Hannah present at all times, of course. I suspect she is the closest person who is representative of what most of my new congregation will be like. I would like to have the opportunity to talk with her about her life, what mattered to her family, how they survive, how they put food on their table, how they solve problems in their lives. We have always had money. If I had the chance to speak with her, I feel it would open the door to a better understanding of the way others live. Would it be intrusive? Would it be insulting to her? Is my idea out of the question? What do you think, Father?'

John surveyed his son silently, thankful that Richard at least understood his lack of experience, and grateful that his enquiring mind had not stopped seeking answers.

'I think,' he said at last, 'that you could do a lot worse. But tread gently at first to find out how she will accept your questions. Your mother and I do not want any friction here. Matilda is here for a purpose and she has excelled all expectations with Hannah, and long may it continue. Do not destroy it.'

Next morning John was struggling with the paperwork his brother had sent down and trying to sort out how to move a double delivery to Bristol that should have come into Lyme Regis. He was muttering even louder on the vagaries of shipping companies when Sarah put her head round the door.

'Richard said you wanted to join us for tea this morning. We are on the terrace as it is such a lovely day. Will you join us?'

John looked up, scowling. 'Stupid ships!' he grumbled, then remembered Richard's intention for tea conversation, and immediately brightened. 'On my way.' He went out with his wife, anticipating more than just a polite morning tea.

Richard, Hannah and Matilda were already seated and talking quietly among themselves, Hannah particularly pleased that Richard was bringing Matilda into their conversation and she responded brightly to his comments. He rose as his mother approached and held a chair back for her.

'They have been asking about the vicarage and how big it is, and I have absolutely no idea. I really have no idea about most of it, other than I have been told that the Parish needs attention of a young and enthusiastic man, and that is apparently me!' They all laughed at him and he continued smiling. 'Father and I are to go up tomorrow to get an idea of what needs attention and return here for the weekend.'

'I may go on to Bristol and see James about shipping and return later still,' John said. 'What are you two planning for the rest of the week?'

They chattered on inconsequently while tea was poured and cakes handed around.

'Have you thought what your first sermon is going to be on?' Hannah asked. 'What will be your first service?'

'I assume there will be a Holy Communion at eight a.m. and I believe the calendar has an eleven o'clock Family Service. I had better brush up on an appropriate children's story from the Bible that I can base it around. No fire-and-brimstone stuff for the first one—hopefully everyone will turn up to see what they have got landed with. A safe one that will keep the children listening, and the parents satisfied. Jonah and the whale or something like that will do.' Richard paused, unsure as how to get Matilda into contributing. John came to his rescue, seeing him hesitate.

'What do you think, Matilda? The rest of us are too used to Richard's ways—do you think he is on the right track?'

Matilda was surprised to be asked and hesitated, trying to work out a safe response.

Richard quietly added, 'I would appreciate your opinion, and you at least will be unbiased.'

Matilda looked over to him and solemnly said, 'Very well, unbiased and honest. You are likely to lose them from the start if you are going to tell them impossible stories. If the children stop listening, then so will the parents as they will be spending their time trying to keep their children quiet in church, and you end up with no one paying you full attention. What you have to do is be honest. Tell whatever story you like, but be honest about it. Just how many people, do you think, really believe that Jonah was swallowed by a whale and came back out after three days and three nights? We never believed it when we were children. We are farmer's children, we know what animals can and can't do, we know what happens when they eat something, and you don't come out with clean clothes. It may well be meant to be told as a biblical fable, but what do you remember of the story? Why was Jonah in its belly in the first place? Where was he when he was thrown out of the whale? What did he do next? What was the point of Jonah's life?

'Can you tell me now his whole story, and what he did? If the whale part was left out of the story, you would probably remember what God's message was, what he wanted us to learn from that reading. But we didn't remember a thing about Jonah, and stopped listening once he was out of the whale, because our minds were fixed on the one part that was, in fact, quite irrelevant to Jonah's mission. We got so fed up having to listen to vicars telling those stories as though they really happened that way, and they just don't ring true to children today. Your congregation will be there to see what you are made of, so be honest with them.

'Since I have been welcomed into your family, I have always been honest with your parents. I can do no other, I would be foolish to try and be what I am not, and I would look even more foolish for doing so, as I would very soon be caught out and that would be the end for me here. The same goes for you there—be honest with them, they want to know you, they even want to like you, but you will shut that door if you cannot give their children an honest sermon.

'Talk about your schooldays when you were their age—there must have been some incident you can tell them about and build a sermon around it. If you are honest enough they will listen, and they will learn, and they will appreciate you opening up to them. As children we got tired of silly stories from silly vicars that had no relevance to us.' She stopped suddenly, seeing the look on John's face. 'I am sorry, I have said too much. Please excuse me.' And she rose to leave.

John stood rapidly. 'My dear Matilda, you have spoken splendidly! Please sit down, I do believe you have hit the nail right on the head. You have expressed with utter conviction exactly what Richard needed to hear, whether he wanted to hear it or not. If he cannot follow such astonishingly honest advice, then he has little hope of making his mark in Timsbury.'

'Well said, Matilda, bravo! I do not think anyone has been so blunt and honest with him in years. You have given him much to think on,' said Sarah, warmly praising her, and astonished yet again at her basic honesty and ability to say exactly what was needed to another of her children.

Richard sat there with his mouth slightly open, nonplussed by the answer so bluntly given. *I will need to be sure I want an answer before I ask her a question again,* he thought, then slowly nodded his head and said, 'Thank you, Matilda, I now understand Hannah's appreciation of you and what a true friend you must be to her. I feel as though I have been put in my place before I got out of it! I do see that I could have very easily made a complete hash of my beginnings up there and I am very grateful for your honesty. You have quite literally given me not only my first sermon on a plate, but told me how I must present myself to the parishioners for ever. I am humbled by your honesty.' He rose and went over to her, and taking her hand, he quietly said again, 'Thank you.' He turned to the others, slowly releasing her hand, saying, 'Please excuse me, I believe I have some rewriting to attend to and some notes to make.' And he made his way to the library and the old writing desk there.

Hannah watched him go and said to Matilda, 'I do believe you have had quite an impact on my dear stuffy brother. I can think of no other person who would have dared to speak so frankly to him; it has clearly given him much to think on. Come, it is too good a morning to sit here, let us go for a stroll. May we lunch in town, Mother, providing nothing else has been organised?'

'I see no reason for you not to, but I would suggest you are home soon after as Richard and your father will be leaving early tomorrow and you have not had much time with Richard. Matilda, thank you, you spoke well and although John and I have held similar thoughts, they had greater effect on him coming from you.' She dismissed them and sent them on an errand while in the town. Watching them go, chattering away as always, she looked at her husband with a sigh. 'Goodness!'

'Goodness, indeed, Sarah. It's almost as though Richard has met his match. Now I must come up with some solution to this shipping nonsense.' He wandered absent-mindedly back to his office.

Richard had ruled so many lines through his jottings for his first sermon that he threw it in the fireplace and started again, and stared at a blank sheet of paper, thinking of the boy he was at school. His hand dropped to his briefcase and pulled out his diary. Turning to that day's empty page, he placed it before himself and wrote, 'Today I met Matilda properly, a remarkable woman, and a wonderful companion to Hannah. I am envious of her, as such a companion for me right now would be a huge benefit and comfort. She was asked to contribute, she looked me in the eye and saw my weakness. She answered and solved my dilemma and gave me guidance that I didn't know I needed. I must have more time with her.'

'Tosh!' he said aloud, 'get the notes for the sermon written down while her words are so clear in my mind.'

And the words flowed.

Chapter 11

1841: Plans for the Rectory

The coach bringing John and Richard back from Timsbury arrived at the Three Cups promptly at 5 p.m. Their walk back up the hill to Fairfield Lodge stretched their legs and exercised their cramped muscles after the eight-hour trip.

Feeling just a little guilty at not alighting from the coach as it passed their house, John reasoned, 'We need the exercise—there is going to be pity all peace when we get indoors with all the womanfolk wanting to know every last detail, and too much of it on things we didn't even bother looking at as being unimportant to us.'

'Never mind, Father, those questions you can direct to me and I will give a bachelor's answer to them. That will keep them quiet!' Richard smiled at the prospect.

'Only possibly, my boy, only possibly. It is just as likely to set them off into a furore of indignation. You had better spend time with them to try and understand how the female mind works. Their logic does not follow ours, and usually to our cost!' This thought cheered John up immeasurably. His grin broadened as he entered the house, now keen to watch the women's reaction to one of Richard's flippant remarks.

'You look pleased with yourself,' Sarah greeted her husband. 'It must have been a very successful trip.'

John hugged her, replying, 'Sadly enlightening is the best way of putting it. Sad as to the state of the place, enlightening as Richard only has to do half the job I believe he is capable of doing, and he will make a strong impression up there.' He kissed the top of her head and added, 'A bath first, then a quiet drink before dinner. We can all chat then.'

Richard passed his mother, giving her a quick hug on the way by, agreeing on the bath as the first stop and to meet in the drawing room later.

Sarah and Hannah were waiting for them when John came in, and he headed straight to the drinks cabinet.

'You have a sherry, I see. I think something a little stronger for myself.'

'You looked so pleased when you arrived—is it going to be easy for Richard to begin up there? Is everything in order?' Sarah asked.

'Not by a long arrow's shot! It is a shambles to my way of thinking, an enormous amount of work ahead for him. But it is Richard's impression that counts, not mine.'

'So what were you grinning so much about when you arrived?'

'Ha! As to that, you will have to wait and see, and I suspect you will know why soon enough,' John replied mysteriously.

Richard bounded through the door full of excitement and things to tell. He looked at his father with his drink in hand.

'Same as you, I think, Father,' he said, nodding at his glass. 'Is Matilda not joining us?' He looked to his mother.

'Matilda has never joined us when we are likely to be discussing family matters. It is not something we have asked of her, as she has always excused herself on her own accord. It is something we have come to accept as her form of politeness, and at times it has been the correct thing for her to have done.'

'She believes family matters are only for the family,' Hannah added.

'Oh,' Richard said, feeling disappointed at her not being there.

John touched his glass with Richard's. 'Here's to you and Timsbury, Richard.' They all drank to his future. John looked at him. 'What's on your mind?'

'What are we likely to discuss before dinner that Matilda should not hear? You asked her opinion on my sermon and she replied with such blunt honesty that I could have been hurt by it. Let us not fool ourselves, Father, what needs doing up there requires some blunt honesty—we have no time for anything else. If you all have no objection to it, I feel no harm can come from her being present. Is there any matter you are going to raise that she should not be a part of, Father?'

'Probably only money. What it is going to cost us should be kept only within the family. Beside that, another woman's opinion would not go amiss. Sarah?' John looked to his wife for confirmation or objection.

She studied her husband's face, realisation coming to her that what John wanted was Richard to be subjected to women's opinions. His life, she thought, had been lived almost completely without them.

84

'On this occasion, I believe she could be with us. We must all be ready to steer any discussion away from private matters. Would you like to go and invite her down, Hannah? She may still consider it too soon to be here though.' Hannah fairly ran up the stairs to get Matilda—she realised the honour that Richard was bestowing on her by asking for her presence, and who understood money better anyway?

Matilda was taking her time to be ready for tea, not expecting to see anyone until then. She was nervous at the invitation that Hannah so breathlessly delivered.

'Come along, Matilda, this is going to save me having to repeat everything to you later,' she said while she brushed out Matilda's hair, and Matilda did up the last of the buttons. 'Leave your hair down—it's so lovely and wavy, it deserves to be left loose and it will save time not tying it up!' She bustled Matilda down to the drawing room, anxious not to miss too much.

'Good evening, Matilda, Thank you for joining us,' Richard said, rising from his chair as she and Hannah came in.

'Thank you for asking me, Richard,' she replied.

'Would you like a sherry?' Sarah asked, determined to keep the atmosphere relaxed and informal. John had already begun to pour it and gave it to her.

'I hope Hannah gave you the choice of coming down or not?' he laughingly said to her.

She replied so quietly that the others couldn't hear. 'Not really!'

John choked back a laugh, and had to stop himself laughing more. 'Please be seated, Matilda. Richard was saying how impressive the vicarage entrance is through the gateway and the sweep of the drive to the house.'

'It's a shame that the gardens and the lawn are so poorly kept. That entrance could be quite appealing.'

'Did you go inside?' she asked.

'Only from the front hall to his study. It was a bit musty, but everyone has his own way of having his office sorted,' Richard replied.

'How did you see it, John?' Sarah asked, knowing of his fastidious tidiness.

'It was a shambles, and smelled quite badly.'

'Didn't think it was that bad, Father,' Richard said defensively. 'You work better in your own comfortable surroundings. I have seen student rooms in much worse condition.'

'Hmmm,' John murmured. 'What do you make of that, Matilda?'

Sarah sat further back in her chair, knowing of Matilda's tidiness and how she had got Hannah to improve her ways. *This will be interesting if she is blunt,* she thought, watching her decide how much to say.

'Richard, that is an appalling attitude to have! It may be all very well for you to think that you can work in a smelly mess, but you are not there for yourself, you are there for your parishioners,' said Matilda. 'If I was one of your flock and I wanted to come to you for help or advice, do you seriously think I would be comfortable confiding in you in the midst of a stinking shambles? Have you lived in a world where impressions don't count? Would you be happy talking with your mother in that smelly mess? What do you honestly think she would do if you asked her to? I don't think she would stop to talk to you, Richard, I think she would dismiss the staff and employ new servants who could keep a clean house. Your own mother wouldn't want to sit down in that room, so how do you expect any other woman to do so? Why have you so easily disbanded the standards your parents have set for you? The vicarage should be a haven for the troubled, not an objectionable test for their senses!' She took a breath and looked over to Sarah, then blushed. 'I am sorry, Mrs Hill, I should not have taken your name so, but he needs to stop being such a stodgy bachelor!' Matilda gulped, hoping she had not annoyed her.

Richard sat surprised at the tirade, not sure how to respond. Hannah started to giggle, and John suppressed his laugh, waiting on his wife's reply.

'Matilda, you were quite right to use my name, it is probably the only one he would pay attention to! I believe your thoughts are equally quite correct and he needs to heed them, although I would almost certainly tell him that I am about to dismiss his staff before I do it. Do you think the present vicar does his counselling there, John?' she said, watching her son's awkwardness.

'I have no idea where he saw people, I didn't see the rest of the house, I didn't really want to. The church or vestry room are the only likely places, and they are not very welcoming. Part of the roof leaks, one door has a broken hinge and it's draughty. It was pleasantly cool on our summer's day, but it must be dismally cold in winter. I fear there will be a substantial cleaning-up bill coming—it all needs doing.'

Richard gathered his thoughts, taken aback by Matilda's ability to get straight to the nub of a situation and show it for its failings and the effect it has on other people.

'I don't deny that the place could be a great deal more welcoming, but where to start? The church should be repaired first, then the vicarage, surely? I will be on my own up there, and will have to inspire a tired parish council to get things moving,' he ventured.

Sarah looked to John. 'You have thought on this, haven't you?' she asked him.

'Indeed, Sarah. I fear that to do it Richard's way will take too long, and likely fade out before very much time has passed. The new young rector's enthusiasm may become a burden more than a blessing if they are asked to do too much, and there really is too much to be done. I believe a family effort is called for. We must all contribute together and show a united effort in support of Richard. I think the soonest Richard has the vicarage and church in good repair, the sooner he can concentrate on what he is there for. Particularly, as Matilda says, where he holds counsel with his parishioners, comfort and cleanliness are paramount. What say you, Richard?'

'Yes, superb, Father. With Mother in charge of the house, we shall take charge of the church. Will Hannah and Matilda come up as well?'

'Try and keep us away!' Hannah said. 'You would like to come up too, wouldn't you, Matilda?'

'I would like to contribute in whatever way I can to help Richard get established, if I may.'

'Excellent!' said John, 'And I do believe Richard will accept your contribution, as you have so succinctly given much already.'

'A toast then,' said Richard as he began to refill glasses. 'To us and to Timsbury—may we set new standards and give others new hope.'

They clinked glasses together, and a bell tinkled next door.

'How opportune—dinner is ready, shall we adjourn to the table?' said John, joining Sarah and watching Richard take an arm each with Hannah and Matilda.

'Come along, fair ladies, let us dine,' said Richard, and the three of them walked away.

His parents watched them go, and Sarah turned to John, saying, 'Your little ploy worked, Matilda leaves Richard in no doubts what he must do. I am surprised at her forthrightness with him, I would have thought she would have been a lot more reserved. They do get along very well and he would never take the way she speaks to him from anyone else. Why is that do you think? Surely not for Hannah's sake?'

'I have wondered that myself. Probably initially it was for Hannah's sake—he will never do anything to upset her, and as Hannah's friend and companion Matilda has been set apart from other people. But now it is more than that—I believe he respects her in her own right. She speaks to him as though he was her younger brother, and when he needs to be corrected, she does it with brutal honesty but with a sister's love. He needs to be shown the error of his ways, and she is not worried how she does it, as a family's love will allow him to take rebuke and instruction. He did ask for her to be present this evening, which surprised me. I think he knows she will not be abashed in telling him what she thinks. Perhaps it is because she is a couple of years older than he is that allows him to regard her as an older sister. Whatever it is, they do get along with each other better than I had hoped, and with Hannah's blessing. The three of them are quite relaxed in their own company.'

They were joined at the table by Sarah Ann in the company of William Hussey. They listened to how the visit to Timsbury had transpired, and Sarah Ann was quite unperturbed with the planned family excursion to clean the place up, volunteering instead to stay behind and run the household. This was clearly not to her parents' liking, but they had to acknowledge the benefits of having her stay in charge. Richard and Hannah were of the same mind, they preferred her not to come as she was never a hard worker, particularly if there were servants about to do it for her. Dinner passed pleasantly enough, with idle chatter over the coming week's events.

It was decided that Richard would travel up on the Thursday coach, giving him Friday and Saturday to meet the vicar's warden and other vestry members, before Sunday's church services.

The final service for the incumbent before retiring was to be the 11 a.m. matins, and he would introduce Richard formally at the end of it. The farewell tea was to be held that afternoon, and he was leaving the vicarage on the Monday with his sister, to live his retirement out with her in her cottage in Devon. John, Sarah, Hannah and Matilda were to go up on Monday's coach and set to work on Tuesday.

John addressed them all as the table was being cleared. 'Your mother and I are going to remove ourselves to my study, we have much to discuss. Richard, will you look after the ladies and William, then join us in an hour? I will say goodnight to you all now.' He nodded his head in acknowledgement and left the room with Sarah.

'I will just finish this wine, Richard,' said William. 'I have things I must attend to before morning. Thank you.' He gave a glass of sherry to Sarah Ann and they moved to the settee.

Hannah and Matilda began discussing what they were going to do to the vicarage. 'But you haven't seen it yet!' Richard pointed out. 'How can you plan what to do to it?'

'Don't be so silly, Richard,' Hannah rebuked him. 'If Father said it was a shambles and smelled, then there is much to be done in cleaning and tidying. Your study will have to be done first as you will have a whole string of visitors wanting to meet you, and that should be where that takes place. Therefore Matilda and I will have to clean it up as quickly as possible. I bet the dust is inches thick! Then there will be the kitchen and bedrooms, we want to be comfortable during our stay.'

'But Hannah . . .' Richard started.

'No buts, Richard, have you forgotten what Matilda said? You and Father will be busy at the church and we will attack your study, won't we, Matilda?'

'That would be the most sensible thing to do, Hannah,' Matilda replied. 'But we must include whatever staff there are there. Just because it is a mess now doesn't mean that they wanted it so. They may well have wanted it cleaner but were always told to leave things alone. You have to give them a chance to prove that they want to work, and get the place tidy.'

'Yes. A very good point, but don't hold your breath that they are going to want to work hard now, after having a lazy time of it for so long,' Hannah said.

'I agree, but if they are tardy then they must go. I think your mother will do a very nice job of encouraging them to work hard or leave. Then she can do the hiring of new staff and show them the standards required, as you would never know how to go about it, would you, Richard?'

'But they will be working for me—surely I should do it?'

'You will be busy at the church with Father,' said Hannah. 'Leave the house to the women, we know best!'

'But . . .' Richard tried again.

'Poor Richard,' Matilda interjected. 'You are fighting a lost cause— you won't win, give in graciously now with some dignity intact.'

'Oh, I just thought . . .' he started to reply.

'Richard, never argue with a lady with her mind made up,' William interrupted. 'Now please excuse me, I must get going.' He rose and left the room with Sarah Ann.

'Why is it that I always feel in the wrong when facing you two?' Richard playfully asked.

'What rubbish!' Hannah said.

'My humble apologies, kind sir!' Matilda teased him, rising to give him a mocking curtsy.

He laughed at them, enjoying their banter. 'I have no chance of winning with you two, but I am indebted to your kindness. I truly thank you both, as I know you have my best interests at heart. Now I daresay I had better join the management team,' he said, nodding in the direction of his father's study. 'I will see you in the morning.' He went to Hannah and gave her a hug and kissed her cheek. 'Sleep well, little sister.' He turned to Matilda and likewise gave her a gentle hug and kissed her also on her cheek quite naturally, saying, 'Thank you again Matilda, sleep well.' He was suddenly quite aware of her giving him a hug back, and of the pressure of her hands on his back.

'Goodnight, my Richard,' she whispered in his ear, caught unaware by the feelings inside her at his touch. She stepped back, looking up to him, wondering if he felt anything as well. He looked down at her.

Goodness, he thought, *what happened there?* He smiled again at his sister and went to join his parents.

'Well Richard, have you deserted the ladies already?' his father said.

'Not quite, they have retired upstairs. I suspect Hannah and Matilda are in one of their rooms planning what I am to do next. Honestly Father, I have no choices with those two together, and they seem to think that they have you organised as well, Mother.'

'Oh really?' Sarah said, surprised. 'In what way?'

'Next week in Timsbury. They have shovelled Father and me off to attend to matters with the church and out of the house. They intend cleaning and tidying my study in a day, so as to be ready for my first visitors. They intend to enrol the help of whatever staff that have stayed on and expect them to work as hard as they will. They see your role, Mother, as the arbitrator of standards—you are to encourage the staff to work hard, or encourage them to leave. Then you are to employ suitable new servants for me!' he finished, to John's burst of laughter. 'I wasn't being funny, Father!' That just made his father chuckle more, and his mother joined in.

'Dear Richard,' his mother said, 'I do believe the girls are being entirely sensible—the benefit of their plan is that it frees me up considerably. It will just take the first hour to assess the value of the staff up there, and another hour for them to go if they don't want to work hard when required. It won't be me who sees them off, it will be Matilda. Could you take her tirade for more than two hours if you were lazy and didn't want to work? I think she will see off the lazy ones for us and encourage the good ones to stay on. I will keep well out of the way as she will temper her comments to suit my ears if I am about, and not give the tongue lashing that I feel she is quite capable of giving. I should be able to find new staff within a day and half, once we know what you may require up there. That way I can come home on the Wednesday coach, as I do not have great faith in Hussey and Sarah Ann to behave correctly in our absence.'

'This is going to cost more than my allowance and the little I have saved. Have you talked of a budget for the work? Have you set any figure on what is reasonable for you to contribute, keeping in mind that I will be unable to repay you?' Richard knew he would not get very far without financial help from his parents.

'Only as far as knowing we will pay for what clearly needs doing immediately,' John told him. 'We have not considered any figure, as we do not yet know just how much work is required. I will open a separate account for you to draw from for renovation work only, and it will be your judgement on how much you spend after we have initiated the immediate needs when we are up there. If something unexpectedly large comes up, you had better contact me first.' John then added, 'Send me the receipts.'

'Thank you for that, it will make it easier for me.' Richard paused, thinking of how to approach his next idea.

'Do you have other money worries, Richard?' his mother asked.

'Not for me,' he started, 'but I wonder how you would feel about giving Hannah a fund to work with? She and Matilda will be on their own once Mother comes home, and they are most likely going to need to make purchases to achieve a clean and tidy home for me. It would be much better if they didn't come looking for us during the day, wanting some money—that would be a waste of all our times. Do you understand my viewpoint?'

'Entirely, and it may prove more beneficial than you propose. It will be good for Hannah to be responsible for her own budget and keep it recorded. Cash or a bank account? What do you think, my dear?' John turned to his wife for support.

'It may be best to set her up the same as you have for me. Let her have a bank account where she can draw a few pounds at a time—that will allow them to purchase their needs from any number of merchants in cash, without having to open accounts with them. It's an excellent idea.'

91

Back in his room, Richard reached for his diary and pen, but his mind wandered.

He was sure he felt then the breath of her whisper and the touch of her body.

He took some while to go to sleep.

Chapter 12

1841: A Growing Intimacy

It became a habit for Richard to take an afternoon stroll with the two girls, often into the town on a minor errand, and occasionally up the Charmouth Road to the top of the hill, then back along the public walkway through the fields to the house. It was on one of these walks that they saw Sarah Ann and William walking the same way, arm in arm, and unchaperoned.

'That's inappropriate,' Richard muttered on seeing them. 'It cannot be allowed.'

On returning home, he promptly told his father of seeing them. John was more than annoyed at this public display and immediately wrote a note to John Hussey, William's father. Sarah Ann, for her part, was not at all amused to be called before her father and voiced her opinion clearly to Richard when they met later: her brother had not a warm blood vessel in his body, and could not possibly understand any feelings for the opposite sex, as he had lived such a cloistered and celibate life tucked away in his fancy schools. What sort of a preacher did he think he would be if he had no feelings, and didn't allow others to have feelings either? When she had finished, she left the room in a cloud of protest, slamming the door behind her.

That evening meal was a stifled affair, and it was a relief when it was over. Sarah Ann excused herself immediately and went to her room. John went to the decanter and poured drinks for them all.

'Something a little stronger tonight I feel is appropriate. It's Richard's last night in this place as his home. You will always be a welcome visitor, my boy, but from now on you must consider that Timsbury is your home.

Be settled there and you will succeed. Make the vicarage feel like your home, and others will likewise be comfortable with you in it. Best wishes, son.'

They drank the toast willingly, each with their own thoughts of wishing him well. Perhaps they all had a little too much in celebrating Richard's future, for his mother soon excused herself; she was feeling the effects, she said, and John decided to accompany her as she was looking a little shaky and pale.

Hannah watched them go and thought she ought to retire as well, which Matilda agreed to, as it would not do to stay any longer on their own. Richard gave his sister and Matilda their customary hug and kiss on the cheek but as Matilda moved her face back, Richard's lips brushed hers and they stayed there ever so briefly, but long enough for Matilda to respond with some pressure of her own.

'Goodnight, Matilda,' he said, dropping his arms.

'Goodnight, my Richard,' she softly replied, turning to leave with Hannah. He stood motionless, watching them leave the room.

Hannah said nothing until they got to Matilda's door, where she looked back to her and said, 'I didn't see a thing, but can you imagine the carry-on if Sarah Ann had!' She giggled. 'I am really relieved that you get along with Richard. I was so nervous that you wouldn't and that would make everything so awkward with the three of us, but I need not have worried, as you both seem to be getting along just fine!' She laughed even more as a blush began to creep over Matilda's cheeks.

'I am sorry, Hannah. I should not have done that, it was unfair, I should have kept my distance from him. It was all my fault.' Hannah pushed her into her room and followed, closing the door behind her.

'Don't be so silly, Matilda. There were two of you standing there and I didn't notice Richard holding back. He needs a good woman and you are the best! Just don't let Father catch you out—he is so strict and so highly moralistic, you would think *he* was the priest! He knows Richard is ignorant with women, and that is why he sent him off to Europe last summer with three of his friends from Oxford. I think he was hoping that Richard would find out about women over there and out of the way, particularly as one of the friends that went with him has no scruples whatsoever, and Father will not allow him back here. Apparently he spent all his time here trying to seduce Sarah Ann and no one is letting on if he succeeded or not, but you do have to wonder, as he left suddenly early one morning with father showing him the door, and Father remained in the most thunderous mood for days and Sarah Ann was hardly seen and never said a word at the table. I don't think that Richard discovered anything at all on the trip as he complained to Father that the fellow was an absolute bounder with no moral fortitude and he would not be disappointed if he didn't see him again!

'I thought it was all very exciting, but Richard wouldn't tell me anything and got quite starchy over the whole episode, and the subject was closed to me. Even the tiniest kiss he gave you was a monumental thing for him to do, and it's so exciting. So don't ever say you are sorry or keep your distance, as no more will come of it, and it is such a relief that he has shown that he is human after all!' She gave Matilda a hug, saying, 'I must go to bed, I think I have had too much to drink like Mother,' and she left Matilda standing in the middle of her room. Matilda put her fingers to her lips and thought of his touch that had sent such a tingle through her.

They were up and away early a few days later, with too much activity for Matilda's nerves to worry her, and there was the new countryside to keep her occupied. By midday, the continual rocking of the coach had lulled her to sleep and her head dropped onto Hannah's shoulder.

Richard, who had travelled there a few days earlier, met them at the Timsbury stop with a horse and cart.

'Not very comfortable, but it will do the job. I will take Mother along, if you two don't mind walking down with Father. It's not very far.'

'The short walk will do us good—have the kettle on ready for us!' John said, and strode off down to the vicarage. When they got to the gates Hannah stopped in her tracks.

'It is rather impressive, isn't it?' she said. 'I do hope that the inside is not as unkept as the outside.' Her mother came out shaking a cloth. 'That doesn't bode well. When was the last time Mother shook a cleaning cloth out the front door for the neighbours to see?'

'Mmmm,' John murmured. 'At least the garden wall keeps the house and grounds private, but I gather she doesn't think there is a moment to be lost.'

Sarah greeted them at the front door with, 'You may wish you had not volunteered to come and clean. I do not know how Richard has been able to sleep in his room—I have opened the windows in your bedroom. I just hope it is a calm night and you can leave them open all night. Come and see.' She led the procession through the house. It was not a cheerful sight.

'There is one bonus for you,' Richard said. 'He has cleaned out all his papers from the study—it's empty except for the desk and two chairs, which will give you a head start with cleaning. On the down side, he has one maid who doesn't live in the house and she is also his cook. She has left some food in the pantry for us to prepare a meal for tonight, but I haven't seen her for two days. I have been busy helping the old boy to pack, and have been staying at the inn until today to give him some privacy on his last days. Why don't we all unpack and then organise tonight's meal? You may want to change where you want to start cleaning, now you have seen around.'

'Sound thinking, Richard,' his father said. 'Perhaps Matilda and I might see what's what in the kitchen so we can get things going. Hannah can unpack for you, can't she, Matilda? Come along then, let's get into it.' He marched off down to the kitchen. 'I'm not looking forward to this,' he said to Matilda. 'I expect it is going to be as disgraceful as we both anticipate.'

It was. The only utensils that had been used were appropriate only for when cooking for one; the bigger pots and pans were dirty and rusted, the oven unclean.

'Oh Mr Hill, this will never do, she has only left enough food for three at best. I could mix up a hash like we do at the farm, but I will need to use the breakfast food as well to make enough, and I don't fancy what that will taste like.'

'Good if we are hungry enough! Do it, Matilda, and we will worry about breakfast in the morning. You and Hannah will have to do some grocery shopping first thing.' They got the oven fire going and had got some heat starting to come through on the top plates when Sarah came in.

'It is going to take some time, Mrs Hill. The fire hasn't been stirred since this morning, is my guess, it will be late by the time it is hot enough to cook with. Mr Hill and I decided that I will make a hash of everything here; he's gone to find me some more coal.'

Sarah surveyed the kitchen sadly. 'Do your best, we will all appreciate it. Clearly we need to find a cook for Richard as this will never do.' She was interrupted by a banging on the door.

'Hello, who's in?' came a querying voice. 'Are you there, Vicar?' Sarah went to investigate and returned to the kitchen with a ruddy-faced woman and Richard following.

'Mother, this is Mrs Hadlow, she is one of the roster cleaners for the church,' said Richard by way of introduction. 'Mrs Hadlow, this is my mother, Mrs Hill, and my sister's companion, Matilda White, who has come up with my sister to help clean. Where are Father and Hannah?' They both appeared through different doors.

'Is something amiss, Mrs Hadlow?' Richard queried, not expecting to see anyone until the following day. She looked around the kitchen, and at what Matilda had started to prepare:

'It would seem so—did you not get my message, Vicar? I have a meal prepared at home for you all. I think the part-time maid took fright at the thought of preparing a meal for five and she is going to give you her notice. Come along then, no point in standing here. I've left George in charge of dinner, and he is no cook.' She promptly left with a trail of very relieved and weary travellers in her wake.

The meal was all the better for its unexpectedness and cheerful hosts. Mrs Hadlow sat beside Sarah.

'I am so sorry for such a dismal welcome and I have such high hopes for your son here. We desperately need some life injected into our church and village, and the vicarage is such a cold place.'

'I have only a few days here,' Sarah replied, 'and in that time I was to organise Richard's staff. It would seem that now he has none. I thought he would need a maid and a cook. He will need two, so that one is always there on the other's day off. You wouldn't know who may be available in the village, would you?' Sarah hoped fervently that Mrs Hadlow was about to save her a lot of time.

'Well as it happens, I may be able to help. There is a little prejudice to overcome, as our last vicar here was not good with his staff, and no one stayed for long. But I can think of a few who would do a good job, providing they could see that they would be looked after. Perhaps I could speak to them all tomorrow and arrange for them to come up to the vicarage on Tuesday morning. You and Richard could speak to them then and they could have a look around the vicarage and make their minds up about whether they want to work there. That may be the downfall, as it is not in the best condition.'

'That would be wonderful, thank you. It will be up to us to show the place as it could be. The girls had planned to clean Richard's study first thing tomorrow, and we will make sure at least one room will ready for visitors. The kitchen will take a little time.' Sarah heaved a sigh of relief. George turned to John. 'The grounds are not up to standard over there. I have a handyman who helps me out here on occasion—good man, knows his plants, got a gammy leg, ex-army, got it out in India, doesn't say much, just gets on with it. Don't want to add to your expenses any more than necessary, but it is an unruly mess.'

Richard smiled. 'That is a fair assessment,' he said. 'It does need some major work on it. What it really needs is someone who can put the time in. It needs full-time attention for some while, I think.'

John nodded agreement. 'Would he be available to do the hours?'

'Can but ask,' George replied. 'I'll find him tomorrow and send him along with the likely maids on Tuesday morning.'

'Well,' said John, 'a splendid evening, out of one starting so badly. Not only well fed, but well on the way with your staff as well, Richard. We are extremely indebted to you both. My heartfelt thanks.'

They returned to the vicarage in higher spirits and retired early.

The next morning Hannah and Matilda attacked Richard's study. By late afternoon, after much rug beating and washing, the room was transformed. They were sitting on the two chairs, exhausted, when the door opened.

'Lord love us! What a change!' Mrs Hadlow exclaimed. 'You have worked a miracle.'

'Well done, it's so much better,' said Sarah. 'All it needs are some books on the shelves and a nice light picture or two on the wall.'

'I will send George over with some books until the vicar gets his own here. I have one picture that might do and a mirror will make a difference, I think,' Mrs Hadlow said. 'Having this room done will make all the difference when you speak with the servants I have in mind.'

And so it did.

By Tuesday night, Richard and his mother had employed two staff, one as a house servant, the other to be the cook and help within the house, both to live in. They were so impressed with what had been done to the study, and so enthralled with Richard's enthusiasm, that they both offered to start immediately and help clean up and take over the rooms that Matilda and Hannah were using when they left. George's handyman also began that week, appreciating a regular income to complement his small army pension, and delighted at the challenge of bringing the big garden back to its former glory.

Wednesday morning saw Sarah take the coach home to Lyme Regis, leaving Hannah, Matilda, and Jane, the new cook, to go on a shopping trip to purchase new equipment for the kitchen and groceries for the larder, all of it to be delivered that afternoon. The three of them set to cleaning the kitchen and scrubbing the floor. Alice, the young house servant, arrived mid-afternoon and joined in the fray. By late afternoon the deliveries had all arrived, including a new load of firewood and coal. Hannah rose to the occasion as the one left in charge, and felt very pleased with herself at capably handling all the monetary transactions.

As they ate their first meal in the vicarage at the kitchen table, Richard beamed his delight at them all. 'You all cannot know my joy and absolute delight to be able to sit at this table and eat such a wonderful meal in my vicarage. It's beginning to feel like a home already.' He smiled at his words. 'I am really pleased that you, Jane and Alice, made yourselves available to join us here so soon—thank you.' They blushed at his attention and praise. 'As for you two,' he said, looking at Hannah and Matilda, 'what else can I say to you, you both know how much I appreciate the help you continue to give me. Thank you as well.'

John nodded in agreement. 'We will just have to toast their contribution with a cup of tea!'

Hannah thanked Jane and Alice, saying, 'You two go home, Matilda and I will clean up the dishes and lay out for breakfast. Could you be here for eight in the morning?' They agreed and soon left. John rose from the table.

'Will you excuse Richard and me? I would like to finalise the list for immediate work on the church with him—it is only a portion of the roof that is a concern. Then I would like to leave tomorrow and go to Bristol and talk with my brother James about materials needed, and the contacts he knows who can provide them quickly here. I may go straight home from there and miss your first service. The girls can travel back on their own.'

Matilda and Hannah tidied up, and before retiring, made a fresh pot of tea and took it into the study.

'We are off to bed. We thought you may like some refreshment,' Hannah said, and gave her father and brother a hug goodnight. Matilda said goodnight from the door, being demure in John's presence. 'We have decided to go home on Monday. We should have most done by then and Jane and Alice will be able to finish off.'

'Very good,' said John. 'I will see you back there.' Richard watched them go, wishing very much he could have given Matilda a hug as well and hear her say 'My Richard' again. It seemed so long since she had last had the chance.

The next two days raced by. Richard spent all day at the church with tradesmen measuring and quoting figures. The others slowly working their way through the house, spring-cleaning each room, emptying out cupboards and wardrobes, and leaving lavender bags in them to be rid of the musty smell. So much had to be washed and aired, polished and cleaned. Exhausted and bone weary, the four of them at last sat around the kitchen table with a pot of tea in front of them.

'I think you deserve the weekend off,' Hannah said to Jane and Alice. 'We are near enough ready for you to do it on your own come Monday. Would you like to start to shift in on Sunday afternoon? Choose which bedroom you each want—Matilda and I will be packed ready to leave early Monday morning.'

'I will come over and cook your evening meal for you though,' said Jane. 'I can't see you stopping long enough to prepare a proper meal, and Mr Richard should eat correctly with Sunday coming up. If Alice would like to help me to prepare tonight's meal and start it cooking, we can both get away a little earlier. Maybe you two would like to have a hot bath before dinner for a change, and then be ready to keep an eye on the cooking when you come down?'

'Thank you, Jane, that will be very helpful. A hot bath now seems quite luxurious.'

Refreshed from their baths, they stepped out feeling completely clean for the first time in a week. They dressed slowly, brushing out their wet hair.

They heard the front door banged shut.

'That smells nice,' Richard called out. Then, 'Where is everyone?'

Hannah put her head out her bedroom door. 'Up here, we are dressing,' she called out. 'Check the pots, we'll be there soon.'

The two women went down together, and Richard looked up at them, surprised. 'Goodness! Don't you both look radiant! Where are Jane and Alice?'

'I have given them time off until Monday. They will move in on Sunday afternoon. It's just us three until then, with Jane coming in to cook the evening meals. They have earned their rest,' Hannah advised him.

'I am so grateful for that,' he said. 'I have bought some wine to go with the meal. Let me race upstairs and clean up as well, and we can have a quiet evening together.' There was much banging and splashing to be heard from him upstairs.

'He is on his own up there, how can he make so much noise?' Matilda asked Hannah, laughing.

Presently they heard his footsteps thumping down the stairs and he burst back into the kitchen. 'I'm back' he announced needlessly. 'I'm famished, let me open that bottle.' He picked it up then put it back down and gave Hannah a mighty hug and kissed her brow. 'I don't know what I would have done without you here this week. You are a blessing!'

'I would have done little without Matilda—it was she who kept us all going. She deserves equal thanks.'

'My apologies and grateful thanks, Matilda, I was not about to leave you out,' he said, going to her and likewise giving her a big hug and kissing her without hesitation on the lips.

'You are welcome, my Richard,' she replied, and he sighed to himself. *I do like hearing that.*

'I wasn't encouraging you to thank her quite as equally as that!' Hannah said, enjoying Richard's sudden embarrassment. 'But she does deserve it!'

'I'll open that bottle,' Richard said, flapping his hands about, not sure which way to turn.

They both laughed at him, at his awkwardness.

'Come on then, I'll serve up,' Matilda offered.

Richard poured them all a glass. 'Here's to us! What a week it has been,' he said, raising his glass, and the three of them acknowledged what they had achieved in that short time. It was the first of several toasts taken during a tasty and convivial meal.

'This is the first time I have relaxed all week. As we will be alone tomorrow, I will finish my sermons then. No more work tonight. Let us relax and enjoy it,' Richard declared, and they did. 'Shall we adjourn to my study? The seats are more comfortable in there. They are about the only ones that are!'

It was some time later, when Richard poured the last from the second bottle, that Hannah stifled a yawn and said, 'Enough! I will never wake in the morning at this rate. I am going to retire these weary bones to bed. Here's to us.' She smiled, mimicking Richard's first toast of the evening.

They stood and clinked their glasses together, and emptied them.

'I agree,' said Matilda, 'to bed.' She took Hannah's empty glass and went to take Richard's. 'I'll wash these and put them away. See you both at breakfast. But not too early!' She left them and went to the kitchen to finish the dishes. She was not long, but Hannah and Richard had already gone upstairs. She made sure all the lamps were out as she went, moving quietly up the stairs to her room. She was surprised to meet Richard coming back from the bathroom.

'Goodnight, my Richard,' she whispered as he drew near.

'Goodnight, dear Matilda,' he whispered to her as he met her, taking her in his arms and kissing fully as never before. She held onto him tightly, kissing him lovingly back.

'I don't want to say goodnight just yet,' he quietly said

'Neither do I,' she breathed in his ear, gently opening his door. She thought they were floating, not aware how they reached his bed, nor how her bodice had come undone, as the kissing never stopped. She could feel her breasts being held and kissed and their excitement growing.

'Never before,' Richard heard himself say, not knowing how their clothes came off, and marvelled at seeing her body before him. He felt driven on, guided by soft hands, and entered her in a rush, hearing her cry out into his shoulder. He couldn't stop the motion of his body, and then suddenly he lay still.

'Oh Matilda, what have I done? That should never have happened,' he said in anguish, but not moving from on top of her.

'My Richard, it needed to happen. I couldn't keep seeing you and not wanting it to happen.'

'But what if you become with child?' His fears were rising.

'Hush, it won't happen that easily. Rest easy,' she whispered, holding him to her, and kissed his ear. She felt him stir again within her and moved with him. This time it was she who could not stop the motion, crying out again into his shoulder.

'Oh Richard, I do so love you.'

'Is this love I feel? I have never been near another woman.'

'I have never been with another man, but for me, I will call it love.'

'So be it.' He sighed, his head dropping onto her shoulder.

'Hey! Don't you be going to sleep, I need to be getting to my own room!' Reluctantly, they parted to be alone in their respective beds, to dream and sleep as never before.

Chapter 13

1841: Ecstasy and Humiliation

Matilda woke slowly, as if from a pleasant dream, and she smiled at the memory of the night. *So that's what Mary was on about,* she thought. *It was worth waiting for the right man.*

She dressed and went down to the kitchen to find she was the first one there. She stoked up the fire in the stove, put the kettle on for tea and started to get the breakfast ready. A bleary Hannah came in behind her.

'I couldn't wake up, just kept going back to sleep. Morning, Matilda. Richard not risen yet?'

'I've not seen him. I think we were all too tired last night and he has probably slept in as well. Take a cup up to him, he will not want to sleep too long. I'll cook some breakfast.' She handed Hannah the tea on a tray and sent her up to her brother with it, and began to poach some eggs. Hannah was soon back, looking worried.

'He is already up and in his study working. He wants to see you—he seems upset,' she said to Matilda. 'He wants to see you alone—why's that?'

'I'll tell you when I come back. Probably wants his sermon tested.' Neither of them were convinced of that. Matilda knocked on his study door and waited for him to call her in.

'You want to see me, Richard. What is worrying you?'

'You know very well, Matilda. I should never have allowed last night to happen—what happened is unacceptable. How can I preach to these people with the example I have set by my own behaviour? I have prayed for forgiveness, but the guilt remains. What's to be done with us?' He slouched down more into his chair.

Matilda walked to the front of his desk, looking down to him, and softly spoke. 'My dear Richard, you are a very learned man, but your life's experiences have come to you in a strange order. There would be few men who reach your age and have not experienced a woman. Last night was not a mistake, nor do I think it was wrong—it was an experience you needed to know. It was not a burden to you last night, and this morning you should be treating it as enlightenment. Do not ask for forgiveness as though it was a sin, but offer thanks for being shown how a woman loves. It would be a sin if either of us was married, if it had held no love. Remember that there were two of us, and we surrendered to each other gladly. We were rewarded with our love. That is a gift, Richard. You worry about preaching to your congregation because of last night's experience; I worry about you preaching to your congregation without it. Half this town are women, well over half your congregation will be women, nearly all the people who come into this room wanting help and guidance will be women, or men here on the insistence of a woman. They will come to you because they expect you to have some experience of life, including last night's. How many do you think would come and open their hearts and minds if they thought you to be young and lacking in understanding? Would they say anything even near what really troubles them? Be grateful that you are no longer quite so lacking in life. Be proud to be one of them, and give them your sermon with love and honesty, and they will return it. Show leadership with an understanding of a broadened life, and they will listen.

'You are the first man that I have considered worthy, and I am glad I waited. I will never deny you, and I will always love you.' She paused, catching her breath. 'I will leave now if I have truly become a burden to you.' A tear began to roll down her face and she bit her lip, trying to control her emotions.

'Matilda,' he said, coming from around his desk. 'Matilda.' He held her in his arms, and finally she continued.

'Last night was something very special. It wasn't a tragic mistake, it wasn't sinful and it very definitely wasn't a burden. Do not treat it or me like that, I couldn't take it. I would have to leave for ever.' Her tears flowed down her face.

'Matilda,' he said again, 'you are not to leave. Why do you see things so clearly when I cannot? How do you always make my problems seem so simple, and no more than another step in my life's education? Maybe it is you who should give the sermon.'

She smiled her relief into his chest, telling him, 'You will be fine— you will surprise them all with what you will say, just don't tell them what we did!'

He laughed, his tension dissipating. 'Thank you.' He kissed the top of her head.

'We should go and have breakfast—those eggs will be like leather and Hannah will be wondering what is going on.' She stepped back and dried her eyes.

'Perhaps you should wash your face before you see her, I have seen you prettier. I will talk to Hannah.'

When Matilda came into the kitchen she was met with close scrutiny from Hannah. Richard was looking at his plate, devouring his eggs and toast, and she served herself.

'Richard has tried to tell me what went on in there. Am I to believe any of it?' Hannah asked her.

'Probably not,' Matilda replied. 'But to tell you now would only embarrass him even more.' Hannah smiled at that, feeling that whatever it was, the problem had been overcome.

They finished their breakfast in companionable silence.

'I am going to rewrite my sermon again,' he told them. 'I feel I am not being honest enough with it.' Hannah laughed at this, thinking of Matilda's bluntness with him. 'I am hoping that you two will attend tomorrow's services—I will be relying on some honest comments. But please sit at the back where I can't see you, as I will surely falter should I see you watching me.'

Hannah laughed at him. 'Stupid man!' she said. 'Did you ever think we were going to stay away?' And they all laughed at that impossibility. He rose and left them, all tension gone.

'Well?' asked Hannah, searching her friend's face.

'Very well, indeed!' smiled Matilda right back, knowingly.

'What!' Hannah squawked. 'You didn't! You haven't! Richard wouldn't! Did he really! No wonder he was so shame-faced this morning! He wouldn't have known what hit him! What did you say to sort him out? Are you all right now?' She gasped at the revelation of it all.

'Yes, yes, yes, yes, yes, no, none of your business, just wonderful. All in that order,' Matilda replied, starting to clear the table.

'I can't remember what I asked first!' wailed Hannah. 'But it seems to have done no lasting damage. I just can't believe he did! He must

105

have felt he had broken every sacred rule—no wonder he was in the dumps this morning. How did you change him?'

'I explained life from my point of view, as any honest woman in love would.'

'That probably confused him more,' Hannah said. 'He took the easiest way out—that as you were clearly happy about it, then so should he be.'

'Something like that,' Matilda agreed. 'Now, Lady in Charge, what are we to do about this house? For all our cleaning, it is still rather shabby and sparse in furnishings. Your father will not see it before we get back and he will want to know how we got on. I suggest we make a list for each room for what it still needs, to be of a reasonable standard. What do you think?'

Hannah thought before answering, 'You are probably right—have everything on it, you mean. Whether it needs new drapes, as Richard's study does, or furniture, fresh paint and wallpaper, floor covering, even bed linen. Then put a cost to it all—he likes having costings done on everything. We could get an idea for that part back in Lyme Regis. He would be impressed if we did that.'

'I will help you get the prices when we get back, but you must present it all to your father on your own. How much money he is prepared to let you spend is a family matter, and I should not know that.'

'It would be better if we made the list up in order of importance. He will see Richard's study, the kitchen and the entrance hall as very important, as that is what visitors will see. Then do the rest of the house as we see it. What about the gardens? Should I list that? Richard and Father seem to have employed the gardener with no direction or instruction,' Hannah said.

'Just do the house—it's what we came up to do. Mention the garden at the end and ask what instructions he has. Come on, a page a room.'

The morning swept by with continual chatter, ideas raised and dropped, colours shared and furniture agreed on. Richard found them deep in discussion in the formal dining room.

'Not interrupting anything serious, am I?'

Hannah explained what they were planning. 'Can we go into your study now that you are free? We want it to be perfectly comfortable for all purposes.'

'Be my guests. Can I contribute?' he asked teasingly of his sister.

'Of course, but do be sensible about it,' she retorted.

'Absolutely, ma'am,' he said, tugging his forelock in a subservient manner.

'Stupid man!' she said of him again. But it proved to be the easiest room to do, as they all agreed on all the changes that needed to be done.

'Good luck with Father,' Richard said. 'Now let's eat, and after, I rather fancy a stroll through town and some fresh air. Would you both be kind enough to keep me company along the way?'

'Of course we will,' Hannah replied.

'Gladly,' said Matilda. 'We have barely been out the door all week.'

They had a slow and relaxed walk, stopping many times to talk with the villagers they met, all wanting to introduce themselves to the new rector, and all promising to attend tomorrow's service.

They ate a relaxed meal, tired and satisfied that all they could have done was done, ready for Richard's true beginning in the morning.

'If you don't mind, I will retire early and read my sermon notes again. I will be up early and I would like to be at the church well in time to be sure all is as I want it. You don't need to be there too early, just make sure you don't arrive late!' Richard kissed them both and bade them goodnight.

'A most satisfying conclusion to a difficult day,' Hannah said.

'Most satisfying,' Matilda agreed.

The next morning they sat through both services, watching Richard in awe.

Hannah proudly acknowledged her brother, so clearly where he needed to be, so confident in his role. Matilda listened in rapt attention, particularly during the family service, where she watched an attentive congregation listen to every word as he gave his sermon. It was about how, as small schoolboys, he and his friends had crept out of their dormitory to raid the orchard on the farm next door. Every boy heard their own story told, every girl knew a boy who had done the same, and they all wanted to know if he was caught or not. The ending of Richard's tale took them by surprise, and every child knew they had done wrong, and that God was not happy with them. There was no mistaking the meaning of the sermon, and every parent knew Richard had got his message across.

They remained at the back as the congregation filed out, each one wanting to acknowledge Richard's impact, each boy feeling that Richard knew whose orchard they had raided, guilt on every face. Each parent smiled, knowing their child had been caught out by the tale.

Hannah and Matilda finally left also, shaking his hand like the rest, but with tears of pride in their eyes at such a warm and convincing service. He could hardly acknowledge their presence before he was swamped by his parish councillors, all offering him lunch, all wanting his attention.

They left him to it and walked back to the vicarage in silence, thinking of the man they both loved.

They were thankful to have Jane and Alice arriving in the afternoon with their luggage, and shifting into their rooms. The distraction helped to pass away the time, but they were also pleased when they left, and they were alone again.

It was a drained and exhausted Richard that finally got home that evening, his dinner kept warm in the stove. They were almost packed and ready for their early-morning departure, and left him to eat his meal in peace and solitude downstairs. When he had finished, feeling slightly more like himself, he called up to them. 'Come on then, you two, let's have it.'

They came down to find the table already cleared and the dishes being washed. They took over, sitting him at the table to sip on a glass of port they had taken from his study.

'There is nothing we could possibly say that your congregation have not already said, and they are the ones you need to take judgement from,' Hannah told him.

He looked to them. 'That's it? Maybe they wanted to flatter me first up, maybe they wanted to get into my good books. Do you have nothing at all to say, Matilda?' he asked her, almost pleading for some comment.

'You were all that I could have hoped for,' she replied quietly. 'You held them all spellbound, every man, woman and child. You told your own story with more honesty than I thought you capable of. Your message was clear from the start and no one could miss it. Your ending was sudden and surprising and I didn't see it coming. You were simply magnificent.' She walked over to him and hugged him warmly, kissing his cheek.

Hannah joined them as Matilda moved away. 'I am so very proud of you, big brother. I have never seen you like that,' Hannah said to him, also giving him a big hug. 'I really do not know what else I can say.' She kissed his cheek.

'Well, that's all right then,' he said with relief. 'Just be aware that it was you two who have kept me in line all this week. That sermon was as much yours as mine.'

'Richard Hill! I must let you know that I have never raided an orchard in my life!' Matilda retorted.

'Neither have I! I made it up from all those dormitory stories I heard after lights out.' They all laughed.

They stayed talking around the kitchen table until late, when Matilda said she had better retire, as tomorrow would be a long day. She rose to leave them, and Hannah nodded, adding that she would follow. Richard went to Matilda and held her in his arms. He spoke quietly.

'You have changed me, you must not leave because of what I said this morning. Goodnight, my dear, sleep well.' He kissed her and looked to Hannah. 'What has she said to you?'

'She didn't need to say anything,' Hannah replied. 'We are too close for any need to explain, but be careful as you are both too precious to me for either of you to be hurt.'

He went to her, saying, 'And you are both precious to me. Look after each other.'

The following morning was a bustle of activity, Hannah and Matilda making sure they had everything packed and lists accounted for, Richard giving last-minute instructions and scribbling notes for his father, and Jane and Alice arriving with the last of their belongings and settling in.

The parting at the coach was a flurry of cases and parcels being loaded, goodbyes and best wishes among them all. The coachman suddenly whistled his horses into action and they were gone.

It was a long time before either spoke. Leaving was an anticlimax to the week, and both felt low in spirits. Neither of them knew what to say, particularly in front of the other passengers, but sat instead looking out the window as Somerset rolled by. Even the lunch break afforded little conversation, and it was with relief that the brow of the hill to Lyme Regis was passed. The coachman stopped for them outside Fairfield Lodge and two of the maids ran across to help carry in the bags.

The next two days were a frantic race around the Lyme Regis shops, asking questions on furniture and getting costs. By Thursday morning Hannah was ready to present it all to her father, she felt confident of what she was going to say, having practised for hours with Matilda in her room.

She went down and knocked on his door, leaving Matilda to wait anxiously upstairs. She entered at his call and sat before him.

'You two have done well in Timsbury—I am extremely grateful, and going by Richard's scribbled notes, he is too. You seemed to cover everything last night at dinner. Now tell me, what exactly have you there for me?' John sat there attentively, not sure if it all wasn't to be a waste of time, or whether there was sense in what she had to say.

An hour later he was still sitting attentively, surprised by his daughter's efforts. She had presented every detail that each room needed, and the reason why. She had given priority for each room in order, and he couldn't fault her on that. The work within each room was also prioritised, each item costed individually so that work could be done to match any available budget he may choose to set. Her plan and lists were faultless. The only option he didn't have was to say 'No'—he just had to decide how much to spend. He sat silently for so long, thinking on his daughter's new confidence, that it was Hannah who broke the silence.

'Father?' she tentatively asked. 'Does it make sense?'

He looked up guiltily. 'I'm sorry, you have given me much to think of. I am very impressed by this whole plan—it is most thoroughly done, and now I have heard you out, it is also quite necessary. There is only one small area on which we may differ, and that is the costing. You have based it on the local suppliers, which is completely reasonable as that is all that is available to you. Up there we can approach bigger suppliers in Bath and Bristol, and we should be able to buy at better terms, which means your budget is very likely on the high side, which in itself is not a bad thing. I need to think this through and speak with your mother on it. Now tell me, how much has Matilda put into this?'

'Rather a lot really. She thought that maybe I should make a list of what still needs doing to give you an idea of what we had got done and the next steps to be taken. Once I started it seemed to grow to what I finished up with. She helped me visit places in town to get prices, as I knew it would be the first thing you would ask if I hadn't, and without them the lists seemed to have no real meaning. She was quite rude to old Mason in the decorator's—she told him his prices were ridiculous for the amount we were looking at. I am not sure we will be welcome back in there.'

John roared with laughter at this. 'She would be quite right—that old rogue adds on to everything, probably saw you and added on more! Would have done him good.' He smiled at what the confrontation must have been like, then added, 'You have done very well with this—I am extremely grateful and proud of your efforts. Would you mind leaving all this with me, and we will talk it over later?'

She stood, relieved it was over and he liked it. 'Thank you, Father,' she said, and left to find Matilda and tell her how it went.

John went to find Sarah, wondering what she knew of the proposal. They spoke at length, Sarah admitting she had no idea at the depth of the work put into it. Finally she said, 'How much of Matilda is there in this, John?'

'I asked her that, fearing too much Matilda, and too little Hannah. Her reply suggests that Matilda guided her along the way, but it was Hannah that did it. It is a huge step for Hannah to have done so if that is so, but I just don't know.'

Sarah looked at him. 'How important is it that you know?'

'It matters in that we need to be able to judge how mature Hannah has become in her thinking, just how far away is Hannah from becoming independent.'

'Then ask Matilda directly. You know how blunt her answer will be— you will be left in no doubts then.'

'Yes,' John admitted and smiled. 'It is that I am almost afraid to ask— her answers can be pointed where you don't expect. Her honesty can hurt.'

Sarah looked over to him. 'That can do you no harm, I'll send her down.'

When Matilda entered his study, John had Hannah's lists to one side and was totalling up figures on a pad. He raised his head and smiled at her.

'Have a seat, Matilda. I'm afraid I need to ask you more of what Hannah has prepared here. I see it as a sudden leap forward in her capability, and, I want to give her more independence with her own money, I want her to be able to look after it, not waste it. What she has produced here is remarkable, it shows clear thought in how to get the most for where the money should be spent—she has even written out all the reasons and their correct priorities, and I cannot fault it. I could not have done it better. What I am asking you is what part of this did you do and what did Hannah do?' He flicked the pages over the table to Matilda. She looked down at them, then up to John.

'We talked on the Saturday morning about what we had achieved and what was still to be done. I did suggest to her that the easiest way was to write a list so that she could tell you how far we had got, and it was clear it had to be done room by room. So we walked around every room and talked about what else could be done easily, to make it look complete. Richard joined us to do his study, so you have his thoughts included there. Hannah did all the lists and assessed how important each was. We spent the first two days back here together in town getting prices. She did most of the talking as most of the merchants knew who she was. I only did the talking with one merchant, who was clearly loading his prices because he reckoned you could afford it. I know a cheat when I see one, and I told him so. You will probably get a complaint about the matter. That is all I did. Hannah wrote it all up, and did the sums. It really is mostly all her own work.'

John nodded and sighed. He looked again at the lists in front of Matilda. 'All of that?' He motioned to them.

Matilda sat quite still, then said almost too quietly, 'Mr Hill, you seem to have forgotten that I can neither read nor write. I cannot understand what is on those pages, I could not have done them.' She paused before continuing, 'I do not think I can help you further.'

She stood and left the room without another word being said, walking up to the privacy of her own room, her hand over her bowed head trying to hide her shame and humiliation.

She sat and cried on her bed.

Chapter 14

1841: A Tragic Morning

'Oh God, John! What damage have you done? We still need her!' Sarah turned and rushed from the room. At Matilda's door she stopped. Knowing Hannah would be the only one who could talk to Matilda now, she moved on to her room, hoping she was there, and went straight in. Hannah jumped at the sudden intrusion and saw almost fear on her mother's face.

'Come!' was all Sarah said, taking Hannah by the wrist and heading back out the door.

'What's happened?' Hannah asked. 'What's wrong?'

'Your father has made a terrible mistake,' she said, arriving at Matilda's door and knocking. 'He has insulted Matilda without thinking.' She opened the door, not waiting for Matilda to call, and went in, still pulling Hannah by the wrist. Matilda turned, surprised at their entrance.

On her bed behind her, her suitcase sat opened.

'Matilda,' Hannah cried and ran to her. 'Don't.' She held her limp friend in her arms.

'There is nothing more for me to do here, you have proved yourself, my dear friend. Now I feel I am in the way.' She said it calmly, but was still smarting by the painful way her inadequacy had been brought home.

'John was not thinking, he meant no malice,' Sarah said. She moved to the bed and closed Matilda's suitcase, putting it on the floor. 'You must stay, Matilda, I require you, Hannah still needs guidance and a chaperone. I will get some tea. Persuade her, Hannah.' And she left them there, trying to remain calm in herself.

'What happened, Matilda, what did Father do? You cannot leave!' she begged of her, and they sat on the bed, her arm around Matilda.

'He wanted to know how much I had done of your plan for the renovations, and I told him. I do not think he fully believed me. He had pushed your lists to my side of the desk and meant me to check through them.'

'Oh no!' Hannah exclaimed.

'He knows I cannot read, but he deliberately asked me to do so. I am sorry, but I cannot take that, from him of all people. He is reminding me that I am not of your standing, I am no longer required.' She paused. 'He need not have done that, he could have only asked that I go. I would accept that without question, there was no need to insult me. So you see I must go,' she finished quietly, wishing for a nicer way for her time here to have ended.

'You are quite wrong to think that, Matilda, quite wrong. Father would not wittingly be even mildly rude to you in a million years! Look at me, Matilda, and please believe what I say. Even I have forgotten many times that you cannot read or write—your confidence that I so envied, your knowledge and your vocabulary are so broad, it makes a nonsense of you being illiterate. Can't you see that?' she pleaded.

Sarah came in with the tea tray. 'Even Mother's ladies think you well educated. One even asked Mother what school you attended, so that she could send her own granddaughter to the same one, she thought your education so well rounded. Can't you see that we all forget at times?' she asked again. Sarah had poured a cup for Matilda and turned to Hannah.

'I think it would be a good idea if you went down and talked the same sense to your father, Hannah. I am afraid that I may become very annoyed with him right now, while you, on the other hand, could make a scene and get away with it. I will sit with Matilda for a bit, until you come back.'

Hannah needed no more encouragement, and left promptly.

'I believe Hannah will express both our views to her father very clearly, if not a little too loudly. I don't mind how she does it, as long as I am not present to hear it. Drink your tea, my dear, although I would like something a little stronger myself—it's been very upsetting.'

Matilda had to smile at the thought of Hannah before her father, and looked to Sarah. She was shocked, as Sarah clearly looked more shaken than she herself was.

'Have some tea yourself, Mrs Hill, it will have to do instead of brandy!'

She found reassurance from her insistence that it was John's lack of manners alone that had led to him saying what he did, and not an intention on their part that she should go. It seemed a very short time before Hannah was back in the room.

'Come Matilda,' she said from the door. 'Wait here, Mother.' She turned, making Matilda catch up to her, half way down the stairs. 'Father has something to say to you.' She knocked just once on his door and went straight in and closed the door behind them. John was pacing the floor, stopping as they met in the centre of the room.

'I am most terribly sorry, Matilda—what I did was completely unacceptable, a level of rudeness that I condemn. Hannah's condemnation of my action was sharply expressed, the magnitude of my error unmistakable. You have become a part of this family and you have helped Hannah to attain such a level of competence that it is hard to remember that there are some things you cannot do yourself. She has told me that you have even managed to give Richard some instruction that has made him all the better for it.' Matilda glanced at Hannah at this double meaning. 'Hannah's work was so thorough that I still doubted you had not had a greater part in it, and you were hiding your input into it. I was forgetful of your abilities, I was forgetful of your continual honesty with me, and it was a stupid mistake. Will you please accept my most humble apologies? Will you please stay with us?' he finished, with the most abject of expressions on his face.

Matilda had been watching him all along, reading his face as much as hearing his words. She held out her hand to him. 'Thank you, Mr Hill, I do accept your apology fully. I will stay on, of course I will.'

John sighed mightily and took her hand gratefully. 'I am most grateful for your understanding,' he said, relaxing a little at last.

'I will leave you now and return to tea with Mrs Hill. Hannah would like to go through her plan with you. Thank you Mr Hill, what you have just explained has meant a lot to me.' She left them standing there and walked a little shakily upstairs to report to Sarah.

When she walked into her room she knew instantly that something was wrong with Sarah.

'What is it, Mrs Hill? What is the matter?' Sarah sat still on the bed where they had left her, her tea untouched on her lap.

'I felt a bit shaky, my dear. I sometimes feel unduly tense inside when I get upset, or overly tired. It passes, I just need to sit a while.' Matilda took the cold tea from her hand, noticing some was spilt into the saucer.

'Do your muscles sometimes twitch as well?'

115

'On occasion—why do you ask?'

'You must see a doctor, Mrs Hill—it may get worse without help.'

'We have, Matilda. It is part of the reason you are here, the part John and I were hoping not to have to tell you. I can only get worse and they can't tell us how long it will take—we don't know how long I will be able to manage running the household. It could be many years yet, we just don't know. John cannot do it, which leaves only Hannah, and unfortunately Hannah never matured, and stayed a flighty schoolgirl who could only buy clothes. We both needed her to become a responsible adult to take over from me, and we couldn't afford to wait. We had been looking for a chaperone and tutor for her for over a year and just couldn't find anyone suitable, and then she found you. It was like a godsend to us and you have worked a miracle on her. Spending last week with Richard with neither of us around has transformed her into the woman we only dreamt of. What you have done for John and me is beyond reward. You perhaps now understand how devastated we were with John's incident this morning. You hopefully will understand why we have not yet told anyone else, even Richard, of my illness. We would like to keep it that way for as long as possible. Now tell me how you knew to ask about the muscle spasms.'

'We had a neighbouring farmer whose wife suffered the same. You looked like she did at the start.'

'How did she fare?'

'She died, Mrs Hill, quite young.'

'I see,' Sarah said.

'What will happen when Hannah marries?' Matilda had to ask the obvious question, something they must have thought of.

'That is an "if" not a "when". If it were to happen, then we are hoping they will live here. It is a big house, and we could easily accommodate them without getting in each other's way.'

'And Hannah would make that work,' Matilda conceded.

'Now if you will excuse me Matilda, I shall go to my room. I will send a maid to clear this. Would you mind putting your bag away before she comes in?' She quietly left.

Matilda returned her room to normality and went into the garden for fresh air and think on the morning's revelations. *What a tragic morning it has been for us all,* she thought.

'Ah! Miss Matilda,' the gardener called to her. 'You have been gone so long, you should come and see this.' He whisked her off on a tour of the garden, and showed her what had now grown and flowered since she had been out there, now over three weeks ago. He picked flowers as he went and gave them to her near the last corner to the garden.

'Put these in your room—brighten any room, they would,' he said, pleased to have her attention again.

Yes, she thought as she arranged the blooms, *they make all the difference, the room is much better with them*. Her thoughts were interrupted by the lunch bell. She was the first there, not expecting to see Sarah, and wondering what had happened to Hannah, never one to be late for a meal. She soon bustled in, with John behind.

'Guess what, Matilda! Father says the plan is to be followed through. He is writing to Richard with a suggested programme for his approval with a start next week. No point in delaying the inevitable, he said. But it is better than that—he thinks we should go back up to manage it and make sure things happen when they should, and I'm to keep my banking account going so that I can pay for things as necessary and not to worry Richard, as he will be too busy doing church work and not give proper attention to it. What do you think of going back up to Timsbury?' Hannah finally took a breath, and looked at Matilda, as though she knew exactly what Matilda would think of being able to see Richard again.

'I think you could manage that very well.' She smiled her agreement to Hannah. 'Have you thought how much time this will take, Mr Hill?'

'As long as it takes. No sense in rushing at it, if it is to be done properly. We will need to await Richard's response, for all we know he may have started on it already. Your mother's not here yet—shall we start without her?' he asked Hannah.

'I saw her a little earlier,' Matilda said. 'She said she would eat in her room, I believe she wanted to finish a letter she had started last night.' John looked at her closely and understood the message.

'I'll take something up later,' he said. They ate and spoke randomly on the refurbishment at Timsbury.

'Father wants me to be sure that the tradesmen we get in keep on with the job and don't sit on their hands, Matilda. You may have to help me be stern.'

'I don't think so,' John said. 'I got a short sharp lesson this morning from you—you have taught her well, Matilda.' Matilda laughed at this.

'As long as she doesn't use too many words and the message gets lost,' she replied.

'She didn't this morning!' John couldn't help laughing as well. He gathered some lunch onto a plate. 'I'll pop up with this for Sarah,' he said, leaving them alone.

Hannah waited for a moment after the door had closed and leant over to Matilda, saying quietly, 'I will write to Richard myself this afternoon, and tell him he had better not have started anything, and that he does need us up there. Then we can stroll into town to post Father's letter for him, and mine at the same time.'

Matilda laughed aloud at her complicity in getting them together again up there.

It was difficult to decide who was the more impatient of the two in waiting for Richard's reply, but at last it came. Then they had to wait for John to say what was in it. Hannah was furious that she had no reply herself; waiting for her father was agony.

It was not until the table had been cleared and tea was served on the side table that John made any reference to Richard's reply, and then it was only to say that Richard had said how much he appreciated their help in cleaning the house. He poured them each a sherry and sat back in a large chair and looked over to Hannah.

'I suppose you would like to know how much he has got done?' he asked, as though it didn't really matter.

'It would be nice to know how much more he has managed in our absence,' she replied as casually as she could.

Sarah came to the rescue, telling him, 'John, do not tease her so. Tell her what he said.'

He smiled at his wife indulgently. 'Oh, very well. He has done nothing in the house at all. It seems that Alice has achieved a little but maintains a high standard of cleanliness throughout, and Jane is of small help to her as she is constantly interrupted by the visitors he has had, supplying teas and cakes for them. She has little time out of the kitchen. His study is desperately short of appropriate seating, he is using the chairs from the kitchen for folk to sit on during meetings, and the changes you all talked of now seem like a distant memory, coming to mind when he wants to use them. He asks if you can come up yesterday?'

Hannah laughed with joy—she could not have asked for a better reply. Her glance at Matilda told her that she was also happy with the reply.

'When can we leave, Father? When is the next coach up?'

'It went up today—you will have to wait until Saturday, which gives me time to settle matters for your arrival.' He smiled indulgently at Hannah. 'You will need to go into the bank to be able to sign for an extra clearance, as you will need a lot more money this time. I think we will leave them now, Sarah, I'm in need of an early night.'

They took their leave and Hannah immediately poured another glass of sherry each.

'Here's to us!' Hannah proposed the toast. 'May we both be successful up there.' She smiled a wicked smile over her glass to Matilda.

'Nothing will happen like that,' Matilda said, but enjoyed the thought. 'There is a full house up there now, remember.'

'The best I can do is wish you well, but I bet Richard thinks of it as well!'

'Hush! Hannah, neither of us should be having such thoughts!' she said, putting an end to the conversation, but still enjoying the tingle inside of her at the thought of seeing him again.

The next morning Matilda again took down her suitcase ready to pack, but this time with a great deal of anticipation. Hannah gave a quick rap on her door and came in.

'Father has given me everything for the bank, but wants a quick word with you before we go into town. I'll be with Mother, as she wants some things done as well.'

What can he want now? she thought as she went down and knocked on his door. She waited for his customary 'come' and went in.

'Ah Matilda, have a seat. Sarah says that she has told you of her illness—I do hope you understand why we have kept it from everyone. We meant no deceit to you, when not telling you the part it played in arranging for you to become Hannah's companion.'

'That is understood. I would not like it to be known from my point of view either.'

'She also said you recognised her symptoms, that you have seen it before.'

'Yes, in a neighbour.'

'You said she died quite young.'

'Yes. She was also much younger than Mrs Hill when it started.'

'Was it bad?'

Matilda hesitated. 'If it is exactly the same, then yes, it was an unkind way to go.'

'Do you think this could be different, then?'

A longer pause. 'No.'

'You understand our need for Hannah to be able to take over here?'

'Very clearly now.'

'I would like you to guide her carefully, encourage her to make more decisions on her own, try not to take them for her. Make her discuss her ideas, though only one head can make the final decision. Try to get her

119

to understand money the way you do—the amount of it is not important, it is how it is used that is. Getting value for it and knowing where it is best put, be it food on the table or stock on the land, or left in the bank. Do what you can to encourage her to achieve all that.'

'It is becoming increasingly easier for her. She did so much more when we were up there before. I will watch her, but you can have a lot of confidence in what she can now do.'

'Thank you. I am sorry to put the private burden of Sarah's illness on you. Enjoy your time up there. Hannah will write to us on progress. Come home when you are satisfied you have finished, and Richard is happy for you to leave. I will give Hannah a letter for him to that effect.'

'Thank you for your trust, Mr Hill.' She rose to go. 'I will pray for you both. Neither of you deserve the anguish that is coming in the bad times ahead.'

'Thank you Matilda, we will appreciate your prayers. Sometimes, my dear, your honesty is very hard to take.'

'The truth too often is,' she said quietly as she left him.

Her sombre mood was soon dispelled as Hannah came down the stairs. 'Ready to go?' she asked, and barely waited for her to reply before heading to the door.

The afternoon was a frantic race to pack, and check through all the notes John had made. Sarah joined the three of them in the midst of the sorting.

'I have an extra parcel for you to take up,' she said. 'I hope it will not be too much of a bother—come and see.' She led them all into the drawing room and pointed to the wall. 'That, I think, will be perfect for Richard's study wall. It is light and refreshing, and he has always admired it.'

It was an evocative watercolour painting of Lyme harbour with the Cobb curving around through the sea.

'That would be most appropriate, my dear, and something he will cherish. Now, how will the girls manage it on the coach?' John said.

'They will manage splendidly, I'm sure. Just wrap it up well, won't you, John?' And she left them to puzzle it out.

'I will get it down, wrap it, and get it to the coach. From then on it is up to you—good luck,' he said grinning.

They stood looking at each other, aghast, doubting that it would even fit into the coach.

Chapter 15

1841: Planning a Comeuppance

The coachman stood looking at the wrapped painting that John was holding, and then at his coach, the expression on his face worthy of a painting in itself.

'Loramassy! Ware 'ee 'avin' 'at gert fiddle faddle ockered thing afore put?'

Hannah looked dumbfounded, not understanding a single word, and John turned to Matilda. She smiled at the driver pleasantly and replied, 'Doan be argify yer rummage on me, be Deb'n maid yu be see'n! 'ee buckle tu on praper lot, Zartain zure go upalong!'

The coachman stood stock still, and gaped at her, then grinned a toothless grin, 'Gid out wi' 'ee! Tis plaized as punch ter 'ere 'ee. Aye, maid. Tis aisy nuff, tis be by 'un,' and he grandly helped Matilda into the coach, and Hannah after her. John watched bemused as the coachman carefully lifted the painting up and put it in behind where he was to sit. John felt in his pocket for a coin and gave the driver a tip, for lunch.

'Tis 'ee thanky much, 'is look to thickee maid, she be look to passel.'

'Thank you,' John said to him, then to Matilda, 'What on earth did you say to him?'

'I told him not to argue any rubbish with a Devon girl and to get on with his job. The tip you gave him means that he will look after me and the picture, or words to that effect. It would seem that he hasn't had a conversation in our dialect for some time, and was glad to have it.'

'What's the picture?' Richard asked, as he met their coach.

'Mother decided it would go on your study wall—it had better, having got it here. It's one you like.'

121

'It's not the one of Lyme Bay is it? I wouldn't have thought she would part with it.'

'Yes,' said Hannah, 'it surprised me too.'

Alice came out to greet them as they arrived, and helped carry the luggage in.

'Hello again,' she said, 'welcome back. Which rooms would you like? Jane has the end one looking out over the back of the garden, and I'm next to her. Mr Richard has the one at the top of the stairs, with the next two empty. Does it matter who has which?'

'I will have the one next to yours, Alice,' said Hannah quickly. 'Matilda can have the other.' She gave Matilda a look with a sparkle in her eye, as if to say, 'Don't say I didn't try to help.' Richard pretended not to hear and carried the picture into the study. Jane came out, wiping her hands in her apron.

'I have a fresh pot on, Mr Richard, where would you like it?'

'Around the kitchen table, I think, thank you,' he called back. The two took no time to unpack their bags and they all gathered in the kitchen.

'The room is so much nicer to go into than when we were here first. Thank you for preparing them,' Hannah said.

'Mr Richard said you would be here today, so it was no trouble,' Alice replied, handing Richard a plate with fresh buttered hot scones on it.

'You can see I am going to put on weight—they keep feeding me,' he said, but didn't hold back.

'Why didn't you answer my letter?' Hannah asked indignantly.

'I didn't need to. You already knew my answer.' She smiled at her brother. He looked at them. 'Do you have a plan of attack?'

'I thought we could work our way through the list as I wrote it room by room,' Hannah replied.

'Hmmm, you will find Timsbury a bit short on suppliers for some things. Uncle James has sent me a list of suppliers he has used or knows in Bath and Bristol. Bath is closer but smaller, it deserves first look. We will need to go in and have a look at them all to get the best deal, and as we are doing that, we should actually buy for all the rooms at the same time, otherwise we will be constantly going back and forth. Have a look here and see what you can find, then we will know where we stand for the rest.'

'That sounds fine, doesn't it, Matilda?' Hannah said

'Yes, but there were an awful lot of "we's" in that,' she said.

'You don't think for one minute that I will let you go to either of those places on your own do you? They aren't tiny safe little Lyme Regis or Axminster, you know.'

'Quite right, Mr Richard,' Jane advised. 'No place for ladies on their own, at all.'

'Clear enough?' Richard said with a smile. 'Come and look at Mother's picture.' He led them into his study, where he had already hung it.

'Gosh!' Hannah exclaimed, 'it goes there brilliantly.'

'I think Mrs Hill knew that all along,' Matilda murmured, and Richard gave her a puzzled look.

'Would you two like to wash the travel dust out and come down for dinner in an hour?' Richard asked them.

'There is plenty of hot water now,' said Alice. 'And Mr Richard had me buy some bath salts for you to soak in. He has been in such a tizz over you coming up since he got the letter from his father. Proper pleased you are here to finish the rooms for him, he is.'

Hannah couldn't hold back her laughter when Alice had gone. 'Proper pleased indeed! He wouldn't make this fuss if I was coming up on my own—I would still be walking down from the coach stop!'

'Of course he would fuss over you,' Matilda said, but was secretly delighted at the attention.

The five of them dined together around the kitchen table, with so much chattering going on that Richard claimed a headache coming on. He received no sympathy at all, but was given a glass of water and had his wine taken away from him. His headache cleared remarkably quickly!

The clearing up and dish washing was done equally quickly, with all of them helping. Jane then suggested that she and Alice retire early to their rooms so that the family could talk on their own in comfort.

'Now don't keep him talking too late, now. It is his long day tomorrow,' Jane reminded them as she left.

As soon as they were sure of not being interrupted, Richard went and held Matilda in his arms and kissed her. 'I have been bursting to do this since you stepped from the coach,' he said.

'I have been waiting for it too, my Richard,' Matilda replied, catching her breath.

'Do I have to leave the room as well?' Hannah asked with a giggle, and they all laughed, glad to be in each other's company again.

'Some more wine, ladies, or would you like a very nice port I have in my study?' he asked.

'The wine will do nicely,' they agreed and he filled their glasses.

'To us, again!' They touched their glasses, all three feeling very pleased that they were together again so soon.

'What services do you have tomorrow?' Hannah asked

'Eight a.m. communion, eleven matins and an evensong. Sleep in and come to matins, but there will be no raiding-orchard stories, just a sermon on the readings.'

'How are they accepting you? Have they been kind?' Matilda asked.

'Amazing, really. Lots of people stopping me on the street, and many coming round here. Apparently bigger congregations and some new enrolments at Sunday School—the two old maids who take it want to try their own stories. See what you have started! All to the good, I suppose, except one boy wanted to know what sort of apples they were that we had pinched.'

'And how did you answer that, with honesty?' Matilda demanded.

'"Very sour!"' Richard responded, to their delight.

'Oh well done, that was a smart answer.' Hannah admired his wit. 'I wish I could think that fast.'

'Not quite so smart really. If you had seen how many times I wrote that sermon, you would know how many variations I had for it for boys, apple colours, numbers and apple types. I had more answers than questions and could have kept going for an hour!' he replied.

'What did he ask next then?'

'Nothing, his mother gave him a smack in the ear, told him not to be cheeky to the new vicar, and dragged him away!' This amused Hannah even more.

'You've had no problems then?' Matilda asked.

'It was difficult with my first counselling visitor—there is just no way of practising for it. I was terrified of making a complete hash of it and making the person even more upset. Fortunately I had recently attended a lecture about the need to have some understanding of women and what the women in my parish expect me to know. The lecture was quite forcefully presented and was easily recalled in my time of need. But other than that, it has been remarkably straightforward.'

Matilda and Hannah had looked at each other at his comment and both smiled inwardly.

'Good,' said Hannah. 'It sounds like the sort of lecture you should attend regularly.'

'I intend to, as the opportunity arises,' he replied, straight faced. But Hannah was having difficulty remaining serious, and Matilda didn't help her.

'Do you have to go far? Are they free?' she asked, looking at both Richard and Hannah.

'Quite close, actually, but I do pay, and willingly.'

This was too much for Hannah. 'Oh stop it! Are you ready for tomorrow?' she said, changing the subject.

'Yes, ready enough. But I will go up now, as it is a long day tomorrow without a break. Would you mind?'

'Not at all, dear brother, we have had a tiring trip and I'm ready for bed.' They all got up, making sure the doors were shut and lamps out as they went. He kissed them goodnight at the top of the stairs and they went to their respective rooms.

It took only the softest of taps on his door for it to immediately open, and she vanished through it.

'I couldn't wait,' Matilda whispered.

'I'm eternally grateful you didn't,' Richard replied.

He was gone before they stirred in the morning.

Only Jane attended communion. She got back to find breakfast waiting for her, with Matilda running the kitchen.

'Sit yourself down, Jane. How do you want your eggs?' Jane was not sure if it was proper for Richard's guests to be making the servants breakfast, and hesitated. 'Poached, fried or boiled?' Matilda asked, to cover her hesitation. 'I've already done Alice's and she is on her way to her mother's home—they apparently attend the eleven o'clock service together.'

'Yes, they do, she'll be back in the morning. Poached please, she has Sunday off,' Jane finally replied. 'He asked if I would leave something available for a quick lunch if he could find time, and then cook a small dinner which I keep warm till he gets in. I spend most of the day with my friend,' Jane explained.

'Hannah and I will attend the matins and will spend the rest of the day here. If Richard turns up he can lunch with us; don't worry about doing anything for him.'

The day was warm and sunny, and they watched in awe again as Richard ran the service smoothly, and chattered with some of the congregation after it. They lunched under a tree in the garden and later found an old table that Hannah used to write the new lists under suppliers. Jane found them still out there when she came back to prepare the evening meal and Matilda went in to help her.

Richard came in late, and as drawn and weary as the first time. They fussed over him, serving his meal, pouring him his port, running a bath for him and putting him to bed. He didn't resist any of it.

It was Richard who was waiting for them in the morning, already having gone through Hannah's shopping lists.

'There is much for me to do this morning—can we talk these over this afternoon? Why not go with Jane this morning and she can show you what the village can offer and what tradesmen we have. I wouldn't recommend the fellows doing the slates on the church roof—that's one of this morning's problems.'

'It will be my pleasure to show them round, Mr Richard,' said Jane, beaming.

But it was the village gossip that proved more valuable. They found out about the roof tilers, who was the best decorator and the tidiest painter indoors, where the locals bought new furniture and where they bought used, and most startling of all, where the original dining room chairs were: sold by a vicar some ten years ago, and now unused in a storage warehouse, part of an estate awaiting probate.

'The solicitor in charge be my friend's second cousin, and they be drinking companions come Friday night. I could get my friend to mention it over a pint, that you wants 'em back and for a reasonable price they be yours right enough. I get him to test the waters like, come Friday, reckon.'

'Jane,' Matilda ventured, 'your friend wouldn't have a pair of britches and shirt my size by chance?'

Jane stopped and stared at her. 'Whatever for?' she asked, stunned.

'I was brought up on a farm, worked on it until recently, and work more comfortably in those sort of clothes.'

'Well I never! Never took you for a farm girl at all!' She looked Matilda up and down. 'Be near enough fit for sure, I'll fetch 'em soon enough.'

Hannah had listened in amazement, completely bemused by Matilda's request, not able to work out what she wanted them for, as she would not dream of wearing them in the house, so where? *Wait and see*, she thought, as Matilda would not want any questions now.

They met up with Richard later in the afternoon, after a procession of vestry members and work foremen. The last one out was the gardener.

Richard's head appeared around the kitchen door.

'Any chance of a cuppa, Jane? Hello you two, want to join me in the study so we can try and plan the week?' And he disappeared again.

'You can leave those potatoes, Matilda, you aren't here to do my work anyway, but you can butter these cream cakes and take them in with you.' Jane busied herself with making the tea.

'Those tilers are dragging a leg, I tell you,' said Richard. 'I can't see up there to know what is going on, but I think there is an awful lot of nothing happening. One of that lot before was their foreman wanting a part payment before finishing. I asked him if he had even started, and he took umbrage, storming out with my cheque.'

'Mmmm,' Matilda murmured. 'Did the day get any better?'

'Only so-so—I am not cut out to deal with the likes of him and some of those tradespeople. Let's forget them—now, how did you get on?'

'Very well, by comparison,' Hannah said. 'Jane was ever so helpful, she told us of who to use with workmen from the village, and who to keep away from, where to buy new and where to buy used, but best of all, she knows where the original dining room chairs are! They are in storage waiting for an estate to be settled,' she finished excitedly.

'Well that solves the chair problem, as long as we can wait. It can take years for these probates to be finalised sometimes. Shame she didn't tell me what tradesmen to use. What else did she tell you?'

'Mainly women's gossip, Richard. But it is gossip we can use,' Matilda said. 'Would you be free for us to go to Bath on Wednesday?'

'I should think so.'

'Tomorrow morning, are you going to the church?'

'I should, I don't trust those tilers,' he replied, frowning.

'It would be better if you could stay away, all day if possible. Could you write your sermon or something tomorrow instead?'

'I could, but why?'

'You are better off not knowing until Wednesday. Have you the letters for the bank, Hannah, everything your father gave you?'

'Yes, in my bag. I didn't want to impose on Jane's time this morning, I didn't know how long it would take me with the manager,' she replied, puzzled by Matilda's sudden change of manner.

'Very good. Come along, Hannah, we have not got a minute to lose.' By now she was almost at the door, with a curious Hannah following behind and an even more curious Richard sitting at his desk.

She rushed Hannah down to the bank and asked for the manager. 'Just follow my lead,' she whispered to Hannah as they went in.

'Miss Hill, isn't it?' he asked politely.

'Yes, and this is Miss White. We have new instructions from my father regarding my account.' He took them into his office. 'He has increased the limit available to me, and we will be in your parent bank in Bath on Wednesday.'

He looked at John's instructions and his eyebrows went up.

'This is a considerable amount, Miss Hill.'

'Yes,' said Matilda, but there is one consideration that needs action with some urgency.'

He turned to Matilda surprised. 'And what may that be?'

'Earlier this afternoon Mr Richard Hill wrote a cheque in the favour of the tradesman working on the roof of the church. We ask you to hold payment on it for twenty-four hours,' Matilda told him.

He looked to Hannah. 'That is most irregular. Do you have Mr Hill's authority, and where is it?' he said, getting rather pompous.

'What is irregular is the manner in which the said tradesman is conducting his business, and the manner in which he is extracting money from Mr Hill's account by presenting Mr Hill with incorrect progress reports. We ask for the delay in payment to ascertain work actually achieved. You withholding payment is by far the tidiest and least disruptive option we have available.'

'I can assure you that it is untidy, and *is* disruptive. Not to mention entirely irregular for this bank to agree to, particularly that you have no written authority to expect us to take such action.'

'Very well. Thank you for your time. We will take another course of action. Please read carefully Mr John Hill's letter regarding the authorising of the release of the limit available to us. You will notice that it does not specifically name your bank. We will take it to another banking company in Bath and use their facilities instead of yours. We will, however, use the authority to close all accounts held with your bank, including Mr Richard Hill's, on Wednesday in your parent office in Bath. Miss Hannah will now write you a note to that effect, so that should you make payment on Mr Richard's cheque that we have asked you not to, you will find that the cheque will be dishonoured. You cannot say we had not warned you of our intended action as we will have your chief cashier witness it. As you can see, this option is untidy and disruptive to us all by comparison. Please give Miss Hannah a page with your bank's name on the top for her note.'

He picked up John's letter of authority and reread the amount to be made available to them. He could not think of another account as large, and he thought of his principals in Bath finding out on Wednesday that the accounts were all to be closed. He visibly paled.

'Please wait one moment,' he said and left the office. Hannah looked at Matilda.

'How did you know all that, how do you know how much money there is?' she asked, amazed.

'Shush! I don't! And you are doing really well. Quickly, take some paper from his desk and start writing as though you are writing what I said.' When he came back in and saw Hannah writing on the bank's letterhead, his paleness turned to a sickened expression.

'Miss Hannah, there is no need for that, truly no need! You have amply expressed the clarity of your options and I agree to the simpler one. I have instructed the tellers that when the said gentleman comes in with the cheque, he is to be sent in to me, and I will hold payment for as long as you need.'

'Thank you,' Hannah replied. 'But it can be honoured tomorrow after three-thirty p.m. That will be long enough for us, will it not, Miss White?'

'Ample, thank you. But another correction.' Matilda turned back to the bank manager. 'The person who wishes to present that cheque is not a gentleman, nor would he ever attain such title. The man is a cheat, sir, and has been cheating citizens of this village for far too long. We will not stand by and let it continue. I will not allow him to practise his deception against Miss Hannah's brother, who is new to his work for the church in this community. Your helpful participation will make a difference to his position tomorrow. Good day to you.'

They both stood and left him, his mouth agape. He felt battered by their meeting and wondered what they had in store for the cheating tradesman. He couldn't wait to get home and tell his wife that one of the most reviled men in town was about to get his comeuppance from a couple of demure ladies of Christian upbringing, one being the sister of the vicar!

Chapter 16

1841: A Job Well Done

Hannah could wait no longer. She stopped Matilda not ten paces from the bank.

'You have to explain everything, including those old clothes!'

'Well,' Matilda began, taking a deep breath, taking Hannah's arm, and walking on, 'the roof tiler is cheating Richard—he is claiming payments that aren't due. Richard has as good as admitted that he knows it but doesn't know how to prove it. Jane, bless her heart, in all her gossip this morning, told us about the tiler cheating everyone in town and cheating on his wife as well. So I decided that there is a way to catch him out at his own game, but I needed you and the bank to help me. I really know nothing of what is in your father's letters, other than that they authorise more money for your account. Your father knows I do not want to know how much money there is, so he has not told me. He just made sure that I realised that we needed to get the letters to the bank before we spent any money at all. But I needed to stop that tiler's money, because he is spending it on his mistress—Jane as good as told us that. It was all bluff with that bank manager. You know I have no idea what is written on those forms, but he didn't either, because I didn't give him time to. But I did know that he couldn't afford to lose a big account—his supervisor in Bath would demote him to teller if he did! So by saying what I did, I got him to do as we wanted. I was relying on you to back me up and poke any piece of paper in front of him when needed, and it worked beautifully. Now we have a tiler on edge because he hasn't got the cash he needs, and he certainly won't go and confront Richard, because he pushed Richard too hard earlier today. He knows

Richard no longer trusts him and he can't afford to lose Richard altogether, and he knows he will get the cash tomorrow afternoon anyway, so he will wait until them. But what he doesn't know is what is in store for him tomorrow morning, which is why Richard must stay away from the church during the morning at least. I cannot afford for him to turn up at the church as it will ruin everything. I need you to keep him home, and I need you with me at the church. That tiler has to know us both in the morning.'

'How am I to be in two places at once?'

'You have to be with me, or more precisely, fifty yards behind me.'

'I am getting very confused—why not just tell Richard what we are going to do, and tell him to keep out of the way?'

'Because, Hannah, your brother is a very honourable and upright man. What I will do tomorrow is deal with a dishonest man, and I am going to have to be a little dishonest myself. I do not want Richard to see that, or even learn of it. He only needs to know the result of it. Which is why he has to stay at home.'

'I see. So how do you propose to give an honest reason for him to stay home?'

'I don't! That's why it's your job!'

'Matilda! That's not fair.'

'I know, we will think of something by morning,' she said hopefully. As soon as they got in, Matilda went to find Jane in the kitchen.

'Hello Jane, I know I am going to be a nuisance, but I will be needing those clothes first thing in the morning. Is there any chance of getting them by then?'

Jane turned and looked at her, hands on her hips. 'There is something you are not telling me, young miss. What is it?' Jane just stood and waited. Matilda stood for a minute, then turned and closed the kitchen door to give them privacy.

'It is very simple. The roof tiler is cheating Mr Richard, as he seems to have cheated most of the villagers and his wife. I intend to beat him at his own game. I cannot climb up onto the church roof in any of my dresses—I need those clothes for that. My life has not always been living in the Hill household, I really am a farmer's daughter, and I have faced worse men than that tiler.'

Jane hadn't moved; she just watched Matilda closely.

'You've got guts, I'll say that for you. I'll fetch them after dinner is served. Anything else I can do?'

'Yes—give me his home address. Is his wife likely to home in the morning? Where does his mistress live, and can you help keep Mr Richard at home for the morning? He must not go to the church—better still, not out of the house.'

'They live in Primrose Cottage, up the Avenue, half a mile from the church. His wife is Anna and she will helping at the mail agents all morning. The talk is that his lady friend is in Meadgate at bottom of Tunley Hill. If Mr Richard is going to be doing his sermons in the morning, then there is little to worry about, as he shuts the door and won't be interrupted. He hasn't come out before lunch yet.'

'Thank you Jane. Just one thing more—Mr Richard must not find out what we are about. He is too fine a man to be tarnished by any deceitfulness that I may take part in tomorrow.'

'I couldn't agree more. I have my own reasons for wanting that disgusting man to be taught a lesson. I will do my part here, rely on it!'

'Thank you Jane,' Matilda said as she reopened the door, just as Hannah came through.

'Richard has agreed to stay away from the church tomorrow,' she said.

'How did you get him to agree? What did you say?' Matilda asked.

'The simplest way. I told him what we are going to do and he would only weaken our argument if he turned up.'

'Oh!' both Matilda and Jane said, surprised at its simplicity.

The following morning was just as simple. The workmen were caught out by Matilda's sudden appearance on the roof. She went straight onto the attack and demanded to know why so little was done, and so clearly not what was reported as done. She then turned on a startled foreman.

'I shall be back here at three,' she told him. 'If this section is not finished, I will withhold payment on your money for another day. I will then visit your wife, either at work or at your home at Primrose Cottage and tell her that you are cashing a substantial sum of money that you plan to spend on another woman in Meadgate. Have I made myself clear?'

He had turned pale.

'You shouldn't be up 'ere,' was all he could say. A worker sniggered behind his back. 'Get about our job, this section is to be finished by three.'

'The whole area that needs repairing will be done by next Wednesday, will it not?' Matilda asked politely. 'You see, I have a need to be in Meadgate on Thursday afternoon, close to the bottom of Tunley Hill.' At this piece of information, he looked visibly ill and watched speechless as Matilda walked back across the plank to the ladder quite calmly as

for all concerned if it were to stay that way. My client has his own reasons for making his inspection rigorous—you can trust him, he will report to you at the rectory.'

'You make it sound as though I have no choice.'

'My dear, it is my recommendation only, I have no wish to interfere against your wishes. But his wife is well liked and at some point soon, someone will talk too loudly in her hearing about a woman who put her husband in his place, and that would be most unkind on her. It is time for you to withdraw from the scene of increasing public interest.' He looked at her kindly. 'I am sorry that I was not up there to witness your discussion with him—you obviously have terrified him. I hear that he has stopped visiting Meadgate.' At that Matilda smiled.

'Then I am satisfied—your man may do the inspection and report to Richard. I am sure Richard will be pleased to hear what he has to say.'

Later, Richard came into the kitchen behind them, beaming immensely.

'Come along, all of you! This you must see!' He led them into his study. 'What more could I ask for?' The new curtains had arrived while they were out and had been hung. They toned in perfectly with the room and the new chairs. The room was complete.

'Oh my goodness!' Hannah whispered in amazement. 'I never realised it would turn out this well.' She took it all in: Richard's books had arrived and were all lining the bookcase, Sarah's painting shone from the side wall, the curtains matched the décor and fresh flowers on the side table filled the room with a soft scent.

'You can be proud of this room, Richard,' Matilda said. 'It looks and feels like a room that you can work in, it has such a nice feeling to it now. The flowers stop it from being just a man's study, it's comfortable. Keep it this way, Richard—your parishioners will talk to you in here.'

He did exactly that—the flowers were kept continuously fresh, the room always tidy and clean.

'I think a bottle of wine with dinner tonight, for surely we have all deserved it by this result,' he happily announced, and they all headed back to the kitchen, to sit around the table there.

The end was actually at last in sight and Richard had been proposing toasts to their successes all evening. Matilda helped Jane and Alice clean up and tidy the kitchen ready for the morning.

'The house has been transformed since you and Miss Hannah came up,' said Jane. 'It's been hectic and tiring, but very worthwhile.' Jane looked around her kitchen, at the new pots and pans, at the shining floor and polished work surfaces. 'Very worthwhile,' she said again. 'But do excuse me, I am all but done in, I shall retire to my room.'

'I shall go as well—I fear perhaps I have sipped too much,' Alice said. 'I am asleep on my feet!'

'You have done well, Alice. Thank you for putting those flowers in my study, they really set it off,' said Richard. She left them with a shy smile on her face.

'Shall we finish this wine off in the comforts of my wonderful study?' Richard asked of Hannah and Matilda.

'Yes, we should drink one of your toasts in the first finished room,' Hannah said. As they entered, they stood in the middle of the room and gazed about. 'It is so much better than I imagined,' she said.

Richard nodded. 'Truly a superb effort,' he went to his sister and put an arm around her. 'I could not have done it without you. Thank you for your unstinting work.' He kissed the top of her head. 'I couldn't ask for a better sister!'

Hannah blushed. 'Aren't you forgetting Matilda? She was the one who pushed to get things done, I had to keep up with her,' she said, looking over to Matilda, who had sat back in the settee.

'Don't discount what you did, Hannah,' Matilda told her. 'You were the one who had to organise all the payments—you even did the ones for Richard as well. You set up the deliveries and did as much as I did. It would be fairer to say that I helped you this week. Your father is going to be very proud of what you have achieved.'

'I couldn't have done anything with the tiler—you will have to accept that success.'

'No one, particularly not your father, will ever find out about that, though, will they?' Matilda emphasised.

'Quite right, Matilda' Richard said.

Hannah held out her glass for a refill, and when Richard had obliged she said, 'Here's to us three. I couldn't ask for a nicer brother or a better friend, Matilda—how can I ever repay you?' She unwrapped her arm from around Richard and went to her to touch her glass in the toast.

Matilda rose to meet her. 'There is nothing to repay me for. I am the one who has benefited the most from our friendship. Thank you for taking me in.'

'Actually, I am the one who has gained the most from all this,' Richard said. 'I have seen Hannah grow in confidence and ability because of you, Matilda. I have seen what you both have done here together—for that I am grateful and I feel closer to you both because of your time up here. So I agree, Hannah, here's to the three of us!' And they sipped some more.

'So give her a hug as well,' Hannah told Richard. 'You have been so cautious near her since we have been back. I shall turn my back if you wish to give her a kiss, if that will help.'

'He doesn't need encouragement,' Matilda said with a giggle, going into his arms and kissing him.

'No, I see that,' Hannah giggled as well. 'I will leave you two alone and see you in the morning.' She strolled from the room, smiling broadly at their appreciation.

They soon followed her upstairs, but didn't part, both going instead into his room, staying together for as long as they dared, lovingly in each other's arms.

Chapter 17

1841: Sarah Deteriorates

It was only a few days later that the two women realised that their reason for being in Timsbury was running out. It was a reluctant Richard who broached the subject of their return to Lyme Regis.

'I should be writing to Father, giving him a day for your return. He will be expecting it soon enough as he has been kept up to date with your progress.' None of them wanted to acknowledge the truth in this—even the maids were enjoying their company—but the end was very much in sight.

'I think Friday would suit—there will be very little to keep you here any longer.' He stood solemnly and left the room.

Matilda and Hannah sat and looked sadly at each other,

'Well, it had to come. It just seems so soon, the time has flown by,' Hannah said, 'and Father did say we were not to stay away too long, that Richard needs to be left alone to get on with his work.' But no matter what she said, it made going sad.

'Then let's make the most of the time left,' Matilda said with glassy eyes. 'No use moping about, let's get on with it.'

By Thursday there was barely anything to do but pack. Everyone was feeling low and it was Jane who got them all to improve their humour, by declaring a special dinner to be served in the dining room.

A cart pulled up to the door and James came in.

'What be you doing here at this hour?' Jane asked in surprise at his appearance, as he had never been to see her at the rectory before.

'I'm on business,' he replied. 'I'm delivering your master's chairs. Done up they be, like new pins!' This news raced through the house, with

Hannah being the first to see if they were indeed to be allowed back into the house. She got to the door as James was lifting the first one down.

'That's nice,' she said, 'but where are ours?' looking past the one on the ground and looking for the older blackened ones she remembered.

'This be they!' James said. 'Cleaned up and restained with new cloth seats. You can see the grain of the timber lovely now.' And indeed you could—seven chairs looking as if they had come off the showroom floor.

'They are beautiful, James. Oh well done!' Hannah exclaimed. Matilda saw them and was equally impressed,

'You can be very proud of your work, James.'

'I be not finished yet,' he said, embarrassed. 'We did this olden one up as well.' He lifted the last one down which had a higher back and armrests.

'Makes a set this does—put this at head of table and you have a proper seating for eight,' he finished off proudly.

By now Alice had joined them outside. 'My! They do look the part, don't they Jane?' Jane stood looking at them, taking great pleasure in what her friend had achieved with the old chairs, and the excitement generated by them all at seeing their renovated state.

'Aye, he has done well,' she said, looking fondly at James. 'Come on then, let's get them in and surprise Mr Richard when he gets back.'

With all their spirits now firmly lifted, the final day became a joyous celebration. The dinner was a huge success, in a room that was transformed. All five of them sat and enjoyed the evening meal together, the serving and clearing shared by them all, all bustling about, all talking at once, or not at all, eating with relish that which they had all helped to prepare. It was quite the most wonderful final night they could have wished for, all sadness dispelled. Richard kept pouring the wine, they all kept making up toasts. The time kept slipping away. Wearily, and much later than usual, Alice and Jane slipped away to their rooms. Richard held up his glass for the final toast.

'To us three!' he said. 'Till we meet again.' And for the first time that night, a tear appeared in the girls' eyes at the thought that it may be a very long time before they were to be together again.

He hugged them both tightly. 'You have set me up beautifully here, and now I must get on with it alone. I will miss you both enormously.'

The next morning was a rushed farewell, which both girls were grateful for, as to linger would only bring more tears. The trip was an hour old before they spoke, each having been filled with their own thoughts. It was Hannah who broke the silence.

'Will you marry him?' she asked quietly.

'Very quickly,' Matilda replied. 'But I don't think it will happen.'

'Why ever not? You clearly love each other.'

'I believe we do,' Matilda acknowledged, thinking of last night as they both gave to each other with no reserve, no concern for quietness, no idea if they could ever be together again. 'We have never mentioned such a thing, it would be very difficult for Richard.'

'Why?' Hannah asked in disbelief. 'You are made for each other, how could it possibly be difficult for Richard? He needs a wife!'

Matilda looked at her friend sadly, realising that Hannah was not taking into account all the facts.

'He does, Hannah, but one that can read and write.' Hannah dropped her head in embarrassment, feeling very foolish for having forgotten.

'Then I shall teach you—he can wait for you,' she proclaimed.

'Dear Hannah, I am now twenty-six. My schooling days have long gone,' Matilda said, wishing she was just six and could start again. 'Whoever heard of some one learning to read and write at my age?'

'That is just nonsense to think like that!' Hannah rebuked her. 'I am twenty-one, and you have taught me how to count money.'

'Not quite, you have always been able to count money. You may not have always been so bright at handling it, but you learnt to count as a child at school.'

'It's you that is being negative now. Are you not willing to even try?'

Matilda thought of what she could gain if she could become literate. Even the remotest chance of learning and gaining Richard's hand in marriage was worth it.

'Of course I am willing to try,' she said. 'But how?'

'The way I did, by repetition. But I promise not to crack your knuckles with a ruler if you make a mistake! We will set up a writing desk in your room where you can practise. No one else need ever know what we are doing. We will start as soon as we get home!' Hannah was full of enthusiasm at the prospect at being able to help Matilda in return for all she had done for her.

The two very tired travellers were welcomed home by John and Sarah, keen to hear the girls' descriptons of the rooms and of Richard's services.

'Perhaps after breakfast we could go through your accounts, Hannah,' John said, 'you can explain where you spent money and why.'

'Of course, Father, I have notes for it all.'

When Hannah saw Matilda at lunch, she couldn't wait to tell her all that had happened with her father during their morning meeting.

'I believe I took him quite by surprise,' Hannah began when they were alone. 'He was most impressed with how well I had kept the books and could account for every penny we spent. He didn't question anything while I went through it all, and when I had finished he said he was very pleased with what I had done in looking after the money, even if we had spent a little more than he expected. He then asked me a whole lot of questions about various things we had done and what each part had cost. But what was most surprising, was that after all that, he said that I had obviously got to the stage of understanding how to keep track of the money; and it was time I had my own account with the bank and my own allowance. This afternoon we will go into town and see the bank manager and set it all up. Isn't that amazing?' she finished breathlessly.

'It is wonderful for you, I am very pleased. You have shown him you can be trusted with money and can use it wisely. When do you think he will go up to Timsbury and see what we have done?'

'They are not going to go until the end of September, unless Richard asks sooner. They want him to settle in properly first. Now, once we have been to the bank we will find the writing desk and set it up in your room.'

They spent far longer than they intended in the town that afternoon, with many folk stopping and asking how Hannah's brother was settling in, and what the house was like.

By the time the dinner gong was sounded they had only managed to find the small writing desk and have it moved to Matilda's room.

The meal began cheerfully enough, Hannah particularly chattering away, remembering interesting items to relate of their stay with Richard. Her sister Sarah Ann took a passing interest, obliged to in her father's company, but contributing nothing of her own activities over the weeks that they had been away. Matilda said little, enjoying Hannah's enthusiasm for what she had done up there, and glanced over at John to see his face showing satisfaction at his daughter's progress.

She looked over to his wife, expecting to see the same expression, and was suddenly sickened at what she saw. Without realising it, Sarah had stood up. Everyone looked at her in surprise.

'Mrs Hill? Mrs Hill, don't try to stand.'

Sarah let out a soft cry, her hand going to her head.

John suddenly looked away from Matilda and to his wife, whose head had started to twitch, her body becoming rigid.

'Sarah!' he cried, rising behind Matilda, who had already got to Sarah's side.

'Don't let her fall,' Matilda told John as Sarah's body suddenly shook with the first spasm. He tried to help her, but was beaten by the hidden strength of Sarah's muscle spasm, and could only soften her fall to the floor. Matilda threw the chair aside and, pulled off a slipper.

'You can't hold her John, let her go!' She struggled to put an edge of her slipper into the corner of Sarah's mouth. 'It will stop soon,' she said to him. 'This will stop her biting her tongue.' She looked up to see Hannah and her sister standing by them, ashen faced.

'What's happening? What's she doing that for?' they cried, shaken at the sight of such violent actions.

'Later!' was all John could say, fear on his face.

'It's going,' Matilda said. 'Get a blanket, Hannah.' Sarah's shakings slowed and stopped, leaving her lying in a tragic position half under the table. 'The stiffness will leave her soon; we will wrap her up and you can carry her to your room.' Matilda removed her slipper and put it back on her foot. John took Sarah's shoulders and slid her into a more demure position, laying the blanket Hannah had fetched over her.

'She will sleep deeply for a while now, Mr Hill, we need to put her on her bed.' Between them they managed to wrap her, and John carried her upstairs. Once she was lying on her bed in what appeared to be a peaceful sleep, she said, 'This can't have been the first one, can it?'

John struggled to reply.

'It is the first one I have seen. She has said she has been feeling poorly and come up to bed, and said no more of it. A couple of times though, when I have looked in on her later, I have thought the bed to be in a very rumpled mess. So it isn't the first one then, is it?'

'Not if it is the same as Jennifer. We can do no more for now. Come downstairs and explain to your girls—they are frightened by what they have seen. Let Mrs Hill come down when she is ready, but I feel tomorrow morning will be soon enough.'

'Yes, very well,' he said, not wanting to leave his wife's side. 'I must talk to the girls. I must write to Richard, but how do I tell him about his mother in a letter?'

It was a completely shattered husband and father who entered the dining room to be met by his two daughters, both still standing where they had been when Sarah collapsed, visibly shaken and scared. John spoke for a long time, trying to explain her illness, trying to explain what the doctors had been unable to explain to him, trying to reassure his daughters that she would be all right again soon, but failing miserably to reassure himself. He tried to say that there were no long-term effects, but the seizures would occur again, and at any time. He said it would not damage her mentally, but could not deny the stigma of the common perception that it was a form of madness. It seemed, he said, that in the past she had had warning symptoms that she was about to have a seizure, and had taken herself to her room. The cruelty was what others would say of her, or to her, should outsiders ever see her have a fit. He stood and wept, his arms hanging by his side, at the thought of any future humiliation she would have to suffer if she had an attack in a public place.

Matilda had quietly filled three glasses with brandy and placed them on the table. She went to John and, without a word, led him gently to his chair and handed him his glass. Hannah and Sarah Ann followed her lead and sat and sipped. Hannah then swallowed the rest in one gulp and looked accusingly at Matilda.

'How long have you known?' she demanded.

'Now Hannah!' John said, jolted out of his gloom. 'Don't speak like that! Your mother and I requested specifically that Matilda say nothing to any of you. She recognised Sarah's symptoms, having known a neighbour with the same illness. Your mother didn't want it generally known, that is all.'

'I would have preferred to have known in advance than to have learnt by witnessing her tonight,' she replied, not placated by his explanation.

Matilda spoke sharply before John had the chance to reply.

'Your mother would prefer not to have the illness, but what we prefer is not always what we get. Preference is a luxury in life, and your mother is going to have very few luxuries from now on. Think about how it has been not knowing, and not having to worry how your mother is when you were not about to help her. Think about knowing now, and that the thought is never going to really leave your mind for the rest of her life. You now share her fear of when the next attack will come, and at times you will wish you were still in ignorance of it. Then tell your father whether you prefer to know it or not.' Matilda looked hard at Hannah. Sarah Ann said nothing, almost frightened, aware of the difficulties now facing their future.

'Perhaps. I don't know,' Hannah said.

'You will, soon enough,' Matilda told her. 'What matters right now is how you are going to treat your mother in the morning, and I am very sure that she will not want your recriminations at being held in ignorance.

She will also not want silly sympathy. She will need you both to be the normal loving daughters that you were yesterday, and not doting nurses. Let her be as she was, and let her explain what she needs from you, and give it.'

John had finished a second brandy in short order, and couldn't think of anything to add, not trusting himself to say too much.

'I'll take my leave. I will go up to her now and take the morning as it comes.'

Matilda soon left the room as well. 'I will see you in the morning,' she said in parting to the sisters. 'Support your mother, don't accuse her!'

Breakfast was a stifled affair, with no one saying much. It was clear to all the servants that something was amiss, but none of them knew what, and their whisperings were far from the truth.

Finally John said, 'Your mother is breakfasting in bed this morning. She has asked that the two of you go up to her at nine. She has decided to tell the entire staff of her illness later this morning, as she wants no ridiculous rumours drifting around the town.'

Sarah Ann and Hannah duly attended their mother in her room at nine, and Hannah found Matilda to tell her that her parents were going to meet with all the staff at eleven in the library.

Hannah said she was surprised at her mother's apparent full recovery— a little pale perhaps, but with no signs at all of the previous evening's vicious attack.

'That is her future, Hannah,' Matilda said. 'Everything will always be completely normal, until the next one, and no one will know when it will be.'

Hannah was still shaken by it. 'Will she die from it? Will we pass it on to our children?' she asked, not sure if she wanted the answer.

'I do not know, Hannah. I can only say what I know from what happened to Jennifer. She was much younger, and her children were much younger. She did die at an age younger than your mother is now, but no one has said it was that that killed her. I don't know about it affecting children you may have, but there is nothing wrong with you and there was nothing wrong with Jennifer's children. From her, there is no reason to believe it will be passed on.'

Hannah nodded. 'Please excuse me, I think I would like to be on my own for a while.'

You poor, poor girl, Matilda thought, *what a load you will carry from now on.*

Some time later there was a tap on her door. John was standing there.

'Would you please come down to my study? Sarah would like to talk with you.' She followed him down and found Hannah already there with her mother.

'Good morning, Mrs Hill,' she said on entering. 'I am delighted to say you are looking very well, almost a full recovery.'

'Thank you for saying so, but I do feel rather drained of energy. My apologies for the incident. I felt it coming, but thought I would stay and outlast its arrival. I was sadly wrong and should have retired and avoided the whole sad event.'

'There is no need to apologise to me, but you need to heed those warnings,' Matilda replied.

'Indeed, my dear, indeed. From what you have seen of your neighbour, was last night as bad as it gets and will they become more frequent? It is useless asking the doctor—he seems to know nothing.'

'I can only relate to Jennifer—you may be different. But yes, they will be much worse and sometimes come on much quicker. She could never remember anything of the event, just waking up later from it. Her shaking got severe and she always carried a cotton-wadded peg in her pocket so that if it happened with someone that knew, they could put it between her teeth to stop her biting her tongue. It would be a good idea if you did the same.'

'Thank you, Matilda. One day I will learn not to ask you a question when I may not like the answer!' Sarah said with a half smile. 'What is the next step for me, do you think?'

Matilda thought for a short while. 'The next step, Mrs Hill, is for you to host one of your afternoon teas. I would invite your usual group with a few extras. Probably next Sunday afternoon would be appropriate, that will give the correct time for the invitations to go out before the event. It will all seem quite normal that way. Hannah and I will be delighted to help host it in our customary way. You shouldn't let this stop you being who you are.'

'She can't! How will she cope? What if another occurs then? The gossip will be devastating!' Hannah exploded.

'Your mother will cope. She is perfectly normal—if she feels another coming, she will leave immediately and go to her room, leaving us to carry on as a matter of course. It will be better for her to tell her friends the truth than leave the gossips to make a meal of it,' Matilda replied as calmly as she could.

'My dear Hannah,' her mother said comfortingly, 'I think it is a splendid idea. It is the way we will conduct ourselves in the future. Now Matilda, let us leave them and attend to this, as John wishes to have a discussion with Hannah alone.' They left a puzzled Hannah with her father. 'You do give me hope for a reasonable future. How well did Jennifer cope as time went by?'

Matilda stopped walking and looked squarely at her. 'You could always tell that she had had another attack—each one left her a little more weary, a little more drained, and she never recovered to her previous level of energy. It frightened her, and many thought she lost hope and died from a lack of will to continue her private battle with "the evils", as she called it. You have lived more and seen other hardships, you are made of sterner stuff, you have a stronger spirit that will sustain you longer.' That was the best Matilda could come up with.

'But it will kill me in the end.'

'Yes.'

Chapter 18

1841–1842: Time to Move On

Life changed for them all that day. A different perspective cast a shadow over them, each having to cope with their own concerns about Sarah's illness and accommodating it into their future.

Sarah Ann was easily the most frightened, losing sleep for worry of how this was going to affect her relationship with William. How would he take the news? Would he want to end it, not wanting to carry on, in fear of continuing the illness through their own children once they were married. How to tell him? It had to be soon, as the servants were bound to say something to their families, and it would get to William or his father quickly enough. *Tomorrow I will tell him*, she decided. *If he wants to end it, then he was never good enough for me.* That thought left her satisfied that she would soon know what sort of man she was planning to marry, and it calmed her considerably.

John and Sarah talked through the transition about to begin for Hannah, both satisfied it was the best course to take, but both knowing it was going to impinge on Hannah's lifestyle earlier than they had hoped. How were they going to establish her new position and still leave her to enjoy the last of her carefree years she had left? Neither wanted to suffocate her youthful enthusiasm, but both felt that they probably would.

There seemed no choice.

Matilda was worried by Hannah when they got together in the afternoon. She had lost the sparkle that always lingered in her eyes. There was a deep solemnness about her, no spring in her step, no continual chatter, her mind elsewhere.

'It is really quite depressing to have your life laid out before you,'

Hannah said flatly. 'There are no surprises left, no adventure in what may happen next week.'

Matilda was taken aback. 'What on earth has made you so sure you know what's ahead?' Matilda asked, amazed.

'Father's long discussion with me. They want me to learn how to run the house, how to keep the domestic accounts, how to supervise the staff. Really how to do everything that Mother does, for when she can't. He even brought up if I were to marry, they want us to live here, so that I will be able to carry on running the place. My life has gone—I'm now my Mother's deputy.' Hannah sank into silence.

'Well, we must work toward you being able to do both,' Matilda said, glad at last to understand what had got Hannah so upset. 'So who is the likely suitor that is after your hand in marriage?' she asked her lightly.

'Oh, no one! You know that. Those who were hanging round have faded away since you arrived—you showed them to be as flighty as I was. I am grateful not to be bothered with their silly attentions, but there has been no one of serious intent worth holding a candle to since. I am beginning to doubt that there will be.'

Matilda turned and put her hands on Hannah's shoulders. 'Now, you know that you cannot tell who may come around the corner, or when. Just look no further than your brother, and how much older am I? Stop looking for a man—the right one will suddenly be standing in front of you when you least expect it.'

'Oh it's not doubting that there may be the right one out there for me that's the worry, it's that I have stopped looking! Since you arrived I have had so much to keep me occupied and learn, that I seem to have lost any interest in finding one. I haven't missed it.' And with a sudden smile, 'I have had you and Richard to watch—that's been quite exhausting enough!'

'Shush! Hannah, someone may hear!' Matilda demanded, but delighted in feeling a tingle inside at the mention of his name in that manner, and her own remembered cries on that last special night. 'If you have to wait another five years for some one as special as he is to me, then it will be worth every minute.' Hannah relaxed at the memory of how they looked at each other when they were without company, and a smile played on her lips at her conspiracy with them in the affair. 'Now that you have a smile again, what else worries you in the future that you don't want to know?'

'I feel that I have been left to hold up the family. It feels that Father has dumped all his problems with his children on me,' she said. 'Some have disappointed him badly, and to be honest, I think they have to. Father set such great expectations on his sons, he dearly wanted to have one at least that would take up the mantle in the family business, importing Baltic timber. There have been generations of Hills in the company, but not one of them will even enter the business in his place. He is so disappointed. Philip is the one who really upset him the most, I suppose. He is the eldest son and was expected to become Father's successor, but he seems to have failed in everything. He walked away from anything to do with the family business, married very young to a shoemaker's daughter, well below Father's social standards, and they already have two sons. We don't hear from him, and Father will not mention him. John is the youngest and rather a weak man; he left school early and couldn't stay here as Father kept lecturing him to make a man of himself. He was almost frightened of Father, I think. He left with a friend and stays away, and is treated much like Philip. Mother has lost several children—John is actually their third son to be named John—the first two died as babies. It must have been terrible for her. Only Richard has done the right thing. Father is delighted with him, he seems to have the brains and determination to succeed, and joining the church is what is expected of a second son.

'As for the girls in the family, Sophie is married to a solicitor in Tiverton, and I think Father has almost as much regard for her husband, Thomas, as he does for Richard. Mary is also married to a solicitor down there, but Father is not very happy with her, as she always tells him what Philip is doing. You can see that Sarah Ann will marry William as soon as she decently can, and will be gone from the house. None of them will show a helping hand here now, and Richard will not be allowed to, Father as good as said it. His long talk with me was my role in taking over from Mother, being able to do everything she does, so the household runs smoothly at all times regardless of how her health is. She will do what she can while she can, but I am to be there at all times.

'Can you begin to understand how I feel about my future? Can you imagine what it is going to be like trying to do things when Mother is feeling really well and wanting to do them herself? She is so strict with the staff and I have never bothered them, so what will happen when I have to give the orders? I am younger than most of them. Can you have any idea how gloomy it all looks to me now? Oh Matilda, I am really going to need your support now, you really will have to help me get through this.'

Matilda gave her friend a hug and said quietly to her, 'I will of course help you as much as I am able. You do have time on your side—your

149

mother will be around for years yet, there is no panic to learn everything by the end of the month! Just take on one role at a time and learn it fully before starting the next—I'm sure Mrs Hill will not push you into anything too quickly. I will do all I can, and I am very sure that they will not expect you to stop doing anything that you enjoy doing away from the house. Do not worry so much—think on how well you did up at Timsbury, as nothing will need doing here as fast as we did things up there.'

In its own measured pace, a new routine established itself into the Hill household.

Morning tea in the drawing room became a ritual, Sarah would sit with Hannah and most times Matilda as well.

Myriad topics were covered, often several times, often on the difference between the two women, and how each saw a situation. Sometimes intense, but never angry. Sometimes as though Matilda wasn't there, then as suddenly one of them would bring her into the conversation, wanting her to put her interpretation on a topic of difficulty. Nothing was ever rushed, much was talk over many days, some forgotten altogether and only returned to weeks later. When it came to discussing the servants, Matilda would excuse herself as it was an area she regarded as personal to the Hills only. It was Sarah who one day asked Matilda to stay when a staff issue arose. She felt that as Matilda would be leaving them at some point in the future, there may very well be some useful instruction for her in how to deal with staff that would benefit her in a future position.

John went alone to see Richard, and returned full of compliments on the transformation in the rectory. He said that he had arranged for Richard to come down for a couple of days every three months or so as a break. He was concerned that Richard would let his life become too much of a routine and he would become dull with it. Coming home would not only keep him fresh but would allow him to see his mother, who had made it clear that she was not prepared to risk such a long and tiring journey.

This news was greeted with undisguised joy by Hannah, and hidden joy by Matilda, even though she knew she would only see him in the company of the family.

His first visit was a blur of activity, from his arrival on the Monday evening until his departure on the Thursday morning. He devoted much time to his mother, whose appearance was much better than he anticipated, but whose tiredness worried him. When she felt she needed a rest she would dismiss him with instructions to take the girls for a walk, something he could never refuse to do.

Throughout his visit, Richard could not stop his mind going back to his mother. She had always been the strong and supportive parent, and now suddenly she was the one needing the support. He quietly worried for Hannah, equally suddenly thrust into being her understudy. He watched her listen attentively to her mother's words; her old, youthful enthusiasm seemed to only show while the three of them were out walking. He prayed that Matilda's stabilising influence would always be there to see her through this time of adjustment, that Hannah's confidence would build again as it had in Timsbury and her cheeky personality would reassert itself. He touched Matilda on the arm only once and both felt the reason for the touch, without being able to express their feelings any more. All too quickly he was on the coach returning to Timsbury, his head crowded with emotions and thoughts, adjusting to so many changes in such a short time.

He jotted some of his thoughts down, and by the time he arrived in Timsbury, he found he had written three of his better sermons for some time.

With so much going on, Matilda's reading and writing lessons never became the regular sessions Hannah had intended. She found it difficult to explain letters and numbers, but felt some satisfaction in getting Matilda to be able to write down the alphabet in order. Her hand was naturally steady, the letters always perfectly formed. But somehow they stumbled on getting the idea of using the letters to make words—they never materialised. The harder they tried, the worse the results, and slowly over the months the lessons became less regular, as other events became more important.

Over time, Sarah's seizures became more severe, but no more regular.

Her ladies' afternoon teas continued without any incidents, a disappointment to two of the most spiteful attendees. Hannah became adroit at caring for her mother when an attack occurred, and little was said of them. Their lives adapted to a new standard for normal, and Hannah's confidence slowly returned.

Christmas was fast approaching, and they all decided it was a chance to lift everyone's spirits by making it a special occasion, more so than any previous Christmas. A huge tree was brought in, streamers were hung across the rooms and entrance, big boxes were wrapped up prettily as though presents, and the house was filled with anticipation. The fulfilment of all expectations was ensured when a letter arrived from

Richard announcing he was coming down for some of the festivities. A merchant from Bath was coming down to Lyme Regis in his own carriage on Boxing Day, allowing Richard to deliver his services on the Christmas day and be with them then, and he asked whether they could put off some of the festival celebrations for a day so he could enjoy them with them.

Never had a Christmas day been celebrated so well, a day late! He stayed four days, to travel back on the Saturday and thereby not missing a Sunday in his church.

It was four days of relaxation for him. He was not disturbed by his mother's frailty, as she seemed to him to be improved. Hannah was much more in control, their mother enjoying watching her manage without fluster, and taking part a lot of the time. Matilda quietly backed them both up, stepping in unobtrusively when required, leaving John to be with his wife more often, confident now that the two of them could handle any situation. John was grateful for the rapport between them and Richard, the three of them often staying up later than anyone, chatting and drinking the evening away.

'Here's to the three of us,' he heard them toast themselves as he was leaving them one night. *Thank goodness for that,* he thought to himself, *they have been my saviours.* He told Sarah what he had heard and they both smiled as they drifted into sleep.

Much later they too went upstairs, Hannah stopping at Matilda's door saying, 'Goodnight Matilda,' then going to her own room, smiling, but not looking back to see where Matilda had disappeared to.

'My Richard' were the only words spoken, all else being given.

The subterfuge was played out during future visits, each three-month gap taking so long to come around, and the days he was there passing so quickly. Hannah took secret delight in helping the two people that meant so much to her take advantage of the short time they could have together.

Nearly a year passed before another change took place in the Hill household. Hannah could by then easily have taken total control if required.

An invitation to attend their afternoon teas was in much demand. Sarah had relinquished much of the household operation to Hannah, and took pleasure in her role of a retiring matriarch. John could not have been happier with the arrangement, but his happiness was to be severely tested.

One morning, Matilda knocked on his door and waited to be invited in. Hannah sat in her room upstairs, waiting for Matilda to return.

'Good morning, Matilda. You look thoughtful—is anything the matter?' he asked, concerned.

'Not really, Mr Hill. I wish to give my notice to relinquish my position here. I am of the opinion that I have accomplished all that I can, and that Hannah has now gained confidence to a level where I can no longer help her. She is now twenty-two and deserves to be left to show what she can achieve without me in the background. I would like to leave at the end of the month, if that is suitable for you.' She sat quietly, her hands on her lap, waiting for him to reply. He sat quite still, looking at her.

'That is a sad thing for me to hear,' he finally said. 'You have become part of the family and I do not want you to leave yet. However, I do understand your attitude, but please reassure me that Hannah's future progress is the reason, and not some difficulty between you.'

'You can be very sure of that! Hannah has become a precious friend and I would like to think that the friendship will continue. I cannot see any benefit of my staying longer, but more of a case of my staying being a hindrance or handicap to her.'

He was silent, then asked, 'And Hannah, what does she think of this? For surely you would never come in here without first talking to her about it.'

'We have been discussing it for a week or two now. She doesn't want me to leave as yet, but realises it is for the best in the long run.'

'Then stay a while longer. I am sure that I speak equally for Sarah as for myself.'

'That would only be putting off the inevitable, and probably make us all miserable for delaying what must be done.'

'How on earth do you believe that staying longer will make us miserable? Your company is anything but miserable!'

Matilda hesitated, not wanting to say what now must inevitably be said.

'Because I am with child, Mr Hill. I must go before it shows. I will not allow any gossip to be in a position to be able to talk about this household in a manner that my staying would invite.'

He sat stunned, words failing to come. Finally, with effort, he said, 'Who is the father of your child? Who is to stand by you?'

'The father is an honourable man who I respect enormously. I have always been honest in all matters with you here, but in this case, I request that you allow me to remain silent about my child's father. Will you allow me to remain until the end of the month now?'

153

'Of course!' he muttered, 'Of course. Does this mean that he will not marry you, to make you an honest women? No honourable man would do that!'

'Please, Mr Hill, no questions about him. He has a future that I would only inhibit. If you please, I will leave you now. Thank you for your help in this.' She rose and left him, and John sat for some time after she had gone, finally rising to go and speak with Sarah about it.

She sat and listened with increasing sadness, finally saying when he had finished, 'You dear man, she is completely right and we must do as she asks. I believe she is being as honourable with us as she knows the father to be.'

'You know who he is?' he asked incredulously.

'Yes, I believe I do. Time will tell, and I will not say more until I am sure.'

Matilda was taken home eighteen days later, two weeks before Richard's next visit.

Chapter 19

1842: Homecoming

There were tears as Matilda and Hannah parted after arriving at the farm. Matilda's mother came out, disturbed by the sound of the gig arriving, to see her daughter hugging her friend in farewell.

'I will go in to the first market of the month—we can meet up that way if you can get in. Please try, we can keep in touch that way, I don't want to lose you altogether,' a saddened Hannah said. 'Richard will want to know.' And she stepped back into the gig for the return home.

'Matilda!' her mother called. 'Mercy be! This is a surprise, be 'ee home for good then?' She rushed up and hugged her daughter in delight. 'Be 'ee job finished then? Whatever will Father say when 'e gets in! Come, come, lets get 'ee inside, and all these bags—you only left with one! You can have your old room and there's so much that's happened for us to catch up on.' Her mother chattered on, unaware that Matilda was still listening to the sound of the receding gig as it clattered on the stones in the lane, her friend and her dreams disappearing with them.

'Yes, Mother,' she finally said. With a heavy heart she lifted two bags and turned to go in, knowing somehow she had to start her life again, knowing that somehow she was going to have to tell her parents that her homecoming was not in the best of circumstances, and dreading her father's reaction. There was nothing unusual in a farmer's girl having a child without a husband by her side—the Delawney girls seemed to have made it an occupation, with barely a male in the valley not succumbing to their charms. There were plenty of brats of unknown fathers in their brood, and no one was bothered. But she knew that her father was going

155

to be more than bothered when he was told and, unusually, Matilda had no idea how she was going to tell him. It made her nervous to think on it, and she messily unpacked her bags.

Dick felt a tightness in his belly, and he stood upright looking over the valley. 'Be not right,' he muttered to himself, putting his sack of apples aside. As if by intent, he walked past Madeline's home, stopping at her gate. She looked out to him, seeing his troubled expression.

'Miss M be home. You'm best ways be visiting her past noon,' and he walked on without waiting for a reply. He didn't bother to knock when he arrived at their door. Matilda and her mother, Mary, became aware of his silent presence as his great frame filled the doorway.

'You'm home proper then,' he said to her.

'Hello Dick,' Matilda said, and stood to hug him. Mary was not surprised to see him within the hour of her arrival. She almost said jokingly, 'What took you so long? She's been here an hour!' But she saw the expression on his face, and wondered what he understood and knew of her return, that was beyond anyone else's reckoning. Some of her excitement left her then.

'My work is done there, it was time to come home,' Matilda said, knowing there was no need to say more, knowing that he would also know who the father was, should they ever meet.

'Aye, tis time to be 'ere.' He hugged her again, smiling down to her. 'Tis right.' And he left them as easily as he had come.

John, Charles and Ann came in together from the farm for lunch to find Mary and Matilda still sitting at the table talking. There was immediate bedlam, a crescendo of questions all asked at once, a flurry of food being brought to the table, excitement of having her home and the telling of events past that they felt she should know.

'I'll be getting upalong to our Mary after, she be wanting to know 'er sister be back,' Charles said in the hubbub. 'She'll be well pleased, reckon.' And he grinned like an idiot at being able to convey such news, as he knew how well she would welcome her sister back, being as close as they were to each other.

Some of the household peace returned when John resumed his farm work, Charles had saddled up and departed hastily to Mary's, and Ann carried on with the housework that she preferred to farm work. It was a short-lived peace, as Mary soon came bursting into the kitchen and, rushing up, gave her sister a huge hug.

'You are back! You could have warned us! It's so good to see you, you won't believe the size of the twins now. When will you be over to see them? Richard is doing very well on the farm, his critics have all been silenced. What was it like in that big house? I didn't think we would ever see you out of it, living in such a comfortable way.' She paused. 'You aren't going back again, are you? Is this a visit or are you home for good?'

'Well,' Matilda replied, 'I am back for good, my work there is finished really. Hannah can practically run the place on her own and . . .' She stopped at the knocking at the door and saw Madeline come in with her two boys close behind.

'So it's true, you are back,' Madeline said, going over to give her a hug as well. 'Is this a visit, or are you here for good?'

Mary laughed and said, 'For good, I've got that much out of her.'

Her mother stood shaking her head and turned to the boys. 'Come along young 'uns, I'll find you a biscuit. It didn't take those three long to get together—there will be no sense from them for a bit till their tongues stop wagging.'

Matilda looked over to Madeline and asked how she knew she was back so soon.

'Dick, of course. He actually said it as though all was not well,' she replied in a low voice so as not to be overheard.

Matilda hesitated just slightly before saying, 'Let's stroll outside, I need to stretch my legs, and it will be nice to see how the garden has faired.' They rose in unison, each knowing more needed to be said, and went outside chatting inconsequentially.

Mary carried on talking of Soap House Farm and Richard's progress until they were safely away from others' ears, when Matilda stopped and told them, 'My Richard is doing well too, too well in fact—I am carrying his child. That is why I had to come home. How am I to tell Father?' She only just held back her tears. The other two were stunned.

'God in heaven, Matilda! You of all people!' Mary finally said, shocked.

'Is he not going to marry you?' Madeline asked.

Matilda gathered her thoughts and told them both the whole story, leaving nothing out. It was Madeline who broke the silence.

'You are going to have a baby born of pure love, conceived by mutual love. That must be a wonderful thing, for my lovely boys are the product of demeaning abuse and I strive to show them that respect and love is what life is about. Your baby will know that already from conception— above all else, keep that advantage for the wee tot.'

Mary had remained silent, thinking hard. Finally she said, 'Father is not going to like it. Once you show he will like it less. We have a little time to find somewhere for you to go, it will be too difficult for you to stay on here. I will speak with Richard when I get home, see what is available over our way. Tell Mother in the morning, tell Father tomorrow evening—you cannot go long without them knowing, and Mother will guess soon enough if you don't say something. We need to keep your Richard's name to ourselves—if Father finds out who the baby's father is he will charge off over there demanding justice for his daughter. If you are sure that you want to protect him, then his name must not go any further.'

'I am very sure I want him kept secret. I love him very deeply, but I cannot have him. I will have his child with pride, no matter what Father says.'

'You could always come and live with me,' Madeline offered. 'Just go out every Monday morning!' She laughed at herself.

'That is a kind offer, but it will not work. It's too close to home and Father,' Mary said before Matilda could accept. 'She needs to be as far away as we are at least. Far enough so as not to have chance meetings with locals, close enough for when needs be.' She looked at Madeline. 'Why Monday mornings?' Madeline put her hands to her face and blushed.

'Still?' they both said to her together.

'For ever, I hope,' she replied, abashed. They laughed then at their mutual conspiracies and secrets they knew of each other.

'I must be getting along back,' Mary said. 'Tell them as I said—you know where to find me. Good luck.'

It was much harder than Matilda thought it would be to tell her mother. Finally, after watching her daughter fidgeting with a tea towel long after the dishes were dry, the older woman said to Matilda, 'What is it love? What be bothering you so?'

'I'm with child,' was all that Matilda could say, lost at being unable to explain more.

'I guessed as much,' Mary said putting a comforting arm around her, 'and by coming home I gather a wedding is not going to take place.'

'No, Mother.' Matilda's head dropped to her mother's shoulder.

'And do I gather that there be a good reason for that?'

'Yes.'

'And you have agreed you two are not to marry? Is he already married?'

'He is not married, he did not know I was carrying his child. He will make a fine husband and father, but his work prevents us marrying. I will not tell you who he is, I love him too much to destroy what he does so well. We shared enough, he gave me enough, for me to live with his memories and his child, I need nothing more.'

Mary held her daughter, knowing her determination, but fearing her future.

'Your father is not going to like this. He has such high hopes for you, he was so proud of you working with the Hills, told everyone. We will tell him over lunch, then he can go and kick gate posts all afternoon to calm himself down.' Matilda smiled. 'We will need to find a place for you, as it will become too uncomfortable for us all here if you stay—but where?'

'Don't worry, Mother, Mary will sort that out with Richard.'

'I suppose that was what you three were talking about yesterday? You will never be left wanting with those two around. I will do the talking with your father—he will be more accepting when he knows you have my support.'

The afternoon unfolded almost exactly as Mary had predicted. John sat stone-faced as his wife told him of Matilda's condition. He glared at all his children, mumbled about this farm not being the Delawneys', nor was it going to be, what did she expect him to do about it, where was the gutless creature that sired the child, no one was going to make an idiot out of him, he expected more of her, thought she knew how to keep her legs together, was going to fix a bleedin' gate. And he left the room in a thunderous mood. Charles looked in surprise at Matilda and said he would go and work at the other side of the farm and keep out of his way. Ann smiled at Matilda, said she hoped that she had a lovely baby, and went to her room to continue with a large piece of lace she was making.

Mother and daughter sat quietly for a while, not sure what to say next.

'I think I need another cup of tea,' her mother said at last, 'want one?'

'Aye, just hope Mary and Richard find something.' She sat upright at the sound of heavy steps coming back to the house. To both their relief, there was a soft tap on the door and a familiar voice calling.

'Miss M?' Dick's head appeared around the doorway.

'Would you like a cup of tea, Dick?' Mary asked. He nodded.

'Thank 'ee Mrs Mary,' he said, and then to Matilda, 'Miss M, you best ways be talking to Mary, she need be getting her Richard to see Thomas Downton upalong Dalwood Hill ways, be just up hill from thems, 'ee could be fine up Dalwood way.'

Matilda smiled her thanks to him. 'That is very kind of you to think of them for me. I might walk over and see them this afternoon, and maybe stay the night. It might help Father calm down if I'm not about.' Her mother was amazed yet again at Dick's instinct toward Matilda.

'I'll walk 'ee a way. I be needing be going up Shute pillars.'

They left soon after, Matilda with a small bag to stay the night, that Dick carried for her. Her mother watched them go, bemused by Dick's continual protection of her, unwavering from when she was a baby and he could not have been much above five or six at the time, and hadn't yet spoken a word to anyone.

It was as if it was meant to be. Dick ended up walking all the way with to her Soap House Farm. Richard saw them coming down the hill from Andrewshayes and called out to Mary, who met them at the gate.

'Hello Miss Mary,' Dick said, then turned again to Matilda. 'I be going now. It be right you be back, no more gallyvantin' for you, I be zartain zure you be home praper now.' He smiled at her indulgently. 'Be all right now, you be seein'.' Both of them understood his certainty that she would not leave the district again, both accepted that she would never marry the man she loved, and would never give up. He wanted to say something to cheer her up some, let her know that her future was better than it looked at the present; he thought of telling her that she was carrying a boy, but knew some women were funny about knowing these things, and kept it to himself. He decided to stroll by in a few days, just to let her know he was there when needed, then held her close, smiled again and left.

They watched him go, and Mary said to her, 'How much more does he know that he doesn't tell you? He was going to say more, you know.'

'Yes, I know that, it happens a lot. He says enough to try and comfort me, but I don't think I want to know it all anymore—some things we don't need to know until they happen. I used to pester him to tell me more when we were much younger, then I would keep it a secret and wait for it to happen and be so proud that I knew before anyone.'

'Has he ever been wrong?'

'Never.'

'How did Father take it?'

'You were right, it's why I am here. I will stay the night if that's all right with you. Mother thinks he will settle to the idea easier if I'm not in the house, and Dick says there is an empty cottage on Thomas Dowton's place upalong Dalwood Hill. Will Richard talk to him for me?'

'Of course, we grazed the field of his last summer. I know the cottage,

160

it has been unused for two years now. Help us milk in the morning and Richard will speak to him then.'

Thomas, it turned out, was happy for Matilda to live in the Dalwood Hill cottage, providing she clean it up herself and pay him a small rental. She could have the few hens that were left, after the foxes had raided the broken chicken coop recently, and she could sell any eggs she may persuade them to lay.

Richard was also a great friend of Jacob French, who farmed at Hawley Bottom and seemed to run Mount Pleasant Farm next door to Dalwood Hill for his father. Jacob had been trying to work both farms for a while as his father was no longer able to do the hard work. He and Richard came to the agreement that Matilda could help him milk a few cows to make the clotted cream that they had missed out on since she went to the Hills, supply him the excess milk and he would pay something toward her rent to Thomas. They thought that once she got it in order, anything she produced from the old garden she could sell in the market to help pay her own way. It was a start at least: Matilda had somewhere to live.

Mary and Matilda were delighted with the arrangement, particularly as they would be less than a mile apart.

Her father just nodded when told where Matilda was to live, passing no comment.

Her mother was relieved at the situation being resolved, pleased that she was far enough away to leave her father untroubled, but close enough for her to come home for the childbirth, no matter what John thought about it. Ann could go up and take care of the place while Matilda was home.

It was a merry group who gathered to clean out the cottage the following Sunday. Richard and Dick shifted anything heavy and kept up a supply of clean water for Mary, Matilda and Madeline, who washed down the rooms and windows and cleaned up the kitchen. Madeline's boys made a game of beating the dirt out of the mats, then running in covered in dust. By afternoon the ground floor was passed clean enough for Matilda to move in; upstairs could wait. Richard and Dick had been busy outside, the chicken run was again secure and the last four hens safe inside it. The gate to the garden was rehung and swung feely. Richard was surprised at how easy it was to work with Dick without a word being spoken—his anticipation of Richard's next move disturbed him at first, but he soon found his readiness reassuring and the work was quickly done.

'The garden's a fine old mess, Dick, but that will have to be another day,' said Richard, then left them to milk his cows. Madeline and Dick left soon after, taking Richard's dray with them so as to collect all of Matilda's belongings and bed from her parents' the following day once the boys were at school.

Mary took Matilda back to their farm for the night. 'It's going to work, Matilda, I believe it's going to work.'

The next morning Matilda helped with their milking and they all went back up to the cottage. They got the stove fire going and stocked the cupboards with the pots and food that Mary could spare. Madeline and Dick arrived soon after with Matilda's goods as well as blankets and other necessities. Matilda was overwhelmed. The ground floor was looking quite homely and comfortable, and they made a start on upstairs. By early afternoon they had achieved enough for Matilda to continue on her own, and sat in the kitchen now warmed by the fire, making tea for the scones that Madeline had brought along.

'I must go soon to be home before the boys,' Madeline said, 'but expect me to be a regular visitor.'

'Except on a Monday, Madeline,' Mary said cheekily. 'I believe we have quite upset your usual morning!'

Matilda quickly settled into a routine. The hens were the first to produce a return for her, safely housed and fed. Three more were added by the end of the first week. Jacob arrived with a few sheep from Hawley Bottom Farm, and drafted out three cows of lesser yield from the labourer's herd and a steer that he put into the orchard to clean up the longer grass around the trees.

On the Sunday she walked down to the village and attended the eleven o'clock service. She entered and quickly sat in the pew straight ahead of her, not wanting to be noticed. Bowing her head, she said a short prayer, then imagined Richard doing the same in Timsbury. She looked up to the altar and thought of him standing before his. Closing her eyes again, she told him all that had happened and apologised for leaving before he came home on his next visit, leaving it instead to Hannah to write to him and tell him of her condition. After the service she left quickly, only offering a brief hello to the vicar, and returned up the hill to her new home.

With every expectation of being disappointed, she went that week to the Axminster market. She knew Edith and Margery would no longer be there, but was pleased to be greeted by many others. Her hopes though were to find Hannah visiting, and in this she was rewarded. They saw each other at the same time, both smiling in relief that neither had wasted the journey. They talked as always, with barely a pause, Matilda with so much to tell on what she was doing, Hannah with news of Richard's reply and her mother's questions.

Poor Richard was at desperate odds with himself, she said, not able to reconcile his position as rector with his future fatherhood of a bastard child. He had written to Hannah that he would declare everything to his father on his next visit home, and renounce his position in the church. Hannah had promptly written back that he must do no such thing, as Matilda had left the household to protect him from such actions. As yet she had not heard back, but assumed that he would do as she advised.

But Mother was another matter, as Hannah suspected that her instinct had told her that Richard was the father of the expected child. Opportunity alone made Richard by far the most likely candidate, but after initial questions, Sarah had kept silent on the subject. Much, she thought, would be discussed when Richard arrived soon on his next visit.

Matilda described the Dalwood Hill cottage and how to get to it along the Dalwood Down Road, and Hannah said she would come out to it, seeing as how she had the gig and it was not but a few miles from Axminster. They agreed that Hannah would try and come out every first Thursday of the month. That way she would be able to keep Richard informed as to Matilda's progress and she could pass back to Matilda messages from him.

Thunderstorms could not have kept Hannah from visiting Matilda on the appointed day. She had so much to tell her after Richard's visit home, and messages from Richard as well. She was not sure what had been said between Richard and his parents, or whether Sarah had pressed for confirmation that he was the father of the child, and she had felt it best that she allow Richard to tell her what had been said in his own time. But when they were alone, Richard revealed only his confused emotions, his inability to accept his position as rector and having had sired a child out of wedlock. His concern was for her well-being. Hannah had reassured him that Matilda was very well settled in her own place and was setting up a smallholding, that she had all the money she had earned from her time at Lyme Regis, and was in a comparatively comfortable position. She told him about her monthly visit and said she would make sure that Matilda was able to keep herself in a satisfactory manner.

Hannah said she would write a long letter to him and describe the cottage and the land and animals she kept. She would tell him how at peace she was, and hoped that perhaps he would gain some peace from the fact that she was more in her natural element there than at Fairfield Lodge.

They both certainly hoped he would, as Matilda certainly was well content with her ever-expanding waist.

Chapter 20

1842–1844: A Child is Born

The winter was gentle on Matilda. She was shielded by the savings she had earned by being Hannah's companion and had only used a small part of it. Her biggest expense was in buying a young cow from Mary and Richard, which was in calf and would be milking in a few months. She had planned on this good cow providing a noticeable increase in milk volume, which would give her the chance to make a better quality of clotted cream. She had been able to sell the small amount that she had been able to make to the village shop, and they had always asked for more.

There were also more hens now, and she not only supplied Jacob and then Mary, but at times some to the shop as well. The orchard had been tidied and dead branches removed, which made picking up the windfalls easier, although the crop of apples had not been great. Jacob took them away gratefully, to add to his for the cider press. If they produced better next year, she could sell what Jacob didn't need to the Cobbledicks, who for generations had made and sold their cider throughout the district. Matilda had figured that between the excess apples, the eggs and some of her clotted cream money, she would be able to cover her share of the tithe to the vicar—one shilling each year—and the agreed rent to Thomas.

The freely swinging garden gate now led to a restored and planned garden. Although it had produced little up to now, Matilda had it ready to yield a crop to envy that from Shute. She was determined to match her strawberries from her youthful days in the market.

Dick had pre-empted Matilda in appearing one day to repair the old barn behind the cottage. She had tried to tidy it up, but the work was too heavy for her and her maternal concern for her baby stopped her from straining too much. In three days, Dick had cleared and secured plenty of space for the cows to winter over in, had safely stored the fodder that Jacob and Richard had sent over for her, and had fixed the large barn door so that she could handle it without difficulty. All the useless rubbish was burnt in a smelly smoky fire and all the wooden scraps cut to fuel the kitchen stove.

Mary was a regular visitor, telling her that she also was expecting a baby later in the year, and Madeline came by at least twice a month. Hannah only missed one monthly visit because of the weather, with news that her Richard was intending to come over on his next trip down, in just eight weeks' time. It was this that reminded Matilda how much she was missing him. She had been kept so busy that she had been able to cope with not seeing him on his previous two visits to Lyme Regis. But her time was drawing near, and her swelling belly was a poignant reminder of their love and times together. Eight weeks could not pass quickly enough for her.

There had been only two setbacks. One was her father's undiminished objection to having her home, and he had made it clear he was not happy about her coming back to give birth to the child there. The fact that the rest of the family were against her having the baby anywhere else did not make him relent. Matilda had by now accepted his position and his shame of her, and would endure his hostility for the short time she would be in his house. Dalwood Hill cottage would welcome her back quickly enough.

The other setback came as a shock. She had become a regular member of the St Peter's congregation, and became known as the new land girl upalong Dalwood Hill on Dowton's place. Some knew her as the producer of the clotted cream that was sometimes available in the shop. Most greeted her warmly enough, acknowledging her presence among them as a fellow worshipper, but not quite getting to know her well enough to begin to invite her in for tea after the service. She wasn't sure she wanted too close a friendship with them until she was well established in her new home.

Even Mrs Beamish, the starchy upholder of all virtues, and parish councillor, who took it upon herself to set the standards on right and wrong, had passed comment that it was nice to see a new young face as such a regular attendee. No one knew what had happened to Mr Beamish, be he living or dead, but it was generally accepted that wherever he was, he was in a much more tranquil place than living under the same roof as his wife. Mrs Beamish was on the verge of making Matilda one of her projects, and involving her more into the church and village life, when she noticed that perhaps Matilda's waist was not as slim as it had been upon first arriving. She held her tongue and watched. Two months later she was sure, and Mrs Beamish had a new project. Such women, she declared, should not be made welcome in God's Church. Such women as her, who was just a land girl but had so many nice clothes, could have only got them one way. She had no husband in sight and was clearly guilty by her silence, unable to name the man behind her now-obvious pregnancy. For all her nice talk she was just some common trollop, who quite rightly was no longer welcome in her parents' home. Such depravity should not be tolerated within St Peter's walls. She niggled away with her equally small-minded friends, trying to shame Matilda into not attending the services, and not wanting to accept Matilda as a resident of such a lovely village as Dalwood.

Matilda showed no outward sign of her rebuttals, but would smile sweetly at her and greet her with a cheery smile, saying, 'Good morning, Mrs Beamish' at every Sunday service. Such brazen pleasantry was more than Mrs Beamish could take and she became Matilda's most bitter foe, which continued until the day she died. She thought that she had ridden the church of Matilda when she didn't turn up one Sunday in March, but Matilda had gone to Mary's instead.

'My time is close,' she said to her sister, 'can you get me down to Mother?'

Her mother scolded her for leaving it so late and Matilda could only agree. She gave birth to a strong boy that evening.

'Be glad 'ee got the hips for it, girl, the lad be lookin' to walk in a week!' she exclaimed at seeing such a big baby, with its mass of black hair. 'Well pleased I be I never had 'em this size.'

They all trooped up to see Matilda sitting up in bed with her baby snuggled in against her. Even her father, against his better judgement, needed to see that all was well for himself. He entered the room and walked to the bedside to peer at the wrapped bundle. Matilda promptly handed him her sleeping baby, and he held him in his large hands against his chest, looking down at him with a glimmer of a smile on his lips.

'The innocent should never suffer,' he said to his daughter gruffly. 'Make sure he doesn't.'

'Not while I breathe,' Matilda replied. 'I want to call him John,' she added, watching her father. He made no indication of hearing, just held his grandson and gazed at him with perhaps a hint of a tear in his eye.

Finally he muttered, 'Aye,' and handed the child back. 'Aye' again as he left the room.

A smiling Madeline arrived early next morning to see the baby, and laughed when asked if Dick had come too. 'Right behind me,' she said. 'He told me last night, all out of breath from running over to tell me.'

For the rest of time she was to stay in their house her father would come in of the evening, wash his hands and face, and walk straight up to baby John's room and hold him quietly for a while and tell him of his day.

Matilda took his actions as acceptance, but not forgiveness. At the end of the week when she was ready to go back to her own home he said to her, 'Take Ann up there with you for a bit, she be more use to you looking after the child while you attend to your place, than she be doing on this farm. Take all her lacing fiddle faddles with you, be no reason she can't be doing that while the bairn sleeps. I'll send the merchant upalong to 'ee to collect her work.'

Ann never returned home. At thirteen she became Matilda's first paid housekeeper and child-minder. The arrangement worked well for both of them—Matilda was free all day to work her small parcel of land, only going into feed him, and Ann was delighted to no longer be required to do farm work. She cooked and kept the house clean, and she simply adored looking after her nephew. Her hands remained soft and her output of lace-making increased; her savings likewise increased as she was now able to keep all the income from it, and added to it was what Matilda paid her.

It was Ann who was the first of them all to meet Richard. He arrived with Hannah, bearing gifts for the baby that had surely arrived. He seemed almost shy to Ann, letting the lady do the talking, but it quickly came to Ann who they must be. She dashed past them to get Matilda from the garden, excited at such important visitors. Matilda came at the run, flustered at being caught in gardening clothes, blushing at seeing her Richard again after so long. She hugged Hannah tightly and flung herself into Richard's arms, not caring what Ann would make of it. Richard held her as tightly, burying his head into her neck. She spoke first.

'I've missed you,' she mumbled into his chest, tears of joy rolling onto her cheeks and wetting his jacket.

'My heart beats again,' he whispered. 'You have gone through too much without me.' He still didn't let her go.

'It was the way it had to be,' she replied. 'No one needed to know.'

'But what of the baby? Are you both well?'

'I am, obviously. And so is our boy. I have named him John.'

'Most appropriate. Do I get to meet him?' She let him go quite suddenly, knowing he must be anxious to see his son.

'Of course you can!' she said, stepping back and taking his hand to lead him inside. Turning, she was met by Ann coming out the door with John in her arms and Hannah clucking close behind.

'He has come to meet his father,' Ann said, holding him out for Matilda to take and show to Richard. He took him gently, as though afraid he would break.

'He has your big hands,' Matilda said.

'So tiny,' he replied, awestruck at the little miracle he was holding. 'A good name, John, and well chosen. Both our fathers will have something to be pleased about by that. How did your parents take your motherhood?' he asked nervously.

'Mother is very supportive, and has never pushed to find out who his father is. But Father is not happy at all. He fusses over John, but lets me know that he expected better things from me.'

'I see,' Richard said. 'Much the same to report. Mother knew without being told that I was the child's father; she has made no judgement on me other than I must support you and our boy so that you are at no disadvantage. Father I had to tell. He was dumbfounded and had no idea that I was the child's father. I am afraid he was extremely angry, bit of shouting went on, I am ashamed to say. Me of all people, sort of thing. Never to see you again, shamed the family even though the family don't know and we mustn't tell them, must be no thought of marriage, even though we already knew that ourselves. I have to take care of you somehow and only Hannah to keep in touch with you. I am afraid it was a desperate scene. Fortunately though, he had calmed down this visit. He knew that he could not stop me coming over with Hannah to see you both, and Mother sends her blessings—there is something here from her for the baby. She misses you, you know. There is no improvement for her.' He stopped talking and put his free arm around her. 'I do love you.' And he kissed her head.

'Would you like to see around my little world?' Matilda asked, and he nodded. She showed them everything, both Hannah and Richard acknowledging her pride in her cottage and garden, her favourite cow and the squawking hens thinking it was their feeding time. They finished inside, where Ann had tea ready to be served and Matilda introduced her.

Hannah raised her cup and said, 'The three of us—sorry, four!' And they laughed at their old toast.

'I have this for you,' Richard said, lifting a money pouch from his pocket. 'I have made it up of small change, as I assume that is how you will use it.'

'Thank you, Richard. I will keep in reserve. As you have seen, I will be able to support us on what I make here,' she said proudly.

'You are very comfortable here, Matilda. It is good that you have Ann to help, but you must never hesitate to ask us for help if you require it. Father would be even more angry if you were to suffer in any way, particularly as you left so quietly, without fuss. I think he is rather fond of you, actually,' Hannah said, knowing how her father had gone on and on about Richard being so thoughtless in his selfish actions, as though Matilda had not been a willing participant. She smiled at his misconception of their times together.

'I will be fine,' Matilda replied. 'I am grateful for your care and your parents' concern. But do please try and visit me again—I ask for nothing but your occasional company and to know how you are all getting along.'

'That is an easy request to keep,' Richard said. 'Hannah will always come as usual, and I will be here as often as my visits allow.'

They departed soon after, Matilda watching the gig disappear over the brow of the hill.

'Do you want me to forget that they were here?' Ann asked Matilda over dinner.

'No, they are people worth remembering. Just don't tell any one about their visit—life will be easier if it stays with us.'

Ann nodded, taking in the contented look on her sister's face as she remembered the man that she had held so tightly that day.

In mid-summer Mary also gave birth to a boy, whom they named Edward. There was little doubt that both sisters were enjoying their motherhood, both confident that they were secure in their own surroundings and future. Madeline's visits became a ritual, and they shared a lunch together, carrying a conversation from one lunch to the next as though there was no break between.

Hannah kept her visits throughout the summer, keeping her in touch with what was happening at home, passing messages back and forth for her parents. Richard only managed one visit before the autumn, unable to get away from Timsbury at any other time.

Ann came back from a visit with their parents with the news that William and Ann had had a daughter who was to be named Elizabeth.

She said, with amusement, that Father was boasting to his cronies that he had had three grandchildren over the summer months, seemingly now forgetting that he was ashamed with Matilda for not having a husband.

Autumn crept in, the garden produced well, and her strawberries were almost her best. She had regular buyers for her clotted cream and the extra eggs. Her confidence grew that she would be able to carry on living there and always be able to pay her way.

This particular day started as any other. There was no hint of anything that was about to happen—she had milked and breakfasted with Ann and played for a while with John. The milk was settling in a pan and most of her usual morning chores were completed. She had only gone inside to be sure that Ann had finished the list of requirements from the shop.

Then there was a heavy knocking on the door. They looked at each other mystified, as no visitors were expected. Hannah had been not a week earlier, and Madeline and Mary never knocked, but just called from the gate waiting for an outside answer and then walked on in. Even Jacob, when he came by, called from the gate now and Dick didn't have to, he always knew where she was. To knock without calling meant a stranger, and a heavy knock meant a man. A little unsure of themselves, they went to the door together. Matilda caught her breath in surprise, stunned.

'What are you doing here?' she exclaimed.

'Not the welcome I had hoped for,' Richard replied

'But Hannah said nothing!' she cried and hugged him.

'Hannah didn't know,' he said softly, realising the fright he had given them. 'Actually, I didn't either until this morning. May I come in?'

'Of course, of course you can, you daft man,' and Matilda pulled him in. Ann had scuttled off to make fresh tea and set out her just-cooked biscuits.

'I have been down and officiated at Sarah Ann and William Hussey's marriage—they went ahead and arranged it themselves with little input from Father and Mother. Sarah asked me to marry them, more to appease our parents, I think, than as an honour for me. Rather hoped a break out here would ease the tension from back there. I was hoping you would be home, as I have no way of getting back to Lyme Regis now, and the coach doesn't leave until morning.' His comment sank in, his suggestion clear. They clung together at the thought of spending more than just a short afternoon visit together. She saw then the bag on the ground behind him. 'I can catch the coach in Axminster so long as I can get in there by eight-thirty in the morning.'

'I am sure you will. John is asleep—it's nice that you can wait for him to awaken to see him this time.' They went in and chattered with Ann, going over what she needed to get.

'I will stop in and see Mary on the way back for a while,' Ann said. 'Probably have lunch with them,' she added, thinking that they would appreciate time alone together. She stopped at the door, looking at his bag.

Matilda came up behind her and said quietly, 'He is staying the night. He is catching the morning coach in town.'

Ann looked at her seriously. 'I will see if I can stay the night with Mary then, shall I?' she said, so as not to be overheard by Richard.

'She will insist on it,' Matilda replied, smiling, knowing the lack of subtlety Mary usually displayed, and sent Ann on her way.

Matilda returned to the kitchen and hugged him again.

'My Richard,' she whispered in his ear.

'You have no idea how I have longed to hear you say that again,' he said, kissing her again.

'I have just longed for you,' she giggled, 'and I don't intend waiting for tonight. Come.' He didn't argue and followed her willingly. It was over quickly, too quickly for both of them. Then John woke and a gurgling chuckle sounded from the next room.

'Do you think he heard us?' Richard asked, bemused.

'He would have only heard his parents' love for each other,' she replied getting up and rearranging her clothes, 'I will fetch him and feed him. Make yourself respectable!'

'What will Ann say to Mary?'

'I don't care, but you had better be ready for her to visit. Ann will never be able to withhold who is here, particularly as she is asking if she can stay the night with her so we can be alone.'

'Good Lord! Really!' He leapt from the bed, tidying himself up as he rushed to the door to retrieve his bag, where he found his hairbrush.

'They won't be here that soon. She will come before milking just to meet you—she knows better than to make a long visit out of it!'

'Really! Does she think I came here for no more than that?' Matilda laughed at his nervousness at meeting her older sister.

The afternoon drifted by. She showed him the garden and they sat under an apple tree in the orchard, watching the clouds float across the sky. John lay wrapped in his blanket between them. She followed the flight of a pair of buzzards, soaring in lazy circles high above.

'See them, Richard? When I was little I used to watch out for them—I always felt everything was in its place if the buzzards were in the sky.'

'Well, everything is certainly in its place today,' he replied, never feeling more content.

'Matilda!' came a call from the gate.

'In the orchard,' she called back. 'It's Mary, come along.' They rose to meet her, Richard carrying his son with pride.

'So you are Richard,' Mary said. 'Nice to meet you at last, I'm Mary.'

'Yes, so I gather. I am pleased to meet you,' he said. Mary stood and looked steadily at him for what must have seemed a long time. Finally she nodded.

'Yes, Matilda, I understand now,' she said to Richard's uncertainty, then she smiled. 'I have brought along a pie for your dinner, you are not going to want to waste time cooking tonight. I am going to take Ann back with me and help with our milking. I suggest that you do yours sooner than later, as you are likely to forget them altogether. Come along Ann, they do not need our company any longer!' And off she strode with Ann in her wake.

'Goodness!' said a startled Richard. 'Did I pass inspection, do you think?'

'Oh very much so. If you hadn't, you would be marching down the road now and Mary would be here making sure you were gone!' They both laughed.

They put John back in his cot and Richard stayed and watched his child sleep while Matilda went out and did the milking. They ate the pie and gazed at each other, hardly tasting it. He cleaned up and washed the dishes while Matilda gave John his evening feed and put him to bed for the night.

'I have something for you,' Richard said, handing her a small solidly made box. She opened it carefully. Inside sat three silver spoons, shining on a deep purple silk base. Matilda picked one out, resting it in the palm of her hand. Engraved on the handle were the initials MW, slightly entwined.

'Richard, they are beautiful.' A tear ran down her face at the extravagance of the gift. 'For the three of us,' she added, 'one each.'

'Yes, but you are the beautiful one. None outshines you.' He rose and held her tight.

That night was the first they spent together without fear of discovery or interruption. They made love with deep satisfaction, then drifted into sleep, until one woke the other with arousing touches and they began all over again, until dawn. Richard dragged himself from her bed to make his way into Axminster, never noticing the chill in the air or the distance he had to walk.

Little John slept soundly through it all.

Chapter 21

1844–1846: A Family Christmas

Matilda's life settled into patterns as regular as the seasons. She considered herself to be comfortably situated, with little to upset her life. She was making a small income from the holding, easily producing nearly all the food they needed. Richard visited four times that next year, not only leaving a purse to ensure she faced no hardships, but leaving her warm inside as well. Hannah continued her monthly calls, keeping her informed on her family, and passing messages back to John and Sarah. She said that her father would ask many questions as to Matilda's well-being, concerned that she never faced any difficulties, and expressed a thought that he himself may visit when passing the area.

She went to church regularly, always taking John with her and sitting in the same pew. The congregation were now divided on her presence, the majority being unconcerned by her background and welcoming. The few who belonged to the Mrs Beamish brigade, which included most of the choir, still devoutly opposed to her inclusion. They gained no more support, but relinquished none either.

Matilda, with innocent delight, always beamed her a dazzling smile and wished her a cheery good morning. This always increased Mrs Beamish's fury and she would storm into the church to fire up the choir into singing rousingly through the hymns. Unfortunately for her, one of the choir was an impishly humoured fellow who had little time for Mrs Beamish, and rather a lot of time for Matilda. Tony was known to be a bit of lad, and would choose a time during the service when he was watched by Mrs Beamish from across the choir stalls to look out to the congregation and give Matilda a quick nod of his head in acknowledgement of her presence. His thinning fair hair would drop over his forehead and he flicked it back into place with his hand, plucking at an eyebrow in passing. Such frivolous behaviour rankled Mrs Beamish in the extreme, and her glare at him could burn toast. His cheeky grin back to her would earn him a rebuke after the service.

It was always worth it, he thought.

Life could have carried on as it was for Matilda, for she was content. But lives end, and when Samuel French died, her world began to slowly change too. There was nothing dramatic about it at first—the changes were small and easily accommodated. But each step got bigger, each demanding more of her, each more difficult to accomplish. It was time and her own dogged determination that saved her, otherwise Mrs Beamish would have had the cruellest of victories.

There were no surprises with Samuel's death, considering his age and health. Neither was it a surprise that Jacob inherited the Mount Pleasant estate.

'Rest easy,' Jacob had said to her, 'you be safe in yer working wiv me. Stay on as 'ee be wiv same arrangement.'

What did surprise her was that shortly after that he appeared again at the gate with the news that he was moving into the Mount Pleasant house.

'Farm not be doing no good,' he told her. 'Me and missus be coming up and staying to be sure work be done praper. Got good chap down Hawley, he and his lad can look after it for time being and easy to check on 'im from 'ere. But thicky mazed git 'ere be no use to man nor beast, 'e'll be working my ways or working yonder ways. When's all fixed and running praper I be thinking on Hawley chap coming upalong and missus and me be going back home.'

True to his word, Jacob and family moved into Mount Pleasant, the labourer being allocated a back room. Matilda almost felt sorry for him, as Jacob set a cracking pace and his shouted orders to him when he got tardy were clearly heard at her cottage.

'Cor,' Jacob said shortly after moving up, 'missus be in right stew. House be bigger mess than farm, chap spends more time hiding from 'er than doing any work. Tickled him up with riding crop when she saw the mess 'e made, 'e only comes in 'cause he's hungry.'

A week later he had gone, 'yonder ways'.

'Can 'ee give a hand with all the milking?' Jacob asked Matilda that afternoon. 'Till new chap starts. Be just for a few days.' So Matilda would milk with Jacob first, then milk her own. It soon became apparent to

Jacob that Matilda was an excellent hand with all the cows—they milked easily and patiently for her. As his cows got used to her, she began milking them in the field as she did with her own, soon milking eight to his six.

'Be a shame to lose her when boy chap comes Monday,' he said to his wife, 'put me last tanner on milk dropping when he takes over milking mine.'

'Then keep her,' she replied bluntly. 'Plain as pikestaff she can out milk any our lot.'

'Oh, aye,' he mused. 'Need pay her proper though, and this place don't return a penny yet.'

'Talk to her, see what she wants. She be doing it right on patch she has, she be no fool, maybe's it be not cash she be needing. She may not want to carry on when lad arrives, anyways. You needs be talking to her, not flapping your jaw here,' and she sent him on his way to see Matilda, amused at his reticence at having to talk business with a woman. She quite liked Matilda, and was one of many who sat on the sideline watching her frustrate Mrs Beamish's attempts to rid her from the congregation.

'More sport in it than a football match,' they were heard to say.

Jacob returned as perplexed as he had left.

'How'd 'ee know she not be wanting paying money?' he asked as he came in the door. 'Not sure if I got a good deal or not! Be mazed what sort of deal I agreed to.' He sat shaking his head and supped at his cup of tea.

'Well? Out with it!'

'She happy to do it, no doubting that. She be wanting to put her lot in with ours to make milking just one job, use more of our fields to graze over, but house them in her barn for wintering, be room enough for twenty in there. She be wanting bigger share of the milk, a third she wants, and new lad to do milking with her, and work for her one whole day a week.' He scratched his head, thinking on it.

'Good.' his wife said. ''Tis fair for both. Herd be better off in her hands and milk yield will go up, she will make more clotted cream and get her money that way, and free labour a day a week. Some of his time with her will be in the fields the cows graze, which are ours anyway, so farm will improve downalong her way without us having to do nowt. You did well.'

'I did?' Jacob muttered to himself, not sure that the wool hadn't been pulled over his eyes by both women. *Nar, missus won't give an inch away where farm concerned*, he thought to himself, and he felt much better.

By mid-summer Jacob had repaired the hedgerows and cleaned the remaining fields. He was more than delighted with the improvement in his herd and the way that his new boy worked with Matilda—he could see her teachings show in his milking style and the way he handled the stock. The boy was thirteen and still not strong enough to do a grown man's day's work, but he was hoping to find an older couple who could take over living in the Mount Pleasant house with the lad living in with them. That way he would be able to return to Lower Hawley Farm, which would always be his main venture and priority.

In the autumn, Mary gave birth to a girl, and to Matilda's great delight, they called the baby Matilda, after her. It was a very proud aunt who held the baby throughout the baptism service.

Barely nine months passed before they were gathered again beside the font in St Peter's church. This time Matilda held a boy named Samuel, a son that Mary had wasted little time in producing.

It was a mild winter that year, cold enough for most, but with a lot less snow. The lanes soon turned to a slushy mud, never freezing for the whole day, but never getting any drier either. Boots remained wet and coats had a permanent hem of brown mud stuck around them. Mary was at her wits' end trying to get clothes dry for Richard and her five children, the eldest not yet five years old. There was a drying rack permanently placed in front of the stove, capturing its heat. The house was perpetually in a state of mayhem, the only place the children could play and stay clean.

Matilda walked into this on one particularly stressful afternoon for Mary, and three-year-old John bounded off to play with his cousins.

'Take some home with you,' she pleaded. 'I can't take much more of this! Please!' Matilda laughed at her sister's beseeching.

'I'll take some of your washing and return it dry and folded, but none of your children. You would be missing them before I got to the corner, and you would be chasing after me to get them back!' Mary smiled at the truth of it, knowing Matilda to be right. 'What do you think of the idea of all of us going home for Christmas?' Matilda asked her. 'I mean all of us, have William there as well with all the grandchildren together for Mother and Father.'

'Lorra Massey! They'd never cope!' Mary exploded. 'My five, your one, that's six, William's three, that's nine children under seven! Father would not be able to handle it, he would disappear and kick gate posts in the snow! Mother would love it though, she will be in a right tizzy till we all left.'

'Well, actually, I was thinking on there being eleven children under twelve,' Matilda added to Mary's surprise. 'I had thought of asking Madeline to come along as well. She spends Christmas on her own with her two every year, and it was thinking about getting her involved in our Christmas that started me on the whole idea.'

'That would be wonderful, Matilda, a perfect Christmas. How were you going to let them know?'

'I have young Joshua Palmer for the day on Friday—I will send him off on Jacob's horse with directions and instructions. He's a bright enough lad to do it right. I was hoping that if I lent you Ann for the day to look after your lot, you could go and see Mother and find out if she is willing. You know that Father will be against the idea if I go through his door.'

'You have been thinking this through, haven't you? But don't send Joshua over—I will go on to Madeline's myself, after seeing Mother. Charles will tell William, as they see each other often enough apparently. It seems that Charles has got himself a lady friend in Colyton and uses visiting William as an excuse to head over that way, as though Mother hasn't worked that out.'

'That's even better. Tell Mother she will not have to cook a thing— between you, me, Ann and Madeline, we will be able to bring it all.'

To Mary's surprise, her father was possibly more enthusiastic for a family Christmas gathering than her mother. For all his reluctance to accept Matilda's lack of a husband, he held nothing back in accepting his grandson—he felt that none of his grandchildren could do any wrong, and he adored them all equally. He was beaming from ear to ear at the thought of having them all together at the one time, Madeline's included, as they were regular visitors. Mary and her mother watched him, bemused, as he paced around the kitchen talking of the games they would all play. Reality would hit fast enough, they decided, and they left him to his quiet expectations.

Madeline was not only delighted with Mary's unexpected visit, but overjoyed at the Christmas her boys were going to have.

'I have time to make each girl a little doll as a present from under the tree, but what about the boys?' Madeline said.

'Oh, Richard will come up with something, he is forever making some toy for our boys. I'll get him onto it. It is going to be quite a day,' she replied, then added, 'We haven't seen Dick over our way for a while, and you've passed no comment—have you seen him lately? Is he all right?'

Madeline looked at her in surprise. 'If he wasn't, wouldn't Matilda know it? I've always assumed that it goes both ways with those two.'

'I suppose you are right. It's never occurred to me that she would know about him without being told—she's never said if she can or not.'

'Well, to satisfy your curiosity, there was nothing at all wrong with him on Monday. God, what a difference he has made to my life!' She sighed with deep satisfaction.

Mary laughed with her friend. 'For that, we are all truly grateful.' She left a laughing Madeline to return home.

The White family Christmas gathering of 1846 was a boisterous success. Grandmother and Grandfather were treated in their own home to a celebration for which they did nothing in preparation. With the arrival of each family came trays of food, already cooked and only needed warming in the stove. Children were everywhere, with grandfather John trying to keep up with each of them, almost to the exclusion of paying attention to his own children. Grandmother Mary followed at a leisurely pace, picking up a fallen child and cuddling away the tears, then returning to the kitchen where her daughters and Madeline were quick to sit her out of the way as they prepared the meal. She was not sure if the children really made more noise than the women in the kitchen, as they all talked away as they worked, with too many conversations going on at once to follow one completely. The men quietly left them all to it and sat in the parlour, supping cider and comparing farm results.

'There be too much food,' old Mary said from her seat. But after they had all eaten, there was very little left. Charles and Richard took the children out to the barn to see the animals and play hide and seek in the hay loft while the women cleaned up. Grandfather John was left in peace as he nodded off in his old chair beside the stove, his youngest grandchild, Samuel, asleep in the crook of his arm.

'Tis been grand,' Mary said, 'and I've not lifted a finger to help. Thank you, all of you. He would say something if he be able,' she nodded towards her husband, deep in sleep, a mellow rumble accompanying his breathing. 'Quite wore him out they have, and never a word of complaint will 'ee hear from 'im!' She smiled indulgently.

They were all on their way soon after, to attend afternoon milking and feeding of their stock, each girl clutching a prettily made rag doll, each boy a little cart. John woke when Mary lifted Samuel from his arm to change him ready for the trip home. He rose and shook the hand of each man, and hugged and kissed each daughter, Madeline included, saying thank you to them all. Matilda was not left out by him, treated equally with the others. His wife shed a quiet tear at the sight of it.

Light had faded by the time Matilda returned home to the cottage, after attending to the animals. Baby John was already asleep in bed, and Ann looked ready to retire as well.

'It was a good day, Matilda. Who would have thought Father would have played with his grandchildren like that? He seems to have forgiven you at last.'

'Christmas cheer, I think Ann. I am not expecting any better treatment when we meet next. It would have been hard for him to have treated me any differently with everyone around, but he is still unsettled by what I have done. Be kind to him.' She left it at that, too happy with the day's events to want to lose any of it.

It snowed again the next day, just enough to put fresh covering over the landscape like a new tablecloth. *Tomorrow I will give the barn a good clean out*, thought Matilda. *I ate too much yesterday and the hard exercise will do me good.*

She set to the job with determination, not wanting to spend all day at it. She talked to each animal as she worked among them, and didn't hear the sound of the horse hooves on the yard outside announcing a visitor's arrival. It was the way the cows lifted their heads in unison that made her aware that someone was out there.

Bother, she thought, not wanting to be stopped in what she was about. Probably Jacob wanting something. She leant the rake and shovel she was using against the wall and went to see what he wanted. As she brushed her hair from her face, she smeared cow muck on her cheek from the back of her hand. Annoyed, she pulled her sleeve over her cheek to clean it off as she went through the door into the bright snow-reflected light. Realising that the man was too tidily dressed to be Jacob, she lifted her hand to shield her eyes from the glare to see better who had arrived. When she heard his voice, her heart raced.

'Hello Matilda, have I come at a poor time for you?' She raced to him where he stood holding his horse and threw herself into his arms.

'My Richard,' she sobbed, holding him tightly, 'What a Christmas this is!' And he held her tightly back, not letting go. Ann had heard the horse's arrival and came out to see who it was. She almost laughed at the sight of them standing unmoving in the snow, the horse looking about. She went over and took its reins from him and led it to a stall in the barn.

When she went back out with the bag from the saddle, they were still embracing in the middle of the yard, and she said, 'You had better come inside or you'll freeze to the spot.' Richard looked up and saw his horse gone and his bag in Ann's hand.

'Oh!' he said, embarrassed, 'you've attended to him—yes, perhaps we should go indoors.'

Reluctantly, Matilda released him and followed Ann inside.

Without a word, Ann put Richard's bag in Matilda's room and went to fetch warm water for her to have a bath. 'I will milk later for you Matilda,' she said at the yet-again-entwined couple.

Richard looked up. 'I don't mean to interrupt farm work—do you want to finish what you were doing?' he asked Matilda.

'No,' came a muffled reply from his chest.

'Then we shall finish it together,' Richard said. 'I have old clothes here for the job.' He released her hold and went to change, with Matilda close behind. He took a while to change, and they both came out with satisfied smiles on their faces.

The barn did get cleaned, and the cows milked, not that either really noticed. Ann had the bath ready again, with Matilda taking her time in it. By dinner both were refreshed and able to include Ann and John in their conversations. Richard thought there was no reason now for Ann to spend the night at Mary's, as there was no longer any secret in the type of relationship he and Matilda shared. He ate heartily and talked a lot, and John joined in with the excitement of the atmosphere around the table, feeling the joy, but not understanding a jot of it. He was put to bed soon after, relaxed in the happy feeling he got from them all. They soon had the plates washed and tidied away, helped by sipping on port that Richard had produced from his bag.

'I think I shall retire, this has all been too rich for me,' Ann said with an exaggerated swoon as she reached the door. 'I shall sleep the sleep of the dead tonight,' she giggled as she left the room. 'Wild horses will not wake me!'

'Wild horses will not let me sleep!' Matilda said throatily. 'Let me check on John, then we can go to bed.' She quickly slipped into his room where he was deep in sleep. 'He's ours,' she whispered, when she felt Richard behind her as he watched his boy in slumber. Then she took his hand and took him to her bed.

They were like young lovers, over eager as though for the first time, and over too soon.

'What happened?' they asked each other in surprise at their almost desperate effort, feeling cheated by its suddenness.

He held her closely, still breathing deeply. 'I have known I will be here tonight for four weeks, and for four weeks I have been thinking of being with you, I could hold back no longer.' His hand slid over her breast.

'Well now that your tension has gone, we can start again more leisurely. We have been doing this for five years now, so I don't think we need rush, do you?'

'Yes, start again, more leisurely, if I can, so soon.' He felt Matilda's hand move down his stomach and then holding him, softly holding, then stroking, his desire building in waves. 'So soon!' he murmured, moving down to kiss her held breast.

'Take me,' she whispered, moving over him, and he did.

She woke first, disturbed. She could hear John asking of Ann why Mummy wasn't up yet, and Ann's mumbled reply of her being very tired and needing rest. Perhaps they could be very quiet so Mummy could rest peacefully. Matilda smiled at Ann's attempt to keep John quiet, but knew that John was incapable of letting anyone rest peacefully while he was awake. She tried to get out of the bed without disturbing Richard.

'I heard,' he whispered holding her afresh.

'No you don't,' Matilda whispered back, slipping out of his grasp. 'Behave!' They both smiled at the improbability of that, but he let her dress.

'Good morning, my young man,' Matilda said to John as she entered the kitchen.

'Good morning, Mummy. Have you milked yet?' he said, much to Ann's amusement.

'Not yet,' she replied, feeling chastised. 'Do you want to help?'

'Yes,' he said and dashed out the door. Matilda was relieved to find that Joshua had already started, with only three cows to go.

'First time I be 'ere afore 'ee,' the quiet lad said. 'You be all right, like?'

'Just a hectic Christmas catching up with me,' Matilda said.

'Aye, as likely as be it,' he said, and gave no more thought to it.

Richard didn't leave until after lunch, delaying as long as he could.

'I will not be able to come down again until March,' he gloomily told her as he left. 'It may even be April. Hannah will keep you informed as always though. I doubt if Father is aware of how much she does for us both—he is happier not knowing, I believe.'

'Take care, my Richard—my love goes with you. Leave me out of

183

your conversations with your father—it's best if Hannah lets him know how I am.'

Matilda did not need to wait until March for more news for Richard, for by then she knew she was carrying another child for him.

Chapter 22

1847: Promotion

Dick confirmed it for her. It was early February when he ambled through the gate and found her in the orchard, picking up the wind-fallen apples for cider making. He could hear her chatting away to John as they worked their way around each tree, leaving filled bags behind them.

'Hello Miss. M, be getting fair crop, be 'ee?' he asked. 'Hello John,' he said, patting the boy on his shoulder as he passed him.

'Hello Dick,' Matilda called over to him. 'It has been a bumper crop this season, more than old Cobbledick can handle, I suspect.'

'Never take that notion wiv 'im, be poor days if that be ever 'appen, 'im's would never sleep at night if 'e got more 'n 'e could make into cider! Cor! Even 'is old dad would climb out of 'is grave to help push 'em through.' Matilda smiled at the prospect. 'Young John be growing up some,' he added, standing beside her. She brushed the hair from her face and looked up to him.

'Yes, and going to attend school later in the year. He will start with Mary's eldest two, Francis and John. He is not going to be like us, Dick, he is going to know reading and writing. I will not allow him to be held back like us.' Dick had been looking at her closely.

'Aye,' he said, not taking his eyes from hers. He lifted his hand to her face and brushed her cheek with the back of his fingers, then softly added, 'You'm be with child, Miss M, gone summer it's time be.'

'Yes, Dick, September by my figuring. I'm happy to be carrying it.'

'Aye, I know that. Be careful Miss M, this one will force changes on 'ee. There be no niceness in some folks, you'm will see that. Enough cares for 'ee to help when 'ee needs it. Take 'em help readily, Miss M,' and he wrapped his great arms around her. 'Take 'em help,' he muttered into her hair.

Matilda couldn't think of what changes she could be in for. She was very well settled in the cottage, living on the land in a perfectly content way, and with no shortage of money thanks to Richard's purses he left with each visit. She realised that the priggish Mrs Beamish would react most strongly at her having another child, but she thought that it was that Mrs Beamish and her cronies were never to find out who the father was that caused most of their annoyance. She couldn't see any reason why having another child would make any difference to her life, but accepted Dick's advice that it would somehow, and she would deal with it as it came.

Matilda gave little thought to Dick's prediction for some time, becoming too engrossed with her small allotment of land and looking after Jacob's cows. It was a bountiful spring, and Matilda loved this time of the year. The welcome warmth of the sun soaked into every living thing, almost demanding that all should appreciate its presence after the winter. The cows milked well on grass that grew with renewed vigour, fields were allocated for hay in the summer, and the vegetables flourished in the cared-for garden.

The first surprising change came when Jacob came down from the Mount Pleasant house with his wife Ann one Sunday afternoon.

'Miss Matilda,' he began hesitantly, 'we be thinking on making other arrangements.' He paused and glanced at his wife. 'We be thinking on shifting back down to Hawley to farm proper. This acreage be repaired to run with easy maintenance from now on's, and proper farm needs me for more time. We be thinking on leaving the lad here and bringing old Morgan and his missus up to work upalong. He works well enough, but a bit mazed he be, and needs steering right. Be 'ee set to run upalong for us and we be seeing 'ee regular like to help as needed? Be 'ee paid for effort, course!'

Matilda was taken aback, and didn't respond at once. Ann, Jacob's wife, spoke in the silence.

'Hawley is slipping behind and we can't afford that. Will you run this farm for us so we can go back down there? We will make whatever pay arrangements suit you. We cannot fault what you have done with the herd and you keep a tidy farm. Jacob will come up at least every two weeks to see what you need and what you want to do over the next while. Will you help us?'

'That is a big responsibility—but isn't there one of the men at Hawley who should be coming up?' Matilda ventured, not wanting to lose this opportunity to prove that she could manage it, but realising that Jacob and Ann would be taking a lot of criticism for putting a woman in charge of the farm.

'We want to keep the good workers at Hawley,' Ann replied before Jacob could open his mouth. 'You have proved to us that you can do it with what you have achieved already. Morgan will do the heavy work, and young Joshua will help both of you. It is no one's business but ours who we put in charge, but with Jacob meeting you at least every fortnight, it will have the appearance of him being the decision maker.'

'Be right Matilda. I be upalong regular, if only for you to tell me what you wants to do, not the other way round. No one will know what's said between us—you worry about the farm, we will worry about the gossips. Be only come from that Mrs Beamish anyways, stupid woman!'

'I will gladly, of course, if you are sure,' Matilda replied.

'Very good,' Jacob said giving a rare smile.

Jacob and Ann were back at Hawley Bottom and Morgan installed by the end of the week. It would be difficult to tell who was the most excited by the new arrangement, Matilda or Joshua, who worshipped her in secret. Matilda was able to tell both Madeline and Mary at the same time and both shared Matilda's excitement, but it was when Mary's Richard came in and Mary told him and he shared her enthusiasm that Matilda knew she was going to be all right.

'We can add Mount Pleasant to the haymaking roster now—that will put our men up by three, an excellent gain for your two fields,' he said, and went off beaming.

After Hannah's next visit, she went home to tell John and Sarah of Matilda's new position with pride. John was particularly pleased that Matilda was doing so well and made a point of telling Sarah so. It gave him more reason to try and get over and visit her, and wondered then if he could get her to visit them, as it would do Sarah so much good to see Matilda again.

It was early summer when Richard was able to visit Matilda. It amused him that his father had added a little into one of his letters to tell him of Matilda's promotion, as though Hannah would not have already done so.

They were lying under an apple tree in the orchard, gazing up at the clear blue sky with the last of the blossom petals falling about drifting in a wafting breeze. The air was filled with scent from the wild flowers growing among the trees and hedgerow behind them. John, about to turn six, was chasing butterflies, trying unsuccessfully to catch one.

'There are your buzzards,' Richard pointed to them.

'Is this not heaven?' Matilda sighed. 'I'm with the man I love, a healthy boy we adore, and all's right in our world.' She squeezed his hand.

'Here?' he lazily answered. 'Do you not mean up there, beyond the blue sky?'

'No silly! That's the easy explanation for children to understand. The real heaven is all around us, it's how we live in this world. Look around you, look at nature's beauty, isn't this how heaven should be? Shouldn't heaven be filled with all the peace and beauty that your life is surrounded by? Shouldn't heaven be how you live your life? Shouldn't it reflect how you are, how you treat others? Do you really believe that you have to wait until you die and meet St Peter at the pearly gates, to know if you are going to heaven or going to hell? Isn't the day of judgement every day, all day? Doesn't every action you take, and every manner in which you treat others, decide whether you are a fit person to be in heaven or hell? And isn't that happening every minute of every day? You set your own standards in life on how you wish to live and how you are judged. God is with us all, all the time. Waiting to die to go to heaven seems a tragic waste of time—why not live your life as though you were already there? The world is a far better place if you do.'

Richard looked at her in surprise at this idea and pondered it for a while, then said, 'That is an interesting way of putting it, unconventional, but interesting.'

'Do you think I'm so very wrong? Let me tell you a story that my grandfather told me when I was little, maybe no more than ten, when I asked him about going to heaven. I was sure that he was going to go there. He took a while to reply, then said that he knew what heaven and hell were like, and he told me this story.

'God had shown him two doors, and he opened one of them. Inside, in the middle of the room, was a large round table. In the middle of the table was a large pot of delicious-smelling stew, that made your mouth water in anticipation. The people sitting around the table were thin and sickly as though they were unfed. Each of them were holding spoons with very long handles, that were strapped to their arms, and each found it possible to reach into the pot of stew and take a spoonful, but because the handle was longer than their arms, they could not get the spoons back to their mouths. It was a ghastly sight of misery and suffering. "That is Hell," God said.

'The next door was exactly the same as the first, and when it was opened, the room had the same large table with a similar pot of delicious stew in the middle of it. The people in there had the same long spoons strapped to their arms, but these people were well nourished, laughing and talking all together. "This is Heaven," God said. "The difference is because of just one simple thing. These people have learned to feed each other, while the greedy ones only think of themselves and stay in Hell. Live your life working in with your neighbours and sharing, and you will always live in Heaven. Be greedy and selfish and you will be always be living in Hell. The choice is yours alone to make."

'I knew I wanted to live always in heaven, and he taught me that day how to do it, and I truly believe that I have done my best to do so. That is why I said, "Is this not heaven," because I have done my best to make it so.' She turned to look at him directly, asking, 'Do you understand what I believe better now?'

He sat silently for a while, his head nodding slowly. 'Why is it you have always given me better sermons than I could write myself? But what about eternal life, the spiritual life after death, how does that fit in? Do you believe in that?'

'Of course there is eternal life for us, but I also believe it lives most strongly in the minds of those who we leave behind, those we were close to while we were on this earth, and how we treated them. St Peter doesn't make judgement on us at the pearly gates, we make it on ourselves while we are here.' Richard again sat quietly absorbing her words, her belief just a step away from what he had been taught, disquietingly so, but also totally relevant.

'For all my years of study, for all my textbooks, I am given a lesson on life in two minutes that is more succinct by one who has never opened a book in her life. You have yet again opened my eyes in my staid world. How many, I wonder, can live constantly up to those standards?'

'You can only judge that for yourself. Take Dick, for instance—he lives a blameless life, and would do no harm to anyone. But because he doesn't speak to folk, because he seems to be a simpleton, he gets shunned by others, and they would say he has no place in heaven. If you were to know him, you would know differently. Others cannot judge, only you yourself.'

'Self judgement can be biased and blind.'

'Then open your eyes. I find it is easier not to tell others what I believe— it saves trying to explain what I don't have the words for.'

'Your words are adequate—it would be others' acceptance of them that fall short. We have a child out of wedlock, you have been accused of having a bastard child, and some don't think you should be part of the village congregation—how do you think that is acceptable to God?'

'Our boy is the result of our love, as is the one I carry. He is cherished and cared for, he is a happy child and will go to school. Being able to read and write will be as natural to him as it is to you. We will see that he is given every opportunity to do things to his best ability. What else would God want us to do for him? Us being married would not make any difference to what we will do for him, or the love we show him. He will be better off than many boys of married parents. Being a bastard child is a title that lesser folk will give him, those who only know envy and hate. We are above that,' she promptly replied.

Richard lay back, wondering how he was going to explain her beliefs to his father, and the fact that they were to have another child. He was sure that he was not going to be accepting of the news.

'Mother would like you to visit her; she cannot make the journey here, so if you are willing to go to her, she will appreciate it. She always found your company and conversation invigorating, she said. She weakens every time I see her, and I fear you will see a noticeable decline. Is there any way you could go over?'

'Perhaps—should it be before I show? Do you want them to know of my pregnancy?'

'I will tell them on my return, there is little point in hiding it.'

'Then tell Hannah to stay home, and I will go there instead of her coming here. Joshua will accompany me and tend the horse. I will use Jacob's gig.'

Matilda did make the visit to Lyme Regis in late spring of 1847. Sarah was alone, as John was in Bristol with his brother. Hannah, Sarah and Matilda spent the few hours that Matilda was there talking continously, with little time to draw breath. Sarah was at her best, clearly far more frail than Matilda expected, but as quick-witted as ever. She delighted in meeting young John, who politely responded at their introduction, but was quick to leave them and play in the huge garden of Fairfield Lodge with Joshua and the gardener. Only very briefly did Sarah make any reference to Matilda expecting another child, saying that she was pleased that Matilda showed such obvious pleasure in motherhood, but also said that it was as well that John had chosen this week to be in Bristol, as he was not happy about the coming event. He had spent some time in his study with Richard, making it clear to him that he should be setting the example of an exemplary leader in his community, not creating a scandal that could erupt at any time. He told Richard he should be finding himself a wife and stopping his philandering ways. Sarah said that John had been rather worked up for days after Richard had returned to Timsbury, and that things needed to be sorted out once and for all.

'Oh dear!' Matilda said. 'Richard and I both know that marriage for us is out of the question, and it has been assumed that he would eventually find himself a proper wife. I never thought he would still be visiting me, but I am truly grateful that he does! I could never deny him, I love him so, but at the same time, I do understand Mr Hill's point of view.'

'Do not fret on it Matilda—Richard has to make the decision on how he behaves and when he marries, not his father,' Sarah said. 'Love is a strange thing and men do behave oddly under its influence. It is not their heads they think with at times. I will settle John down soon enough, he gets quite het up over family matters.'

Matilda was quiet all the way home, thinking on the sad frailty of Sarah's health and her determination to keep control of it. Clearly she could not survive without Hannah's constant help, she admitted that she no longer ventured away from the house, afraid of an attack out in public and the humiliation it would cause John by others' lack of care and understanding that she was ill, not mad. Hannah was her saviour, selfless in her care for her mother, the management of the household, and source of all news.

Matilda spent no time worrying on how long Richard would keep on seeing her before he relented and found a wife to suit his role in Timsbury. She would enjoy to the end whatever he could give her, irrespective of what John thought of their situation.

Joshua left her to her thoughts, in awe of the house where Matilda had lived, and nestled a sleeping John under his arm.

The routine work on the farm soon dispelled any dwelling on thoughts of what Richard's father would insist that Richard do. Her developing waist slowed her down, imperceptibly, week by week.

Almost with devilish glee, she made Mrs Beamish aware of her pregnancy, aware that she would be abuzz with indignation over her condition, and still no one having the slightest idea who the father could be. Every man in the area came under scrutiny and suspicion, all inevitably dismissed as unlikely.

Once the hay was brought in on the local farms and all the labourers returned to their own land, Matilda and Mary decided the time was right to enrol the boys into the school. John and his cousins Francis and John Hoyle were duly presented to Herman Bowditch, a musician by trade and now Dalwood's school master. His background of holding people's attention and entertaining them with his performances meant that his lessons were equally entertaining, and the young minds were soon grasping the basics of reading, writing and arithmetic.

Ann at first found it difficult not having the young John scampering about the house and demanding her full-time attention.

'Poor Herman,' she said to Matilda. 'I feel sorry for him having the two Johns arriving at the same time.' Matilda laughed.

'Don't worry too much,' she told her, 'the next one is not far off.'

The next one was a little closer than she thought, and arrived with few warnings before dawn on 16 September. With the minimum of contractions, Matilda gave birth to a bellowing girl.

'If it's a girl, I would like her to be named Matilda,' Richard had said that spring day under the apple tree, while she had only thought of boys' names. To have a girl was not a possibility she had thought of.

Chapter 23

1849: The Seeds of Literacy

The next two years seemed to speed by. The farm became a flow of seasons, each with its demands of work to be done. Matilda had become quite accepted in the community. Her reputation for her clotted cream never waned, while her ability to harvest the best from the fields was being noticed by neighbouring farmers. Jacob was even acknowledged for his astuteness in putting her in charge, and she had just persuaded him to allow her to plant one field with corn the following year as a trial, as there had been a shortage that year.

Her first thoughts of the future came about because of John's success with his learning at school. There was little she could do to support him with it, and it became clear to her that daughter Matilda would need to go to school as well if she was not to follow in her mother's footsteps. Matilda was determined that should her daughter fall in love with a man of education, her own lack of education would not be a reason for them not to be married.

At this time, education was a privilege that seemed to extend to only a few of the girls of the gentry, but when Matilda voiced her intention to Herman to see how welcoming he would be to have the young Matilda attend his classes, his immediate enthusiasm for her future attendance overwhelmed her.

'My dear Matilda, of course she must attend! Literacy for girls is not the exclusive domain of the upper class! My word! If I had my way, every child from the age of six in the parish would be in my school. Our papers bring us news from around the world at greater speed, our boundaries are expanding, the Empire grows. If our youngsters today do not learn to read and write they will never enjoy the opportunities that will come their way with increasing frequency. She must come and learn! She really must!'

'Thank you, Herman. That is very pleasing to hear,' Matilda humbly replied.

'Pleasing? My dear, it should be a Commandment! I will teach anyone who has the desire to learn. Even you!' he boomed.

'Herman! Really, I am in my thirties and well past the learning age.'

'Absolute codswallop! Learning is a state of the mind, not a state of the body! A supple mind will easily learn—age is irrelevant. Do you mean to tell me that you are not learning new things on that farm yonder? Are you not the one to sow corn for the first time on that land? Is that not learning?'

'That's different. That is farming matters, not words.'

'When you can accept the fact that there is no difference, that learning is learning, be it herds or words, sows or sums, come and see me then, and you will be surprised. You won't be the first and you won't be the last adult I have taught.' With that he wheeled away to attend to the children, calling back over his shoulder, 'Think on it, Matilda, it will help your children.'

She thought on it all the way up the hill back to the farm. Helping her children was what mattered most to her. But learning herself? The idea terrified her, and by the time she was home it was well into the back of her mind.

Other family events helped keep Herman's offer from her thoughts. Her two brothers had recently announced their news: William and Ann were soon to add to their family, but most exciting of all was that Charles was at last going to marry his long-time love, Lucy. His late-night trips home from Colyton were about to end. Matilda and Mary teased him relentlessly, and wagered that a family must be on the way. Charles denied every charge, claiming innocence in such activities, but a blushing Lucy could not hide the fact that perhaps some practice had taken place.

'There is no family coming as yet,' she quietly told them. 'A bit surprising, in a way.'

Sadly for them both, they were never to have any children.

One day, Thomas Downton called. He rarely did so, other than to collect the rent. But here he was, obviously in a troubled state, and the rent was not due.

'Miss Matilda, I wonder if I could have a word?' he asked awkwardly.

'You had better come inside,' she offered, fearing he was about to tell her he wanted the cottage back. He sat uncomfortably at the kitchen table, and told her of his predicament.

'I be needing to raise some money for home farm, I be needing to repair the barn and rethatch home, 'twas leaking something desperate winter gone and Mother won't take no more. I tried everything, and only option I got left is to sell off this cottage.' He wiped his nose noisily. Matilda could see her haven being lost to her and her children. She hid her fears and waited for him to continue. 'I be real sorry, Matilda, but bank give me no choice. Your rent don't give me what I needs, so's I needs to sell to pay for repairs.' He fell silent. Matilda's mind raced, everything was about to be lost.

'When is this to happen?' Her voice quavered.

'Tis in motion now. Mr Bond said I must offer it to you first, as you be in residence, but I needs an awful lot, he told me what I must ask for it. I says you have two children and just be farm worker, you couldn't afford it.' He looked completely dejected, knowing the terrible news he had just delivered.

'Who is Mr Bond?' Matilda asked, for something to say. The fear of losing so much clouding her thinking.

'He be legal man in Axminster, young chap, calls himself an attorney, whatever that means.'

'How much do you need to find?' she asked, more from curiosity and the need to fill in the silence. He told he, and her heart raced.

'Thomas, could I ask you to come back tomorrow, before you take this any further?'

'Anything, Miss Matilda. I knows this be a terrible shock. Missus sent me up straight aways like, she knows you be in a tight corner now, and needs time.' He left her quickly, not wanting to stay, having delivered his dreadful ultimatum.

Matilda rose and went to her cupboard. She knew exactly how much money she had come home with from the Hills, and she hadn't spent a penny of it. What she was unsure of was how much she had from the purses that Richard always left. It was from these that she bought her cow and all the household expenses, but it was into it that she put what she made from selling clotted cream and eggs. She put it all out on the table and counted it. Three times more she counted it. Seventeen shillings short. She almost cried.

Look to your friends, Dick told me, she thought. But what friends would know of buying the cottage? Who owns their own place that knows of buying? Madeline? But Madeline was already in her home before her husband died. Jacob, next door? She shied from talking to a neighbour on such personal matters. Then it came to her—Francis Turl, a family friend who owned Umborne Farm, next to her parents. Francis had been running the farm for several years now, and would listen and give good advice. She didn't hesitate. She cleared the table and rode over to him. He was delighted to see her, and set her down with his wife, sending their children packing outside. It took him less than ten minutes to solve her problem once she had finished her explanation. With tears of joy, she rode home and waited anxiously for Thomas's visit the next day.

Thomas was surprised at his happy reception. He was even happier with Matilda's offer, even though it was two pounds short, the rest to come later.

'I will have Mr Bond come and call on you to make it legal and safe,' a jubilant Thomas said, and then hurried in to Axminster to see Mr Bond. Mr Bond arrived the next morning, dapper, proper, and barely a speck of dust on him from his three-mile ride out. Matilda was taken aback by his appearance—she expected all legal people to be old and dusty, but this chap was but a boy, 25 if he was lucky. He smiled at her expression.

'Miss White,' he politely said, 'my age has no restrictions on my qualifications. Shall we proceed?' And proceed they did. He carefully explained exactly what was to happen, and what the document he was writing said. He had long ago given up trying to understand how so many of his clients could not read or write, yet could count money with extreme accuracy. The terms of the purchase as Francis had suggested were agreed; Charles William Bond, Attorney of Axminster, counted the money Matilda presented, and signed a receipt.

In March 1849, Matilda became the owner of Dalwood Hill cottage, together with the outbuildings, garden orchard, in all, covering about four acres. She was the first member of the White family ever to own her own land.

She was in awe of what she had done, and told no one. She was unsure how to.

It was on one of Hannah's visits that Matilda learnt that Richard was to come down imminently, probably as soon as next week. Hannah was not sure of the content of Richard's letter to his father, nor what he was coming down to Lyme Regis to talk with his father about, but her father was certainly in an awful mood, snapping at servants, and short with Hannah. He had been seeing a lot of one of his political friends, a man who had visited their house on a number of occasions of late. All that had been said of him was that they shared several points of view, including concerning overseas developments. All that she had got from Richard was that he was doing well in Timsbury, and that his congregation had grown tremendously. She was looking forward to seeing him and finding out what was up with Father. She left Matilda earlier than usual, wanting to call in on a household supplier in Axminster who had short-supplied their last two orders.

'I'm getting as bossy as you!' she said, laughing as she left.

Matilda couldn't stop smiling at the thought of Richard visiting soon. He would be the first to know that she now owned Dalwood Hill. But her next visitor was entirely unexpected and shocked her—she didn't expect to see him again, and he had aged so.

He arrived one day when Ann came running out to the barn, calling out to her.

'There be an old gentleman in the front room wanting to see you. He be a stranger!' she announced, concerned.

'What's his name?' Matilda asked, quickly wiping her hands in her apron.

'I didn't hear it clearly, but I think he said Hill.'

Matilda headed to the cottage, taking her apron off and brushing back her hair as she went. He rose from the chair as she entered.

'Good Morning, Matilda, I do apologise for my unannounced arrival. I was in Axminster and took the opportunity to see you for myself. I do hope I am not stopping you from some important work.' He bowed slightly in his formal manner.

'Mr Hill, this is a surprise. Is Mrs Hill all right?' she asked, thinking he had come with bad news of her.

'Sarah is quite well, no more so than when you visited her. I am most grateful you made the effort to do so—she spoke of nothing else for the following week. It is not her that has necessitated this visit.'

'Some tea perhaps,' said Matilda. 'You may wish to refresh after the ride out. We can talk over some tea, I'll get Ann to make some.' She turned to the door and called to her sister. Little Matilda appeared at the door with her. 'This is my daughter, Matilda,' Matilda said, introducing her to John. John looked down at her quite solemnly, then smiled as the small girl shyly smiled up to him.

'Would you like to help Ann make the tea?' Matilda said to her daughter, an offer she quickly took and skipped from the room. They sat and Matilda added, 'You will miss meeting John. He is at school, where Matilda will also go, when old enough.'

'It is right that they should attend,' he said, then sat still for a moment, studying the toes of his shoes in thought. Quietly he began talking. 'There are matters that need to be tidied up. There are situations I am not happy about. Of paramount concern to me is the welfare of my grandchildren, all of them. Not all of my children have managed their lives as well as I would like, and I do not want my grandchildren to suffer for their parents' foolishness. I am in a position to improve their futures for them, beyond what they would be if left to the lack of standards displayed by my children.'

'There is no need to worry for *my* children!' She bridled at the insinuation that she was not capable of looking after them.

'My dear! My dear!' John quickly apologised. 'I meant no insult to you. I have no doubts of your abilities in these matters, but I will return to you and your children in a moment, with your permission. I have other grandchildren at great risk that are on my mind. But Richard is not above reproach.' There was a gentle knock on the door and Ann came in with the tea tray, little Matilda followed carefully carrying a small tray with a plate and a scone on it. She placed it on a table beside John, then scampered out.

'She is quite delightful,' John said, smiling, 'a credit to you.' When they were alone again, he continued, 'My son Philip has acted most disgracefully, with little concern for those around him. He has two sons, 13 and 15 years of age. Philip has no prospects and is a wastrel, so I have arranged for the boys to go out to New Zealand and begin new lives. It's a new country, a treaty was signed but ten years ago with the local Maori for peaceful settlement. The boys will be going to the South Island to a region called Canterbury, and money has been put aside for them to buy land. There is someone going out with them who will suitably set them up. There is nothing for them here, and their father will only waste whatever money I give them if they stay in this country.'

Matilda was shocked.

'But they will be only fourteen and sixteen when they go. Is that not too young?'

'Were you to know their parents, you would not think so. Young, perhaps, but not so young. Lads that age are in our armies, being killed. Whole families have died of starvation just across the sea in Ireland, where the potato famine has wiped out so many, and it is reported that a great number of them have left the country to settle in new lands like America and Australia, many of them going without living parents. We live in a blessed part of our land here—by comparison, the worst we suffer is a heavy winter. Those grandsons of mine will forever live in a heavy winter if I do nothing. I am prepared to go to these lengths to save them and give them a chance.'

'I must accept what you say—I am in no position to criticise your generous efforts to give them a better future,' Matilda said.

'They will be very well looked after out there, and Richard will control their money from here. But it is really Richard that I wish to speak of with you. This situation is not correct,' he said, choosing his words carefully. 'There are standards that must be met as rector, and he is not doing that. He should never have allowed a situation to arise where he has a child out of wedlock, but to have two is appalling. Should it become known in Timsbury, or anywhere for that matter, he will be ruined. I told him as much the last time he came down, and instructed him to find a lawful wife. He has recently written and told me that he is considering relinquishing his position and moving here to farm with you as husband and wife.'

'No John! He must not do that! He must stay where he is and do what he was born to do.' Matilda stood in shock, hands to her face as she paced to the window, a sob in her breath. 'He must not do that. I will refuse to see him.' A tear ran down her cheek. John rose and went to stand behind her.

'I did not mean to upset you—I had assumed that he had spoken of such things with you.'

'We have never spoken of marriage—we both know it could not happen with him as rector. There has never been a hint of him coming here to farm with me—he would make the most terrible farmer, he could not adapt, he would be most miserable within six months and regret ever giving up Timsbury. That misery would then turn on me and the children. You must stop him from doing that. You must! I love him too much for such ruination of what we both have.' Now there was a steady flow of tears. John took a large handkerchief from his pocket and handed it to her.

'Please calm yourself, Matilda. I am sure Richard will come to see it as a reaction to my instruction, and that it holds no sense at all. I had no idea that it was never spoken of between you—I thought it was something the two of you were anticipating doing one day. You will need to make your attitude clear to him next week. But you do understand the predicament I am in and the need to have it corrected?'

She turned to him, composed again and dry eyed. 'Mr Hill, I have never asked anything of you, or expected anything from Richard. You were most generous while I lived at Fairfield Lodge and Richard has been most generous since. He always leaves a purse with each visit, although I didn't need it. "For the children," he says each time. I am earning enough from working Jacob's land, and Jacob is pleased with what he also gets from it; he has said the situation here will not change in that regard. Richard and I have known that we cannot wed—I could not be a rector's wife and run his affairs while being unable to read or write. We have talked of him getting a proper wife and yet he does nothing about it. He knows I will not stand in his way. I will never refuse him here, I love him too much to deny him when we meet those few times each year. When he does find a suitable bride, then he must attend her alone and I will see him no more. That is all that I can do.'

John was silent for a while, thinking.

'Matilda, as it has always been, you clarify a muddled situation with your disarming honesty.' He paused. 'That was the second time you have called me John—both times have been when you have been in a uneasy situation and have needed me to pay close attention and help you. I found it acceptable on both occasions, and would be pleased if you could do so from now on. Very few people use my Christian name, and I would like you to carry on doing so.' He turned from the window and looked at her.

'I did not think that you would have noticed the first time—I was embarrassed for some time after that, hoping you had not. When you said nothing of it I assumed that your attention was firmly fixed on Mrs Hill's seizure.'

'Her name is Sarah, as you well know. The time has long gone since you should have been using it in her company. You are the best medicine for her, and I would be grateful if you were able to visit her again, perhaps more often if possible. But as for Richard, I do understand love, you know; I do not have a frozen heart. But what are we to do?'

'I can only do what I always do when he comes. I always ask after Timsbury matters, and that includes any introduction of likely brides. He has never shied away from the subject and tells me of those presented to him by doting mothers. I don't think he is avoiding the issue, but it seems that there has been no suitable possibility on offer. You could ban him from coming here to see me,' she added as an awful afterthought.

'That would never work, and you know it. It's not as though he isn't in love with you as well. I just hope his love for you is not making him turn a blind eye to the possibilities up there. I pray that this situation doesn't destroy him.'

'He is a much stronger man than that. But privately, John,' she found she could call him by name with surprising ease, 'I am surprised every time he comes here. Each time he leaves I believe it to be the last, that he will realise he must present himself correctly in Timsbury. But each time he arrives I am overjoyed with his presence, I have no way of stopping that, it flows to the very core of my body. I am happy for our love to run its course; when it ends, it ends.' Matilda looked at him. 'What else can I do?'

John just slowly nodded his head. 'Nothing, my dear, nothing. I suppose I have an answer to my problem but not a solution. He is going to be even more busy for some time now. We are to extend the church. Richard is writing to the Church Building Society for permission to build on a new chancel with transepts and applying for a grant to do so. If it is approved he will be truly occupied and we will see less of him for some time. I have arranged funds in support of the application.'

'That is wonderful! Do you think I will need to go up there and make sure the roof is done correctly this time?'

John couldn't help himself, and burst out laughing. 'My dear, I fear for the whole of Timsbury, not just the roof workers, should you appear up there.' He chuckled on at the story he had been told by Hannah from their stay up there. 'While I am here, would you show me the farm?'

'Of course. Come along,' and she headed to the door, eager to show him what she had achieved, and tell him of her plans for the future. John walked beside her, taking it all in. He was impressed with the tidiness of the farm and her obvious satisfaction and comfort at being there.

'This is home to you, isn't it Matilda?' he mused. 'As much as Timsbury is to Richard.'

'Precisely, so I don't think either of us could live, forever happily, in the other's world,' Matilda admitted.

'With your permission, of course, I would like to visit Jacob to see if there was any way I could secure your tenure here. I would not like to see you lose what you have built up here.'

'There is no need for that, I am quite safe here. Farm land stays in families hereabouts, and neither Jacob nor Ann would sell a family asset.'

'Hmmm, I would feel more assured of that if I could talk with him.'

'By all means do so. But shouldn't you be concerning yourself with securing Hannah's future, not mine?'

'What do you mean? Hannah is quite secure where she is,' he asked, bewildered.

'For now, like me, she is. But what for her future? What has she got when her mother goes? Even worse, what if you go first? How is she protected then? She enjoys what she is able to do for you both, she enjoys running the household, but that will not last for ever. What will she replace it with when you have both gone?' John stood stock still, looking straight ahead.

'She will inherit her share of my estate. There will be ample money for her then.'

'You have avoided the answer, John, and you know it! She will stay with you to the end, then what? She will have nowhere to live and nothing to do to replace what takes all her time now. You must look after her now so that she has something in place once you have gone.'

He turned to her and gave her a soft smile. 'You never relent for her, do you? A firmer friendship I am yet to see. I do know what you mean, and I had never thought of it, which is why I tried to dodge an answer. I should have known better than that with you.'

'Then you will think of something for her?'

'Yes, Matilda. I will think of something. Why do I feel like a chastened child?'

This time it was Matilda who laughed aloud. 'I'm sorry, John. But you seem to have been trying to help everyone but the one person who you depend on the most.'

'Perhaps you are right. But now I must leave you. Please call on Sarah.'

'Will you call here again?'

'I think I will, but only when I feel I can take the pressure from you. You are very strong on your own ground, you know.'

This time they both laughed as he took his leave. Matilda leant on a gate and gazed across the fields, lost in thought at all he had told her. Did he mean to say so much, she wondered—he had never said so much about his family to her before. He was clearly very troubled by it all and he hadn't just come out to chat about them to her. She could only think that he had come to tell her that she was to see Richard no more. The affair was at an end. But what had changed his mind? Why did he step back from that ultimatum? She would just have to wait for Richard to arrive, she decided, and pushed herself off the gate and went about her work.

Richard arrived, a little tentatively at first, unsure of how Matilda would receive him following his father's visit. His father had told him nothing of what they had talked of, except he knew they would have discussed his intent to join her on the farm—something he would have preferred to broach himself. There was no difference in Matilda's welcome; she threw her arms around him and kissed him at length.

'Hello,' he was finally able to say, before she kissed him again. She lessened her grip on him a little and looked into his face.

'Hello, my Richard,' she said and kissed him again, stopping long enough to add, 'your father came by,' and smothered his lips to stop a response. This time she felt him harden against her.

'Yes,' she said to him, and all other thoughts left him.

Later, she mockingly scolded him. 'What were you thinking of when you told John that you were going to join me here?'

'He was being pompous! I was reckless in answering. Not a wise thing to do with him. He told me I was not to see you again, he wrote and said he was coming to see you. I gathered from that that he was going to tell you that I was no longer coming to visit.'

'I think he was, but he never said it. Why did he change his mind, do you think?'

'He has said nothing on the subject, it must have been something you said that stopped him.'

'It must have been my outburst about you coming here, that I wouldn't allow it. I was a little forthright with him.'

'That would do it. It must have been some visit—Mother said that when he came home he went straight up to her room and said, "She is going to call us John and Sarah! And is going to come and see you again!" As though he was presenting her with the Crown jewels. Poor Mother had no idea that he was even going to visit you, and it was only that he went on to talk about us that she realised that the "she" was you! Do I gather that you will not have me living here with you?'

'You are a silly man! How long would you last doing farm work? How long before the farm boundaries enclosed you in boredom? Yours is a bigger stage than this, and if you were only half way honest, you would admit it.'

'You are right as usual. What a muddle we are in. I just cannot contemplate a world without you, even with the little we see of each other. I do look at other women up there to see if there is a wife for me among them, but none can hold a candle to what you do to me. None give me a flicker of a possible candidate. What's to do?'

'I'm sure one will flicker for you one day. What will happen, will happen—you can't force the issue. In the meantime, we have each other to enjoy.'

He told her of the plans for the church and the difference it would make, and of his mother's pleasure in being told that Matilda was going to visit again and how she looked forward to it.

She told him then that she had bought the cottage and surrounding land, of how she had paid for it from what she had earned while at Fairfield Lodge and the sale of eggs and clotted cream. She told him of the two pounds to be paid later, and the security she had gained for their children. She told him of the farm's progress and the plans for next year. He was immensely proud of her, and told her so. Then they walked across the back field to meet John coming home from school, like most boys, hearing him before seeing him.

John told Richard of his days at school, of the things he was learning, and Matilda watched them talking, suddenly realising what she was missing out on.

Having bought Dalwood Hill, surely nothing was impossible.

She would see Herman the next day.

Chapter 24

1849: A Belated Education

Matilda timed her delivery of clotted cream to William Edwards, the village grocer, so as to be passing the school when the children would be playing in the yard. That way she hoped to find Herman outside as well, and to stop and speak with him then would seem all the more natural. She wanted no one to know what the purpose of their meeting was about, and a coincidental meeting whilst passing the school gate suited her very well.

He was however, nowhere in sight. She paused at the gate to look for him, but was only greeted by 'Hello' from a number of the children who knew her. She walked on to the village shop feeling despondent, her courage failing her. 'Stupid woman!' she told herself. 'Learning's not for you, you are well past learning age, no matter what he said.' She crossed the footbridge over the ford and saw a pair of ducks paddling furiously for cover. *Pick your spirits up girl!* she thought. *Remember who you are and make a job of selling these to William. You don't want old Ma Beamish seeing you sad.* With that, she lifted her chin and strode purposefully to the store. She was raising her hand to open its door when it burst open and a rushing figure nearly collided with her,

'Pardon Me! Terribly sorry! Rushing back to the tyrannical hordes!' It was Herman with a parcel under his arm. 'Oh, it's you Matilda, why haven't you been to see me?' he demanded.

'Herman, I . . .'

'Can't stop now, the hordes will have sealed the doors before I return to keep me out!' He looked at her basket. 'Clotted cream, yes! I will be up after I release the monsters to collect some, no excuses now.' And he whirled around and was gone.

Surprise and relief swept through her. *So I am to learn*, she thought as she entered the shop.

'That was a bit close, Matilda,' William said. 'Looked like he was going to fair charge through you all the way to the school before he noticed you at all!'

'Was a surprise, indeed. But the basket is intact,' she said, handing over the pots of clotted cream.

'I have some empty ones here, I'll just fetch them.' He went to his back room, coming back with a bag of his special little pots he liked to sell her cream in. 'I'm selling out every day lately, could you do more?'

'From next week I could, maybe another four pots.'

'Very good! yes, that will do nicely. You know that daft Beamish woman will only buy clotted cream in these pots, thinks they are special I bring in from outside the parish. She told me once that she would never have any of yours, much too common. Will only take the superior product in these pots—I laugh every time! No wonder her husband took to his heels first chance he got, she be no better than fresh cow droppings herself.'

'Mr Edwards!' she said, trying not to laugh. 'That is a terrible thing to say,' totally failing to hide her smile.

'Aye, true. But she doesn't half get up my nose at times, just like fresh cow droppings! Now be on your way before you get me gossiping!' He handed her her pay for the cream and she left with a lightness in her step, chuckling under her breath.

Herman arrived shortly after John, having first raced home to tell his wife, Frances, of his new campaign to teach Matilda to read and write, and gather some material to do so with.

'Be careful with her,' she warned him. 'Not everyone can learn at your speed. Be patient.'

'Balderdash!' he boomed. 'I think she is quicker than both of us put together!' And off he went, like a knight on a mission.

However, he did heed his wife's words, and approached Matilda and her desire to learn with great care and diplomacy that would have astounded his wife, had she seen him.

'Now Matilda,' he began, once they were alone in the drawing room, 'to begin we shall start right at the beginning. There will be things that you didn't know you knew, things that you have been using and recognising that are part of reading. They will all help to make learning easier. The hardest part is learning to write the words down correctly—misspelling a word in English will often give the reader the wrong meaning to what you meant. The English language is a bastard, and I mean that in its true sense—it is a bastard because we have taken so many pieces from other languages and put them into the English language. That makes it harder to learn; the rules of forming words and sentences have become jumbled so that the bastard bits can fit in to make our English work.

'I am not going to teach you as though you were a pupil in my class; instead, I am going to teach you how to write down what you already say in conversation. When you write, you will write it as though you were talking directly to that person, and they will read it as though you were standing in front of them saying it. You have no need to learn any words—your vocabulary, the number of words you use naturally, is extraordinary, far beyond that I would expect to find from someone living a farm life. More surprising to me is the correctness of your sentences— you speak very well according to those bastard rules I referred to. I do not have to teach you any of the rules of the English language—you already know and use them in your speech. It is part of what I meant by knowing things you didn't know you knew.

'So our job is quite easy, really. I will show you how to spell and write what you already say. That means we first need to know the alphabet. We need to be able to write each individual letter and know what each one sounds like. When you know that, you will then be able to take each letter in order to make the word you want to write. You will get to a stage where you will say a word and you will hear each of the letters needed to write that word down on paper. It will only come with practice and repetition. Have I made sense so far? Have you understood what we need to do?'

'Yes, Herman, but you have made it sound simpler than I fear it will be.'

'I hope not. So to the alphabet and what it looks like. Twenty-six letters in their own order going from A to Z. Watch over my shoulder as I write and say each letter.' He sat and wrote A, saying aloud, 'A.'

'I know the ABC,' Matilda said behind him.

'What! Good Lord!' He bounced up from his chair, excited. 'Say it to me. Please say it to me, in your own time.' Matilda thought for only a short time, then beautifully recited the entire alphabet without hesitation. Herman just stood there, his mouth gaping. Finally words came to him. 'How can you know it? You said you had no schooling—how did you learn it?'

'I made a good friend in the family I worked for in Lyme Regis. I was there to be her companion, and in return, she decided to teach me to read and write. That was the first time I have said it from before John was born. We only got as far as doing the ABC though.'

'Can you write it as well?' he asked in anticipation.

'I used to be able to,' she replied, sitting at the table to try. She got herself comfortable and picked up the pencil. 'A,' she muttered, gripping the pencil nervously. Slowly the letter was drawn and she looked at it, unsure. She wrote another A. 'Better,' she murmured again, and looked up to Herman for assurance.

'I would have accepted the first one,' he reassured her. 'Carry on with the rest, as best you can without stopping or repeating one to do it better.' He walked away from her so she could concentrate on her own, and stood looking out the window. Sometimes there were long pauses while she said the letter she was up to several times, trying to conjure back to her mind what it looked like. Finally he heard her say 'Zed' and give a sigh. He turned to her then, and she looked up.

'I have done it as I remember it—is it right?' He walked over, trying to suppress his excitement that she had got this completely right as well. He took the page and checked her work.

'When did you last write the alphabet, Matilda? Have you written it since being in Lyme Regis? What? Seven years ago, John is seven now, isn't he?' He was looking at letters that were evenly constructed and spaced, better than he had seen in a long time. Matilda just nodded her reply, not sure if she had done it correctly or not. 'Your friend must be a meticulous person, she set a high standard of tidiness and clarity of letter formation. Have you not practised at all since being here?'

'No, not once. Is it good enough?'

'Good Lord!' he said, finally lowering the page to look at her. 'My dear, this is quite amazing, I did not expect to be at this stage for months. Very well done, Matilda, very well done, indeed!' He stood, beaming a huge smile at her.

'Thank you,' she said pleased that she had got it right. 'I feel quite exhausted from the effort.'

'Quite so! Now for the next step, I have only brought with me material to help you learn the alphabet—I never expected this,' he said, looking again at her page of writing. He pointed out a few of the letters. 'Some show your hesitancy of remembering how they were shaped.' He picked up the pencil and wrote beside them. 'This is how these ones need to be, touching here, and here.' He showed her the slight differences that made them correct. 'I think you may be holding the pencil too tightly, trying to squeeze the life out of it.' He gave her the pencil and took another page. 'Start again on this page.' She held the pencil in a tight grip again. 'Softer,' he said, leaning down and loosening her index finger. 'Have all your fingers that tight.' She tried it, but the pencil wobbled. 'Just a bit tighter.' She tried again. 'Feel comfortable with it,' he said, and let her write some more. Finally he stopped her. 'That is very well done. I think enough for today. I want you to practise writing the alphabet; at the end of every row put the pencil down and pick it up to start the new line. That way you will get used to holding it with the right pressure, and you will not slowly tighten your grip as you would over many lines. I want you to write the letters more quickly, but not lose anything of their shape. I want them to be as tidy as your first effort, but take half the time. Will you do that?'

'Yes, Herman.'

'When you feel confident for the next lesson, get John to let me know.' He smiled broadly at his pupil. Then a thought struck him. 'Better have him tell me that you have some clotted cream for us. It may sound silly, but we don't want all and sundry knowing you are having lessons to learn to read and write. Most think you already can, you know.'

'How much do I owe you for the lesson? We didn't discuss that before we started.'

'Pay me? Why, in clotted cream, of course. Yours is by far the best we have ever tasted. A pot per lesson. Agreed?'

'No, two pots each time. You underestimate your service.'

'Done! But you underestimate your ability to learn.'

He happily left her with his payment in clotted cream, eager to tell his wife of the unexpected abilities of his new pupil.

'Frances! Frances!' he called as he strode through to the kitchen. 'You will never believe it! She even began with the letter A inset from the margin as though starting a new paragraph, each letter even across the page, each in straight columns down the page. Her hand is perfect and she has no idea of the ability she has!'

'Be calm, dearest. Were you gentle with her? You didn't go on like you do with the children?'

'I believe not. I rather suspect that I would have been told off if I had.'

She smiled at the likelihood of it, and continued to prepare the meal.

Matilda spent a while each evening practising as she had been instructed. Eventually she felt confident enough to have John tell Mr Bowditch that there was some clotted cream ready for his wife. The next lesson was short: they walked around the farm and he made a list of the things they saw. Barn, cow, gate, grass, tree, and so on, until twenty things were listed. Back inside, he sat her down with pencil and paper.

'I want you to write out this list again, each time picture in your mind what each names. But really think as you write them how those letters make the word, how the sound of each letter fits into an order so the word appears. Do you understand what I am asking?' he asked.

'I believe I do.'

'Very well, when you find you can spell those words and see the letters making the word, I want you to right down two things we saw out there but I haven't written down. There was the wall, and the hedgerow. I want you to write down how you think they should be spelled by listening to how you say the word, then put down the letters to make that word. Let me know when you are ready.'

He left her, hoping he had not taken a too big a step for her.

Matilda had many interruptions with her lessons, often becoming dispirited because words were not spelled as they sounded. She became frustrated at the combination of letters making different sounds, and sometimes the same letters in different words making different sounds. More than once the page was screwed up and thrown across the room, and she would storm out in frustration. On occasion Herman would arrive unasked, concerned at the passage of time since the last lesson. The lessons were getting further apart.

She told no one what she was doing. Her frustration at wanting to learn yet being unable to do so at the pace she wanted to was pulling her into a silent gloom. Herman noticed and made each lesson shorter and easier, hoping for her enthusiasm to return. Mrs Beamish noticed her lack of confidence and subdued attitude, and rejoiced at the apparent beginning of Matilda's downfall. Mary noticed it and wondered at her sister's reluctance to talk. Dick felt it, and eventually told Madeline something was not right with Miss M.

Madeline wasted no time in getting over to see Matilda for herself.

'What's wrong, Matilda? What has happened?' She asked bluntly. She could see Matilda composing an answer that would cover the truth and added angrily, 'Dick told me there is something wrong with you. Don't ever try and tell me Dick is wrong! We both know he would not be, and we both know it has got to a worrying stage for him to come and tell me, and then tell me to come and see you and not come himself. So we both know that he knows he cannot help you himself this time. So tell me, Matilda, if only for Dick's sake—you owe him that!' She defied Matilda to do anything but tell her the full story.

Matilda looked to her old friend, and tears began to run down her face. Without a word, she rose and went to the desk, opened it and took out some pages. Silently she handed them to Madeline, then went to the window.

'I have been beaten, I have failed to do something I need to do for my children. I am now afraid that I will not be able to help them as I should. I am afraid that I will lose them, or they will fail because of me. People like Mrs Beamish will have their victory over me after all, believing that children like mine should stay out of school and remain on farms as lowly labourers like their unmarried parents do.' She caught her breath with a sob. 'My children deserve better than that.'

Madeline was looking at the pages of letters and words, at the misspelled but phonetically correct lists.

'Have you done all this?' Madeline quietly asked. 'Does anyone know?'

'No one knows. Mr Bowditch, the school master, has been trying to teach me for months. It was good at the beginning, but then I just stopped learning. I cannot understand spelling, I cannot understand how the same letters in groups can make different sounds in different words. Or how different letters make the same sound in other words. I was so sure I could do it, but now I have forgotten what I had learnt to begin with. I am confused, and now I am making mistakes elsewhere. I even left a gate open yesterday, and Joshua had to bring some cows in from the lane. What if Jacob found out? I could lose my place on the farm. Dick said to me before Matilda was born that my baby would bring changes, that people would be nasty and I would need help. Now it's happening.'

Madeline went to her and hugged her, thinking, *No wonder Dick sent me instead of coming himself—he knew what Matilda was doing was beyond his understanding.*

'Why didn't you say something? You know that Mary and I will always help you. Why didn't you ask?'

'I wanted to be able to show you when when I could, I wanted you to know when I handed you a letter I had written. It was to have been a secret surprise. Now I know it will never happen.'

Madeline went and picked the pages up and read them again. 'I think you will get there, I think you have done more than you think you have. I can remember that I was a better reader than writer; I often misspelled what I had just read. Bit by bit, letters and sounds started to make sense. I would always get some things right, and always some things wrong. It took a long time for the things I got wrong to get less, and to do more things right. And you have done all this in only months, while I was years at school learning. Didn't Mr Bowditch ever say how long it would take?'

'No, I never thought it of it either. I thought it would be like the farm, where everything happens within a year—each season has its own events, all events are complete within the twelve months. I thought learning would happen the same, but now I'm going backwards.'

'Learning never stops, I learn all the time. Aren't you the one who is going to put corn in here for the first time? Isn't that learning? Are you expecting to get a bumper yield the first year?'

'I do not know how good the crop will be, I can only hope it will be sufficient to make it worthwhile. But I do not expect it to fail,' she replied.

'That is my point exactly. Learning is the same—you work to get a worthwhile result. It may take years to get really good results, same as at school. No one is at school for just one year and has learnt it all, it takes years. You need to understand that it will take years for you to get really good at reading and writing. Mr Bowditch was very naughty in not explaining that at the beginning.'

Matilda could not hide her smile and look of gratitude. The thought of Mr Bowditch being very naughty was indeed a funny thought.

'It's just that I have never taken so long to understand anything,' she said, feeling better.

'You have never had to learn anything as complicated as the English language before. Did he not say it would be hard?'

'He did say it was a bastard language with jumbled rules,' Matilda said, using the word that always made her cringe.

Jumbled is not half of what I will give him, Madeline thought to herself.

'We must tell Mary—she has to know what you are doing, otherwise she will just keep on worrying why you are out of sorts. Get the sherry out—we are going to drink a toast to the success you already have achieved in your lessons, and to the many more that you will have to come.'

'Sherry! It is only eleven o'clock in the morning!'

'Sherry! You deserve the honours!'

And indeed, they toasted the honours well.

Herman glanced out of the classroom window and excused himself to see who the stranger was.

'Herman Bowditch, school master. How may I help you?' he said as he walked up to Madeline.

She stood and looked straight at him. 'I am Madeline, an old friend of Matilda's.' He saw in her eye the glint of hardness she had for the defence for her friend. 'You are teaching her to read and write.' He was astounded that Matilda would have told anyone. 'You failed to tell her it would take a long time. She expected to be totally competent within the year, as she is with everything else she does. She is now floundering with all she faces because she feels she has failed in what you are teaching her. You have to rectify that this afternoon, before Matilda loses her confidence any further, particularly with her children, but on the farm as well. She must suffer her loss of confidence no longer. Have I made myself clear?'

Herman was shocked at the revelation.

'Of course, ma'am. Of course. How did I not see it?' But the conversation was over, as Madeline had turned and was walking away while her courage held. She felt herself shaking from the tension inside her, afraid he might call her back for her temerity in speaking to him like that, for she was still afraid of men, particularly strangers. *Where are you, Dick?* she thought as she headed up the hill towards Carters Cross. *I need your strength—if only you could feel for me as you do with Matilda.*

She had no need to worry. He was waiting for her barely a mile along the road.

Chapter 25

1850–1851: The Letter

It was over three tumultuous weeks in late summer that Matilda was fully restored to her confident self. That ever-present smile twitched again at the corners of her mouth, the sparkle in her eye that hinted of secrets she knew and that the gossips didn't, but yearned to.

It began with the birth of Henry, welcomed with delight into the world by Mary and Richard. They were delighted to have him, and delighted more that he would be the last.

'Six children are enough, anyway,' Mary told Matilda later. 'I can't have any more. Richard says that's a challenge to prove the doctor wrong, once things have healed. I fancy he thinks he will be performing more often—I wonder if he can keep up with me?'

'Mary!' Matilda exclaimed. 'You shouldn't talk like that!'

'I doubt very much if your Richard gets much rest from you when he arrives!' She slyly dug her sister in the ribs.

'Mary!' Matilda exclaimed in embarrassment again. 'Don't say such things!' She blushed furiously in the face of her sister's accurate statement.

After church that Sunday, the curate said to Matilda that he was looking for boys to join the choir. Would she allow John to join, and perhaps his cousin as well? She accepted on the spot, as John showed immediate interest at the idea.

'Excellent!' he joyfully said. 'That's five. Jacob's lad is coming, as well as James Small's two boys. That is splendid, first practice after school on Wednesday. Under Tony's supervision, of course. So good to see a continuation of family support in the congregation. Don't you think, Tony?' he added as Tony walked past with his wife.

'What is it that I think, Curate?' Tony asked impishly, and his wife Susan tugged at his sleeve, telling him in a loud whisper to behave himself in front of the curate.

'That we have three good families with boys for the choir. Young John White here with his cousin, Jacob French and his lad Samuel, and Timothy and John Small. All yours after school on Wednesday—perhaps your lovely wife would like to help organise them as well?'

'Oh, I see,' said Tony with a cheeky smile to Matilda. 'I have a choir made up of Small White French boys!'

'Tony!' Susan scolded him, 'that is not the right thing to say!' But Matilda could not help but chuckle, and the curate set off to repeat the new name for the boys' choir. In total innocence, the first group he told included Mrs Beamish. She bristled with indignation at a further inclusion of 'that woman's' children in the church, a reaction that Matilda saw, and it lifted her spirits even further.

Mary Rapsey, the victualler at the Tuckers Arms, saw it all as she passed them by, and she gave Matilda a hearty smile. 'I think that puts you back ahead!' she said, nodding back to where Mrs Beamish stood as though rooted to the spot. 'Can't stop, must open up for lunch trade and beat those two reprobates to the door!' Matilda turned and saw Robert Pike and John North watching Mary's progress toward her inn over the road. Both had their caps replaced firmly on their heads, hands in pockets and a look of thirst in their eye, following the morning's service.

'Thank goodness some things never change.' she thought.

Hannah arrived on the Wednesday, full of excitement, and was more so to find her friend restored to her usual cheerful self.

'The most amazing thing has happened!' She couldn't wait to begin to tell Matilda her news. 'Father has arranged an endowment for me! I'm to have my inheritance now. He thinks that I have limited my opportunities of finding a husband or establishing my independence by staying at home, helping look after Mother, and running the household. He and his brother have given me a block of shares in their company, James Hill and Sons. I can sell them back to them over the next two years in equal lots at the end of six-month intervals. What I do with the money is up to me, and they are both full of ideas of what I can invest in that would be more interesting to me than timber. Uncle James said that by making it four separate payments I can't lose it all at once if I make a bad choice! But it is such a lot of money, Matilda, more than I realised would ever be mine. I have no need to have to work now when

Mother and Father go.' She finally took a breath, her face alight with excitement and confidence with the knowledge that her future was safe.

'That is very good news, Hannah. I am delighted for you, and I am so pleased that your father has made these plans for you now.' She gave her a hug, thinking back on the conversation she had had with John when he visited, what now seemed so long ago.

'It's more than enough to live on—I could buy a dress shop if I wanted. Imagine me owning the shop instead of buying everything in it for my own wardrobe! I've started reading the newspapers for properties and interest rates—it all needs to be put in safe investments, as it will be two thousand pounds in all. I'll show Uncle James that I will not lose any!'

'Be prepared for him to be right,' Matilda said warily. 'You cannot be too careful. I have lost money on what I thought was safe. I bought a fine heifer from a good line of cows, but the one I bought never came into season, she never calved. A cow that doesn't have calves is no use to a farmer and I lost that money on her. It is very easy to lose money, even with the most honest intentions of all those involved. With that amount of money, you had better be prepared for very good-sounding offers to be anything but. You will be better to leave it in your banking account if you are not absolutely sure.'

By now Hannah had a huge smile on her face, barely suppressing laughter.

'What have I said that's so funny?' Matilda asked her, puzzled.

'It's just that you sound so much like Father. You have said what he did, almost word for word!' And they both laughed at that.

'Is there no man in sight for you yet, then? There will be if they know how rich you are!'

'None of any interest at all,' Hannah replied, with hardly a touch of sadness. 'I don't think much on it, actually. I was never happier than while you were with us and I had your company, and I strangely have not yearned to have your company replaced by a suitor. There is time enough yet.' She dismissed the subject as unimportant.

'Heard from Richard lately?' Matilda asked hopefully.

'Yes, just last week, or rather Father did. The people Richard wrote to to do the extension have approved the work and have given a grant of eighty pounds. Richard was frustrated that the grant was so small when he had applied for a hundred and seventy-five pounds and ten shillings, as they already had five hundred and thirty pounds that he had raised. Father has written to him to just get on with it and enclosed an order for the balance. It will take three years to complete the enlargements. Can you imagine how magnificent the church will look then?'

'It will be a church that Richard deserves—he is going to be extraordinarily happy with it,' she said. 'How is your mother?'

'You need to visit her again—she had a terrible seizure last week, I thought it would never stop, and she slept so long after it. It was so cruel having to watch and be unable to help. It was fortunate that Father was away with Uncle James at the time and did not have to witness it. He seems to take it personally, as though it is his fault that she suffers. He has become quite intolerant of outsiders who come to the house. A vestry member came to the house last week and sat staring at the door as though he expected Mother to come charging through it and attack him in a mad frenzy. Father virtually threw him out of the house as soon as his business was done. "That man is an ignorant fool" he told me later. "He is not to come into this house again!" If Father keeps this up, we will have no visitors at all!'

'What about her tea-party ladies? Do they still visit her?'

'Oh yes, "the widows", as Father calls them, come every second Sunday. Five of them are regulars and are very good for her, but you are different. She seems invigorated after your visit, so could you make it soon?'

Matilda did. She was saddened at Sarah's deterioration and wondered how long it could go on for. But Sarah's disposition in Matilda's presence did not reflect that of an ill woman—she chattered gaily on many topics, delighted that Matilda was there. She told Matilda that her two grandsons had left on their voyage to New Zealand. John was hoping that they would return in years to come, as fine, mature young men, having made their fortune in the colonies, and ready to take over the family business. Neither of them ever returned to England, preferring to stay in the new land, to raise their families there.

Barely three weeks after Henry's birth, Matilda started to make sense with spelling. While Herman watched, she wrote her first complete sentence correctly. Herman whooped for joy, his arms flapping in the air like a seagull trying to take off. In his euphoria with Matilda's breakthrough, he rushed off home to tell Frances of the success, leaving the clotted cream behind.

He rather meekly returned the following afternoon to collect it and continue the lesson.

Matilda felt now that she would succeed in the end, rarely ever again dejected at making spelling mistakes, or annoyed at the slowness of

217

grasping the principles of spelling, even though it would be another year before she could write that letter to Madeline, and even longer before her spelling ability approached her vocabulary.

Instead of Madeline being given the surprise, it was Hannah who was handed a letter when she visited Matilda that following year. Hannah looked at the vaguely familiar handwriting on the folded sheet of paper that had her name on it. When she opened it and began to read, realisation hit her.

'My God! Matilda! You have done it!' Tears ran down her face in joy at her friend's achievement. 'Father is going to be very proud, and Richard, have you written to him yet?'

'No,' she said, 'no one. I need you to write down his address for the envelope. I do not know how to do that yet.'

'Give me an envelope, and I will write his address on it, as I do when I write to him. If you keep this one, then you will always have one to copy from so you can keep on writing to him. What a surprise he is going to be in for!'

'I don't have any envelopes. I never thought I would have a use for them. I learnt so I could help my children.'

'I will send some to you, along with some nice writing paper. I will address two envelopes, one for Richard and one for Father. You must write to Richard immediately—I will tell no one, it will be a big surprise for them all.'

The next week, in November 1851, the very first letter arrived bearing the address,

> Miss M. White
> Dalwood Hill
> Axminster
> Devon.

Matilda sat and held it, unopened, amazed that such an event could happen. When she finally opened it, she found the addresses as Hannah had promised with a short note beseeching her to write to Richard quickly, as she was not sure she could refrain from telling everyone of Matilda's new-found ability to read and write.

It took Matilda twelve days to write her letter to Richard. When it was finished she had a list of words she was not sure of the spelling and asked Herman to check them. He corrected only two.

'Now I can write my letter properly—thank you, Herman,' she said proudly.

Almost without thinking, he asked, 'Who are you writing to?'

But Matilda froze at the question, her fear at having to answer palpable.

'A friend,' she quietly answered. 'Just a friend.' She avoided his enquiring gaze. He looked over at her table and saw Hannah's addressed envelopes and it dawned on him who the recipient was to be. He gently took her arm and lifted her face to look at her.

'My dear, if you are writing to the man I think you are, then you must not post the letters from the village. There is not a soul who knows who the children's father is, but if you hand that letter over the counter, the whole village will soon know. You cannot allow that to happen.'

Matilda almost wept. After all the effort to learn to write, and the joy of being able to now write to Richard, it was all in vain. She couldn't post them.

'I will post it in Axminster! They don't know me there,' she exclaimed in relief. 'But it will have to wait until Thursday week. I don't go in often.'

'Other people do—I know the ghastly Mrs Beamish for one posts her letters in Axminster. She doesn't want our local man knowing who she writes to. It would be just your luck to be in there at the same time.'

Matilda's excitement subsided again. 'It's not fair—what am I to do?'

Herman rubbed his chin in thought. 'Well,' he said, 'I could do it for you. Frances and I have quite a lot of correspondence for all sorts of things, and we could include it in a bundle of ours. That way it would pass through unnoticed. Frances writes with a fairly round hand like yours. Would you trust me with it?'

'Yes, Herman, of course,' Matilda said, relief flooding through her.

From her first letter to Richard to her last, Herman dutifully fulfilled his role, and never at any stage was the ploy discovered.

Richard was tired from a frustrating day of dealing with builders and obtuse parishioners. He looked at the pile of letters on his desk that he hadn't touched and thought of going through it in the morning. He flicked at the envelopes and pulled one out, recognising his father's hand. The next one down had an unfamiliar style, with very correct and open lettering. Out of curiosity, he opened it and read.

An hour later he sat there still, the letter in his hand, and he re-read it yet again, the tears flowing down his cheeks. She had written in an almost formal way, telling him of events since he was last there. It was hardly a letter from a lover at all, but he had cried from the first two words.

The letter began 'My Richard', and his hands had dropped to his desk in shock. He read those words over and over, before he progressed into the rest, and read it in its entirety. Then he read it all again. Her news in the letter barely registered—his mind was pounding with the incredible revelation that she had learnt to write, that she was now able to read. He couldn't stop himself thinking over and over, 'if only'. If only she could have done this ten years ago, things would be so very much different. They would be married, she would be living in this house with him, with their two children. It would be a home. 'If only,' he said aloud, and read the letter again. As he read this time he could hear her saying the words as she wrote, could hear the pride in her voice at conquering such an impossible task. Her pleasure in being able to help John with his school work, and the pride that their daughter, still two years from attending school, would be literate. She would be able to help her learn and grow up into a world that had opportunities that Matilda herself had only dreamt of till now. The letter was one of joy and promise for their children, with never a hint of what might have been. No trace of 'if only'. He suddenly felt abashed by his own selfish thoughts of what could have been, embarrassed by his envy of what they had missed out on.

He put the letter to one side and reached for a clean sheet of paper. But instead of writing a reply to Matilda, he wrote the most powerful and stern sermon he was ever to deliver. He wrote of one person's achievements and its effect on others close to them, he wrote of envy and jealousy and their wasted emotions, of missed opportunities and the need to leave them behind. He wrote of acceptance of others' achievements and the responsibility of each individual to attain their own level of excellence and not complain or be jealous of those missed chances.

He prayed most fervently that he could at some point in his lifetime achieve as much as Matilda had against the odds, by writing those two pages. He wanted to tell his father and started to write to him. Words failed him, and in the end he sent him a letter of just three words.

'Matilda can write.'

It was four days before he could settle and write a composed reply to her. He placed her letter in the endpapers of the big old Bible that lay on the shelf behind him.

John had also received a letter from Matilda, equally formal and with much on her children. There was some on the farm and the results of planting the corn the previous year. She would not do it again, she said, for although it yielded a quite reasonable crop, and the price was better than she expected, it used too much land for too much of the growing season. She had to buy in hay from some of the profits of the corn, as she hadn't produced enough herself because of the corn field. Ploughing and resowing the field back to productive pasture had used the last of the corn's profit.

John, like Richard, sat in his study and reread the letter several times in total amazement. Finally he went up to Sarah's room with it. The strange look on his face as he entered made her ask nervously, 'What is it, dear?' He silently handed her the letter, and sat while she read. Slowly, very slowly, a smile began to play on her lips and a tear welled in her eye. She read it again. 'Will she ever stop surprising us?' she asked.

'I would not have thought it possible for her to learn. What will Richard be thinking? She would have written to him first.'

'Dear John, your son will be thinking the same as you are. If only she had always been able to write, they would be married now. That is not what she is saying in her letter, she is only talking of what lies ahead, not what may have been.'

'I have seen her on Jacob's farm—it is her world, as the church is Richard's. She even said as much to me, that to have married Richard would have been wonderful, but a part of her would forever be farming with her beloved cows. Matilda has accepted how she must live, but I very much doubt that Richard will be as settled once he receives her letter.'

'Richard is at times too stuffy for his own good,' his mother said. 'He is quite secure in Timsbury, he just needs a proper wife, as Matilda readily agrees. By comparison, how secure is Matilda on someone else's land?'

'Safe enough. I have spoken with Jacob, and he says she can stay there as long as she likes. For ever, hopefully. She tends the land very well. She does own the cottage, she has that security.'

'For someone who has taken bold steps to ensure the future of your other grandchildren, you seem to be taking a big chance with these two. John and little Matilda are equally our grandchildren, even though they be out of wedlock. What are you going to do to secure their future? It is stunningly obvious that Matilda is going to extraordinary efforts to help provide for them a better future—and all that you are going to do is ask Jacob to keep her on! She and the children deserve much more than that!'

'What else can I do? He has clearly stated that she is safe there.'

'Sometimes, John Hill, for all the businessman that you are, you cannot see the obvious. Jacob is happy for Matilda to be there because he doesn't

221

need it, she keeps it tidy for him and he derives a small income from it. At some stage there will be another farmer who does need it and will offer Jacob enough to make it worth his while to sell. What of Matilda then? How safe are our grandchildren when that happens, as it surely will? Can she support them on just four acres?'

'That is beyond our hands. I will face that situation when and if it arises. What else would you have me do?'

'Really, John! You do exasperate me at times. You must buy the farm first, then Matilda and the children will be truly safe.'

He sat quietly, thinking on the possibilities of it. Sarah would not let him rest. 'It will cost you nothing compared with what you are spending in getting the boys to New Zealand, and the land you are paying for out there. It will only compare with one wall of the church extension for Richard, and would hardly make a dent in what you are giving Hannah. It would not surprise me in the least if Hannah didn't go and buy the farm herself for Matilda, if she were to be made aware of all the facts.'

'Very well! Very well!' John reacted. 'Let me think on it, there may be a way. But not a word to anyone, particularly not to Hannah!'

He rose and left the room, rubbing his forehead as though trying to conjure a solution. Sarah watched him go and smiled. *Well, Matilda,* she thought, *perhaps I have managed to do something for you this time. That would be nice.* And she settled down for another fitful sleep.

Chapter 26

1852–1853: A Future Assured

The autumn seemed never to end. Balmy days with only blustery winds hinted of a winter late in arriving. Then, in three days at the beginning of December, it arrived, making up for lost time. The wind continued unabated, driving a freezing snow into every crevice, blowing doors open, flurries of snow reaching far inside, and robbing the warmth from the house. Animals huddled in barns to keep some warmth, and cold hands milked reluctant cows. Hay was brought from lofts to sombre stock that were reluctant to move from a warm position to eat out of necessity. When they did eat, it was to produce their own warmth, not milk. Clothing and boots quickly became saturated, giving little protection and barely getting dry before the stove overnight, before being pulled on again in the morning, to check on the stock.

Christmas came and went without much joy, fresh drifts of snow blocking lanes to those who intended to attend the day's special services, and forcing folk to stay indoors. Then the wind stopped suddenly, and a clammy calmness and quiet hid the menace of the plummeting temperature. The weight of the freezing snow broke branches from trees and a babbling brook froze solid. It was the bleakest start to a new year, that was a week old before there was any sign of people venturing beyond their farms.

A week before Charles found his parents dead, frozen before a dead fireplace. Another two days before he, or anyone else, could get out of the Umbourne valley and up the hill over to Dalwood to tell Mary, Matilda and Ann of their parents' passing. There were several deaths, and not just of the elderly, that winter. More funerals were held than any other service over the next two weeks. John and Mary White's funeral was as sombre as the rest, and was attended by few other than family. The vicar at their service in Shute had become immune to emotion, their funeral a repetition of the one just finished, another to be conducted that afternoon. He knew them all, but he was drained of sorrow.

Charles and William emptied the old cottage of their parents' last belongings and left Shute Marsh Farm for the last time, leaving it clean enough for the next farm labourer to begin his new job.

'I wish whoever it be well,' William said to his brother. 'It served us all well enough—we had our share of laughs here, dornnee reckon, brother?'

'Aye,' Charles replied, unable to hide the tears of sadness for his parents. He turned and led his horse, with its laden cart, away.

It was the end of January before Jacob came up to see how Matilda had faired, almost six weeks from his last visit, and unaware of her parents' death. There was only one consolation that they were grateful for: if Matilda had grown the corn in the last season, and not the year before as she had, then she would have been desperately short of winter fodder and would have had no way of getting any more. Not having to face the consequences of deciding which of her treasured stock to slaughter gave both of them some little comfort.

There was almost unheralded jubilation when, at last, the first of the spring bulbs poked their green tips through the snow, the first sign of colour in long, drab months. Herman ventured the furthest first. Having cleared the school building of snow, he was out rounding up his pupils.

'We begin classes on Monday.' His booming voice could be heard from farm to farm. 'I got up to you, you can therefore come down to me! There are to be no excuses, school has been closed far too long and there are lessons to be caught up on. Come along.' He called on each child personally.

Not a child was absent on Monday, which didn't surprise Herman— he knew there wouldn't be a mother anywhere that wouldn't be pleased to have her child out from under her feet after such a long confinement in the house.

Within the week, the bulbs were in bloom and colour sprang from the hedgerows. Birds sang, and the sun began to shine again. Farmers ventured around their land, clearing drains on their sodden fields. Life started to resume normality at last.

The last of Matilda's gloom lifted when she heard his voice calling from the gate.

'Matilda! Matilda! Where are you?' She dropped the fork and ran out to greet him.

'My Richard!' she called, and flung herself into his arms, eventually releasing him to tether his horse and care for it. 'I'm mucking out the barn, come and help, I won't be long.' But Joshua came quietly to her side.

'I be finishing here if you like, Miss Matilda. I be doing feeding then, just milking later I be needing your help for, if you want to talk with your gentleman visitor,' and he moved off, not looking over at the visitor, not wanting to be able to say who had come by, should he be questioned at a later date.

Richard smiled at Joshua's absolute loyalty to Matilda.

'Thank you, Joshua,' she said to him just as quietly, going on into the cottage with Richard.

'I could wait no longer to see you! Your letter was the biggest surprise of my life—I am so very proud of you. Mother and Father run a close second, and Hannah has kept it a secret for so long. My word! You have certainly created a buzz within the family. How did you learn?' He stopped, breathless, beaming with pride at her.

'The school master, a Mr Herman Bowditch, taught me in secret—no one found out. It was the most terrifying thing I have ever done. It nearly beat me, there were times when none of it made sense, but my friends helped me through. I did it for the children, but mainly for our Matilda. I will be able to help her when she goes to school, where she will be taught properly. She will not be left to grow up with my handicap, I will not allow it! I have missed out on many things and I see no good reason why she should as well. Fortunately, Herman is of the opinion that it is important that girls are educated as well as boys, and that all children should attend school.'

'He sounds like a man ahead of his times—many think it, but few will do much to try to achieve it. You are lucky to have a teacher of such vision.'

Little Matilda came screaming out the door as they approached, with her brother in hot pursuit.

'No! No! You can't have it!' she squealed, and almost collided with Richard. They both came to a sudden halt at seeing him.

'Oh,' said John, not sure how to proceed. 'Good morning, sir,' he offered, hoping to have picked the best response at being caught chasing his sister inside, when he had been told many times not to.

'He's chasing me, Mother!' Matilda put in, hoping to shift blame while holding the evidence of why she was being chased behind her back.

'Good morning, young man,' Richard said. 'Good morning, Matilda.'

'What have you got?' Matilda asked her daughter, knowing where the cause of the problem lay.

'Nothing,' the little girl replied as her brother took his toy from her hand, and they both sidled back inside.

'Children!' Matilda said, exasperated. But they were well gone, knowing that their mother would allow their escape so she could spend her time with her visitor.

Ann made them tea as they told of each other's news. Richard reported on the progress of the church extensions, Matilda on the farm, of her visit to his mother, and his father's visit in the autumn, some four months ago. An odd visit, she told Richard, for although his father had been very interested in what she was doing, he had seemed more interested to be on his way to see Jacob French before setting off home.

Richard tried to show no alarm at this, for he knew very well what his father had in mind, and the purpose of his visit to Jacob. He wondered how Matilda would take the change of circumstances when John told her, and wondered why he had not already done so. He knew very well that ultimately his father was working on separating them for good, and having him married off with a legitimate family, so why was he delaying telling her his decision, now that presumably everything was in place?

'What are you thinking? Your mind just went out the door,' Matilda asked.

'Oh nothing really, just something for the future, too early to say yet,' was Richard's weak reply.

'I don't mind your surprises,' she said, not convinced that he was revealing all he knew. He smiled at her, thinking that she was not going to like this surprise.

'The real surprise, my dear, is your learning to read and write. Not something I would have considered possible, I have never known an adult to learn. It is a most extraordinary feat, and I love you for it. Your first letter was a revelation—I have read it many times, and still weep.'

'Oh you silly man, there is no need for that. I have written to your mother quite often, sometimes only a page, though.'

'Yes, she has told me. Many times! She gets so much from them— even if only you were to send her half a page, she would be grateful. Always keep her up to date with what the children are doing, and the animals, particularly your favourite cow. It makes her feel involved, as though she still matters. I'm afraid that she gets very low at times.'

'Poor thing, I shall try to write to her each month, there is always plenty to tell her—it's just that when I do write, I seem to be short on time to tell her everything. Hannah fills in most after she has been here to visit. How is Hannah really doing?'

'My dear Matilda, you are a fine one to ask! You would know her better than all of us. She has always told you more, and shared more secrets with you than anyone. Father feels he learns more from you about her than he does living in the same house with her!'

'There are times when I think she is missing out on life. Is there no man calling on her?'

'None. There have been enough knocking on the door, but they don't get much of a welcome, so they don't come back. She seems quite content not to have to worry about men in her life. She is so very involved with the household, running some of Father's affairs, and looking at investments with her own finances.'

'I'm very glad of that.'

Richard laughed. 'You should be! Father told me of your thoughts on the matter—he would never have done anything for her if you hadn't put the idea to him. Good heavens! I quite forgot! I have a note for you from him.' He pulled a letter from an inside pocket and handed it to her. He watched her as she read it slowly, carefully taking in each word as though she was still astonished she could read, and finding her new-found ability an exciting venture.

'He is coming by next week. That is nice, seeing the two of you so close together.' They chattered on, time slipping quickly by, and Richard finally had to take his leave.

John didn't arrive until the end of March, and then in the company of Jacob. She saw them riding down from the furthest field across Mount Pleasant, with Jacob pointing here and there as they approached.

'Good afternoon, Matilda,' John called brightly when they got to the home gate. 'Came by Jacob on my way here—he is very happy with how you managed your way through that horrendous winter. Are you equally pleased?'

'Hello John,' she said, pleased to see him and hear that Jacob was happy with her work. 'Hello Jacob—we haven't seen so much of you since the thaw.'

'Aye, no lass. Been as much clearing and putting right downalong as up here, I guess.' He mumbled his farewell to them both and rode on.

'Looks like you could do with some hot tea,' Matilda said to John. 'Come on in. How is Sarah?'

'She is very well, and thank you for your letters to her, truly great medicine for her.' He pulled off his riding boots and followed her into the kitchen in his stockinged feet, to sit at the table. Little Matilda came in and quite nonchalantly went and climbed onto his lap and told him of the baby rabbits in the back field. He sat listening, bemused at the confidence of the child.

'She will be attending school in May, although she will not be six until September. Mr Bowditch wants to begin a class for new children then, with them all starting on the same day. He feels it is easier for them to begin together as a group, with no stragglers coming in at odd times. I have to say it can't come soon enough—she has too much energy for Ann and me. Herman can give us some peace!'

'You have done well with them. I am delighted that she will go to school—your school master has quite a modern approach to education, it seems. Jacob told me much of your winter. How well are you placed now, with so much of your reserves depleted?'

'We are well placed. Richard still always leaves a small purse behind when he has been. I have told him it is not necessary, but he insists. "Just in case," he always says. "For the children." The farm is going well—I was very lucky last summer with a very good growth for hay, and that got us through the winter. If I had tried the corn last year, I would have been in all sorts of trouble and short of winter fodder. Although there was a temptation to carry a couple more cows last year, it's as well we didn't, for we could not have kept them through the winter. I may keep two more pigs from this litter though, they will add to the pantry for next winter. I will need to build a bigger sty for them to do it properly though.' She talked on enthusiastically on the coming year, then as openly on Richard's coming year, and the progress of the church extensions. Like everything else, it had come to a halt during the harsh winter months.

John listened carefully to it all, baffled as to how Matilda could discuss Richard's separate life in Timsbury so proudly. It was very clear to him that she saw no possibility that they would ever live together as man and wife, and that both would continue their own lives, a county apart.

But it was equally clear from both of them that their love for each other was still strong. He had no concerns for Matilda and her ability to continue successfully on the farm, but he did have concerns for Richard and his ability to continue as rector, with his separate family, who he clearly loved, and his inner turmoil of conflicting morals with his relationship with Matilda and his standing in the church. John watched Matilda as she worked in the kitchen, aware of the debt he owed her for her time in helping Hannah become the responsible adult she was now, and the comfort that she gave Sarah. The undiminished support she showed Sarah was enormously effective on Sarah's emotional stability. With such a debt, how could he proceed and stop Richard and Matilda from seeing each other again? But how else could he force Richard into a proper respectable marriage? He had done all the preparatory work, the legal documents were being drawn up ready for signing. But he was unable to tell her what was about to happen.

'You have gone quiet, John—is everything all right with Sarah?' said Matilda, afraid that she had fallen further behind. He was grateful of her misinterpretation of his silence.

'She is as well as when you saw her last. It is just that there are many family issues to be settled and my mind wandered, I do apologise. The boys have settled well in New Zealand—Richard is in control of their finances and will make monies available as suitable land becomes available to purchase. It takes quite some time for news to come from them, and it would be useful to have quicker communications. Now I must take my leave, but I would like to call again quite soon, as I have business in Axminster to attend to next month. Perhaps as soon as the end of April.'

'I look forward to it—Hannah may be out before that.'

'There is one matter that would give me comfort in knowing. Have you a will written to cover your cottage and what needs to happen should you have an untimely death? You have a valuable asset and the disbursements for your children need to be recorded. Have you done this?'

'No—is it really necessary?'

'Yes, and you need to think of two good people to act on your behalf should something unfortunate happen to you. Who handled the purchase?'

'Charles Bond in Axminster, and it was an old family friend who advised me on how to purchase it.'

'Then they would make excellent executors. With your permission, I will call in on Mr Bond on my way home, and advise him of your needs.'

'Thank you, John, that is kind of you to think of it.'

Matilda's will was written on 22 May 1852, and remained unchanged.

But Hannah did not arrive. She wrote twice, both short notes and a little off hand, Matilda thought; she hoped her friend was not ill. She had little time to dwell on it, as there was much to do on the farm.

Demands were up for her clotted cream from William Edwards in the village store, and old Morgan had got to retiring age and he needed to be replaced with someone younger and able to do a day's work on the farm.

It was surprise when she got a short note from John saying he would like to call on the last Sunday of April. It seemed no time since he had been there last. But when he did arrive, he was in a sombre mood.

'I wonder, Matilda, if Ann could take the children for a walk. There is much that I need to say, and I would prefer if we were not interrupted, as it is all quite complex.' Surprised at his request and his formal approach, she quickly had them away, going to see Mary as a surprise visit. When they had gone, he sat at the kitchen table and took from his coat pocket a bundle of folded pages.

'This will take a while to explain,' he began. 'I will say it all, but please interrupt if you don't understand something, though please hear me out. Last year I told you of my difficulties in sorting out the family. Among my concerns are you and Richard. I was satisfied that you were in a safe position, but that Richard was not making the progress he should, and I had decided that I would put into place a set of circumstances that would separate you two permanently. That has obviously not happened, but some things have. Sarah pointed out to me that your position was not secure, that Jacob could sell this farm at any time, and you would lose all your income. To save that situation from happening, she advised that I should buy the farm myself, and leave Jacob as a sort of guardian over it for you.

'To this end, I purchased the whole of Mount Pleasant estate in the April of last year and swore Jacob to secrecy as to the change of ownership. I requested that he took only an advisory role, leaving the decisions to you. I had several visits with him over the last twelve months to gauge your progress. To say that he was impressed with your standard of work and stock management would be an understatement. My plan was to give you the ownership of the Mount Pleasant estate on the condition that you were no longer ever to see Richard again.'

Matilda paled at his words and was about to speak, but he held his hand up, not wanting to stop now he had started. 'Things have changed over the year, and there are new considerations. It would be fair to say that it is Sarah alone who has changed what is to happen.' He picked up the pages before him. 'This is a debenture. It is a legal document that describes what is to happen with this farm, and how it concerns you and the children.' He opened it out and she saw the pages of writing, some of it in big capitals, and most of it written rather untidily compared with her own hand. Her eye fell on her own name on it. 'It was written up by my solicitor in Bridport, a Mr James Templar. I am afraid that it is difficult to read, as it written in legal terms, and many of the words will not be familiar to you, or to me for that matter! Let me explain it as best I can. It is a document between myself, you, your children Matilda and John, and Richard. I release my ownership of Mount Pleasant to Richard and his heirs, specifically in here, to you and the children. The farm and everything on it, is for your use for the rest of your life, so long as you remain single and unmarried. Young Matilda will receive an annual sum of ten pounds should you die or marry, until she dies or marries. After your death or marriage, young John and his lawful heirs have the use of the farm for ever. Should John not live to be twenty-one and have no lawfully begotten children and you also have died, then the farm returns to Richard for his use, but young Matilda will still receive her ten pounds, and she will have legal rights to claim it if the payments are late arriving. It says a lot about dying, but that is to cover a premature death. What it does say is that the farm is yours for your own use until you die of old age. When that happens, then it is John's until he dies of old age, then it is his legally begotten children, and so it goes on.' He finished and looked up at her. 'Do you follow what it means?'

'Yes,' she very quietly said, quite daunted by the responsibility of the offer. 'I did not know that you have owned the farm for some time. It is a generous thing to do, but does it mean that Richard and I are now stopped from seeing each other? Does it say that? Is that why you are giving the farm to me? So that we are safe and Richard can put real effort into finding a wife, knowing that we are secure down here?' She looked hard at John, demanding a straight answer. He returned her look and put his hand on hers.

'When I bought the land from Jacob last April, it was my intention that he would oversee your work here, and tell me when he felt you could run it on your own. At that time, I was going to give you the farm on the condition that you and Richard were never to meet again. From the day Jacob was paid out last year, he and his wife have had nothing but praise for your ability to run the farm. I made an agreement with them that they would keep the sale quiet and act as advisor only for one year. I wanted to be sure you could do it on your own. Not only have you proved your capability to do so, but you also learnt to read and write, primarily to help your children. You have brought them up very correctly, and you are having them attend school. You have conducted yourself in

231

an exemplary manner, and have never revealed who the father of your children is. You have never asked anything of us or Richard. You have maintained your friendship with Hannah, something that has helped her more than you can possibly imagine, and you have maintained your support with Sarah. I can personally reassure you that your letters and visits have been gratefully accepted by both of us. There is nothing more I can possibly ask of you. There is nothing in this document that requires you not to see Richard again. Sarah is most insistent that such a requirement would be unduly cruel. She is of the opinion that you will not object when he finally finds himself a wife.'

'That is correct. Both Richard and I know that one day he will marry and have a proper family life, and we hope we will both be ready for it when it happens, for we both know we will never be able to see each other from that day on. But, please God, not just yet, we are both unable to let each other go this soon.' A tear was on her cheek.

John watched her dab it away. *What a wretched situation to be in,* he thought. *Do they believe they will be less in love when he finds a bride?*

'I can do no more for you, Matilda. Keep this document in a safe place, keep talking with Jacob. You now know you are safe for ever, your children equally so. I am proud of what you are doing for them, for they will always be my grandchildren.' He stood to leave. 'Thank you for everything, Matilda. Visit when you can, but keep writing to Sarah, won't you?' He held his hand out to shake hers on their agreement. She went to take it, then stepped inside his arm and gave him a hug instead.

'Thank you for what you have done for us. I am not sure that it has really sunk in yet. No one in our family has ever owned a farm before. Your grandson, our John, will be the first man in all the White families to be a farmer on his own land. His children will grow up on land that will be his family land. I wonder if you realise just how big a gesture you have made.'

He smiled down at her. Unused to being hugged, he hesitated before hugging her back.

As he was leaving, she added, 'We won't let you down, you know. These grandchildren will know what's required of them. And Richard will marry.'

He waved back to her. 'Yes, Matilda. I have learnt not to doubt you.'

Chapter 27

1853: The Weight of New Responsibility

Mary French saw Matilda coming down the lane and could tell by the way she walked, with her head down, that she was clearly troubled. Concerned, she went out to meet her.

'What is it?' Mary said as soon as she was close. Matilda looked up, surprised at seeing Mary ahead, surprised that she was already at Hawley Bottom, her mind so full of yesterday's visit that she had been oblivious of her walk down, and the time it had taken.

'I had a visit yesterday from Mr Hill. He told me that he had bought Mount Pleasant from you last year.' She didn't know at all where to start with what had happened.

'You had better come inside, Matilda,' Mary said. 'Jacob be milking half hour yet.' She settled Matilda at the kitchen table, putting the kettle on to boil.

'He has given the farm to me, for the children,' Matilda said into the silence.

'Please don't think badly of us, Matilda. It was what Mr Hill demanded. We consoled ourselves with the fact that you would own the farm at some time, but we always felt that we were being dishonest with you, as though we were doing something behind your back.'

Jacob came through the door and saw the troubled women. He guessed the reason.

'What be for, then?' he asked.

'You knows well enough,' Mary said. 'Mr Hill told Matilda yesterday.'

'Well I hopes you be not wanting me not to come upalong for farming talks no more then, Matilda. Be sad if you be wanting that to end, it be

233

as useful to me as to you to hear what you be on about doing yonder,' Jacob said as he sat at the table beside her, ready for his breakfast.

Matilda looked at Jacob, relieved.

'I want nothing to change. It's that suddenly I am responsible, not you. It was the surprise of it all. The responsibility.'

'That be settled then, I be upalong as always. No business of other folks, I reckon.' Jacob started in on his breakfast as though nothing had changed. Mary looked quizzically at her husband.

'What do you mean, no business of other folks?'

Jacob munched on his mouthful, puzzled at what his wife couldn't understand. 'Well,' he finally said, 'what business is it to other folks who owns the farm? They can find out in their own good time. It be up to us to keep quiet on it still. Be time for Matilda to get used to the idea first, tis no small step for her, you know. When she be comfortable with what she be about, then those that needs be can find out.' And he filled his mouth again as though to close the subject.

Mary looked at him with approval. 'Sometimes, Jacob French,' she said, 'you surprise me, and say just what is required first.'

Jacob was puzzled further. ''Tis bliddy obvious, in 'it? Matilda don't need no busybody interference, dornne she now? Lets be as they are, maybe year or two afore needs be telling. What matters is Matilda is allowed to get on with it, suits us both that ways, dornee reckon, Matilda?'

'Yes, Jacob,' she replied, comforted by his support, 'to carry on as normal. I was feeling quite isolated, and slept badly.'

'Daft woman!' he exclaimed, 'No farmer works isolated. If we stops talking and working together, well, all us farmers would fail. Dornee work no different, dornee tell a soul, times will sort themselves out.' And he returned to his breakfast.

'Thank you, I feel much better,' Matilda told them.

'Then get back to your farm,' he told her. 'And you owe us some clotted cream for that advice!' he added with a rare smile.

Ann and Joshua were both relieved to see a smiling Matilda coming back across the fields, a definite lightness in her step. She went about the day's work as though its bad beginning had not existed.

That evening, beside a turned-up lamp, she wrote to Richard. She told him of his father's gift and much of their conversation. Towards the end of the letter she realised that not much of what she had written would be news to him, and said so.

He recognised the writing on the address when the mail arrived, and opened it first. He smiled at her initial trepidation at being the landowner, and laughed when she realised that what his father had done would not be news to him, and that he must have known about it for some time. He smiled at her parting line of asking if he had found a bride yet, which was immediately followed by her finishing words, 'with all my love, your Matilda'. He read it again, then locked it away in the bottom drawer of his desk, where he had decided he would keep all her letters.

Sarah had also received a similar letter from Matilda. She smiled at her acceptance of John's intent in giving her the farm. Sarah looked over at her husband, saying, 'You did the correct thing for Matilda and the children, John. She writes well of your talk to her.' She read on, quoting the passage where she told Sarah that she regularly admonished Richard regarding his search for a proper wife, and asking Sarah if he had given any indication to her that he had done so.

John laughed at this. 'I very much suspect that it will be Matilda who hears about a possible bride before we do!'

Hannah was the most relieved that the farm issue had finally been completed. Knowing, but not being able to say anything to Matilda, was a burden removed. Now she could chat away as she used to, no longer having to watch her words in case she gave anything away.

Matilda was surprised at how quickly the farm ownership became accepted in her mind—probably, she thought, because nothing had outwardly changed. Jacob came regularly to see her, and filled her in on how Mount Pleasant could fit into this year's haymaking roster of farms. Nearly all these matters were normally settled over a jug in one of the pubs, and what Jacob didn't hear, Richard, her brother-in-law, would find out for her, as she never frequented the inns. Her lines of communication with her neighbouring farmers were well set out, her position on Dalwood Hill accepted.

Richard was likewise jubilant in his new surroundings, as his latest letter revealed. The church extensions were at last complete. The interior now seemed huge by comparison, he wrote—it felt as though they had more than doubled its size, although they hadn't quite done so. He praised the skill of the architect—the whole church interior flowed from vestry room to pulpit, with no clear demarcation where the gallery ended and the new enlargement began.

'What St Mary's now is, is a tribute to the dedication of commitment given by everyone from Revered Barter, who put so much into getting the ruined St Mary's rebuilt over 25 years ago, through to the efforts of our present group of workers. This is a house of worship that will be remembered by all those who visit here.

'There is more to be done yet—I have plans for the windows behind the altar and to its sides. I want to replace them all with stained-glass illustrations of saints, including, of course, St Mary. These take enormous time to be made, and it will be years before they will be installed. But that is for the future; now we are all delighted with the result of nearly three years of work. We are having a special dedication service next month. Father will be attending alone, as Hannah will not leave Mother in anyone else's care.'

John visited within a week of returning home after the dedication service, he was overwhelmed by it.

'Matilda, it is a joy to behold!' he told her. 'Richard took me in the day before the service to show it all to me. Even empty of people, the church holds you in an atmosphere of the peace of the sanctity of prayer. The dedication service itself was a most moving experience—the church was filled with an expectant congregation, some having to stand along the sides. Richard followed the choir in and as he bowed before the altar cross, the sun rays played down on his back. It was quite a moving scene. He chose the hymns well, all rousing and joyful, and we sang our hearts out. His sermon was on participation and cooperation, of contribution and reward, of personal effort and community satisfaction to the betterment of every person who is willing to do whatever they can. He likened himself to a conductor of an orchestra, who stood and waved his arms about, but without the orchestra there would be no music, only silence. Without all contributors, there would be no new church, only an empty gallery. He is a powerful speaker and a wonderful leader of his flock.

'After the service, no one wanted to leave, everyone wanted to shake his hand. There was hardly a villager not present. He was most humble in their congratulations on the enlargement, and very quick to point out that nothing would have happened if everyone had not played their part.

'I was so very proud of him, and told him so. "Rubbish, Father," he said. "Merely doing what I am begotten to do, performing my duty as is God's wish."

'He will be down in a week or two for a break—I have no doubt you will hear most of this again from him, as will Sarah.' He paused in thought before continuing, 'How are you getting on? How have people taken to your new ownership?'

'I am doing very well,' Matilda replied, her mind still with visions of Richard in his church. 'No one knows that I own it. Jacob and I have carried on as we always have. Folk will find out when time is right, and by then it will be too late to make any comment at all. I am comfortable with that.'

'Probably the wisest way,' John said. 'But what about your family?'

'Haven't told them either, simpler that way. The right occasion will come when it will be accepted without fuss.' She felt awkward at not having told them, and changed the subject. 'Did you find a wife for Richard while you were up there?' she asked.

'No, although I did glance around. I am afraid that I agree with Richard in that I did not see a really suitable lady at all. There were a few casting a longing look in his direction, and a couple of ghastly mothers cornered me to push their daughter's case. But none of any consequence. I fear that Richard must look further afield, and he gets pity all chance to do that.'

'And your brother James, has he no associates with suitable daughters available?' Matilda teased John.

'Have you been talking to Sarah? She said the same thing not a week ago,' he said, surprised, and Matilda laughed at his reaction.

'No. It's just that he is the one in the family that travels so often between Bristol, Bath and London. He would see far more of the appropriate society than any of you.'

'As it so happens, I have recently written to James on this very subject. At Sarah's insistence, I might add.'

'And did you tell James that there was no need to rush?' Matilda added coquettishly.

'Women!' John exclaimed, 'Will men ever understand them?' He evaded the subject by saying immediately, 'Now tell me about the farm. What are you planning before winter sets in?'

They spoke amiably of Matilda's plans, of Jacob's thoughts of using a new bull the Wakelys had bought, of how she would be milking two more cows from next spring and fattening two more bullocks for the village butcher from this year's calves.

John knew little on the practicalities of farming, but enjoyed listening to her talk so confidently on matters so close to her heart.

She then told him of her growing confidence with writing letters and the wonder it still gave her that she could communicate with others in this way. Only her eldest brother had any writing and reading skills, and they were limited. Her sister's husband, also a Richard, was the only other person who could read and write, which is why they all were sending all their children to school. There was not a single child that would not be educated.

'I am sure you will use those skills more as the children grow,' John said. 'We have seen a much improved style to your letters. Sarah really enjoys them, quite relaxed and chatty, she says.'

'Thank you, John. Most times they are quite easy to write, but sometimes they are very hard, the words just don't seem to come.'

'Keep writing, Matilda. The more you do, the easier it becomes.'

He left soon after, satisfied that she was quite settled into her life at Dalwood Hill, just as he had noticed Richard becoming equally settled into his life in Timsbury.

Richard's next visit was a whirlwind of excitement about the church, how much the children had grown, how well she was doing with the farm, the ease she now handled the ownership of Mount Pleasant estate, his plans for the stained-glass windows around the altar.

'If Father was impressed with what is there now with the big gold cross, imagine what it will be like with all those blues, reds, greens, golds and yellows. The richness of all that colour behind the altar will adorn the inside with light and warmth that will only enhance the church even more.' He paced up and down the kitchen as he spoke, his enthusiasm reflected in his movements.

Little Matilda sat beside her brother listening and watching, trying to work out what his church had that their own St Peter's didn't have. 'We have all those things already,' she said. 'Why don't you?'

Richard stopped in his tracks, looked down at his daughter and laughed aloud.

'Just like your mother! Straight to the point! Well my dear, it's like this,' and he sat and told her all about rebuilding the church, how it had spanned over twenty-five years and the number of clergy who had been in residence to see it through.

'Then they should have looked after it in the first place!' she retorted, much to Richard's delight.

'Pity the man that marries her!' he jovially said. 'What chance will he have?'

Ann came to his rescue. 'Come along you two, we have clotted cream to deliver to Aunt Mary, and your cousins are waiting.'

In the sudden silence following their departure, Matilda and Richard looked at each other, smiled, and moved into each other's arms.

Chapter 28

1853–1855: Deaths of Two Friends

The people who were important to Matilda were told of her ownership of Dalwood Hill Farm within a few months, and respected her request for privacy on the matter. Most would not know for years. Her brothers were pleased for her, but a little jealous. They were not told who her benefactor was and only guessed it was somehow tied in with her time with the Hill family. Only Mary and Ann knew, and they were the only two who were ever to meet Richard. Somehow, that seemed appropriate to them all.

Over the next two years Matilda established the farm's routine and stock levels, and comfortably ran it with two labourers. She had no need to work the farm to its maximum—its easy sustainability and adequate income suited her work ethics.

In safe keeping, and mounting up, were the purses that Richard always left behind, now worth a tidy sum on their own.

'There is no need,' Matilda always told him.

'For the children,' he always replied with a smile, and Matilda would add the latest one to the total.

'They will be grateful,' she would say.

Hannah came less often to visit. With Sarah becoming weaker, she was more reluctant to leave her. They wrote more often to each other, with Matilda also sending a letter to Sarah at the beginning of each month, but not always receiving a reply.

Richard received a letter most months, still dutifully posted by Herman. He read them several times, then sat and replied immediately with his news. In one he wrote with amusement that he had been invited to a meeting and dinner with his uncle James in Bath. Present was a local businessman and his daughter.

'Now Uncle James is in on the act of finding me a wife!' She could almost hear him laughing as she read it.

His visits to Dalwood were treasured, his anonymity remaining intact.

Madeline and her boys were regular visitors through the summer months and always present for haymaking. Ann, Mary and Madeline were the caterers for the workers in the fields, producing meals for those outside from Matilda's kitchen, Matilda herself preferring to be in the fields herself. In the evening, a huge meal was served to everyone, with ample cider to wash it down. At the end of each day, the four of them would talk on for hours and far too late into the night, considering the next day's early start.

Then they would move down to Mary and Richard's farm and do it all over again.

Dick would be there for at least two of the days, having also to help on his father's farm. He would appear to work with Matilda quite often and stay half a day, quietly chatting to her and taking great comfort in how settled she was. When he was ready to leave, he would amble over to her, give her a loving hug with his arms wrapped around her, kiss the top of her head, and wander off without saying goodbye. Matilda knew he would never turn up on a Monday, and teased Madeline quite unmercelessly about it. Madeline would offer no response, just blush uncontrollably and smile knowingly.

'I would hope not!' she once replied, but Mary and Matilda both jumped on her reply and teased her all the more.

They were two good years, the winters gentle, spring full of promise followed by glorious summers.

It was 1855, and the children were growing fast. John was now twelve and acting the young man, Matilda turned eight and the pestering little sister. Both were doing well with schoolwork, and both were absent during haymaking. Herman was quite used to his school roll dropping to nearly a third at this time of the year, where children of all ages were called in by family to help bring in the hay.

Dick could help Matilda for just the first day that year, his father needing him at home as he was short of labour.

It was the third and last day for the haymakers on Mount Pleasant. The last field was being cleared with hay being pitched up onto drays to be carted to an open barn, everyone hot and sweating from the midday sun, heads bowed over their forks and rakes, concentrating on what they were doing.

No one saw Matilda drop to her knees, clutching at her chest. But they all heard her terrible scream, 'NO!'

When they turned to her, she was trying to get to her feet, one hand pushing herself off the ground, and they ran to her. Young Joshua, as ever, was working closest to her and tried to help her up.

'It's Dick!' she cried to him, still doubled over as though in deep pain. 'Get me Jacob's hack.' He ran for his life, never questioning her command. He threw a halter over the horse's head and rode it out to Matilda, who was running to meet him. She quickly replaced him and galloped out onto the lane towards Shute.

Madeline came out of the house at the sound of cantering hooves going by, to be met by Joshua. He said without being asked, 'It be Miss Matilda, she be struck down in top field and called for a horse. She said it be Dick! She be gorn to him, I reckons.'

Madeline visibly paled, her hands going to her face and feeling suddenly quite sick. Mary came out and saw them—there was something obviously terribly wrong. Madeline turned to her, saying simply, 'It's Dick. She's gone to him.'

Mary went to her and put her arms around her, saying quietly to her, surprised, 'It works both ways, then.' She went on, 'We will have to wait for her to come back; only she will know where he is. Come, we will need to help finish in the field, and tell the men what that was about.'

But there was no need for any explanation when they reached the haymakers; the strange relationship between Matilda and Dick was well known among them—they had grown up with it. That it should work both ways was unquestioned. They spoke quietly among themselves, assuming that such a reaction from Matilda could only mean Dick had suddenly died.

Matilda had ridden hard through to Shute village, past the lane up to the church and school, and taking a later lane down to the back of Burrows fields. She had no thoughts of where she was headed, turning the horse instinctively towards where Dick lay. Through an open gateway and over the crest of the hill she pushed the tiring hack. Ahead, she saw what she knew she would find.

Several men were standing beside an old cart. Upon it was Dick's great body. His father looked up at her approach, shaking his head.

'Be too late, Miss Matilda. He went sudden like. Just grabbed his chest and groaned something. Dropped like a stone where he be stood.'

Wordlessly, she dismounted and walked to Dick's side. She took his hand in both hers, tears flowing down her face.

'You great lump, Dick Burrows! You nearly took me with you,' she cried, and laid her face on his hand.

'Aye,' murmured one of Matila's old neighbours, 'that be what he called out, he called for "Miss M", like he done since they be chillens.' The men silently moved back, leaving Matilda and his father by the cart with Dick.

All the workers looked over then at the body of the simpleton, as they all took him to be, and at the woman who had been his only friend since she was a tiny child.

'Tis not for our knowing 'ow she be 'ere so quick,' they muttered. 'Tis best left unsaid, I reckon, 'nuf stories about without us saying she be 'ere so soon. Best ways we finish off and then drink his passing.' With unspoken agreement, they moved off to resume their labours.

Matilda walked beside the cart as his father took him home for the last time. They were met at the door by Mrs Burrows, who broke down at the sight of her son on the cart. Matilda's presence was taken as an assumed expectation.

The old man looked over to Matilda and said sadly, 'There be no way I can lift 'im indoors on me own. Stay as you wish, but I needs someone to tell vicar for funeral and fetch lads from field to carry 'im inside.' Matilda looked over at the sobbing mother and knew he couldn't leave his wife now.

'I'll do it, there is nothing I can do for him now.' She swung herself onto the hack and left them in the yard, inconsolable with their son. Matilda let the hack plod back the way it had come and was met by the men from the field.

'Reckoned on 'em not being able to lift 'im in,' one said to her as they passed. She rode on in silence, only nodding to them, having nothing to say.

She stopped outside the vicarage in the village and told him what had happened. He shook his head in sadness and looked at Matilda, knowing of their friendship.

'God has taken the wrong son. That one did no one any harm. Funeral on Wednesday, then, Miss Matilda.' And he went to collect his things before heading out to the Burrows' farm.

Matilda rode slowly home, letting the horse pick its own pace. She felt empty, alone without her protector. She began thinking of all the times he would just appear when she needed him the most. Sometimes he would not need to speak—just being there was enough. She wondered at how she was going to react when next she thought of him and wanted his help, at the sorrow she knew she was going to feel.

She thought of Madeline. It was Monday, and predictably she had been late arriving this morning. How was she going to feel on Wednesday? How was she going to cope next Monday? She tried to work out how many years Dick had been 'tending her garden' on a Monday, but gave up, unable to concentrate. His passing would affect Madeline as much as herself, but the problem was that Madeline was not going to be able to show it. Her tears started again, this time as much for Madeline as for herself, for she had lost as much.

They were waiting for her at Dalwood Hill. Ann kept the children away and let Madeline and Matilda talk alone. It was an hour before they came out of her room, and Mary was waiting. She went and hugged them both.

'Richard has taken the boys home with our lot,' she told Madeline. 'Stay the night here with Matilda. We will bring them up here in the morning after milking—you could go home then, but not now. You need company as much as Matilda.' She hugged them both again and left to go and look after her family.

The funeral was an extraordinary event. The church as packed with folk who had spent their lives giving Dick none of their time. Most still thought of him as an idiot, but none could disregard how he had always been so different with Matilda, and none could understand it. His presence, they all knew, would be missed. It was going to be strange not seeing him about. If asked, none could really say why they attended the funeral, they just felt they should.

The Burrows all sat huddled together, heads down. Only Dick's mother sat upright, eyes wet, but unwavering from the massive casket that eight had carried in.

Across the aisle sat three women in black—Matilda in the middle, Mary and Madeline on either side, giving support. At the burial the order was changed, but nobody noticed. It was Madeline in the middle, almost being physically held up by Mary and Matilda. It was during the service that Madeline began to succumb to grief, desperately trying to suppress it. Matilda felt her shudder and put an arm around her, knowing her pain. Of those who noticed, it was seen as typical of the support the three friends had given each other over many years. They left together, and went to Madeline's home. Her boys silently greeted her with a hug and sat her in their drawing room, then went to make them all refreshments. Mary produced a bottle of brandy, to fortify themselves, she said. But they wept silently on.

The rest of the week passed in a numb habit, doing what needed to be done, none of them contacting the other, too deep in their own thoughts. Matilda grieved at the loss of her friend; the possibility that he would die before her had never been anticipated. She had taken it for granted that he would always be there for her, and it should have been Dick that buried her, she thought, his final act of service to her. Her reverie was only broken when she sat for lunch on the following Monday, suddenly remembering what should have been happening that morning. She rose from the table, saying with sadness, 'I must visit Madeline.'

Mary had been thinking of how Madeline was coping all that Monday morning, but was unsure how to approach her. Finally, in disgust at her own prevarications, she headed off to see her.

Madeline had retired that Sunday night dreading the next day and how she would see it through. Once the boys had left for school, a horrible silence fell over the house, a silence that was amplified by the absence of any movement outside. There was no squeak of the garden gate opening, no crunch on the gravel path as his boots would have trod their way to her door. No gentle voice talking quietly to her. Nothing. She hadn't moved from the breakfast table, just sat numbly staring out the kitchen window, hoping to catch his shadow. She thought of that early day, when she had sat here to write a list of plants for the garden that he was to suggest. How he had stood beside her as he named the plants, but she had stopped writing and could not take her gaze from him. That list was never completed, and in the need to do something, she decided she would finish it now. She collected pen and paper and sat to begin. She looked to her left to where he had stood, and began to write. But it wasn't about plants.

'This is to you, Dick.'

She began, surprised at the words that appeared before her, and pleased with them. She decided to continue with them.

'I am thinking on those early days when you came into my wrecked garden to tidy it up for the children. You did not talk to me then, not before I interrupted you behind the hedge. What a day that one was, I scarcely believed you would ever talk with me, and the rest of that morning was unbelievable. How did it happen? I have often asked myself. I can remember every minute of it, I hardly slept for fear of forgetting it. You came into my life to repair my garden, and you ended up repairing me. Did Mary and Matilda know that would happen, do you think? For all the years of delight you gave me that followed, it was that first touch I gave you that sent tingles all through me, and I remember it best of all.

I sit here now and begin to tingle again, even though we will never touch again. I remember how you carried me . . .'

She wrote on, committing that day to paper, and blushed at her own writings when she had finished. She carefully folded the pages in half, bound a ribbon around them and put them safely away in her room.

She returned downstairs feeling far more settled, but was shaken to hear the garden gate squeak. She dashed to the door. Matilda and Mary were surprised at her sudden appearance as they approached.

'Oh, it's you two,' she exclaimed, feeling silly with her ridiculous expectations.

'Who else?' they asked, and then realised themselves what must have flashed through her mind.

'Just us. To check on you.'

'I'm glad, come in,' she said cheerfully. 'I am doing very well.' she told them what she had done. 'They are put safely away,' she added.

Mary and Matilda were delighted to find her so strong, so confident within herself. They wondered why they had been so afraid she wouldn't be.

Madeline wrote more each Monday morning. Dick was never forgotten, but as the months passed, Madeline found she had less to say, less need to write to him, more comfortable in his absence, more confident she could carry on without him. She wrote the final page in October that year and added it to the thick bundle she had made. For the final time she tied the ribbon around it all, and knew what she would do with it.

Madeline called out to Matilda as she came in through the garden. Ann met her and told her that Matilda was up yonder field where badgers were seen—they wanted to be sure that there wasn't a sett up there. She went up to meet her and on the way back to the house she explained to Matilda what she wanted her to do.

'I don't want my boys to find them. But I just can't destroy them, I want them somewhere safe. It's as though that while they are safe and close by, then so is he. Who else could be a better guardian of his memories than you?'

'But what of them when one of us dies?' Matilda asked practically.

'If you go first, then have my name on them so they come back to me. If I go first, I want you to give them to the wife of whichever of my boys marries first. It's all right for a woman who knew me to read them, but not a man, a man would not understand.'

Matilda solemnly put them in the same safe place that she had put her debenture from John. In her own round hand, she wrote what was to happen to them as Madeline had outlined. Only once was she tempted to read the letters, but stopped when she realised how deeply personal they were.

Barely had a month passed before she got a shattering letter from Hannah.

'Mother has died. Would you be able to come to her funeral on Friday, 11 a.m.'

That was all it said, brief and filled with pain. Matilda knew the loss and emptiness she would be suffering.

Joshua, always near, said he would take her in Jacob's gig. He got her there early.

There were a few she recognised inside, and some acknowledged her, but not many. She expected the church to be filled, but it wasn't. She sat in silence, thinking of the Hill family that had taken her in to be Hannah's companion, and all that had happened since then. She thought mainly of Sarah, her quiet courage throughout her illness and the horrible uncertainty of it. When would the next seizure come? Would it happen in public? Would she survive it? Just how long had she left to live? Was she in fact going mad because of it? Matilda wondered if she could have written more often, made the effort to visit regularly, but it was too late to think that now.

The organ began to play softly, and the family came in. John led them, and he looked haggard. Some she didn't know, but Hannah and Richard came in together. Hannah looked defeated, Richard strong, supporting her. Lost in their own thoughts, they didn't notice her, not even looking around to see who had come.

The service was sombre; two men spoke of Sarah, and her sons and others she didn't know carried the coffin out. Matilda left with the rest of the mourners, and it was John who saw her first and touched Hannah's shoulder. She turned to see Matilda and went to her.

'Please come up to the house before you go home after the burial.'

'Yes,' Matilda replied, 'after the burial.' Joshua came up beside her. 'I am going back to the house, will you meet me there?' she asked of him.

Matilda walked behind the other mourners to witness the burial. She arrived at Fairfield Lodge with those who wished to continue to the house. John stood at the door greeting those who came. He looked almost dazed, only muttering his thanks to the condolences offered. He was shaking Matilda's hand before he realised whose hand he was shaking, and he brightened marginally.

'Thank you for coming, Matilda, it is right that you should be here. I had not noticed you earlier.'

'I understand, Mr Hill. I needed also to say goodbye to her.'

'Talk to Hannah,' he said, half as instruction, half as dismissal. He turned to the next person as they arrived at his door. Hannah saw her coming toward the drawing room and went to meet her. Saying nothing, she took Matilda's hand and led her to her father's study.

'We will not be interrupted here,' she said, and closed the door behind them. Alone, she broke her resolve and cried, holding tight to Matilda. Between tears she said that Sarah had suffered several seizures over the last two weeks, each one seemingly more severe than the previous. The last one she never woke up from—the doctor said her heart could take no more. Finally, poor Sarah was at peace. The torment was over.

They were still holding each other when the door quietly opened and more softly closed. Neither of them appeared to notice, neither moved. They accepted his arms around them both, each putting an arm round him, silent for some time. Calmness settled on them.

'The three of us,' he said, finally breaking the silence. 'We should talk, but we need to see to the guests—Father will need our support. We must write to each other soon, it would be best.'

Richard left them to find his father, and a short time later, John came into the room.

'Hello, you two,' he said, walking up to them. 'I am very pleased to see you, Matilda, and it would please Sarah to know you were here also.'

'It would have been wrong for me not to be here, considering all that you have done for me,' Matilda said.

'She suffered badly over recent weeks. Would it be such a terrible thing to say that I am relieved it is over for her?' he asked.

'No, John. That is understandable, it must have been quite horrid for you all.'

'Indeed. Thank you for what you have done for her. Now I must return to the visitors. Stay here a while longer with Hannah. Write to me, Matilda—I would miss your letters no longer arriving.'

'Of course, John. I would anyway, as you should know how your grandchildren are doing.'

Hannah walked with Matilda to the door to bid her farewell. Richard watched her leave and could only nod at her parting, not able to acknowledge one guest more than another. Hannah hugged her at the top of the steps and looked down to where Joshua stood, cap in one hand and the reins in the other.

'Thank goodness you have the silent Joshua to see you safely home,' Hannah said. 'Write soon.' And she sadly turned to attend to the remaining guests.

Chapter 29

1855–1860: A Wedding among the Next Generation

Matilda was surprised when Mary told her that their elder brother had given up being an agricultural labourer and had moved into Colyton.

'Be never make a future that ways,' William had told her. 'But menfolk will always sup an ale of an evening, particularly in good company. And they pays for the privilege!'

He and Ann had taken over as innkeepers at the Country House Beer Shop in Butts Street. They both agreed it was the best move they could have made. John, their eldest, had been a quick learner at school, but being that little bit older than the rest, had become bored with it and left, initially to help his father. William had other ideas though. He felt there was little for the boy in following in his footsteps and had sent him off to learn a trade as a sawyer. Thomas, their next son, could not be moved from farm life, and stayed on labouring on the farm when his parents moved into town. Elizabeth moved with them but had nothing to do with the inn. She was showing her skills as a lacemaker, her young fingers creating some splendid patterns.

Mary and Richard's boy, John, had also left school, and was helping on their new farm at Dickens Marsh. Samuel would be leaving school by the end of the winter as well, and Richard was having concerns about being able to keep both boys occupied. He was quietly looking for placement for them elsewhere.

Matilda's John would be leaving school at the same time as Samuel, but she had no thoughts for him other than keeping him on her farm. He had shown an aptitude for farming and wanted to begin as soon as his mother would let him. Matilda, however, was going to be sure he had received all the education that Herman could get into him, and he was not going to be allowed to leave before Herman said he could. Little Matilda enjoyed school and playing games with the other children. It was not unusual for her to be on the same side as the older boys as she was so fleet of foot and took the bumps and knocks uncomplainingly. William Edwards, four years her senior, always picked her for his side. He reckoned on her being the fastest child at the school. William was named after his uncle who was the village shopkeeper, and the old rogue in the shop regularly teased Matilda when she took in her clotted cream, telling her that she would have to watch those two.

There had been changes for Matilda as well, on the farm. Joshua had returned to Jacob's farm at Hawley Bottom, where he was given a more senior position. He was sad to leave Matilda's side, but he knew he had to take the opportunity when it arose. Matilda had employed James and Mary Ousley, a young couple to help her. Mary was a Dalwood girl, and James had come from Hawkchurch to help her father, and had never left. Matilda knew that her John would soon be working with her, and she had often thought that she would offer to have Mary's John with her as well. Mary had said on occasion that she was not sure how they would be able keep all the boys at home, but didn't want them too far away.

For most of that year, Hannah became a regular visitor, often staying a night or two. Since her mother had died, she had been feeling lost and without purpose. She had spent so much time looking after her and running the household that she had never realised how much time she had spent doing each. When Sarah passed away, time hung heavily on her. The passing months only seemed to increase her feeling of a lack of purpose.

John sent her to Matilda to give them all a break, having warned Matilda in advance just how morose Hannah had become over recent weeks. But Hannah had stayed only the one night, saying she needed to get back. John sent her up to Richard a week later, knowing she could not come back from him so quickly. Richard, forewarned of her early return from Matilda's, planned a number of things that Hannah could help him with. One, he happily told her, was to accompany him on another dinner appointment that Uncle James had booked for him with one of his investors and his daughter. This raised Hannah eyebrows.

'Why?' she asked.

'He is finding candidates for my prospective bride! Father had a word with him, and he has taken my cause to heart. I have a dinner appointment at least once every three months—surely he will run out of likely ladies soon?'

'Then I will certainly chaperone you. I will sort them out, and I certainly know who Matilda will think to be good enough for you.'

'Oh dear!' Richard sighed. 'I fear poor Uncle James may rue the day he was pleased he invited you along as well.'

In that day's mail was a letter from James, concise as usual.

'Richard,' it read, 'To clarify this Saturday, not the usual prospective bride nonsense. This is a civic gathering of Bath business men, important you attend for your own benefit as Rector of a local town. It will undoubtedly enhance your position. However, there will be ladies present and one could be of interest, but on this occasion, she is of secondary importance for the meeting. Bring Hannah. Regards, James.'

'My!' Hannah said on reading the note, 'not one for wasting words, is our uncle James. Does he know of Matilda and the children?' she asked Richard, thinking she was going to have to stay until next week now.

'I have always assumed not. I never mention her and he has never raised the matter. It would be best if she is not mentioned.'

'Very well. What am I to wear at this function?'

'Something nice,' Richard suggested.

'That's very helpful.'

'Well, you know what I mean, whatever is in fashion.'

'I have not come here with anything fashionable. Tidy for church, that is all. I will need to buy something for the occasion, and that means a trip into Bath. Will you accompany me?'

'Not to buy dresses I won't! Susan can have a day off, she can go in with you. I have a sermon to write.'

Susan was the head servant, and took her duties seriously. Going to Bath for the day to accompany Miss Hannah to buy a gown was another duty. But within ten minutes of boarding the coach for the seven-mile trip into Bath, Hannah had amply clarified that this was not a duty. Buying a gown was a pleasure, and Susan had better learn to relax and enjoy her day off. She was to offer constructive comment on the gowns available, be a willing companion and not act as a servant. She was to take the return coach to Timsbury if this was too much for her. Susan liked her job too much to lose it, and quickly discarded her servant's role, acting the confidante to the rector's sister.

Saturday night was a great success. James and his wife were there to greet them, and Hannah quickly relished the atmosphere and occasion.

251

It was a very long time since she had been in such a formal and illustrious gathering. Not since Sarah had first become ill. A shiver ran down her back at the thought of her mother, but Richard was already being introduced to those around them and she, likewise, became part of the evening. With her hand in Richard's arm, she felt wonderful, so many women complimenting her on her fine gown.

At one point they met the prospective bride—a quiet word in Richard's ear from James indicated the likely lady. Hannah was instantly sceptical of her chances, but carried on a polite conversation with her for Richard's sake.

When they were safely away she whispered to him, 'Was she really the one?'

'Yes, she was better than most.'

'Heavens, she will never do!' Hannah exclaimed.

'Thank goodness for that! I was worried you would like her.'

'I can see I will have to take a hand in this. Clearly James has no idea what's required and you are not helping by not taking any action.'

Richard was instantly cautious, thinking James to be the lesser of the two evils in looking for a bride for him.

'I have looked, you know. Even Father acknowledges that the choice is not to be found in Timsbury. I don't often get the chance to visit Bath. You know I am not entirely without intent.'

'Good! Then if nothing else, we can begin to eliminate the rest of those present. You have to start somewhere.'

'You came up for a break for yourself, not to find a wife for me,' he mildly protested,

'Perhaps, but this is much more fun. Come along!' And she guided him to a group close by.

They were having supper when Hannah admitted to the enormity of the problem.

'I must apologise, Richard. I thought finding a suitable lady would be easy, but all we have met are well-to-do women with empty heads! There is barely a brain between them. What are we to do?'

'I am pleased you can now see the problem. This has been what it's been like all along. I couldn't live with one of them. Seeing Matilda only three or four times a year does me more good than living every day with one of this lot would!'

'I would doubt your sanity if you could live every day with one of them,' she giggled.

'After supper, would you mind if we left for the night? I would like an early return home in the morning—you know I like to be early at the church.'

They left the supper room to bid goodnight to James, and Hannah excused herself to attend the ladies' room.

What first took her attention was the soft lilting accent that she couldn't place, and then the freedom of an innocent laugh. She turned to see a young woman with, presumably, her mother. The mother caught Hannah looking at them, and she felt she should say something to make her looking acceptable.

'I am so sorry for staring, but your accent took me by surprise. I couldn't place its origin,' Hannah said to them.

The mother smiled. 'That's quite all right, I thought you were looking at us for making too much noise,' she replied. 'Occasions like this can be so stuffy!'

Hannah relaxed. 'I quite agree, and there is nothing wrong with happy noise, especially laughter. And I haven't heard any in there,' she said, indicating the reception room. The mother nodded.

'Allow me to introduce ourselves. I am Sarah Boyd, and this is my daughter, Catherine. My husband is out there being the businessman that he is.'

'Hello,' Hannah said. 'I am here with my brother, Reverend Richard Hill—I am Hannah. It's a pleasure to meet someone here who knows how to laugh!'

Catherine smiled gratefully. 'I find these events rather trying. Father insists I attend, as he is intent on finding me a husband. I mean—look at them! There's not an eligible one among them, they are all too old!' She laughed again. 'Mother and my father are from the Midlands, and I was born in Wales and have lived most of my life there, which rather accounts for my accent.'

Hannah couldn't help laughing. 'I'm sorry, I shouldn't have laughed like that. It's just that our uncle is out there with Richard—he invited us to attend in the hope of finding Richard a bride! Unlike you, though, Richard is older—he is forty-three and I feel he has left it a bit late. There have been many mothers present their daughters, but they all have been rather empty-headed as well, and no use to Richard. Totally impractical when it comes to being a rector's wife with Parish duties.'

Catherine laughed delightedly. 'Doesn't that sound familiar, Mother? I am twenty-four and father thinks I've missed my chances. He presents these idiots who have pots of money and nothing to think with, some have been quite horrible. Once we have been left alone to get to know one another, they just want to grope me. It's as though I have been presented to be bedded, with no other function in life.'

'Catherine!' her mother interjected. 'That's no way to speak.'

'Mrs Boyd, I am afraid that I must side with Catherine. That was exactly my experience at her age. I was not supposed to have any other use to them. I think you expressed it quite succinctly, but only among ourselves.'

'You never married then?' asked Catherine. 'Why not?'

'I do apologise, Hannah,' Sarah interjected again. 'Sometimes my daughter is not very subtle in her questions, and a little too personal.'

'It was not said rudely, and a fair question considering the context of our conversation.' She turned to Catherine. 'I never met the right man when I was looking, then Mother took ill, and I lost interest in finding anyone. I spent my time looking after her and running the household. Now, I'm afraid, I am too independent and would not want to be tied down. Father has generously made me of independent means, so the need for a supportive husband has gone. I have a very good friend who was my companion for many years, and we are always in contact. She is on a farm with her children and it is a pleasure to visit them there. That is all I want. But Richard needs more, he actually needs a wife to make his role in Timsbury complete.'

'And the husband that I want must let me be myself, not a subservient wife, following meekly behind,' Catherine said.

'We have a similar problem. It's been delightful to chat, Hannah, but we really must be getting back.'

'Of course. Richard wants to leave now anyway. We are staying here in the hotel, and will be leaving early to be back for his eleven o'clock service.'

'I may see you at breakfast then,' said Catherine. 'I usually rise early, and we are staying here as well.'

They made their farewells and went to join the men. Richard was keeping an eye out for her, having been cornered by a hopeful mother.

'Ah! Hannah. Come along my dear, we must be going. Do excuse us,' he said to them and made his escape.

'Yes dear,' Hannah said.

As they left they heard the daughter accusingly say to her mother, 'I thought you said he wasn't married!'

Both Richard and Hannah smiled broadly at their charade.

Sarah and Catherine saw Hannah leave with her brother and glanced at each other. 'Shame he is so much older, he's quite distinguished,' Catherine said.

'Yes, such an age gap,' her mother agreed, but not without hope.

At breakfast the next morning, Hannah was only slightly surprised to see Catherine come into the breakfast room.

'There is Catherine now. The one I was telling you about last night. Shall I ask her to join us?' Hannah said.

'If you would like her company, I have no objection. If she is as sensible as you think, then she will not hold us up in leaving, will she?'

Hannah went to meet her, and the two women returned to the table. Richard rose as they approached.

'Richard, this is Catherine. My brother, Richard,' Hannah said, and they resumed their seats.

'Thank you for inviting me to sit with you—it so nicely does away with unnecessary attention,' Catherine said.

'You are welcome,' Richard replied. 'I gather from Hannah we find ourselves in a rather similar situations—we have families trying to get us married off.'

'Oh, she has said that much.' Catherine blushed slightly at their mutual predicament. 'I'm afraid I am rather weary of the constant array of men Father seems to find that he thinks will be suitable for me. It is a bit of a bore.'

Richard smiled broadly at this. 'We should compare notes! What similarities do we have from our fathers in particular, in the hopeful candidates they choose for us, and our reaction to them? You as a young lady and me as an older man. I would guess they would be very close.'

'Probably identical, Richard,' she replied smiling at the idea, 'although not so demeaning for you, I think.'

'I am not so sure,' Richard said with a look to Hannah. 'What difference would you put between being pawed and being groped?'

Catherine spluttered on the tea she was drinking at Richard's candid reply. 'Good heavens, Hannah! Do you tell him everything?' she managed to say eventually.

'He is my brother,' Hannah said with amusement.

'I didn't think rectors spoke like that,' Catherine said, now fully recovered. 'I thought men of the cloth were supposed to be a stuffy lot.'

'Not my brother,' Hannah said laughing, 'although he usually waits to get to know someone first, and not over breakfast!'

'Well that's a relief! Are your sermons just as forthright?' she asked.

'I try to be illuminating—I have had a good coach,' Richard said, trying to work out why he had made such a brash statement to a young lady he did not know.

'Then perhaps I should attend one of your services, to see if I keep listening all the way through it. The local man is completely tedious!'

'Do you live in Bath then?' Hannah asked.

'I do,' Catherine said. 'The rest of the family have recently moved to Weston-super-Mare from Wales. That is why we stayed the night here in the hotel—Mother and Father will go home later today, after they have delivered me safely back to Lambridge.'

'Did your father think your prospects of finding a husband greater here, in Bath, than in Weston? Did he set you up in a house here?' Hannah asked.

'No. I left home for some peace!' Richard and Hannah could not help but laugh out loud. 'I share a house with some friends who are all studying here. It's all very proper, otherwise Father would have dragged me back home. I suppose I have a greater chance of finding someone here, but I am not desperately searching, I can't see what the rush is. Mother is very supportive and has helped a lot in getting me here, and she knows the family I'm with.'

'You have a remarkable freedom for a young lady, Catherine. Has it caused you any problems?' Richard asked.

'Not to me, but a couple of the suitors that Father found took exception to it, and thought it made me a loose woman! Indeed! Some thought the other way, and it made me more attractive as I was available to them without restrictions. They soon got the message! So many men are so demeaning in their attitude to me, it's as though I shouldn't have any intelligent thoughts of my own. That my body should begin at my shoulders and stop at my knees!'

'So very true, Catherine,' Hannah said.

'Not all men, surely?' Richard asked

'Too many!' Catherine retorted.

Their cooked breakfast arrived, and they all ate heartily in easy silence. They chatted briefly after, with Hannah excusing herself to finish packing her bag. Catherine rose with her.

'I should leave as well—Father would have a stroke if he saw me sitting alone with a strange man.'

'Yes, I suppose you must,' Richard agreed reluctantly. 'I will see to the bill,' he told Hannah, and they all parted.

They were nearly home before Richard made any reference to Catherine.

'Quite a surprising young lady, that Catherine. Refreshing views. It would be useful if she was fifteen years older,' he mused.

Hannah was smiling to herself, having waited for him to pass some comment.

'Do you not think so, Hannah?' he asked for confirmation.

'It made my evening very gratifying. I wouldn't worry about the age difference, it is only a measurement of years, not compatibility.'

Richard raised his eyebrows, but made no comment.

Hannah was to stay for two more days before leaving to go back to Lyme Regis. It was just as well, as a letter arrived addressed to her in the care of the rectory. Puzzled as to the unknown hand, and who should be writing, she opned it with some trepidation. She read it in complete surprise, taken aback by its content, but thoroughly delighted.

It was from Catherine, thanking her for her company in Bath, and for making the evening and breakfast so much more enjoyable than she could have hoped. She gave her address, and asked if she would be visiting Bath again before returning home to Lyme Regis.

Hannah folded the letter thoughtfully. *Am I reading too much into this?* she asked herself. *Is Catherine wanting to come to terms with the age difference, wanting to meet again with Richard to test her feelings further?* She wrote to her father, saying she was staying another week, and would be home on Monday's coach.

Then she wrote to Catherine, saying she would indeed be in Bath again during the week, probably Friday, and could they meet?

Over dinner that night, she told Richard she would like to stay until the following Monday, if that would not put him out. She would like to go into Bath again to do a little shopping that was not available to her at Lyme Regis. Richard was delighted to have her company longer and said he would accompany her into the city on the Friday.

Without waiting for a response from Catherine, Hannah wrote to her again, suggesting lunch at the same hotel that they had stayed at, and told her that Richard would be accompanying her if that was of no inconvenience to her. She added the last bit with a wry smile.

The lunch was all that Hannah could have hoped for. Richard was surprised at Catherine's appearance, coming in the door as she did with two of her friends. Hannah stood and greeted them and invited them to join them. Mysteriously, though, Catherine's two friends had to decline, citing a lecture as their excuse, and Richard was relieved.

Lunch lasted three hours. On the way home he was silent all the way, finally saying aloud, 'There is no point to it. She is far too young.' Hannah was deflated. Catherine was perfect for him, but he couldn't see past the nineteen-year age difference. But she knew what she must do next.

John was delighted to have Hannah home again—being alone in the big house with only servants for company was making him depressed. Her arrival lifted his spirits immediately, and they talked constantly. But she didn't mention a word about Catherine.

Two days later she went to visit Matilda. It was a very different Hannah that arrived at Dalwood Hill, and Matilda was delighted with the change. The old Hannah was back; gone was the weary and saddened Hannah following her mother's death. This Hannah had a purpose, and Matilda very soon realised what it was. Hannah told her every detail about Catherine, and the stumbling block Richard had about her age.

'I shall write immediately, while you are still here. We will compose the letter together—he must see the sense in it. He must ask her to marry him—he cannot afford to let her slip by.'

They wrote and rewrote until both were satisfied with the result. He would find it very difficult to argue against both of them, Matilda's conviction evident.

Hannah posted the letter on her way home, knowing full well what turmoil must be going on in her friend.

Matilda cried all night. She knew that, finally, her Richard would be lost to her.

Richard read the letter several times, recognising both his sister's and Matilda's influence in its writing. But the message was clear, and he had to admit that Catherine was the only woman to have taken his eye in the last twenty years since meeting Matilda. His concern was how others would see the age difference, not himself, as he was past the point of worrying about it any longer.

But it was what he had to do next that filled him with dread. To give Catherine any chance of success, there must be no reminders of Matilda in the rectory. Slowly, and with great sadness, he opened the bottom drawer of his desk and removed all of Matilda's letters, holding the amazing triumph of a formerly illiterate woman in his hand. He looked at the bundle with pride, turned, and one by one, fed them into the fire.

Matilda's presence left the rectory in a bright flame, for she was surely that to me, he thought.

Richard wept that night. He finally accepted that Matilda was unable, any longer, to be part of his life.

Richard and Catherine Elizabeth Boyd were married on 10 July 1860, in St Saviour's parish church, Bath.

Chapter 30

1860–1863: The Children Grow Up

Matilda was not alone in facing turmoil within the family.

Ann had been living with her sister at Dalwood Hill for seventeen years now, and had settled into a comfortable role as housekeeper and lacemaker. There was little need for her to look after Matilda's children anymore, as Matilda the younger was now thirteen and quite the young maid. Ann would probably have stayed as she was had she not made a rare attendance to church with Matilda and the children. After the service, they were chatting with the elder Chapple couple, bidding them farewell, as they were retiring from the farm, allowing for the boys to take over.

'What are you going to do?' Matilda asked them.

'Move into Axminster,' the old man said. 'Be got ourselves a nice place in there. Easier on Mother.' He nodded to his wife, whose limp seemed to grow more pronounced each passing month.

'We thought it for the best,' she acknowledged. 'Will miss the girls though.' She was referring to her daughters-in-law, who were always at the ready to help her.

'May have to get a maid in to help her,' he added. 'Needs a hand at times, she does.'

At this Ann joined the conversation. She was the quiet one in the family, and tended not to be very forthcoming. So her comment surprised them all.

'I could come in if you are looking for a maid. Now that Matilda's children have grown, there is little to keep me upalong. I do more

260

lacemaking than anything for Matilda, nowadays.' Matilda was taken aback at this, assuming that Ann would be there for ever.

'You could,' was all she managed to say.

'Tis a pleasant thought,' the old man said. 'You would be easier on the ears than them girls—they talks to drown a babbling brook!'

'I would take that as a blessing,' Mrs Chapple said. 'You would be such good company.'

It was settled there and then. At the end of the month, Ann moved into Axminster with the Chapples as their maid. At the age of 37, she moved out of a family home for the first time, and into full-time employment.

Mary and Richard had their own family troubles. Their eldest son, John, was helping on the farm, but rebelling against his parents, the work, and anything else he could pick an argument with. Of late, he would go out at night to drink cider with a troublesome village lad that the constabulary had their eye on. Mary went to her sister in desperation after he had been brought home one morning in a dishevelled drunken state by the village policeman.

'He won't listen to us anymore,' Mary told Matilda in anguish. 'Will you talk to him? He has always listened to you.'

'I will do better than that. Pack his bag and send him up here. He can have Ann's room and work for me. He and my John have always got on, and I will pay him labourer's wages on good behaviour only, otherwise he will go without.' By dinner that night, John had his bag unpacked and Ann's old room arranged to his liking. Matilda expected him to work as hard as she did, and he accepted the challenge. The two Johns made a good team, often trying to outdo the other in some of the heavy work.

Young Matilda had left school and had taken after her mother with her ability to work with livestock. She was particularly as adept at milking, but impatient at making clotted cream. It was not unusual on a Sunday afternoon to find the Edwards lad, William, coming by to see the two Johns, but spending as much time talking with the young Matilda. Even when he was given the job as a gentleman's servant at Shute Manor, his appearance every second Sunday afternoon was no longer commented on. Matilda just watched her daughter a little more closely.

William's son John had moved away from Colyton to Membury, and then on to Chard. Still a sawyer, but restless in nature, he would send Matilda a short note on where he presently was. She always replied and told him of what the rest of the family were doing. He came to regard her as the one in the family who cared, and had some understanding of his restless nature.

It seemed all too soon that Mary's second boy, Samuel, also left school and came to live with her as well. He was not such an active lad as the others and was often the brunt of their jokes. It was almost an accepted move when he became the house servant, staying indoors rather then working outdoors with the others. This helped Matilda a great deal, as she had no desire to be inside doing housework.

Hannah still visited, but less regularly, writing short notes on what was happening in the Hill family. She told of her father's apathy since Sarah had died, and of a decline in his health. It made no difference to his demeanour when Sarah Ann and her husband William Hussey and their two boys came to live at Fairfield Lodge with them. The only truly good news she had was that Richard had finally approved the designs for the church windows to go in around the altar. He had unspecified plans as to when they would be made and installed, and Hannah mistakenly thought it was a matter of budget. Richard, however, had other events in mind. The windows were to be commemorative, and were to be assigned as time dictated. Hannah also let her know that Richard and Catherine were expecting a baby.

In an odd way, it was a relief to Matilda that Richard was starting a new family. Her envy of Catherine's place in Richard's life still hurt, but it was confirmation to her that he was taking his marriage and new responsibilities seriously. He needed to have a legitimate family, and his father received the news enthusiastically. It was a great relief for John that Richard was to have an heir, a correct family line that the Hill inheritance would continue through, via his favoured son.

But John was not to see his grandson born.

He died at Fairfield Lodge in the September of 1861. Hannah was shattered, and burdened with grief. She had lost her purpose in life, with the household disbanded, no father to attend to, no servants to supervise, no home to stay in. Immediately after his funeral, she went to Matilda and stayed a few nights to get away from her brothers and sisters.

They had all sat through the reading of the will, listening carefully for what they would receive, only Richard and Hannah already knowing what it contained. It was only afterwards that the others realised that Hannah had not been mentioned in the will at all, and she was the one who had stayed home and cared for their parents alone. Philip, particularly, was dumbfounded. He expected nothing from his father, the feud between them never abating. To get fifty pounds a year was more than he expected, but for Hannah to get nothing outraged him. Now she was 41 and single, with nowhere to live, what was she going to do? In embarrassment they avoided the subject, relieved when she left to stay with a friend.

Neither Richard nor Hannah could find any reason to enlighten them of her own, now well-established, wealth.

When she was sure that all but Sarah Ann and William would be left in Lyme Regis, she returned. Together the three cleared the house, sold what was not needed, and three weeks later left the house for the last time.

Sarah Ann and William Hussey continued to live in Lyme Regis. Hannah went initially to Timsbury with Richard and Catherine. It was Catherine's mother, Sarah, who took Hannah into her care and returned some purpose to her life.

'You must come over to Weston-super-Mare,' she told her. 'We have settled there very comfortably. Perhaps to be beside the seaside again will help you settle, and it is not so very far to Richard.'

Hannah agreed and found lodgings. She had lost all interest in owning her own home and being required to run it. She soon took on a maid, partly to save her from the drudgery of housework, and partly for companionship. She could well afford it, as her investments gave her a most satisfactory income. She wrote to Matilda often, keeping her informed of her new way of life, and of Richard's. She told her of the birth of Richard, the first child for Catherine and Richard, and the shared pride they all had.

Catherine's mother Sarah would quite often go and stay with them for a couple of nights, and she went to help her daughter with the new baby and gain confidence in her role as mother. Catherine needed little help, but did enjoy her mother's company.

It was as well she was there, as an unpleasant surprise caught Catherine at her most vulnerable time.

Richard and Catherine were in his study quietly talking over the day's events. Baby Richard was tucked up for the night, Sarah had retired early and the house was at peace. Catherine stood behind her husband, her hands on his shoulders as he sat at his desk, notes for the sermon before him.

'I am going to make a family chart,' she said, 'for our family, now we have one to start it with. Have our parents at the top, then us without our brothers and sisters, then a line for our children across the page.'

'Goodness, Catherine, how many children are you wanting us to have?' Richard asked in mock surprise.

'Enough,' she said, laughing. 'I do rather like the process, you know. Are you ready for bed yet?' she asked coquettishly.

'Goodness!' he exclaimed again, still not used to her very forthright manner when it came to matters of the bedroom. He turned to stand and hold her, but she stepped back, teasing him.

'We could keep it in this old lectern Bible—you have no other use for it have you?'

'No, it's not been touched for years, it's too brittle. I just can't stand the thought of putting it out after its years of service in the old church.' Catherine had put her hands under its edge to feel its weight and looked sadly at its very faded and worn front cover. She rolled it over on its spine to see if the back was in better condition, but its broken spine could not support its weight and it flopped over with a thud, leaving just the back cover in her hand. Some loose sheets of paper slipped from the endpapers and fell to the floor. Surprised, Catherine picked them up to return them in place, giving them a curious glance as she did so. It was an old letter, she realised, and a casual glance suddenly gripped her attention. It began, 'My Richard'. She looked at the other page and asked him, 'Who is Matilda?' in a fragile voice. Richard went cold. He stood rigidly, having forgotten he had not taken her very first letter from its hiding place and put it with the rest.

'Who is Matilda?' she asked again. 'It is clearly to you that she writes,' she said as she read the pages.

'Yes, yes. Let me explain. Please sit, Catherine.' He began to pace the room, making a complete mess of explaining anything. It was more than Catherine could take.

'I have heard enough for one night,' she said, beginning to cry, and hurriedly left the room.

Richard felt as though his heart had stopped. His hidden past exposed, he stood as though rooted to the floor, immobile as an oak tree. He tried to gather his thoughts, to compose what he needed to say to her in a sensible order, to explain his past so it may be in some way acceptable. She had read all of the letter, she would now know of the children. She would surely end the marriage; it was over before it really had a chance to begin. He was doomed through his own folly. He had no idea of the passage of time, only vaguely aware of the door opening behind him.

'We should talk, Richard,' a voice said quietly. He turned to see Sarah in a heavy robe, bringing Catherine in behind her, holding her hand.

'Shall we all sit? Perhaps some port, Richard, would help.' He numbly handed them each a glass with a generous measure in them. Sarah quietly continued, 'I have always been curious about your past, Richard. Your parishioners hold you in awe, you could do no wrong by them, you have always conducted yourself in the most exemplary manner. But you are also a man with forty seven years of living behind him, and never married. I found that mystifying, as you were obviously extremely eligible. Why was there no woman in your life? Your conduct with Catherine has always been correct, but your confidence with her showed you had not lived a life of a monk. So where was she? Who was she? Why were you not already married to her? This letter from Matilda explains rather a lot, I feel. I have persuaded Catherine to listen to what you have to say, before she makes any rash decisions of her own. Perhaps some honest confiding before marriage would have been in order?' Sarah finished softly, betraying no emotion.

'Yes, yes. You are right, of course. It is a long story. Perhaps from the beginning, then.' And he began to tell it, sometimes sitting, then rising and pacing the floor, his great hands waving about trying to explain a difficult part. Mother and daughter sat side by side, never letting go of the other's hand, never once interrupting.

Finally it was told. He was exhausted. He stood before them.

'What will you have me do?' he asked of them. The silence was not immediately filled.

'That is between the two of you,' Sarah said. 'I understand your dilemma, Richard, you must have loved her a great deal, and she must love you more to have given you up so you could marry Catherine without ties. I think I will leave you now, for you two need to come to terms with all this.' She turned to her daughter. 'Think carefully, my dear, before you make any decision. For you have an honest husband who loves you, and that is not to be taken for granted in this day and age.' She rose and quietly left them.

They did talk, right through till dawn. With the new day, they began their life together anew. All the while, Catherine had been holding Matilda's letter.

'I will take that,' Richard said at last. 'Let me burn it now.'

'No,' she said. 'I will keep it. It needs to be kept, it represents too much of who you are. It will be a reminder for me of the man that Matilda made for me. Now come to bed, my love.'

They didn't get there. As they went up the stairs they were greeted with little Richard's cries for his first feed of the day.

Richard was to remember Sarah's intervention that night with appreciation, for it was his mother-in-law who had smoothed the way for Catherine and he to be married, throughout that year of courtship.

While their marriage strengthened, so did another love flourish.

William Edwards could hold back no longer, and young Matilda was not going to relent to his desires.

'If you want that, then marry me!' she teased him.

'Very well, I will!' he replied. 'Now let us practise!' And he grabbed at her before she could escape his arms. She was caught, not unwillingly.

They duly married in Shute on 13 August 1863.

It had been a tumultuous few months for Matilda. There were highs and lows, excitement of her daughter getting married, as old William in the shop had continually told her it would happen, and the sadness of the likelihood of her moving away. There would never be enough money from William's employment to support the two of them, and her daughter had not been able to get work close to him. It seemed inevitable that moving away was their only choice. It was Jacob who solved the problem for them all.

'Be nine acres next Lower Hawley going if young 'ens wants it. Be cheap on rent and take a bit o' work to come good again, but theys be young, and hard work never did anyone any 'arm. Boy be going soft in servant's job, put some colour back in 'is cheeks.'

Both Matildas were delighted: Mother kept her daughter close by, and daughter was able to stay on a farm and work with her precious animals.

'Just like her mother,' her aunt Mary ofttimes said.

Within months of this, Matilda received a letter from John, William's son. It came from Parkhurst, at the army barracks there.

'Dear Aunt and Cousins,' it began, as he always started them. 'I have enlisted in the army. I had got as far as Dorchester in May with plenty of work for the summer, but by September there was nothing left again. There was a recruiting officer in the pub drinking with us lads offering a quid in our pocket if we joined up. I am hoping the army will satisfy my restless nature as he has promised us a life of adventure and travel to overseas countries. He talked of being in India by this time next year. At present we are learning rifle drills and how to hit the target. Some of the lads call me Snow on account of my fair hair, which is all right. One smart mouth called me Snow White, for which I loosened a tooth or two for him. This got me on report and a fine for misconduct with a lecture that we are not here to fight each other, we have a higher calling. Does this mean I have to fight taller people? Please let Mother and Father know where I am, and as usual pass back to me any news. Your affectionate nephew, John.'

He wrote once more at Christmas, with greetings. He told her that his regiment was due to sail to India in the new year, an event he was very much looking forward to. He told with enthusiasm of his short time so far of army life, and his ability as a marksman. Life had real purpose now, he said. Matilda gave the letter to her own John to read; he only grunted, 'Not for me, farming be my life.'

But her nephew John Hoyle read it avidly before handing it back. That evening he went home to see his parents. The next morning Mary came up to see Matilda with the news that her John was going to join up in the same regiment as his cousin. It was not the best news she wanted to hear, hoping that he would stay. He had been far more happy at Mount Pleasant with Matilda than at any other time, and going into the army seemed to be a backward step for him. But he would not be moved from the idea.

By the end of February he was gone.

Hannah's letter was bubbling with excitement. Richard had commissioned the altar windows months before and they had arrived. Workmen would have them installed by the time her letter arrived. The windows were magnificent, vibrant in the richness of their colour. They comprised a set of three windows, with Christ the good shepherd holding a lamb with two sheep at his feet. In the windows on either side of him were St Peter and St Paul. But what he had told no one was what he had put as a dedication. Written underneath across the three windows was:

'To the Glory of God and in Memory of John and Sarah Hill of Lyme Regis This window is erected AD 1863.'

'I wept when I saw them,' wrote Hannah. 'They are the most beautiful windows in any church I have seen. Richard beamed with pride when he showed me. He also showed me the designs for the windows on either side, but refuses to say what their dedication will read. There is to be a special service for them in two weeks. I shall write when I return from it.

'They also have another son, named Francis. Catherine is a picture of health and they are well suited.'

Matilda smiled, thinking of how proud Richard would be, standing at the front of his church, with the new windows glowing behind him.

Thank you, Catherine, for giving him so much.

Chapter 31

1863–1871: Tragedy at the Rectory

Richard had taken some care in rewriting his will. His previous will was amended immediately after his marriage, but made no mention or allowance for any children that may be born in the future. Now they had two sons, and he wanted to have conditions describing the inheritance benefits that they were due. Satisfied at what he had written, he called Catherine into his study for her understanding and approval of his revisions, before having it legally scripted and signed.

She read it carefully, then laid it on her lap and gazed thoughtfully out the window.

'It is restrictive and does not cover all your children fairly.' She finally said. 'You have named Richard and Francis because they are here, now. You mention children to come and their possible guardianship should we both die. I approve of Hannah taking care of the girls we may have, and William the boys. But are you sure they are all you wish to bequeath to?'

Richard was puzzled.

'I am not sure I understand you. How can I name children we have not got yet?' He paused. 'We are going to have more, aren't we?' he asked with a cheeky grin on his face.

'I am quite sure we will,' Catherine replied happily. Then she added, to his shocked surprise, 'But what about your other two children, John and Matilda? Is there no responsibility to them?'

Richard was speechless, confused. He fumbled for words, as there had been no reference to them since the all-night talk when her mother was present.

'They cannot be mentioned, as no one knows they exist in our family. Only you, your mother, Hannah and I know of them. And they have already been looked after—Father bought the farm for them. No, it's out of the question. They cannot be included.' He was quite emphatic.

'I do not agree. No matter what has been done for them already, they are still your children, you follow their progress. Hannah makes sure you know how they are doing, she does it quietly and without fuss. But since our talk, I let her know that I now know as well. She tells me some things as well. Surely you would have wanted to be at your daughter's wedding?'

Richard was stunned—was there no end to the mysteries of women and what they said among themselves?

'I did say a prayer for her, and it would have been nice to attend. But I couldn't, as Matilda has never revealed who their father is. It would have broken a confidence with them all if I had attended. It would break it now to include them here,' he finished, but now he was certain that Catherine already knew how to make allowance for them.

'I would be disappointed if you didn't make an inclusion for them. You can do so and still keep their existence unknown. You have mentioned Richard and Francis and then your future children. I want you to rewrite that to say, "for all my children". Your trustees will know only of our children, and they will therefore be the only beneficiaries. You and I will know it is meant to include Matilda and John, even though they will receive nothing. It is your thinking of them, and in a subtle way acknowledging them as part of your family, that is important.'

'It is a vague description for a will, it is too open. Legally, it would not be allowed.'

'Try it, Richard. When they object to the wording, say then that is how you want it to read. I'm sure they will accept it, if you explain that it will mean that the will doesn't need changing every time we name another child.'

The will was duly written as Catherine wanted. The phrase, 'for all my children' remained in its final version, none of them specifically named. Only children born to Catherine, however, inherited from Richard's will.

Matilda was able to relax more with her labours on the farm. John was a strapping man, tall like his father, but more solid and strong. He was joining in with the decision-making, voicing his opinion, but always allowing his mother the final say. She had told him that 25 was soon enough for him to have the final say—provided, she added with a wicked grin, she agreed with it. At 23 he was happy to wait.

His sister couldn't wait, though. Her exuberance was difficult to hold; she had proudly produced a baby girl, and from that day on stopped calling Matilda Mother, but called her Grandma instead. Grandma was not sure she liked it as it made her sound old, and 51 was not old. But she was delighted to be a grandmother, and she fussed over baby Ellen at every opportunity.

Matilda maintained her role with the milking—she was unequalled in getting the most from the cows, and unrivalled in producing her clotted cream. She could afford to take her time in delivering it to the village shop now, stopping by to leave a pot and chat with Frances Bowditch. Herman was no longer giving her lessons, and her letters to Richard had ended with his marriage, but Matilda regarded it as her continual thanks to them, for she continually appreciated the gift of being able to read and write as he had taught her.

William Edwards continued to support Matilda in every way he could. The big-hearted grocer was never short of village gossip, always ready to chip away at Mrs Beamish and her grip on the vestry members. He was forever telling the story of John's winning repartee with Mrs Beamish at choir practice. Not having succeeded in driving Matilda from the church, she turned her attention to her son, making needling comments at any chance. It was at a late choir practice that she said, loud enough for her cronies to hear, 'What of your father, John? Does he support you?'

John lifted his gaze to her eyes and replied, just loud enough for others to hear, 'What of your husband, Mrs Beamish? Where is he?' And he gently moved away. Mrs Beamish turned puce, the veins in her neck bulged, and her friends turned away, leaving her standing alone. She never challenged John directly again.

Matilda was overjoyed to receive a letter from her nephew John, all the way from Poona, in India. It was the first letter he had written since he had been home on leave from Parkhurst, before sailing out.

He apologised for not writing earlier, but there had been a great deal of moving around. He had done well for himself since arriving in Poona— he was the marker for the 45th Regiment and had office duties as well, because of his tidy handwriting. He surprised her by telling her that he had got married six months ago, to the Quarter Master Sergeant's daughter. He had a scare when she went down with a fever, but she survived when many did not. Cholera was endemic where they were last year, and they were obliged to move camp to a safer location. They lost some seventy men in just three weeks to it, fine young men being stricken down and dying, some within the hour, and most being buried without a coffin because they couldn't get them. He mentioned that he was learning the local language, and finished with the amazing information that he was 21,000 miles distant from England. He gave his address, and told Matilda that just a one penny postage stamp would convey her letter to him.

Then, in different handwriting, was an added note requesting a letter with family news, and extending love to John and Matilda and herself from her ever-affectionate nephew, John Hoyle.

Matilda was just delighted with the letter. It was the first time that there had been any contact from Mary's John, and she was very pleased that they had met up. She immediately set off over to see Mary and Richard and give them the good news and find out what they wanted to say to their son.

The next day she went down to Colyton to see William and Ann with the letter and learnt what they wanted to say to their son. When she got home she wrote both letters and sent them off.

Within the week all of Dalwood had caught up with how the two Johns were doing in India. Many old friends wanted news to go to them in her next letter, and she duly made notes to add so as not to forget anyone.

It was after church the next Sunday that William Edwards took her quietly aside, saying, 'Someone would like to talk with you,' and he led her back toward his shop. By the footbridge over the Corry stood a woman she did not know. William introduced them, explaining that the stranger was from Membury. She had a son serving in India who was all but lost to them as neither she nor her husband could read or write, and they had no other family who could. They had heard that Matilda had received a letter from India, and could she write to their son for them?

Tears came to Matilda's eyes. She could imagine how she would have felt if her John was serving overseas like that and she couldn't write to him. She told her that she only had her nephew's address, but she would write to him, giving him the young soldier's name and where he had lived. Hopefully he would find him—working in the regiment office may help him to locate the lad.

It worked. By the end of the following year she was writing to seven soldiers for their families who were in a similar situation. When a letter came in she would take it to the family and read it to them, and they would dictate another to their son. Matilda continued to do this until she died.

A sad letter arrived from Hannah, telling Matilda that Sarah, Catherine's mother, had died. It was a terrible blow to all of them, as it was Sarah who was the bond that held the family together. She had been ill for several months without reprieve, and the insidious cancer had finally taken its toll. Catherine was devastated, Richard distraught. He had become very fond of his mother-in-law—she was always supportive, always ready to help. She had been staying with them when she asked to be taken to their doctor as the pain had increased. He had kept her in the nursing home in Clevedon, just for a couple of days to get control of the pain before she went home. She died on the second day.

Just three months later, Richard had the second set of windows installed in the church. They showed St Luke carrying a bull and St John holding an eagle, as brilliant in colour and detail as the first three. The dedication below said:

'To the Glory of God in Memory of a Beloved Mother. Whitsunday June 9th 1867: For So He Giveth His Beloved Sleep.'

Richard held a memorial service for Sarah when the windows were installed. In the front pew sat Catherine, cradling their baby Isabelle. Next to her was Richard, aged five, then Francis, aged four, and Edith, aged three. Little Catherine, aged one, sat on her grandfather's knee at the end. Robert was grieving badly, completely lost without his wife beside him, his grandchildren a lone shining light in his darkest days.

Matilda wrote back to Hannah expressing her sorrow. The loss of a loved mother was always a terrible blow, an irreplaceable link gone from the family structure.

She tried to lighten the mood of the letter by adding that her John had taken the eye of a lass in the parish. 'Her name is Anna Batten,' she wrote, 'and she is certainly smitten by him. However, John does take after his father in that he is slow and steady before meeting his bride in church. He will be very sure of her suitability to be his wife before he makes any proposal. The only thing that I am sure of is that Anna will wait for him; I only hope it is not too long a wait.'

The wait was indeed long—three years—but John was not to be rushed. His sister teased him unmercifully, and produced her third child before he took Anna to the altar.

It would be 1870 when Anna would say yes, and she would move up to Dalwood Hill. It was worth the wait, it was what she wanted. Of all the people involved with their wedding, it was John and Anna who were the calmest, the least anxious on the day. Their only concern was to say their vows, put a ring on each other's finger, and go home. Just a day in their lives, an event in the day.

'Tis no bother,' he laconically told his mother, 'we be back in time for afternoon milking.'

'You will not!' Matilda exploded. 'You will spend time alone together after your wedding. Be sure of it.'

'Aye, mother,' John sighed, then with a wicked grin through his beard, 'alone in back bedroom.'

'John White!' Matilda stood looking up to her son's smiling face, 'you will do as you are told.'

'Mother White,' he replied, 'I will do exactly as I am told. By my bride!' He put his great arms around her, burying her in his hug. 'Dornee fret so, just make the day right for Anna.' Her argument was lost. Anna had long ago made it clear that she wanted no frills, just to marry John and move into Dalwood Hill.

The day was brilliant, the village festive. It was the longest awaited wedding the villagers could remember, and they all joined in. The church was packed, the ceremony joyous. They were cheered across to the Tuckers Arms, where a wedding breakfast was held. Toasts were announced and much was drunk.

No one noticed when the newlyweds left, no one could remember when they last spoke to them. Suddenly folk just noticed they were no longer about.

They had quietly slipped away, back up the hill to the farm and into the back bedroom. The room they kept until the day they died.

Some of the happiness of the day came through in the letter that Hannah, who attended, wrote to Richard. He smiled at their relaxed approach to the occasion and their self-assurance that all they needed was to exchange vows. The celebration was for everyone else. He read with satisfaction that Matilda had made John the head of the household. The farm was now his responsibility. He nodded his head at the wisdom of Matilda giving their son the authority to live to her standards. He sat and worked it out—John would be 28 now, a suitable time for him to be in charge.

Catherine came into the room and watched him reading. He looked up and smiled to her.

'It's from Hannah, she tells of John's wedding.' He handed her the letter. She read it through, smiling occasionally.

'It sounds as though it was a jolly wedding. Will you write to Hannah and ask her to pass on your best wishes to them?'

'I think I must. Matilda has done everything very well. She has brought up the children without mishap, and now they are both suitably married. I owe her a debt.'

'Would she think so?'

'Undoubtedly not! But I am grateful, nonetheless. It is unfortunate that I cannot acknowledge the fact.'

'I think you can, Richard. I believe that if you think enough now about what Matilda has achieved in bringing up those two children for you, then you will have a beautiful sermon to deliver on the subject next Sunday. No one need know the source of the inspiration for your address.'

Richard looked at her, astounded.

'You quite scare me at times. You have no idea how similar the two of you think, outwitting me in what I should do.'

Catherine smiled. She loved him so when he looked so vulnerable.

'I am pleased I am worthy of my predecessor.' She handed the letter back. 'Now write a sermon to make us both proud.' And she quietly left the room.

Richard wrote with a passion and pride. He wrote in praise of motherhood and supportive parenting. He wrote of giving responsibility to growing children. He wrote thinking of Matilda and acknowledging Catherine. He thought of their family, now numbering seven. He delivered the sermon to an engrossed congregation, and Catherine dabbed away her tears of pride.

Matilda quickly settled into a life of delegating her responsibilities to John. The transition from mother to son was smooth, seamless. She spent more time in her beloved garden. She firmly held onto her role of caring for her precious cows, and milking her favourites. John made sure there was no heavy work left near her, and sternly chastised the labourers should they allow Matilda to tackle something she shouldn't.

She had earned her right to an easier life, he told them—watch out for her. And they obeyed.

William Edwards was also handing responsibility to his son. He was retiring from the village grocery—it was time for the young ones to stand on their own feet, he told her.

'We be going to live up Danes Hill, Maria and I, nice and quiet Deanes Villa be.'

But their lives up there were soon to be disrupted, when they took on a lodger, an extraordinary one.

'Be obliged to really,' he told Matilda later. 'He be from my sister in Lyme, and she be too old now to handle 'im, being as how her husband been gone now years back. Strange old set up it be: Marian was married to army chap, he fought in Peninsular war with Wellington and got involved in getting Prime Minister's family out to safety in England. One of the sons was a sharp barrister in his day, but then lost it all, went dooladdly in the head. Prime Minister didn't want to have embarrassing son on his hands, so asked Wellington for help. Wellington got hold of his old staff officer, my brother-in-law, retired out through injury, and put it to him to take on this chap for a fee—Pedro Valdez be his name. Well, he settles in Lyme Regis with sister and husband, but brother-in-law wasn't too long for this world, carried too many war injuries. My sister carries on with this Valdez chappie regardless, good money in it for her. But she be past it now, she got a good ten years on me, oldest in the family. So I tells her we be retiring from grocery and next thing she set to and send 'im on to me to look after. What can you say? Poor fool can't look after hisself, and family don't want him back in Portugal, so here he be, upalong with us. Queer old world isn't it, when a chap likes 'im ends up in Dalwood.'

'How can I help?' Matilda asked, 'Is he difficult?'

'Not at all, real quiet and easy. His English is none too flash, feel sorry for the poor sod really. Help? Just make sure we don't run out of your clotted cream!'

Richard could not believe the ease with which Catherine conceived, and the glow it brought to her face while with child. It was a total joy for her to say to him that there was another one on the way—it would be their eighth. He shook his head at the wonderment of it. Barely had his first-born been married, than he was told that he had another child due next summer.

The rectory had lost all serenity long ago; only his study was sacrosanct. He marvelled at his wife's energy. At times he found the combined tumult tiring, but Catherine never faulted. She was his treasure without a flaw.

Her pregnancy progressed smoothly as usual. In June she felt an odd twinge, and the doctor told her to slow down, only six weeks to go. Two weeks out and Richard thought she was apprehensive. He took her back to the doctor, who prescribed complete rest. The last week she spent in bed.

'I could do with Mother right now,' she told Richard one night.

'So could I,' he replied, holding her hand.

The nurses watched her, now forever cautious.

Then her waters broke.

'It is the worst birth,' she cried, gripping Richard's hand in pain, and then it was over, no more pain.

A baby boy was born, crying weakly into the world.

Then, slowly, weakly, Catherine began to drift out of it. The bleeding could not be stopped.

She died within the hour, never regaining consciousness to see her baby. Through effort, they kept the boy alive. Richard found no consolation in that. His world was shattered, he could find no justification for losing her. His faith stretched to its limit, he shut himself away.

Hannah and Robert arrived on the same coach, barely finding anything to say to each other during the trip.

Hannah spent her time with the children, and Robert pulled his son-in-law from the depths of depression.

'For the children, Richard. You cannot abandon them like this. Grieve, but grieve with them! Help them get through it, as they can help you. You understand death, they do not! Her death will scar them more than you—you must start to heal that scar now. Not when you feel like it! Pray, Richard, as never before! You have lost your wife, do not lose your eight children as well. You must help them now, not later. Come on, man. Go and tuck them into bed and read them a story. They need your reassurance that you will not leave them too.' He quite literally dragged Richard to his feet and pushed him to the door.

Richard read to them that night, but could recall none of it. It was a start. He made sure he tucked them in every night, dried their tears and eased them from their nightmares. The healing had begun.

Hannah stayed, easily taking control of the household, as though she had never stopped after Lyme Regis.

Reverend Lord Richards, friend and fellow rector from nearby Farnborough, came over to take some of the services. He conducted Catherine's funeral, barely being able to control his own grief at her passing.

The funeral passed in a haze for Richard, numb to the core of his soul, reacting only to the needs of his children.

He took his first service again three weeks later. It was to baptise his new son. He named him William Blundell Boyd Hill. He prayed for the boy to gain strength.

Robert returned home after the service. He was exhausted and could help no more.

It was the nurse, Emma Gillett, who rose to the challenge of this beleaguered family. At 38, she was only a year older than Catherine, and probably because of that, they had become friends. She was determined that Catherine's hard work and love of her family should not be wasted. She began to pull them together, backed constantly by Hannah.

Richard took all the services, burying himself in church work until three in the afternoon, then devoting himself to the children until he put them to bed. Then, many weeks later, he spoke with Hannah.

'We must do this on our own now. Could you leave us to try, but be ready to come back if we falter?' She left them, worried, and returned to Weston-super-Mare.

She wrote to Matilda, telling her of the tragedy that had occurred. Matilda replied immediately, and sent with it an open letter to Richard, sharing his grief and encouraging him with strength to carry on. She asked Hannah to give it to him when she thought the time would be right.

Nothing came from Richard for two months, and when a letter finally arrived, Hannah opened it with trepidation. It held surprising news. 'Please come in three weeks, for the 22nd of the month. I am to dedicate the last two windows.'

Hannah already knew their design. One was St Matthew holding a child, the other St Mark holding a lion. She guessed who the dedication would be to.

When she arrived she was pleased with how well they were all doing. Richard, in public at least, was almost his old self. She gave him Matilda's letter and he thanked her for it. 'Please pass on my thanks,' he said. The packed service was moving.

Under the new windows was the dedication:

'To the Glory of God in Memory of a beloved Wife & Mother July 29th 1871.'

Hannah left Timsbury full of hope that the family was well on the road to recovery. Richard again had a focus on his children and his congregation, and life, although a little unsteadily, was returning to normal.

Hannah was confident that the approaching Christmas would help them enormously. The New Year would be a time to begin afresh, time to enjoy the cleansing of the winter snow.

Chapter 32

1872–1873: Death Comes to the Young and Old

Richard always felt January to be a miserable month. The cheerful goodwill of Christmas had departed, the short, cold days and a further covering of snow smothered enthusiasm. It was a month when his nose never seemed to stop running, the choir had colds and their attendance reduced to a hardy few. His congregation was made up of only the most devoted, who sat in a church that barely sustained any warmth. He made his sermons shorter and as cheerful as his drained imagination could muster.

He worried about William. His baby had not gained much strength, and the winter months were hard on him. It was a deep cough that had Richard concerned; the doctor could not relieve it, and advised to keep him warm and well wrapped at all times.

Richard would hold him to his chest, patting his back, as he walked about the rectory.

'Spring will be here soon and the sun will shine again,' he spoke quietly into his baby's ear. 'We will play outside with the rest of your brothers and sisters, we will all feel much better then. This horrible month has but four days to go and each day of February will improve, just wait and see! Now isn't that something to look forward to!' He smiled at the child as Emma took him to put him down for the night. Richard watched him go and then began gathering the rest of the children, to take them to their beds and read them a story.

He no longer slept well himself, with only short spells of deep sleep, then suddenly awake, breathing rapidly. No recollection of what woke him, no remembrance of dreaming. Calmness coming only when he recalled Catherine's loving face, and could hear her telling him to be brave, that he was doing well with their children. At times, sleep would not return and he would rise and go to his study. He would read and write his sermons, make notes on who had asked his attendance, on what he had to do.

Ofttimes, Emma would come in with a cup of hot sweet tea for him, more often than not without a word being exchanged between them, so routine had their habits become to each other, the mutual acceptance of the burden they now carried.

When she came in this morning, Richard didn't feel a need to look up, but carried on writing. It was when she stopped after closing the door that he felt her anguish, and saw her holding the well-wrapped baby. The baby boy was silent, no cough, no sucked breath.

A coldness swept through Richard as Emma said quietly, 'He's gone. In his sleep.' Richard rose in a trance and took the small bundle from her. 'I'll fetch the doctor,' she said. 'I'll not be long.'

When the doctor entered the room Richard was still standing there, baby William's face wet from his tears. Emma went to the other children, and each, as they were ready, went to their father.

All too soon, the Reverend Lord Richards was officiating again for Richard. His service for the burial of baby William, just six months old, was moving. Richard's pain was there for all to see—now mother and child were gone. Hannah came and stayed again, pushing her brother to carry on, to show love and comfort to his family. Hannah fussed over them all, but spent most of her time with the girls. At eight, Edith was the oldest girl, and valiantly tried to help her with the younger ones. She acted as grown up as her young years would allow her. She idolized her aunt, always close by her, ready to assist.

It was to form a bond between them that would stay strong throughout their lives.

Hannah did not write to Matilda until the end of the month, bereft of the energy or thought to manage it sooner.

Matilda was devastated with what the letter contained. She could only imagine the pain that Richard was going through. She thought carefully of how to reply, as Hannah was still at Timsbury, and there was a chance that Richard would see her letter.

One of the maids gave Hannah her letter when it arrived, and then went into Richard and gave him his. Hannah read it in her room and nodded at how Matilda had written it. She went downstairs with it in her pocket and joined the others. That evening, when Richard came down from settling all the children, the two of them were alone, talking about the day, and the possibility that Hannah should return home soon. Yet again a routine was being established within the stricken family, and the need for Hannah to stay was diminishing.

'Perhaps in a week,' Richard said, 'with plenty of warning for the children, so they can get used to the idea. They will not feel as though they have been abandoned, particularly if we talk of your next visit before you leave.'

'The end of next week then—say Thursday.' She paused. 'Matilda sends her condolences—I received a letter today. It is mainly her thoughts for you and the children. You can read it if you wish, or shall I just read some sentences?'

'Read just the relevant lines,' he replied. Hannah did so, which was most of it.

'Here, read it yourself. There is no need to be shy about it. She writes it as though to an old friend, nothing more.' She handed it to Richard, who took it uncertainly. He looked at Hannah quizzically, before reading.

He sat quietly for several minutes. When he had finished, he sighed and said, 'She writes well. I appreciate her concern for how we are managing and her correct assumption that you will be here for us. She knows us well. I am grateful.'

'So what shall I say in reply? Or do you think that perhaps you could write in reply yourself? You have written every other reply to the condolences you received.'

'Yes, you are right. So why do I hesitate in replying to her?'

'She wrote to you as an old friend, nothing more was intended. Reply in the same manner, intend no more. Just how many old friends do you have, Richard?' She knew the answer was not many.

Richard looked at his sister intently.

'There can be no going back. Our past is safe where it is. It must remain so.'

'She is just an old family friend from Lyme Regis days, thinking of you at this tragic time. What would our parents have you do? Would they have you ignore her? It is a very respectful letter—why not answer it with equal respect? Do you have anyone you can call a friend, new or old? I have seen no sign of one. You have your duties here as rector and people associated with that, but none are your friends that you could confide in. And you have a precious family here, who desperately need a caring and devoted father. I believe you should write to her.' She gave a short laugh. 'The three of us again! Perhaps writing to her as a friend will help bring a balance into your life. Put a perspective back into everyday living that will help you get through those dark days that will continue to sneak up on you.'

Richard did write. He found it easier than he thought, for he wrote it with Catherine's help, as though she was sitting beside him, encouraging him what to say and what to leave out.

Matilda was surprised to receive a reply directly from him. She could feel the pain of finding himself alone to bring up the children; he was frightened at the prospect and responsibility. For the first time he understood what Matilda had achieved, and he would be doing it without the prejudices of the villagers around him, as she had had to put up with. He would face no hypocritical comments, no slur on his character. By the end of the letter he acknowledged that his future was going to be easier than hers was. When he had signed the end, he felt much better, as though his own future was much clearer.

There was a much happier man at the breakfast table in the morning. It began to rub off on the children, and Hannah and Emma smiled at the change.

It was spring when Matilda next wrote to Richard, and the letter held the hopes of a new season. She told him of the flowers now blooming in the hedgerows, of her three newborn calves and the bumper crop of apples. Her son, she told him, had begun to brew his own cider, and his first attempt had tasted ghastly, quite unfit to drink. It promised to be a long summer, she thought, the farm would prosper with it. Her garden burgeoned with flowers and vegetables, her strawberries never failed to be the envy of other gardeners. It was always a good sign when the buzzards nested in the area. She wished him well for an equally prosperous year.

Their correspondence continued, writing as only two old friends in their late fifties would.

It was a good summer for both of them.

Richard regained his confidence, and lost the pallor of depression. Hannah visited often, and the children began to stay with her at the seaside.

Matilda grew content with John running the farm, leaving her with as little as she cared to do. Madeline visited regularly, her boys now both married and living locally, in Shute and Colyton. Mary would join them regularly, and the three would pass a day quite easily. Mary's son Samuel had returned to work on their farm at Dickens Marsh after a long period of working for Matilda. He had settled down a lot since his elder brother had gone into the army. He was married now with two children. Madeline was was soon to become a grandmother.

Autumn soon came, and winter even quicker. Matilda had no love of the cold—she was sure that the winters were getting longer. She tired so much more easily.

'Just your age, Mother,' John told her. 'Old folk always feel the cold more. Winter be no longer, nor colder than before. Put another coat on,' he advised her mischievously.

She softly boxed his ears, smiling. 'That be no way to talk to your mother!' she said. 'And I have no beard like yours to hide behind!' She left him there laughing. 'I have cows to milk and feed even if you have no work to do other than give lip to your old mother.'

The winter came on regardless. It was never too bad up to Christmas—with that joyous season to look forward to, the bad weather seemed to be easier to take. She always wished for a fine Christmas Day, a sunny day was perfect. They would all walk down to the village for the morning service, and from the brow of the hill look up and down the valley, almost to the sea at Seaton. It was pristine, covered in a white blanket of snow under a blue sky.

Most times, though, it was like today, grey, overcast and gloomy. At least there was no wind. The church was always filled with warmth and smiling faces, the service cheerful, and everyone staying back for a tea and cake before going home. There was a lot of chatter, often requests for something to go in a letter for a son overseas. She had written to all of them early in November, in the hope that they would be received in time for Christmas.

It was January that she detested the most. There was no euphoria of Christmas spirit left, and nothing to immediately look forward to. Spring was a long way off. The winter winds took advantage of her misery of the month and seemed to blow harder just to spite her. Darkness arrived earlier and lingered longer. It tired her out, and sat heavy on her shoulders.

Still the animals in the barn needed feeding, and three cows to milk. Wearily, she shrugged her shoulders and went out to them. She leaned into the harsh wind, shivering against the biting snow flurries that dogged every footstep toward the barn.

'Is there anything more mean than a January wind?' she muttered to herself, thinking that she should have put on a heavier coat. She pulled at a stray lock of hair from across her eyes, and tucked it back under her headscarf with frozen fingers. 'Cheer up,' she scolded herself, 'get this lot done and soon enough be back indoors. Anna will have dinner ready and the warm fire will set you right.'

Matilda pulled hard on the barn door that again was dragging on the ground of compacted snow, wishing John would do a proper job of digging the snow away. As if to prove there was no obstacle, the wind slammed it shut, shunting her into the barn and smacking her painfully on the elbow. 'Dornee wonder what will go wrong next, you foolish woman.' A tear trickled down her face from the numbing pain.

The cows looked over to her in soft recognition, pleased with her appearance as it meant fresh fodder and the relief of milking. Matilda went to replace hay first, and found there was none left below. She felt annoyance at having to climb up to the loft and fork more down. *Even colder up here*, she thought, gaining no warmth from her efforts. She dropped the fork down and steadied her self for the first step of the ladder. It felt harder to her to go down than to climb up. She began to fill the racks with the fresh hay, taking longer and longer to reach the end, puzzled by her lack of progress. She sat and rested a while, thinking maybe John was right and she was getting old. 'Foolish woman!' she muttered again, 'Get a move on, sitting hereabouts is doing you no good at all.' She had to push herself up, suddenly fearful of the effort it took, doubting her strength to finish the job. She vaguely felt light-headed as she toppled forward, but felt nothing as she fell to the ground, with illogical thoughts running through her mind.

Getting too dark soon, she thought, and looked toward the barn door. 'Who's there?' she tried to call. 'Help me up.' She was sure now of his silhouette—of course he would have come. She raised a hand up to him, wondering why he didn't take it. She looked up to him again. 'Please,' she begged of him.

Vaguely, she heard him say, 'Be your time, Miss M.'

He turned and left, and with what little strength she had left, she let her spirit go with him.

'Go and help your mother,' Anna told John when he came inside. 'She is taking too long tonight.'

He found her there, lying as though asleep, her favourite cow standing over her trying to nuzzle her into movement.

He wept. Then carried her easily indoors.

The church was packed for her funeral, and many wept throughout. Mary, Madeline and Hannah sat at the front. They made a forlorn trio. John had written to Hannah and told her of their misery and loss, and would she be able to attend? There was never any doubt.

Matilda was buried in the graveyard beside the church.

No one noticed the inclement weather, their attention focused on the coffin and the woman who had won their respect. As they drifted away from the graveside, no one looked back at the last person to leave, nor they had noticed him standing alone at the back of the church, unmoving, tall, and proud of the woman they were all farewelling. He watched her two children, clearly shaken by their mother's death, but obviously proud to be her children. His own pride of their stature had him wipe a tear away. He remained unnoticed among the mourners, until Reverend Ashe returned to the church after the committal, and saw the lonely figure by the grave. He took him for a man of the clergy and made to go to him, but the stranger looked up and shook his head, then walked away from the church. He turned into Lower Lane and climbed into a waiting coach. Hannah took his hand as tears flowed freely from them both. She spoke at last.

'They will be fine—they are both adults now, you need not worry about them. But always be proud of them.'

They left Dalwood for the last time.

Epilogue

Mrs Beamish felt that she had scored a point by not attending Matilda's funeral, but no one had noticed. Deflated and full of vengeance, she blocked a headstone being erected.

John was not overly perturbed. The time would come, he told himself. 'There be a better place for her memorial,' he told his sister.

He had a plaque carved. it was simple and honest.

MW
1873

He had it plastered into the garden wall at Dalwood Hill, near the gate that Dick had put in for her.

It remains there still, well weathered, and just readable. It would be her only memorial, as the headstone was never erected.

Author's Notes

I have listed the main characters in alphabetical order in an attempt to clarify their relationship to Matilda. There are only three totally fictitious people in the book; Edith and Margery in the Axminster market, and Mrs Beamish in Dalwood. Every other named person existed and was occupied as I have described. Two others are alive and well today, I just shifted them back 150 years to help the story. I hope they don't mind too much.

I make no apology for how I have portrayed the people in the book—they are as I found them. Accept them as I have had to.

Included in the list are some items that I have mentioned that deserve notation.

Beamish, Mrs. She is entirely fictional, but has many characteristics that we all recognise with those who have a 'holier than thou' attitude, and whose background would stand very little scrutiny.

Burrows, Dick. Not exactly his correct surname, but close. Not to be confused with the Burroughs or Burrows of Dalwood. I found reference to him and his personality in Madeline's letters, and some comments from present-day family. They would have preferred some of their more notable family members to have been mentioned as well.

Dalwood Hill Farm. This was known as Mount Pleasant in Matilda's time. Through her grandson's period, Mount Pleasant became known as Higher Way, and the home cottage land as Dalwood Hill. It is recalled by all those who have lived there as having a very comfortable feel to it. Even the present owner, who is not a White family descendant, told me it was the most homely cottage they had lived in.

Fairfield Lodge, Lyme Regis. It stands high on the Charmouth Road. Since the Hills' time, it has been owned by the Mountbattens, was a Barnados home, and now serves as a retirement home.

Hill, née Boyd, Catherine, 1835–1871. Just 36 when she died in childbirth, leaving eight children under the age of nine. Richard was 55 when she died. It is odd to recall that when they married, Catherine was the same age as Matilda was when Richard and Matilda first met.

Hill, Hannah, 1820–1901. She lived at Weston-super-Mare until after her brother, Reverend Richard Hill, died in 1883. She then moved to Exeter and boarded there. She never owned her own home, but lived off the interest of her investments. She always had a servant living with her, and almost constantly had one of her nieces living with her as well. She never married. In her will she left the bulk of her estate to her nieces, Richard's children, Edith, Catherine, Isabella and Sarah. Fifty pounds only was given to Richard's sons Richard and Francis, and also to her sister Sarah Ann. Her only other niece to receive anything was Isabella Rendle, who lived with Hannah in Exeter for many years. She remained close to Richard's family until she died, particularly to Edith, who was an executor to her will.

Hill, John, 1786–1861. Richard's father. Born in St Petersburg, Russia, he carried on with the family business of importing Baltic timber. He was far more forgiving of Richard's behaviour than he was of any other member of his family.

Hill, Richard, 1816–1883. Rector of Timsbury, father of Matilda's two children. Educated at Blundells School, Tiverton, where he gained a scholarship to Oxford University. He spent seven years at Balliol College, gaining his BA in 1838, converted to an MA in 1841. Then he gained the rectorship in Timsbury. He married Catherine Boyd in 1860. When Catherine died, his main help with raising his very young family was the nurse, Emma Gillett, who stayed on with him. They did a superb job, as all stayed home in Timsbury and were educated there. All, that is, except the youngest, Charles, who went to a boarding school in Weston-super Mare, almost next door to where Hannah was living. At the time of writing, I had not traced any of their living descendants. Richard completed the extension of St Mary's Church and installed the stained-glass windows as described, largely using the Hill family money. Another stained-glass window was added after his death by a grateful congregation, and can be found to the front right of the church. It is of St Mary, holding a lily. His final will, written eleven years after Catherine had died, asked for his estate to be divided, 'for all my children'. Hannah was the only one alive who knew of Matilda and John, but she was not an executor of his will. Richard is buried in the St Mary's churchyard, Timsbury, with his wife, Catherine, their baby boy William, and daughters Isabel and Edith.

Hill, Sarah. 1779–1855. Richard and Hannah's mother. Cause of death, epilepsy. She was from Tiverton and a descendant of the Blundell family, the greatest of whom started the family fortunes and established Blundell School in Tiverton.

Hill, Sarah Ann. 1817–19?? Hannah's sister, married William Hayter Hussey—a wedding not entirely approved of by her father. She had two sons.

Hoyle, Richard. 1814–1895. Married Mary, Matilda's sister. Mary and Richard worked as agricultural labourers all their lives, first at the Soap House, then at Dickens Marsh. Finally, in 1880, long after Matilda had died, they worked at Dalwood Hill farm for John, Matilda's son.

Madeline. Everything I have written of Madeline came from a collection of letters she wrote after Dick's death. They were in a box that had not been opened in fifty years, and when I was directed to it by a delightful elderly lady who is the present carer of them, I was clearly told that I could use whatever I liked from them, providing I did not reveal the family name. I was to leave them as I found them, in the box, tied with a very old ribbon. Hence, Madeline is ever only Madeline, which is her correct Christian name. The letters are explicit, to a point that I felt that they should be read by women only. Little of my imagination was needed to write about her, and, of course, Dick.

Mount Pleasant Estate. The original name for all the land Matilda was given, some 45 acres, including all buildings and stock. It became known, as it is today, as Dalwood Hill Farm. The original Mount Pleasant Cottage became known as Higher Way, and is now a horse stud farm.

Old Bell Hotel. No longer exists, but did stand proudly in Axminster square.

St Mary's Church, Timsbury. The church and windows are as I describe; they are glorious and well worth a visit. The events I tell of Richard's first arrival there have been based on recorded expenses. The rectory and its garden stand as I describe; the layout inside is supposition.

St Peter's Church, Dalwood. Historic and beautiful, what I have said of it exists. I could only find the record of Matilda's burial, but not the location of her grave. There are headstones for all her descendants buried there.

Shute Marsh Farm. Where Matilda and all her siblings were born and brought up. My thanks to the present owners, who welcomed our visit and gave us an early photo of it.

Silver spoons (mentioned in Chapter 20). I know where only one of them is kept. It is probable that they were shared by Matilda's two children after her death, in which case daughter Matilda would have inherited one or both of the others.

The debenture. This is where the search for this story began. I am grateful to Sara and her team for finding it among old archives. It is now safely stored. For all its old legal phraseology, you can feel the pain John Hill took in trying to correct what, to him, must have been a horrendous situation his son was in.

Tony and Susan. A real enough couple involved in the church and village life, and very much alive. I just shifted them back a few generations!

Valdez, Pedro de Alcantara Travassos, 1827–1887. Buried with an ornate headstone in St Peter's churchyard, Dalwood. All the Portuguese Prime Minister's sons were brilliant in their chosen careers, including Pedro while a barrister. What sort of father was he that he hid his son away in a remote English village after Pedro suffered a mental breakdown?

White, Ann, 1823–? Matilda's young sister. She never married, continuing with the Chapples until their death. She remained a housemaid all her life, including a few years' service in London.

White, John, 1839–? Matilda's oldest nephew, William and Ann's son. Served in India, Abyssinia, Natal and Transvaal. His letters to Matilda did not always reveal his true situation. His story is another book.

White, John, 1843–1906. Matilda's son and my great-grandfather. He farmed Dalwood Hill all his life, as did his son, Arthur, and his son Noel before moving to Worhams. Noel's son John farmed there, and Noel's daughter Susan also lived for a period at Dalwood Hill. There are descendants still living in Dalwood.

White, Mary, 1789–1852. Matilda's mother.

White, Mary, 1809–1891. Matilda's older sister. Married Richard Hoyle, and their children were, Francis, John, Edward, Matilda, Samuel, and Henry.

White, Matilda, 1814–1873. My great-great-grandmother. Mother of John and Matilda. I hope I have done her justice in this book.

White, Matilda, 1847–19?? Matilda's daughter, married William Edwards. Soon after her mother's death, they moved to Hampshire and were farming on Fern Hills Farm, Laveys Titchfield, Hampshire in the early 1900s. I ran out of time to trace her family to more recent times.

White, John, 1786–1852. Matilda's father.

White, William, 1813–1886. Matilda's older brother. Married Ann Denslow, and was an agricultural labourer for a time, but took over the Beer House in Colyton in 1850s, until he died. He also became a roading contractor around Colyton.

Author's Request

I didn't have time to trace present-day descendants of the children of Richard and Catherine Hill of Timsbury, nor of Matilda and William Edwards of Hampshire, before writing this book.

I would be delighted if anyone should recognise their family's history recorded here, and would like to contact me.

Please contact the publisher, or me directly via my email, 94jag@xtra.co.nz.

David White
Matamata, New Zealand